Rugged ranchers looking for love...

His Ranch Or Hers

Roz Denny Fox

The Lawman's Christmas Proposal

Barbara White Daille

MILLS & BOON

First Published 2016
First Australian Paperback Edition 2016
ISBN 978 1 760 37395 5

First Published 2015
First Australian Paperback Edition 2016
ISBN 978 1 760 37395 5

FSC
www.fsc.org
MIX
Paper from responsible sources
FSC® C001695

Published by
Harlequin Mills & Boon
Level 13
201 Elizabeth Street
SYDNEY NSW 2000
AUSTRALIA

Printed and bound in Australia by McPherson's Printing Group

His Ranch Or Hers

Roz Denny Fox

MILLS & BOON®

Roz Denny Fox's first book was published by Harlequin in 1990. She writes for several Harlequin lines and her books are published worldwide and in a number of languages. Roz's warm home-and-family-focused love stories have been nominated for various industry awards, including the Romance Writers of America's RITA® Award, the Holt Medallion, the Golden Quill and others. Roz has been a member of the Romance Writers of America since 1987 and is currently a member of Tucson's Saguaro Romance Writers, where she has received the Barbara Award for outstanding chapter service. In 2013 Roz received her fifty-book pin from Harlequin. Readers can email her through Facebook or at rdfox@cox.net, or visit her website at korynna.com/rozfox.

Dear Reader,

The theme idea for the *SNOWY OWL RANCHERS* books started when I read a great article in *National Wildlife* magazine about a study done on snowy owls in the lower forty-eight. Snowy owls used to nest only in the cold lands of the far north. The study shows these gorgeous birds are having to travel farther afield for food and nesting.

Book characters generally come to me in the night. Odd as it may sound to people who don't write down stories that pop into their minds, the town of Snowy Owl Crossing is fictional, as are all of the people who populate *His Ranch Or Hers*, the first of three connected books for the Harlequin American Romance line.

I hope readers come to love the owls as I have and also develop a fondness for folks like Zeke Maxwell, Myra Odell, and their friends and family who live and work in my fictional Montana ranching community.

As always I love hearing from readers via mail at 7739 E. Broadway Blvd #101 Tucson, AZ 85710-3941, or email: rdfox@cox.net.

Sincerely,

Roz Denny Fox

DEDICATION

I want to thank the hardworking editors at Harlequin who have so kindly shared my vision for the Snowy Owl books and others. Always to Paula Eykelhof and Kathleen Scheibling. Also to Dana Hopkins, and to Victoria Curran for whom I have written stories for the Harlequin Heartwarming line. Harlequin books across all lines are my favorite books to read.

Chapter One

Myra Odell parked the tractor in the implement barn and went out to the fenced acres of grass. Recent rains had greened the pasture nicely. Good. Maybe tomorrow she'd bring the new crop of young animals down to ready them for market. Her neighbor Hank Watson had offered to truck them to the stockyard before winter storms hit northeastern Montana. With August close to the end, she'd still hoped for a few more weeks of decent weather. But all morning the sky had looked ominous. She'd gotten fairly good at predicting weather disruptions. She'd grown up in this country, and for most of her twenty-eight years she'd spent summers here on Flying Owl Ranch with her dad's parents. Three summers ago she'd come to help out Gramps, who's health had declined after her grandmother passed away the previous year.

Rather than return to teaching high school math in Great Falls that year, she'd stayed to run the ranch she loved. Her mom fussed about it, but truth be told Myra liked cattle ranching way more than teaching. Although after losing Gramps, the loneliness took some getting used to. Thankfully, she'd made friends with neighbors and some in the nearby town of Snowy Owl Crossing. And Gramps said she was a born rancher. Which was good because Myra saw herself spending the rest of her life right here.

Stepping down from the last rung of the split-rail fence, Myra checked her watch. She could feed the two saddle horses she kept for herding cattle before driving into town to grab staples in case the *Farmer's Almanac* was right about them getting an early snow. She might drop in to see a couple of her girlfriends, especially Jewell Hyatt, to ask if she had any news from the state. Their committee had put in a request to designate some local land as a snowy-owl habitat.

A waterfowl preserve was already adjacent to a nearby lake, but snowy owls nested in tall fir trees too often being logged off. The birds weren't yet endangered, but everyone in the area who loved watching them raise their young knew the owl population was shrinking. Quite a bit just since Myra had made her home here.

The horses whinnied a welcome. Both stuck their heads over their stall doors to see if she'd brought apples or a carrot in addition to their daily rations. Today she had neither, but they made do with muzzle rubs.

She left the barn and was heading toward Gramps's aging Ford pickup when her cell phone rang. Myra dug her phone out of her jacket pocket and was surprised to see her dad's number on the screen. She rarely heard directly from him as he tended to let her mom or her younger brother, Eric, touch base for the whole family. Her folks owned a much larger cattle ranch off the highway that ran between Miles City and Billings. Because it was rarer still that any of the busy Odells took time to phone during a weekday, worry knotted in Myra's stomach as she swiped the bar to answer.

"Hello, Dad? Is everything all right at Rolling Acres?" Myra heard the tremor in her voice and took a deep breath to dispel her concerns.

"Everything is fine. I have good news. Lieutenant Maxwell is here."

"You mean the guy who saved Eric's life in Afghanistan? I didn't know he was out of the hospital."

"Zeke, that's right. He's out of the VA hospital after an extensive stay after he saved Eric's life."

"Doesn't he live on the East Coast?"

"Yup, he was renting an apartment in Boston, where he grew up. Seems his folks have retired to some island."

"Eric told me they'd kept in contact. I recall him saying the lieutenant had to have his left shoulder and elbow rebuilt. It sounded serious. I think Eric felt some guilt because the guy got hurt saving him and the others."

"I don't know that he felt guilty. Certainly grateful. Your mother and I can't thank him enough, either."

"For sure. So what's he doing in Montana?"

"That's really what I called to tell you. Zeke's

friends and family have all left Boston for other opportunities. Eric thought he needed cheering up."

"So you invited him to visit. That's thoughtful of you guys."

Myra's father cleared his throat. "Actually, kiddo, your mom and I had this brilliant idea to gift him the Flying Owl. With Dad gone and you needing to get back to the job you went to college for, we dug out the deed. As co-owner on Dad's trust, it was simple to have Don Jarvis draw up a new deed. I sent it off to Lieutenant Maxwell last month. At first we didn't hear back and so weren't sure he'd accept. Then yesterday he showed up to ask if it was legitimate. I assured him it is. Expensive as land is, nothing on earth can ever equal the worth of him saving Eric's life."

Myra's ears started to buzz. She wasn't sure she'd processed everything she thought she'd heard her dad say. Turning around, she sat heavily on the old truck's running board. A sick feeling gripped her stomach and washed over her. "I…I love the Flying Owl. Wh… why didn't you call and discuss this with me?"

"Now, honey, your mother and I know you felt obligated to stick around and help your gramps. We appreciate all you did to make his last years easier. He was a lost soul after Mom died, and I was tied down here. Like your mother keeps telling me, you've dedicated enough time in that out-of-the-way place. This way, you have a week or so before a new school year starts to look for teaching jobs. You deserve to get back to living and working in a city where you'll meet young men and women your own age."

Myra couldn't force the plethora of objections past her constricted throat.

"Honey, did I lose you?"

"Uh, no," she managed to rasp. She swallowed a bunch of times and swabbed at tears trickling from her eyes. She heard doors slamming in the background on her dad's end, followed by loud male laughter. "Dad, you don't understand—"

He cut her off. "Listen, hon, Eric and Zeke are back from riding ATVs around the ranch. Zeke's joining us for supper, and he'll spend the night. Tomorrow he'll drive to the Flying Owl. That gives you this afternoon and evening to pack your stuff and take any mementos from the ranch you want. I figure he'll arrive by noon. Maybe you'd be so kind as to give him a quick tour of the ranch. Afterward, come stay with us until you get a job offer. We haven't seen enough of you," he said, his tone gruff with emotion.

Myra remained at a loss for words. She loved her family. She didn't doubt they loved her. Possibly she was partly to blame for this awful turn of events. After all, she'd never told them how much living here and running the ranch meant to her. "Sure. Bye, Dad," she managed to whisper past a growing lump in her throat. She quickly disconnected and buried her face in her hands.

Numb, but not one to wallow in self-pity, she decided to get on with her earlier plan of going to town.

If this wasn't all a bad dream, she had friends to notify of the sudden, colossal change in her life.

As she drove the two-lane road toward Snowy Owl Crossing, gray clouds obscured the jagged tops of the mountain range she loved. With its rock-strewn mountains, patches of evergreen trees and gentle hills flattening into rich farm and ranch lands, this area had everything. She hurt to think of leaving it.

The town had a single major street lined with businesses. At one end sat a combination grocery store–post office, at the other, a very busy feed store. Myra remembered a time Main Street wasn't paved, when she'd spent summers here as a young girl tagging after Gram and Gramps. Little else had changed about the weathered wood stores, except for a new generation of proprietors.

She parked near the coffee shop owned by the mother of one of her good friends, Lila Jenkins. Only a year older than Myra, Lila was already a widow with a nine-year-old son. Following her husband's death, Lila had begun working part-time for her mom. She also owned a bed-and-breakfast that catered to fishermen, but she was struggling to keep it afloat.

Still discombobulated by her dad's call, Myra hoped a strong cup of coffee would help snap her out of the pain gripping her.

As she entered the cheery, warm café, it surprised her to see a couple of her other friends seated at a back table. Jewell Hyatt, born and raised in Snowy Owl Crossing, now served as the area's main veterinarian. Shelley Price was a few years older than the other women in the Artsy Ladies group. Her husband was a park ranger and she taught ceramics out of her home. Shelley made beautiful items for the November bazaar they all participated in to raise money for the snowy owls.

Lila emerged from the kitchen, saw Myra and smiled. But Myra's heart sank. Saying goodbye, telling her friends she wouldn't be able to finish her projects for the bazaar this year would be harder than she'd imagined.

Spotting her, Jewell stood and beckoned her to their table. "Gosh, Myra. Sit down. What's wrong? You look… I don't know, sad-eyed. Not exactly sick, but not well."

Myra pulled out a chair just as Lila reached them. "Can I get you something? I made chocolate pie today. I know it's your favorite."

"Just coffee. But hurry back," she said, sinking down on the chair across from Jewell. "I've got news. Bad news." She shed her jacket as Lila dashed behind the counter to pour coffee for herself and Myra. As soon as her friend returned, Myra blurted out everything she'd learned from her dad's call.

For an elongated moment her three friends looked stunned. Then Lila leaned over and hugged her. "Is there nothing you can do to change your father's mind?"

Myra blinked away a sudden rush of tears. Not trusting herself to speak, she shook her head.

Jewell reached across the table and squeezed her friend's arm. "Let's think a minute. You say your dad jointly owned the ranch with your grandfather. So as awful as it seems, I guess he has a right to give the property away. Too bad you can't just run this new guy off."

Lila glanced at the others. "Dare she even try running off a former Green Beret? They're tough. Plus, he saved her brother. That makes the guy a hero, right?"

Myra paused before drinking from her steaming mug. "How would I even run him off?"

Jewell clasped her own cup. "Maybe you won't have to run him off. Didn't you say he's from Boston? Managing a cattle ranch isn't like doing a bunch of sit-ups. Even if he led a squad or a platoon or whatever they call it, I don't think that compares to keeping a herd of cattle alive during a Montana winter. What's to say he'll stick it out?"

Shelley, who'd been quietly sipping her tea, smiled. "That's brilliant, Jewell. Myra, why not volunteer to stay on and help this dude like you did your grandpa? Only, you let him do all the dirty, messy chores. Get my drift?"

Myra brightened then frowned. "The folks want me to stay with them while I apply for teaching jobs. They'd probably veto any notion of me sharing a house with a stranger. Even if he did save Eric's life."

Lila leaned forward to stare at Myra. "You're an

adult woman. I work part-time for my mother, but she has no say over my private life."

The others all nodded and Myra blew out a noisy breath. "You make good points. But my parents paid for my education. I never talk to Mom that she doesn't work in how I'm wasting my time tucked away here. She likes living nearer Billings where she has access to big stores and such. City amenities we don't have."

"But that's not you," Jewell stressed. "It's your life. And you know we'll all be disappointed if you leave."

"Not as disappointed as me," Myra admitted, thinking it over. "I usually hire help with haying and branding and such. High school kids from neighboring towns or the reservation. The Flying Owl doesn't have a bunkhouse, so Gramps never kept full-time hired hands. I suppose if I didn't take anyone on this winter, this Lieutenant Maxwell would have to do all the worst chores himself."

"That's right," Jewell said with a smile.

"But I don't know much about him. Eric spent a year under his command. They kept in touch after they both left the service. I can phone my brother and ask if it's safe for me to live under the same roof at least long enough to see he doesn't ruin Gramps's ranch." She perked up the more she talked.

"Now you're sounding like the Myra we all love," Jewell said, grinning. She lifted her coffee mug and all the women did the same, touching their rims in solidarity.

Myra set money on the table for her coffee. "I need

to get to Hadley's store before it closes to stock up on a few things. Zeke Maxwell is due in sometime tomorrow morning. I'll see how our meeting goes. Then I'll phone one of you."

"Zeke? Is that short for something?"

Myra shook her head as she shrugged into her jacket. "Dunno. Eric's mentioned he has a twin brother, who travels the world hunting gems. And I think their parents retired to the Caribbean. I know he bunged up a shoulder and elbow saving Eric and other men while under enemy fire. And for that my dad gave him the Flying Owl." She made a face.

Shelley patted Myra's hand. "Tonight I'll burn a candle with the hope he sees right away that he doesn't fit in. The hard work and isolation in Snowy Owl Crossing might well be too much for him."

"Thanks, everyone. I'd best get moving. I probably still should gather the family albums and put them in a box. And drag out my suitcases. I can't make this visit goodbye. However things shake out, I'll come see you all again." She left then before the tears that sprang to her eyes could fall.

THICK CLOUDS THAT had blanketed the mountaintops for most of the previous day had blown in overnight. By 10:00 a.m. stinging snow had dusted and showed little sign of letting up.

If it continued for long, Myra knew she'd need to haul hay out to the herd. But she wanted to wait for the new owner to put in an appearance. Boy, that title almost gagged her. She had phoned Eric last night. When she'd asked if his former lieutenant suffered from any post-traumatic stress problems, he'd laughed and said Zeke was a solidly good guy through and through. Her brother asked why she wanted to know, but she hadn't told him. Really, she hadn't made up her mind. She'd yet to search online for teaching jobs. She felt qualified to hire on as a ranch hand, too. But with the flat economy, not a lot of ranches were advertising. At least none in the immediate area. She had checked on that.

While she could delay ferrying hay out to the main herd, she didn't want to put off bringing the young steers down from the summer lease in the foothills. Too bad the grass that yesterday had been so green and lush was now white with snow. If need be, she could clear a few patches with her snowblower.

Donning boots, a ski hat with earflaps and a Sherpa-lined leather jacket, Myra tramped to the barn. At the sound of an engine, she glanced toward the private lane. Not recognizing the big black Chevy pickup sporting off-road tires, she assumed her nemesis had arrived.

The man who emerged from the pickup—newer than Gramps's old Ford by at least a decade—looked to top six feet by a couple of inches or so. Bareheaded in a snowstorm, his dark hair was cut military short. He did wear boots and a far-from-new bomber jacket with some insignia patches sewn on the left side. The US flag stood out. It was hard not to notice that his shoulders were broad, but as he strode toward her she detected no sign of an injury to his left side. He walked straight as a telephone pole, a thirtyish guy in perfect shape. So if the VA had put him back together, they'd done a bang-up job.

He stopped a foot or so from her. "Hi. I'm Zeke Maxwell. You must be Myra, Eric's sister."

She lost track of a few seconds as she gazed up into warm dark brown eyes fringed by to-die-for long, thick eyelashes. Caught assessing him, Myra fumbled worn gloves out of her jacket pocket. That gave her a moment before answering as she bent to retrieve one from the snow-covered ground. "Is Zeke a nickname?" she asked, blurting out the question Jewell had asked yesterday.

The man wrinkled his nose. "Ezekiel. A family name that got passed down through generations. As twin A in a set, I drew the short straw. I still haven't forgiven my mother, so you don't want to call me that." He pivoted in a slow circle, dusting snow off his head as he took in the house, barn, sheds and corral before circling back to examine Myra from head to toe. "Why are we standing out here in the weather? I could use a cup of coffee and a fire to warm up."

"The house is unlocked. Coffee's in a thermos by the pot. I'm heading out to drive the cows and yearlings down from the foothills into that enclosure." She stabbed a finger, which he followed without moving his head.

His right shoulder rose slightly then fell. "Give

me a minute to grab a hat and gloves from my truck and I'll join you."

"Being from Boston and all, do you even ride? Do you need me to saddle your horse?" she drawled.

"Unless you give me a nag, I won't hold you back." He spun on a heel and stalked back to his pickup.

Myra tugged on her gloves, flipped up her jacket collar and stomped into the barn. She should probably apologize, but really, if he thought one ran a ranch sitting by a fire drinking coffee, the Flying Owl would be in shambles before spring thaw.

Marching to the back of the barn, she led Cayenne, a sorrel mare, out of her stall and had the saddle on and cinched as Zeke appeared in a Boston Red Sox ball cap. *His ears were gonna freeze, but he'd learn.* "You get the black gelding," she told him. "His name is Ember. Saddle's on the rack. Bridles are on the wall peg." She took one down and settled it over the sorrel's head.

He flashed her a glance, as if he had something to say, but then yanked up the saddle, smoothed the blanket over the gelding's back and settled the saddle as easily as if it were an everyday occurrence. Same with the bridle.

In silence they left the barn. Zeke mounted while Myra closed the barn door, then she, too, swung into the saddle.

Zeke let her lead. As they moved from a trot into a canter, he pulled alongside. "Feels like we're in the middle of a snow globe. Is snow usual this time of year? Will it last? At supper Eric said the weatherman predicted mountain snow. Your dad scoffed."

"The almanac shows it could last a few days. It's early. As a rule, the first snowfall is late September or early October. If this is a harbinger of what's to come, it could wreck winter-wheat crops."

"Do you raise and sell wheat, too?"

"Ranchers raise, cut and bale wheat, grass and alfalfa for cattle feed. Lose a crop and you either have to buy grain at outrageous costs or sell stock you can't afford to feed at a loss." It was plain he didn't know diddly-squat about ranching. Maybe Jewell was right, maybe he'd opt out. She wasn't a fan of feeding the greater herd by hand this early in the season. But if it made him leave, she'd say, let it snow.

They reached the foothills where her stock huddled in a cut between the hills that blocked the windblown snow. Myra rode past them, uncoiled her rope, swung it around and yelled "Hi yi yi" several times. Startled, the animals bolted away from the noise.

"What do you want me to do?" Zeke called.

"Watch for stragglers. Make noise to bring 'em back into the fold. I see some have my neighbor's brand. We'll take them in. He can collect them when it's convenient. Hank Watson runs the Bar W. He's kindly volunteered to truck my yearlings—uh, your yearlings—to market shortly. If you see the slant R brand, that's Dave Ralston, your other neighbor. He's a good guy to know. He rents out his baler. A ranch this size can't afford to buy one."

Zeke bobbed his head.

Myra noticed he rode well, and he brought in a number of strays as they rode down the hillside and made their way to the large enclosure. Subconsciously she'd hoped he'd screw up.

As the ranch came into sight through falling snowflakes, Myra raced ahead, hopped off Cayenne and opened the gate.

Without asking, Zeke hung back and drove the cattle through.

"Phew," he said, swinging down to help Myra shut the gate. "I see they're pawing up the snow to get to grass. Good they know to do that."

"Yep. The snow is slacking some, but we still have to take hay out to the main herd. We'll go put our horses up, hook the big tractor to the flatbed and load up twenty or so bales."

"Okay."

Myra couldn't help but notice he sounded unsure. Maybe she should let him stop for coffee. On the other hand, if she kept the pressure on, by nightfall he could give up.

"Just unsaddle Ember. I'll brush both horses down and feed them later. We need to get the hay distributed while it's light."

Again Zeke followed orders.

Myra fetched the tractor and hooked up the flatbed. Backing the trailer into the barn, she climbed a ladder to the hayloft and began tossing down large bales.

"Do you need assistance?" Zeke asked, squinting up at her.

"You could straighten them on the trailer. If I don't have to do it at the end of pitching off twenty bales, it'll save us time."

He stepped up on the trailer and that was the first time Myra noticed he greatly favored his left arm. She heard him grunt as he hefted the heavy bales one-handed. For someone her size—and at five-seven she wasn't petite—moving bales took knowing how to leverage the weight. Obviously it was the same for a man with an injured arm. She debated telling him to leave the stacking for her, after all. But she didn't want to insult him. When she left, the work would all fall on him unless he hired help. Maybe he had a disability pension that would help cover costs. She and Gramps hadn't had extra money to work with.

"I'll drive the tractor this time because I know the route," she said once they were ready. "You can sit on the bales. See, I've fitted one like a chair so you won't bounce off." She'd thought Zeke might laugh, but he had begun to look weary. And a dense fog had settled down, covering the mountains.

"Feels like we've landed on an alien planet," Zeke hollered after she fired up the tractor and drove into the whirling mist.

So he did have a sense of humor. Myra tossed him a smile over her shoulder.

It took about half an hour to reach the pasture where the Angus heifers milled about on either side of a coulee. A bull stood in the brush beyond the fence. Stopping, Myra took her cutters out of the toolbox welded onto the tractor. Crawling back across hay bales, she cut one open, stood and spread hay into the draw. Big, snorting, drooling cows immediately jockeyed for access to the new hay and began to eat.

Taking his cue, Zeke snipped open the next bale and manhandled it farther along the natural trough. "Listen, this will go quicker if you drive the tractor and I do the bales."

Taking pity on him, because Myra saw it wasn't easy for him to do the lion's share while favoring one arm, she said, "We can take turns. I'll drive the length of this coulee. There's another like it a few hundred yards over nearer the stream. We'll catch it on the return trip. Oh, wait. Can you drive a tractor?"

"I learned to drive anything with a gas pedal and a steering wheel in the army, and we had to improvise if either of those pieces got shot out."

She hid a grimace but nodded. It'd been over a year since her grandfather had been able to help her with any of the heavy chores. Working in tandem with Zeke cut the time by more than half what she'd thought it would take to attend to the herd.

"How many cattle did we just feed?" he asked as she broke apart the last bale.

"A hundred fifty, plus or minus any that wandered off or were taken down by coyotes. There are close to a hundred moms with yearlings that we put in the grassy pen by the barn. Those youngsters will be sold before true winter sets in. You calve in the spring, sell in the fall."

Zeke looked around at the snow falling in earnest. "This isn't winter?"

She rolled her eyes. "Far from it. For a Montana winter you're talking snow too deep to trek through. Once the calves are shipped, you'll bring the main herd down to pastures around the barn. Even then it can snow so hard you'll have to take grain out on a sled. Every day you'll break the ice on the water troughs."

He hunched over the steering wheel and followed their earlier tracks back to the barn. Parking, he let the motor idle. "What next?"

"I'll store the tractor and see to the horses. Then I'll go in and start supper. Why don't you go on to the house and get settled. I cleared out Gramps's bedroom and put fresh sheets on the bed and towels in the bathroom. It's the room to the right of the living room. My bedroom is at the back of the house. I could pack up and head out tonight, but with this storm I'd rather wait until morning."

Zeke studied her as he took his ball cap off. "I thought maybe you'd spend a few days showing me the ropes. But we can discuss that later. Tell you what, I'll take KP duty tonight while you finish up out here. Then we can talk, and maybe you'll go over the ranch accounts. Your dad said you kept the books and your mom jumped in to tell me you're a high school math teacher."

"I was. I won't turn down your offer to cook. It's my least favorite chore. The kitchen is old and small, but at least everything is functional and stocked."

"Your father mentioned the house might need some work. He said not much has been changed since he was born and raised here."

"I like it as is. The roof doesn't leak and the fireplace works. So do the showers."

"Uh-huh. It's snowing harder. How much time do you need, so I know when to have supper on the table?"

"An hour should do it."

He tipped his cap and made tracks for his pickup.

Myra climbed onto the tractor, ratcheted up the engine and backed the trailer into its spot in the shed. She watched Zeke take two duffel bags from under his pickup's canopy and hike on to the house.

Sighing, she went in to take care of the horses, dialing her brother on the way to inform him that due to the snow she wasn't leaving the ranch just yet. She contacted Eric instead of her parents because she still resented how they had given away a ranch they should have known she loved.

HIS EARS STUNG from the cold as he walked into a warm house he now owned. It all still felt surreal to Zeke. Particularly since he hadn't realized the house would be occupied by Eric's sister. He'd spent half a day with her, but as yet couldn't pigeonhole her. Figuring her out became more difficult once he entered this home. At his first glance around the living room, on nearly every flat surface in the living room sat dollhouses. *A grown woman had dollhouses?* They were all so elaborate. On closer inspection he saw not all of them were complete. Several had walls but no roofs. A few were unpainted. Taking care not to knock into any of them with his duffels, he located the bedroom Myra had mentioned. He flipped on a light switch that lit two bedside lamps. The big bed, covered with a thick quilt, looked inviting. Thankfully, the decor was neutral. No frills. Having noted ruffled curtains on some of the dollhouse windows, he hadn't known what to expect.

Since he'd promised to cook, he dropped the bags and found the kitchen. *Vintage* didn't begin to describe the space. Outdated but spotless. He didn't see a microwave, and the stove and fridge were surely older than his thirty-one years. He opened cupboards and took stock, then peered inside the fridge. A clicking sound, like dog toenails striking the linoleum, had Zeke straightening and looking around. The noise was coming from the corner where the back door was, behind a dinette set with four chairs. A pen fashioned by baby gates held a quilt, plastic toys, metal dishes of water, lettuce and some kind of pellets. Therein roamed a pig. A pig. Small and white with gray spots. A door with a doggie flap opened onto what looked like a screened porch.

He was still shaking his head in disbelief when his cell phone rang. Plucking it from his pocket he saw his twin's number. "Seth, buddy, where are you this month?"

"I'm back in Afghanistan. My gem contact phoned to say his men found an area of pure lapis. I flew in yesterday to have a look. He was right, and it's rare to find lapis without occlusions, so we're dickering on price. I got your text saying you were going to Montana. The family of one of the guys you saved gave you a ranch? Is that true, or did you injure your head as well as your shoulder?"

"It's true. In fact, I'm there now. I spent my first afternoon hauling hay to cattle in a snowstorm."

"You're kidding! What do you know about ranching, dude?"

"Nothing. But Eric Odell's sister—his folks are the ones who gave me the ranch—she's been running the ranch. Their grandfather owned it before he died. She's a teacher, and Eric's parents told me she wants to get back to her career. But I had to admit, trekking after her today I saw how much I don't know. I had hoped she might stay awhile to give me pointers."

"But?"

"But…then I came in the house. She's got dollhouses everywhere. Like, is it a fetish? And, Seth, I discovered she keeps a pig as a house pet. Now I wonder if she's been tucked away in this remote spot to hide the fact she's eccentric, to put it mildly."

His brother laughed loudly. "If you have the deed, kick her out. Hire an old cowboy to teach you what you need to know. Seems to me you've stepped into a sweetheart deal. I'm envious that you get to live in wide-open spaces. Sometimes I'm so tired of eating and sleeping in hotels."

"Take a break and come visit me. We can learn how to run a ranch together."

"Maybe. Not for a while. I have this lapis I want, then I'm off to Tanzania. Tanzanite is getting scarce. I've got a friend who has staked a claim that he's sure will yield a vein. I haven't actually done any digging in months. It'll be fun."

"Yeah, yeah. I've heard this song and dance from you for years. You don't want to set down roots. You've got the wanderlust, bro."

"Hmm. We'll see. It gets to be a hard-knock life. Email me pictures of your ranch. It'll remind me what it's like to have a home."

"Sure. I'll take some after this snowstorm passes. You take care. Especially in the Hindu Kush. Our forces have drawn down. It's less safe than when you visited me there."

"So I hear. We'll keep in touch. Good luck with Pet-Pig Woman."

Zeke grimaced, gave the round little pig a last glance then started fixing supper. Midway through preparations, he heard the front door open and close, and then footsteps going toward the back of the house. Then he heard water running and figured Myra had opted to take a shower. It was probably something he should have done, he thought as he found dishes and set the table. Were they really going to eat next to a penned pig? *Apparently so.*

It wasn't long before Myra appeared in the doorway. She wore slippers, clean jeans and a checked flannel shirt, and her shoulder-length, tawny-gold hair fell in damp waves around a face scrubbed clean of makeup. Zeke hadn't paid such close attention before. Framed in the doorway, she seemed younger and prettier than he recalled while she'd dragged him through a snowstorm.

"Wow, something smells good. Can I help? Oh, I see you've even set the table. Sorry I was so long. I took time to oil the tack. Saddles and bridles are expensive. Oiled, they hold up better in the weather."

Zeke shook himself loose from eyeing her. "Your timing is great. Go on and choose where you normally sit. I'll bring everything to the table."

Myra crossed the room and pulled out a chair. Like magic, steaming dishes began to fill up the table. Her mouth dropped open. "You made scalloped potatoes and green beans with almonds?" She blinked up at Zeke as he set a basket of homemade biscuits in front of her, followed by a slice of sirloin steak he pulled out from under the broiler.

"Dig in while everything's hot," he said. "Oh, wait." He snapped his fingers and turned to rummage in the fridge. "I saw butter somewhere."

"In the top compartment on the fridge door."

He carried the butter dish to the table even as Myra broke open a hot biscuit. "These are as flaky as my gram used to make. Mine are like lead weights. Everything looks scrumptious. Where did you learn to cook like this?"

"Before I joined the military, I worked in restaurants. I also pulled my share of KP duty prior to getting into a Green Beret unit."

"I'll do dishes tonight, but I draft you to fix breakfast." Her mouth was full when he shot a deliberate glance toward her pet pig.

"I've never had bacon or ham on the hoof, but I guess I can make do." He smiled crookedly as he cut a slice of steak.

Her fierce glare made plain that Myra wasn't amused.

Chapter Two

"Orion is a hundred percent pet." Myra's tone was challenging. "Our local vet found him when she responded to a tip about a family who skipped town in the middle of the night leaving a goat, a donkey and a young indoor pig to fend for themselves. Some call him a potbellied pig, but he's really a micromini. Jewell knew I didn't have a dog or cat, so she talked me into adopting him."

"Jewell?" Zeke looked blank.

"Our vet. You'll meet her. She takes care of animals large and small, plus she heads the committee trying to obtain a habitat for our snowy owls."

"I see. In the developing world, I got used to seeing animals in people's homes that you never see in the US. Really, the quilt and squeaky toys in his pen tipped me off that you weren't raising him for food."

"Teacup pigs and microminis are intelligent, curious, funny, affectionate, clean animals. Orion was good company for Gramps, and now me." She paused, her fork in the air. "I expect Mom will pitch a fit when I show up at their house with him." Myra's agitation showed in the short, stabbing cuts she made to her steak.

"Uh, hey, I forgot to pour coffee." Zeke rose, went to the counter and picked up the pot. "Do you take cream or sugar?"

"No."

"Look, I was teasing about the pig. I didn't mean to upset you." Zeke poured their coffee and returned the pot to the burner.

She dropped her utensils and picked up her cup. But when their eyes met over the rim, Myra hurriedly averted her gaze. "Nothing to do with the Flying Owl is a joke."

He gestured with his cup. "I…ah…don't know a lot about cattle ranching."

"No kidding."

Leaning back, Zeke studied her, his expression pensive. "It strikes me you weren't prepared to have me show up today to take over."

Her eyes flashed. "Take over? Listen, you fixed a great meal. I want to enjoy it."

"No problem." He took a second helping. "I'm just getting way different vibes from you than I got from your family. Your mom went on and on about how anxious you are to get back to teaching in the city."

Myra took more green beans, knowing she was being uncharacteristically surly. "My parents think I should be anxious. Especially Mom." She couldn't seem to stop resenting Zeke. But soon the only noise in the kitchen was the ticktock of the old wall clock and Orion rooting in his dish.

Zeke drained his cup and got up for more coffee. Retaking his seat, he said, “Is it safe to ask you about the ranch finances? I don’t want to cast aspersions on your dad, because he and your mother treated me really well. But did he give me an albatross? I can see the house needs work, but my brother said the land must be worth a lot.”

Myra’s heart gave a kick. She hunched forward. Had he given her an opening to lay it on thick and convince him the ranch was a dud? *She couldn’t lie. It wasn’t in her.* She took her time before looking him in the eye. “To my dad, who left here at twenty-five when he got married and began to build his own spread on a ranch that belonged to my mom’s parents, this has always been the old home place. As Gramps aged, he set up a trust with my dad, his only child. Were you insinuating you might want to sell?” Trying for casual, Myra took a drink.

When Zeke continued his silent regard of her, she gestured with her free hand. “I’d be willing to go to the bank and see what they’d allow me for a loan to buy you out.”

“You? I thought you couldn’t wait to get back to your teaching career.”

She shrugged lightly, not wanting to give away how badly she wanted to own this ranch. “Having lived here three and a half years, I’ve discovered I have a knack for ranching. It's probably too late to get a teaching spot. Schools start soon."

"I wasn't thinking of selling. But if not teaching, what will you do?"

Myra shrugged again. "Maybe one of the bigger ranches needs a cowhand."

Zeke toyed with his cup, then grinned. "On my drive here, on the other side of a town called Miles City, I saw a sign on a fence post. At the time it made me laugh. 'Housekeeper wanted. Must be able to drive a tractor and work cattle.' Maybe you'd do."

She got up and started gathering their dirty dishes.

"So, no comment?"

"Miles City isn't Snowy Owl Crossing. And I'd be leery of a job with that description. The term *housekeeper* could entail more side activities than I'd care to take on."

"Like what? Oh…oh! I get you." He blushed. "I'm not usually that slow on the uptake."

It was her turn to stammer in embarrassment. "Uh, I actually meant it might mean the rancher also needed a nanny to take care of his kids."

"Yikes! Are you kidding me?"

"No. At the grange hall it's not uncommon to hear of some cowboy-rancher's wife he met on the rodeo circuit finding ranch life not so glamorous after they have a couple of kids."

"It does seem life out here might be lonely. How close is the nearest neighbor?" he asked, sliding from his chair to bring his dishes to where she stood loading the dishwasher.

"A…a mile or so from here." Myra straightened. Their arms brushed, surprising her because she hadn't realized he'd gotten so close. She stepped back and almost fell over the open dishwasher door.

"Hey, hey. Careful." Zeke grabbed her upper arm to keep her from taking a spill.

Caught between his close, warm body and the dishwasher, her breath hitched and her pulse quickened. She breathed a sigh of relief when he let go of her arm and moved aside.

Her cell phone rang. Myra recognized her neighboring rancher's number. "Hank, hi," she said, stepping away from the sink. "Is everything okay at the Bar W?"

"It's good. I thought I'd check on you. I was in town picking up supplies and I heard a rumor you were leaving. I'm running trucks to market in a few days if the snow melts—and the weathermen predict it will. Do you still need space for your stock?"

Myra pinched the bridge of her nose. She should've known her business would be all over town. The café wasn't empty when she talked to her friends. And gossip was a mainstay of any small town. "I… We still need a truck. I helped the ranch's new owner trail cow-calf pairs down to our grass pasture today. Are any of the Jarvis boys home? Lieutenant Maxwell is going to need help sorting, and certainly help sending cows through chutes for vaccinating, parasite treatment and pregnancy testing."

"Lieutenant Maxwell? Is that the soldier hero who saved Eric's life? Your grandpa Cal mentioned him."

"He's one and the same. Dad gave him the Flying Owl." She made an effort to not sound distressed.

"Hot damn! Where does that leave you, Myra?"

"I'm still figuring that out. About the Jarvis boys…?"

"Two are off at college, and I guess you didn't hear that Gordy, the high school junior, broke his leg playing football. He's in a cast."

"Damn." Myra frowned at Zeke, who'd finished loading the dishwasher and leaned against the sink cabinet watching her.

"The yearlings have to be weaned for market," she went on. "I can do that since some of the money from the sale is slated to pay off the last of Gramps's banknote. When will you have room on a semi?"

"Day after tomorrow. I can be there to load up by nine."

"Okay. Oh, and Hank, I drove down a couple of Bar W heifers and calves, and a few of Ralston's that mixed in with my herd. Working in snow I figured it'd be easiest to bring them all in."

"Dave rented my truck for tomorrow. I'll ask if he'll send a cowhand over while you're cutting."

They reiterated a time for loading and said goodbye. Myra tossed her phone on the counter. "What was that all about?" Zeke asked.

Myra put soap in the dishwasher and started it running. "It means you're stuck with me for a few more days at least. Unless you can pull a cowboy out of your hat. There are calves to get to market and bills to pay. Hank only charges for the gas it costs to drive from here to the stockyards. You won't get a better deal in your lifetime. Plus, greenhorn that you are, you need to see and help with a process that gets done every year."

"Okay. But does that mean you have to forgo finding a teaching job?"

"I told you, it's probably too late now to secure a fall opening."

"You did. You also offered to buy me out. Greenhorn I may be, but I'm not ready to sell. Not until I know if I have what it takes to be a rancher. Just so we're clear, I had what it took to be a Green Beret."

"Touché." She opened the fridge and pulled out some fresh lettuce from the keeper, crossed the room and set it in Orion's bowl. She rubbed his ears and the pig all but smiled.

"Is he full grown?" Zeke asked.

Myra shook her head. "He weighs about fourteen pounds. Jewell says the full-grown micromini probably ends up twenty pounds."

"Do you have a dog to help herd cattle and the like?"

"Not now. Gramps had a beautiful border collie. Lucy gave out before he did, and he'd had her for so many years he couldn't fathom loving another dog.

He made fun of Orion when I brought him home. But it wasn't long before I noticed him talking to the pig. And Orion liked to sit with Gramps in his recliner." She smiled at the memory.

Zeke smiled back. "Look, if you're not champing at the bit to get to bed, can we talk bookkeeping? I already know from listening to you speak with the neighbor that I have a lot to absorb about what goes on outside. But if I don't understand the economics I'll be sunk before I start."

"It's a boring subject, but if we brew another pot of strong coffee I'll give you some hard facts and walk you through the software I use."

"We'll have to load that onto my laptop, I guess."

"Good idea," Myra said, dumping what little coffee remained in the old pot. Then she prepared a new one. "In the meantime, I'll get my laptop. We can work at the kitchen table. There's a desk in the third bedroom, but it shares space with all of my dollhouse materials and jigsaws and stuff."

"About those dollhouses…?" Zeke's voice trailed off, but his question hung between them.

Myra sifted a hand through her hair. "I'll deliver the finished ones to another member of the Artsy Ladies before I leave. I don't know what I'll do with the half-completed projects, or the unused material and equipment. But never fear, I'll clear everything of mine out."

His forehead wrinkled. "I'm afraid I'm still in the dark here. Who are the Artsy Ladies?"

"Some of us formed a group to sell crafts and hopefully save the snowy owls for which the town is named. They've always nested in timberland running through Canada and the US. The owls are sacred to our local Native Americans, too."

"Okay, I get that," Zeke said.

"They're gorgeous. Wait until you see them in flight, or in their nests if you ride up to the woods. Sorry, I'm getting off track. About the dollhouses… Our veterinarian was born and raised in Snowy Owl Crossing. She first noticed a decline in the owl population when she came home to open her vet practice. Right after I moved here to help Gramps, she organized a committee to look into securing a state wildlife refuge for the birds. It takes money to fight for anything like that. Asking for donations to buy expensive land went nowhere in a bad economy. So some of us decided to hold a Thanksgiving bazaar and all sell crafts. Profits above material costs go to fund our effort. We named our group the Artsy Ladies."

"I counted a dozen dollhouses. There's that big a demand for them?"

"You'd be surprised. People come from miles around to buy them and the other handmade wares."

Zeke looked skeptical.

The coffeepot gurgled. "If the houses bug you, I'll make time to haul them away. I'm sure someone can store them until the bazaar."

He held up a hand. "It's okay. I didn't understand.

Why don't I pour our coffee while you get the computer."

"Okay, but prepare to be bored. People born to ranching, like my dad, keep a lot of these facts and figures in their heads. As a math major, I'm different. I like spreadsheets." She left and came back with a laptop. "Even Gramps said keeping a spreadsheet helped us not to overspend. But so you know, some years you make a profit and some you go in the hole. It's imperative to be on good terms with your local banker, who'll float loans to tide you over in bad years. Notes you pay back in a year when stock prices are up and you haven't been plagued by a horrid winter or summer drought." Myra fired up the computer just as the lights flickered.

Zeke shot a glance at the ceiling lights.

"Don't worry, we have a generator if the power goes out. Lanterns and flashlights, too."

He pulled a chair around to her side of the table and sat.

His body heat warmed Myra, but left her stumbling over giving him basic costs for cows, feed, bull, labor, transportation, vet and other supplies. "In a fantastic year still only eighty percent of our cows wean calves. Heifer calves weigh less than steers, which bring less money. See this column. For last year I adjusted the amount we earned in stock sales. This year I'll do the same when we ship." She discreetly edged her chair away from his.

Seeming not to notice, he said, "Hmm. You broke

even the prior year, but lost money last year. Is that typical?"

She waved her hand to indicate that it varied. "It's better than average for a small operation. A big cattle ranch like Dad's can run four or five years in a row on borrowed money and then have a huge windfall. In an up year you buy equipment or roof the barn. And there goes the profit."

"At the risk of sounding obtuse, why keep on keeping on?"

She sat back and shut down the program. "I guess it's for love of the land. There's not much open land left. I can't explain it, but ranching is a job that gives you a sense of freedom. Isn't that what you fought for? I know it's why Eric went into the army."

Zeke reached up to massage his wounded shoulder. He didn't answer her question.

"That's enough lessons for tonight." Feeling too close to him for comfort, Myra abruptly got up, closed the laptop and carried her cup to the sink. "I see it's still snowing," she said, looking out the kitchen window. "It's lessened some, but not totally. So it's time to take another batch of hay to the cows."

"Really?" Zeke frowned.

"Snow and cold pulls weight off an animal fast. In winter or like with this early snow, it's day and night feeding. Cattle raising is almost always a seven-day-a-week job, Zeke. There's also night work during calving. Grab your coat, and if you don't own a hat with earflaps, there are extras on the rack by the front door."

Myra went to the front door and pulled on her boots, jacket and hat. She picked up a big flashlight and led the way to the barn.

Zeke, who'd had to rush to keep up, didn't say anything until after they'd loaded the trailer again and he sat shivering on the hay. "If I wasn't here," he called to be heard above the tractor noise, "would you be doing this alone?"

Myra briefly glanced back. "Yes. I've gone solo the last two years, once Gramps's arthritis got so bad he couldn't take the cold." From her companion's pensive expression, she actually wondered if he might seriously be contemplating returning his gift. If that happened, she needed to phone her father in the morning, to be square with him. He needed to know if Zeke didn't want the ranch that she did. She didn't expect to be willed any part of Rolling Acres, so the Flying Owl was it for her. Eric would benefit from her parents' holdings. Most ranches could only support one family. If one sibling had to buy out the interests of others, it put a hardship on the one left. Sometimes that person couldn't afford to get married and raise a family.

That made her wonder if Zeke Maxwell had a steady girlfriend or even a wife stashed away in Boston or some other port of call. If so, that person most definitely wasn't a ranch woman, or he'd have said so—wouldn't he?

Because all things to do with Lieutenant Maxwell gave her heartburn, Myra stopped thinking about him. Instead, she concentrated on signs that told her she was still on the right path to reach the herd.

It was spitting snow when the first bunch of cows came into sight. Stopping, Myra let the tractor idle and passed Zeke the cutters. "Will you toss this mob some hay, please?"

"How much?" He rose stiffly.

"I could say as much as they'll eat. But until we see what all is left tomorrow, we won't know if we gave them too much or not enough. Just free a bale and scatter hay as I drive along."

Zeke cut the first bale open. "Are these different cows than those we already fed? I thought we'd be tossing hay in the same places."

"You should try to feed in different spots so the manure doesn't get so deep in one area. Saves you from having to spread fertilizer around when the snow melts, plus it gives cows a clean table to eat, so to speak. If we had to have an early snowfall, this is a good area for the herd. There are plenty of draws and shrubs to shelter them from the wind. And the stream's not in danger of freezing over. Water and feed are the two essentials. After you separate the cows from the yearlings and Hank transports them, you'll drive these cows and the bull down to the pastures nearer the barn. I'll try to show you those pens tomorrow."

"When do you move them back up here?" he asked

right before she revved the tractor and they headed to the next grouping of cows huddled against the biting wind.

"After these heifers drop their calves in the spring. Usually that's March and April. I suppose I can make a chore list," she called back to him, trying not to sound exasperated. But the man was a total novice. What had her father been thinking? Had he been blinded by the fact Zeke had put himself in harm's way to save Eric that he gave no thought to what might befall the Flying Owl? That kind of selfless heroism did deserve recognition, but darn, couldn't her dad have called in some markers and found Zeke a job in Billings or maybe with the Stock Association? Her grandfather and her dad had both once been officers.

Zeke remained strangely silent throughout the rest of the hay distribution. Perhaps he was too cold to talk. The snow petered out. As they drove home, the sky cleared to patchy clouds. The silvery moon popped in and out of the clouds. Those were the quiet beauties that never failed to touch Myra's heart. She wondered what was going through Zeke's mind. He never said a word.

It was well past midnight when she once again unhitched the trailer and stored the tractor in its shed.

Zeke broke his silence. "I'd think times like this would be when you'd want to have a dog. What if you run into trouble out there in the dead of night?"

She cocked her head and guided him to the house. Stamping snow off her boots at the door, she said, "I have my cell phone and there's good service all over this ranch. But if you want a dog, Zeke," she said, opening the door and shedding her hat and jacket inside, "I know Jewell would be more than happy to hook you up with a healthy pet. I can ask her to drop by tomorrow or the next day. We need vaccine for the heifers. If you want my advice, don't let her get you a puppy. You're going to have plenty to learn about the ranch, which won't leave time to train a puppy."

He nodded. "How much sleep do you get?" he asked tiredly.

Myra took pity on him because he did look beat. "I know I tagged you to fix breakfast, but how about if tomorrow I handle that? In fall and winter we eat breakfast around six. Spring and summer earlier."

"I'll set my cell-phone alarm. Is there a towel I can use in the bathroom?"

"Yep. And the bedding is fresh. It's all new, actually. Courtesy of my mom. They stayed here for Gramps's funeral."

Zeke returned his borrowed hat to the rack, excused himself and made a beeline for his bedroom.

Myra was weary, too. Probably she was more tired for still laboring under the shocking news that she needed to turn over her beloved ranch to a stranger. To a man who, however heroic he might have been on the battlefield, was green as a gourd about cattle ranching. Going to the kitchen, she picked up Orion, whispered her thoughts to him and carried him to her room.

LATE THOUGH IT WAS, Zeke needed to shower. He hoped the sound wouldn't keep Myra awake.

Letting hot water beat down on his back and the sore shoulder that still bore scars from his surgeries, his mind drifted. Myra Odell of the curling blond hair and somber, whiskey-colored eyes, was a dynamo. She was nothing like her sibling. When he'd acquired Eric on his combat team, the kid had been fresh-faced and kind of unsure about everything. He'd never have made a career soldier.

Zeke shut off the water and toweled dry. He thought about Myra going out in the snowy evening to load a trailer and haul hay into a stark, cloudy night. Eric hadn't shirked any duty to which he'd been assigned, but he hated night patrol. He went out of his way to trade night duty for any number of undesirable tasks. Maybe that all stemmed from growing up feeding cattle on nights like tonight.

Checking his clothes as he emptied his duffels and hung things in the closet, he noted that while he'd brought long-sleeved shirts and knit Henleys, he didn't own anything flannel. He made a mental note to buy flannel shirts, long underwear and a Sherpa-lined jacket like Myra wore. August had yet to end and both times he'd ridden out with her he'd frozen his fanny.

He fell into bed, wondering if he did have what it'd take to be a rancher. His twin had called this a sweetheart deal. Even he'd considered it a windfall when the papers from Jack Odell had arrived. Now he wasn't sure.

As he lay on his back, staring up into total blackness, it crossed his mind that he could sell the cows, cattle or whatever one called them. And use his army disability pay to live out his days here rocking on the back porch he'd glimpsed. From his drive up, he could see that the mountain range behind the property held a certain gray and purple majesty.

Forget it. The still-rational part of his brain reminded him how stir-crazy he'd been during his recovery and later in Boston when he hadn't found a job. He wasn't cut out to do nothing. So what were his options? No clear idea came to mind because the warmth of the soft bed and the day's unfamiliar exercise overtook him and he slid into sleep.

LIGHT POURING INTO the bedroom woke Zeke. At first he felt disoriented, until the room coalesced around him and he remembered having come to the ranch. The Montana ranch he now owned.

Even as he kicked off the covers and sat up, his phone alarm chimed. And he smelled something cooking. Sausage, maybe.

Climbing from the bed caused pain in more areas than his injured elbow and shoulder, and left him feeling as if he'd aged overnight. It had to have a lot to do with manhandling hay bales, or perhaps bouncing around on a tractor-pulled flatbed. That last trip out to the herd had been an especially rough ride.

How had he gotten so out of shape in ten months? The six he'd spent in VA surgeries and rehab, and the four he'd spent pounding the streets in Boston job hunting? Before that, he'd jogged Afghan hills carrying a loaded M16 and a fifty-pound pack.

Zeke told himself to stop being wussy. After dressing, he made the bed, and after washing his face, left his room—only to fall over Myra's pig. The creature was chasing a rubber ball down the hall. To keep from stepping on the pig, he lurched to the side, but slammed into the door frame. It shook the house and hurt his right arm—thankfully, not his healing left one. All the same, it prompted a colorful array of swearwords.

When he regained his balance and glanced up, Myra stood in the kitchen doorway, spatula in hand.

"What in the world happened?"

"I tripped over your silly pig."

"Sorry. I let him out to exercise when I know he can't go outside. Will you put him in his pen? I have sausage and potatoes warming in the oven. Now that you're up I'll fix the pancakes."

She disappeared from the doorway, her voice floating back to Zeke. He gingerly picked up the round little pig and was surprised when the animal snuggled under his unshaven jaw. Zeke hadn't expected a pig to act like a puppy or for those ears to be so soft.

Feeling a bit awkward, Zeke scooped up the ball, too, and did as Myra asked, carrying pig and ball to the kitchen pen, where he deposited them.

"Thanks. I'll fill you a plate and you can wash up. I'm happy to report yesterday's storm has passed. Can you hear the snow melting off the eaves? A weak sun is rising. Unfortunately it'll make everything slushy and slick."

"What's on our agenda for today? If the snow is melting, does that mean we don't have to haul hay out to the cows?"

"That depends on how strong the sunlight gets. There's still grass in the hills. There's also more shade, and the cattle may stay in the shelter of coulee brush. I'll check to see if better weather is predicted. If so, we can take out a few cakes of protein supplement to tide them over until the grass is visible again."

Zeke dried his hands on the kitchen towel she handed him. "Okay," he said agreeably, taking the warm plate of food from her.

"I'll bring the coffee carafe to the table so we don't have to hop up and down."

Zeke watched her dump a teacup full of lettuce, carrot and an apple slice into the pig's heavy metal bowl before she brought her plate and the coffeepot to the table.

"Is that all you feed…what did you call him?"

"Orion. And yes," she said, settling down after pouring them both coffee. "He's a miniature. I'm not fattening him up for market. A pig will eat all day if you let them. Jewell said it's no different for ones bred as house pets. He eats scraps in small portions. I have to keep his water bowl full always. And so you know, while we're here, never give him salty treats, avocado or chocolate. That's why I have child locks on the bottom kitchen cabinets. If he's loose he opens cupboards."

"I wondered about that yesterday." Zeke looked up from his plate. "Does he sleep in the pen at night?"

"I have a dog crate in my bedroom with his night blanket."

Zeke shook his head and tucked into his food.

"If you get a dog before I leave here, you'll have to feed him in the barn. Orion would gorge himself on dog food, which is way too rich for a mini pig."

Swallowing the last bit of sausage, Zeke picked up his coffee. "I'm still not clear on what all you say is on today's agenda. I recall you told your neighbor we'd get stock ready for him to take to market. Do all ranchers work together?"

"I'll start with basics about our community. The reservation borders town on the east. Sioux, mostly. It's a community in itself, similar to Snowy Owl Crossing. They farm, ranch and guide hunters and fishermen. Like local ranches, the Flying Owl is a cow-calf operation. We get calves in the spring and sell them in the fall." She paused until she saw Zeke nod as if he followed her explanation.

"Calves are ear-tagged at birth to make sure they don't get separated from mothers. Pairs are sorted and calves branded before we move the herd to summer range. I've found it's easier to keep heifers with calves to eventually be sold in an area with access to a bull so they'll produce again. Those that didn't calve this year spend time with a rented bull in summer. Hopefully to produce calves. That's what'll happen to some of the ones we fed yesterday. Have I stopped making sense? You look mystified."

He placed his knife and fork across his empty plate. "It's a lot to take in. Are there books that teach cattle ranching?"

"Books?"

Zeke gestured with his cup. "Yes, in boot camp we were issued technical manuals explaining much of what a new recruit needed to know."

"I suppose there are books. Aren't there books written on practically everything?"

"Yes, but if you didn't learn all the stuff you spout off the top of your head from a book," he said, frustrated, "how is it you know so much?"

"I was born on a ranch," she pointed out, standing to collect both of their plates. "Summers from my earliest memory I spent right here tagging after Gramps. Oh, sure, Gram taught me canning, jam making and cooking. But I learned all I've ever needed to know about running a ranch from helping Gramps and Dad do the work."

"Okay, so listen. I'm having some thoughts here. Yesterday you said it's too late for you to get a teaching job this fall. What would you charge to stay here and work for me until a math job comes your way? I can follow you around and learn what I need to know to keep this ranch running like it does now."

The dishes clattered in the sink where Myra dropped them. She spun toward him, her mouth agape. "Wor… work…for you?"

Zeke sucked his bottom lip between his teeth then released it. "Didn't mean to take you by surprise. I do own this ranch now," he said gently. "If it's a title you want, how about we call you the ranch manager until I get up to speed?"

Myra's cell rang, and she snatched it off the counter. "It's, uh, my dad. I'm sure he's calling to see if I'm headed to Rolling Acres. I only spoke to Eric last night. I'll be right back."

Zeke heard her say hello as she walked down the hall. Then her bedroom door slammed and he was left in a kitchen devoid of noise except for Orion rooting for food in his almost empty dish. Bending, Zeke rubbed the pig's large pink ears. "Shocked her I did, Piggy Pal. It sounded like a good idea to me." He finished his coffee, replaced the pot on the burner and put the breakfast dishes in the dishwasher. Myra still hadn't returned, so he went to shave. Although, if it was as cold out today as yesterday, maybe he should grow a beard. But he didn't like them because he'd been required to have one for so long. He'd needed one in Afghanistan to blend in with locals. Not blending in could have gotten him killed. Once he separated from the military, he'd stayed clean shaven, and considered it a luxury. Passing a hand over his prickly cheeks, he detoured back to his room.

Chapter Three

Myra said hello, but didn't acknowledge that she knew it was her father calling. She was still majorly upset with him. It felt right to give her bedroom door a hard push.

"Myra, it's Dad. Your mother asked me to call to see if you'd be home for lunch. We thought you'd be under way already."

Pacing around the bedroom that had been hers off and on for many years, Myra weighed her answer. "Actually, I won't be home for lunch or anytime soon."

"Why? Eric said you had more snow than we did, but I saw on the morning news that the highway is clear. You shouldn't have trouble driving."

"The weather has improved. But, Dad, you turned the Flying Owl over to a total novice. I can't walk away and let the ranch fall into ruin."

"What do you mean? It's not a working ranch anymore. Your grandfather told me he was trapped under a mountain of medical bills after Gram died. That's why he sold what was left of his herd and offered a chunk of pasture to a neighbor."

"What are you talking about?"

"I told him to sell the whole shebang and come live with us, but he refused. When you went to help out, I didn't press further. So up to now I've ignored your mom's unhappiness over the way you put your career on a back burner. Frankly, with Eric in a war zone and making sure Rolling Acres stayed in the black, not needing to worry about my dad's health and well-being took a load off me. But, honey, you can stop feeling responsible for the Flying Owl. I paid the estate tax and the last payment on Dad's banknote. Giving the property to Lieutenant Maxwell frees us all up."

"You paid Gramps's banknote? Why? I'm about to ship last year's calves. That revenue is earmarked to cover the note and sustain the ranch until we sell next year's calves."

"Come on, Myra. How many pregnant cows did Dad own? Twenty? Although I can't fathom why he didn't sell the lot. His asthma and arthritis were so bad when we talked shortly before he passed away, he admitted he hadn't walked out to the barn in almost a year."

"He didn't need to, Dad. I managed the ranch. I grew his herd. He had around a hundred head when I moved here. We didn't sell any. This year I'll be shipping almost that many calves. Our overall herd stands at close to three hundred."

There was a long silence. Enough for Myra to think she'd lost the connection. Suddenly her father yelped an explosive "Why am I only hearing about this now? Isn't that something you should have told me at Dad's funeral?"

"You didn't ask." Myra crossed to her bedroom window. "As I recall, you guys were in a rush to leave and barely stayed for the reception my friend from the café in town helped prepare."

"I'm sorry about that, honey. You know Rolling Acres was in the middle of calving. With Eric and me at the funeral, it only left two ranch hands to handle a four-man task."

"You didn't hear me say I was in the middle of calving, too? Thank goodness two of my neighbors helped out, which is what neighbors in Snowy Owl Crossing do."

"Honey, I didn't call to argue. I honestly had no idea Dad didn't sell off his herd. But I'm good with you keeping the funds from your stock sale to tide you over until you find a teaching job. Instead of staying with us, you may want to rent an apartment in Billings or Missoula, whichever city you think offers the best opportunity for you. Of course your mom and I would rather you be in Billings. That way you can come on holidays to visit. Oh, your mom is just saying come stay over summer breaks, too, until you find some significant someone, get married and start a home of your own."

Myra recognized the smile in his voice that surely

came from her parents' long-standing wish for her to get married. She wasn't in any mood to humor them. "You still aren't hearing me, Dad. I'm not leaving here. Not yet. I love this ranch. I realize we all owe former Lieutenant Maxwell a debt of gratitude. But he knows zero, zippo, not one thing about cattle. What happens to the Flying Owl, not if but when he flounders? When he realizes he's in over his head, I want to be here to carry on. Then I'll do my level best to convince Nate Gooding at the bank to lend me money to buy Maxwell out."

"That's preposterous, Myra. Do you have any idea what that land is worth? The property taxes alone are partly why I decided to gift the ranch to Eric's friend."

"And it never entered your mind to ask if I was interested in keeping the ranch? Aren't Eric and I the only two in line to inherit from you and Mom? I assume he'll take over Rolling Acres. I thought this was my legacy."

"But…but you went to college when your brother chose the military. Before his obligation was up, he saw it was a mistake. He told us he'd be returning to the ranch. At the risk of sounding old-school, Myra, ranches belong in the hands of a competent man."

She'd heard this before, but it still irritated her. "I can't believe you said that. And man though he is, Zeke Maxwell is about as far from being a competent rancher as I've ever seen. The one thing in his favor so far, he's begun to see it himself. This morning he offered me a job managing the Flying Owl.

At the time I wasn't sure I wanted to work for him. Now I think I'll stay and hope by spring our city boy tires of Snowy Owl Crossing's isolation. Sorry, Dad, I've gotta run. Hank Watson is trucking our calves to market tomorrow, so I've a full day's weaning ahead of me."

Hearing her dad sputter as she removed the phone from her ear, Myra disconnected. Fully expecting a callback from her mother, she tossed her phone down on her nightstand and charged out of the room.

She almost bowled Zeke over as she rushed into the living room. He was bent down peering inside one of her completed dollhouses.

"Sorry I spent so much time gabbing with Dad," she said brightly. "Grab your gear. Time's a'wasting. We need to get busy sorting calves."

"You look flushed. Is everything all right?" Zeke hurried after her, pausing to pluck his coat from the rack where he'd hung it by hers the night before.

"I'm fine, just running late." She stepped out onto the porch and pulled on her boots.

Zeke followed her out and shut the door. "Will I need the hat with earflaps again?" he asked, watching Myra set a gray cowboy hat atop her taffy-colored waves.

"Separating calves from their mothers is sweaty work. You can probably get by wearing your baseball cap. Most ranchers favor a cowboy hat." She left the porch and was met by a cold blast of wind. "It's gonna be chilly when we begin. You won't want to let body heat seep out through the top of your head. In this country it's always smart to start the day wearing a hat."

He went back inside and came out with his baseball cap.

Pulling on her well-worn leather gloves, Myra spared a moment trying to decide which part in today's process Zeke would find hardest or would least like. Aware she probably hadn't heard the last from her folks, the sooner Zeke got the message he wasn't cut out to be a rancher, the quicker she could buy him out. The bank ought to grant her a loan, especially once she proved she had taken on the ranch in a downturn and set it on a profitable course.

Was she being too mean? Engineering chores to help Zeke fail? No, she decided. Not if he figured out on his own that he was a fish out of water.

Zeke caught up. "I assume we're taking the littler animals away from the bigger, older ones. Do we do that by hand or on horseback? I've only seen something like that in Western movies. Cowboys always rope the calves. Of course, I've never handled a rope for that purpose."

"For what purpose have you handled a rope?" His statement shook Myra from her own thoughts. She hoped he wasn't going to say he'd hung anyone. Most of what she knew about Green Berets came from having rented a couple of violent war movies for her grandfather.

"We used ropes for scaling cliffs, or sometimes to assist a buddy up into a chopper."

"Ah." *Thank goodness.* "Well, for this task I'm not riding. I don't want to tear up the grass since we'll bring the mama cows back to the corral to feed once they're vaccinated and checked for new pregnancies." She climbed up to the second railing on the fence that surrounded the milling pairs. "See those two smaller corrals?" She let Zeke climb up beside her before pointing.

"I like using two smaller corrals to separate yearling steers from heifers before we drive them into Hank's semi. Steers weigh more and so earn more at the feedlot. And some heifers we keep, but we need an accurate count." She angled a glance at the man whose shoulder brushed hers. "You do know the difference between a steer and a heifer by looking at them, don't you?"

His mouth thinned to a droll line. "I realize you think I'm a total dunce. I was about twelve when I learned all about the birds and bees."

One quick perusal of his handsome face and she didn't doubt his declaration. She imagined he'd always had girls shamelessly chasing him. How else did city kids learn about mating? Girls like her, raised on ranches, took anything related to birds and bees in stride. She didn't blush at comments that she'd seen send her city college friends into red-faced giggles.

"Good enough," she said. "I'll start out driving a calf toward you. And you'll plant yourself between the two small corrals. If I send you a steer, shoo him into the larger of the two pens. Scram heifers into the smaller one."

Zeke jumped down off the fence. "I'm glad you didn't say left or right, because then I'd have to ask if I'd be facing you or facing the pens."

"You'll want to keep your back to the railing between the little corrals as much as possible. Not all mama cows will be happy to have us taking away their offspring. They've been known to head butt, kick or bite."

"Sounds grim. And you do this every year?"

"Twice a year. The first time is after calving ends. You'll sort mamas and babies and deliver them to the same range we brought these pairs down from yesterday."

"I doubt I can find my way back to that spot. Listen, I hate to pressure you, but have you had time to give any thought to my job offer?"

Myra climbed down and opened the gate, giving him room to pass. "I am considering it. I mentioned it to my dad. My parents will fuss. They sent me to college to… It doesn't matter." She waved a hand as if to erase the comment. "Let's get started."

"Now you have me curious as to why they'd be keener on you attending college than I sense you were to go," he said and cocked his head toward her as he wiggled his fingers into his own gloves.

From the trouble he was having, Myra thought his gloves probably hadn't dried overnight. Wet gloves could be miserable. *He'd learn.* "My mother's not the biggest fan of ranching that ever lived," Myra murmured. "She grew up on Rolling Acres and wanted to leave and see the world. Her senior year of high school she went to a grange dance, met my dad and they fell in love. I've always suspected she wanted me to live her fantasy. Relocate to a city, meet and marry a doctor or lawyer…anyone but a rancher. She still loves my dad to pieces, but she's always told Eric and me that ranch life is too hard. Remember I said you'll get few days off. And forget vacations. But I'm not like my mom. I'm a fan of ranching."

"Why did you go to college, then?"

"Don't most kids want to please their parents? Dad expected Eric to follow in his footsteps. They argued when he joined the ROTC. I thought one of us shouldn't disappoint them. Now Eric's back to help Dad. It turned out he didn't like being in the army any better than I liked being a teacher. Funny how life intervenes. Did you always want a military career?" It was a casual question asked as they made their way around the inside perimeter of the corral.

Zeke laughed. "Sure, after vowing I'd be a policeman, a firefighter or a pro baseball player." He sidestepped a cow patty. "Having a twin breeds early competition. Growing up, we each swore to become what the other claimed he wanted. We fought when we played over who got to be the firefighter or cop. In high school and college we both played baseball. I quit the team my junior year and hung out with some guys in the National Guard. Seth took a science class that turned him on to minerals. For the first time in our lives we went our separate ways."

"You must not have had pressure from your folks. What business were they in?" Myra immediately wished she could take back the question. She didn't want to know personal stuff about the man she wished would go away.

"In a way Mom influenced Seth some. Instilled in him a desire to see the world. She ran a travel agency for twenty years. Mom was forever flying off to one part of the world or another. Dad was an insurance agent, able to work from home. He mostly oversaw us and ran the house."

Unable to drop the subject, Myra asked, "Are you close to your brother now?"

"We're reconnecting. We got the need for competition out of our systems. By the way, I invited Seth to the ranch. But I looked in that third bedroom and it resembles a carpentry shop."

"It kind of is, with my dollhouse patterns, material, jigsaws and Dremel tools. I sand wood and cut doors and windows in there, but if I stay on I can move them. When's he coming?"

"I don't know. He gave me a list of gems he plans to acquire in various countries prior to attending some major gem show."

"Okay. Sounds as if I have time to clear out my stuff." Moving into the herd, Myra drew Zeke's attention to cows and calves with brands other than the winged owl. “We have to hold those pairs aside. If one gets by you, we’ll finish cutting then drive him back out. It’s possible Dave Ralston will be by to collect his stock this morning. Hank said Dave’s scheduled to take his calves to market today.”

“Let’s get to it. I’m cold just standing around.” Zeke shrugged his shoulders as if to make his point.

“You have to be quick on your feet. You’ll open the proper gate when a steer or heifer comes close, and shut the gate fast once the calf is inside.”

“Will they try to come back out?”

“Yes. If their mama bawls enough.”

“All right. I’ll have to learn as we go.”

He didn’t know the half of it. She felt sorry for him, but why should she go easy on him? Her goal was to make him see he wasn’t cut out to be a ranch owner.

She chose a steer that wasn’t too far away from Zeke, let out a yell and slapped the surprised yearling on his rump. Startled, the animal bolted right toward Zeke. The man proved to be agile, sidestepping to open the gate, and they had their first steer penned.

“Good job,” she called, although she hadn’t intended to give him encouragement. Selecting a skittish young heifer, Myra repeated the process. She noticed at once that Zeke had more trouble opening the left-hand gate. Eric had said Zeke had undergone multiple surgeries on that arm. Myra expected him to complain or ask her to go easy on his injury. But he didn’t.

She could make it harder on him if she chose to

drive a series of heifers toward him one after another. But she wouldn't. She wasn't spiteful. It'd be different if he was totally able-bodied. What didn't help was how able-bodied he looked. Tall, pleasingly muscular. Long legs fit nicely in blue jeans. No cowboy boots, but boots. Dang, he could pass for a rancher. That alone probably softened her feelings. Softened her to where she sent him two or three steers for every one heifer, giving him time between to massage his left arm.

She was about to ask Zeke if he wanted to swap jobs when the mother cow of the last steer they'd sorted bawled, pawed the ground and with head down, charged Zeke. He had turned away to shut the gate.

"Zeke!" Myra shouted. But he didn't react in time. The cow's wide head slammed Zeke on his lower back, striking his shapely butt. As the cow's head came up, Zeke flew through the air.

Myra winced at the impact, as if that helped absorb the hit. Of course it did nothing.

Because the angry cow didn't appear ready to give up and trot away, Myra stripped off her belt and darted around other pairs. She smacked the errant animal lightly with the leather strap before mama cow could launch another attack on the man slowly picking himself up off the wet grass.

"Are you okay?" Myra asked after the offending mother left Zeke and plodded to the fence in search of her missing youngster. She continued to be vocal.

Chuckling, Zeke brushed blades of grass and mud off the knees of his grass-stained jeans. "You did warn me. We'd had such success I guess I got too cocky."

"You can't let down your guard," Myra chided gently and glanced up as a red truck hauling a triple horse trailer pulled down the lane to stop outside the corral. The slant R logo was on the driver's door, which swung open to reveal a compact man in his midfifties.

"Dave Ralston's here," Myra told Zeke. "I wondered if he might show up today. That semi will be filled with his calves headed to market. He can transport his two cows and the calves that are mixed in with ours, too. Uh, yours."

"You don't have to keep correcting yourself," Zeke said, straightening to limp over to greet a neighbor he had yet to meet. "I think technically these are your cows, cattle, stock. Whatever you call them," he added lamely to Myra, who matched his stride.

"Pairs," she said firmly. "Dave, hi. I'm glad you're here to get your animals. I've had trouble keeping one of your steers from being sent to the breakout corral. He's a curious little fellow." Because Dave glanced at Zeke, she hurriedly introduced the men.

They shook hands and Dave cast an eye around the property. "Hank told me Jack Odell up and gave you this ranch, sonny. You're a lucky duck if ever one lived. You're sittin' on a gold mine here."

Myra's stomach dropped. She tried to discreetly

jab her elbow into Dave's side. "He doesn't mean that literally," she rushed to inform Zeke. "Granted there are abandoned gold mines out on BLM land. Occasionally we see in the news where someone running cattle on a leased pasture falls through rotten boards covering some old mine or another. I've never run across any on Gramps's property."

"What's BLM land?" Zeke asked.

"Government owned. It's under the control of the Bureau of Land Management. You won't need to deal with them." She continued to glare at Dave.

The older rancher's brow furrowed in a slight frown, but as Myra's steady glare didn't diminish, he shut his mouth.

"Can you back your rig around and drop the ramp?" she queried him.

"Yep. I brought a lariat. Figured if I rope the calves you can help wrestle them into the trailer. Get the calves in and the cows will follow."

"Sounds good. While you turn your truck around, Zeke and I will cut out your two pair."

"Get Hank's, too. He's at my place helping my son load the semi for market."

Myra flashed Dave a thumbs-up as he climbed into the cab.

"I see what you were telling me about neighbors helping neighbors. I hope they'll all accept me," Zeke said, following Myra's lead in separating out the pairs with the Bar W and slant R brands.

Myra pretended she hadn't heard him. She didn't

want Zeke to get buddy-buddy with any of the neighbors. She wanted him to throw in the towel ASAP.

In his younger days Dave Ralston had been a champion calf roper. After he slid out the metal ramp, he came into the pen swinging his rope like the veteran he was. It sang through the air and settled over the head of one of his young steers. Digging in his boot heels, he pulled the stubborn animal out of the enclosure.

"Zeke, I'll shove the calf from behind, if you'll close the gate after us."

He hurried to comply, but froze when Myra stepped right in a gooey brown pile on her way to pushing the animal up the ramp.

"You must not have grown up around cows." Dave grinned down at Zeke from the trailer entrance. Freeing his rope, he jumped down. "Better get boots you only wear when you work stock. Guess Myra didn't tell you these small mounds of cow pucky are nothing compared to what you'll wade through when you start jamming mama cows through the chute for pregnancy testing, vaccinations and parasite treatments."

Zeke gave an offhanded shrug. "I ran into my share of chicken and goat droppings in Afghanistan. I felt bad Myra didn't see it in time to avoid landing in it."

"Afghanistan, huh? Is how they portrayed our role in *Zero Dark Thirty* for real?"

"Dunno. I never saw the movie. I tend to prefer

Westerns. Is what they show of a cowboy's life accurate?"

Dave uttered a deep belly laugh as he opened the gate, swung his rope again and this time captured the calf with the Bar W brand. "I 'spect the majority of Westerns get gussied up so the studio's star or even stuntmen and -women don't break something and sue the film backers." Shortening the rope, he marched the calf out of the pen.

"Figured that might be the case. You're handy with that rope." This time Zeke helped wrestle the calf up the ramp, leaving Myra to close the gate.

And he was careful to step over the aromatic pile that sat squarely at the base of the ramp.

"I started roping an old stump in front of our house from the time I was knee-high to a jackrabbit," Ralston said. "You can probably learn if you put your mind to it and practice."

Myra shaded her eyes and snagged Dave's attention. "You'll have to show Zeke how to fasten the calf to the railings inside the horse trailer. He's new to all of this."

"'Pears to me he's a smart fellow," Dave responded, flipping his rope off the second calf as Zeke prodded it on into the trailer. "A guy who defended our freedom in a wild-and-woolly war zone can probably see how you secured the first calf. Don't be so hard on him, Myra."

She dropped her hand, turned and stalked into the pen, careful to bite back sarcasm that would expose her real feelings. Working alone, she cut the third calf out of the larger herd and chased it along the fence to where Dave had only to reach over the railing and drop a loop around the bawling youngster's head. The mama issued a series of angry snorts. She chased after her calf, so it was a simple matter of making sure she didn't plunge off the ramp as she followed her baby up and into the trailer.

With the neighbors' stock all loaded, Myra went back to culling her calves. She looked around for Zeke and saw him standing by the truck jawboning with Dave. Since this was a task she'd done by herself for the past two years, she herded a yearling right up to a gate, opened it and quickly shoved the animal through. It was definitely more time-consuming doing it without Zeke's help. But she wasn't about to tell him that.

And what were they talking about? Ralston liked to gab. She wished he'd shut up and leave. Not only because she needed Zeke's assistance but because keeping him from making friends would ensure his isolation. If she remained his primary contact, it'd drive home the knowledge that whenever she left he'd be on his own.

Her friends had suggested he'd throw in the towel sooner rather than later. But there he and Dave were, yakking, gesturing, grinning like best buds.

Indeed, he seemed in good spirits when he wandered back after Dave drove away.

"I can see how this job would be easier if the person doing it knew how to rope these little buggers," Zeke said. "Dave said he'll teach me the basics, and all it'll take for me to get proficient is practice. Isn't that cool?"

"Huh," she grunted, shoving another heifer into the correct pen. "Roping is harder than it looks. I never saw the need to waste time learning."

"You don't think it'd be better to be yanking calves around from the front end? I saw what you stepped in when you pushed that one from behind."

She shut the gate and leveled a look at him. "If your aim is to avoid landing in manure, you don't want to be on a working cattle ranch."

He bent his head and tipped his baseball cap forward. "Dave said he was surprised to see you sticking around to give me pointers."

Her jaw hardened. "Really? Did he say why?"

"Well, he said you were third or fourth generation to run the Flying Owl. He said it jokingly but sort of insinuated everybody around here believed that before you turned loose of the land, a coroner would have to pry the deed out of your cold, dead hands."

Shock rippled through Myra. Zeke was clearly waiting for her to deny what may not have really sounded like a joke to him. For a second she debated telling the truth. How her heart broke when her father phoned to say he'd gifted the ranch to someone without one shred of ranch know-how. But what good would it do? Zeke had the right to send her packing.

And she cared too much for the future of the Flying Owl to turn her back on it.

"Dave is quite a joker. He probably thought I could hear him. My name isn't and never has been on the ranch deed. Gramps and Dad put the property in a cotrust after Gram died. Listen, all this palavering is getting us nowhere. We have a lot of calves left to sort out."

Zeke pulled back his sleeve and checked his watch. "Isn't it lunchtime? At least, Dave said he was going home to have lunch before he drove his calves to market."

"I'd hoped to get halfway finished before we broke for lunch. But if you're dying to eat, I guess we can put in a longer afternoon."

"How many more to make half?" he asked, sparing a look around the pen.

"Twenty should do it. Hey, I forgot that maybe you're hurting from the head butting you took. We can take a break if you need to rub on some liniment."

"Are you having me on? Isn't that a horse treatment?"

"It works for people's bruised, sore muscles, too. Really, I swear I'm not giving you hokey advice."

"Well, I do hurt, so I might try it. I figured by morning I'd be black-and-blue in a spot that might leave me standing up to eat for a few days." He gingerly rubbed his back pocket but laughed all the same.

"Okay, you've convinced me to break for lunch. Gramps said the sooner you get liniment rubbed on an injury the faster it heals. He used it liberally on his arthritic wrists and knees. I'm sure there's a giant bottle under the sink in your bathroom. You take care of your owie and I'll fix tomato soup and grilled-cheese sandwiches."

"You're on, even though I haven't called any injury an owie in thirty years."

Myra had left the enclosure and turned to study him. "So how old does that make you?"

"I'm thirty-one." He made sure the gate was latched. "I frankly don't recall anyone in my family using the term *owie*."

"Don't get all bent out of shape about it, Maxwell. It's not an assault on your masculinity." She laughed as she dashed up the porch steps and toed off her boots. "We can refer to it as a pain in the butt, if you prefer. I mean, that is the part of your anatomy the cow hit, right?"

"You're rougher than some of my recruits. I'm not going to dignify that with a yes or no. Let's refrain from talking about it at all."

"I wasn't planning on calling the story in to the *Snowy Owl Weekly Gazette*. For the record," Myra said as she hung up her jacket and tossed her hat on the hat rack by the door, "you aren't the first rancher to take a head butt from a mother cow in an uncomfortable spot, and I doubt you'll be the last. Prepare yourself to have it happen again. And you may not have a soft grass landing next time."

Zeke hesitated in hanging up his bomber jacket.

"Hey, did you just call me a rancher?" His smile carved a dimple in one cheek. "That's the nicest compliment you've paid me since I got here. Give me ten minutes to find that liniment. I'll even brew the coffee for lunch." He whistled, crossing the living room.

Myra wanted to call him and take it back. Zeke Maxwell was nowhere near having earned the title. On the other hand, no one else had heard her slip of the tongue. And the smile her words sparked was pretty terrific. So much so, her own smile lingered while she flitted about the kitchen talking to Orion prior to heating soup and preparing cheese sandwiches.

She couldn't remember ever having a man's simple smile make her stomach flutter. Or maybe she was just hungrier than she thought.

Chapter Four

Myra took a minute to give Orion some snuggle love, freshen his water and bring him a veggie snack before she washed her hands and assembled everything for lunch.

Tomato soup steamed on the stove, and she put two cheese sandwiches in the electric fry pan. Suddenly she smelled the pungent odor of liniment, warring with the more savory scents. Startled, she spun toward the door. Even though she knew Zeke planned to treat his bruises, tears unexpectedly filled her eyes.

In two giant steps, Zeke grabbed her and gripped her arms. "What's the matter, Myra? Did you burn yourself? Run cold water over the area. I'll watch the food."

"I didn't burn myself. Sorry, it's the liniment." She smudged the heel of her palm over her weepy eyes.

Zeke took a step back from her sheepishly. "I should apologize. That stuff has helped, but it sure stinks."

Myra shook her head. "It isn't the liniment smell, Zeke. Or I suppose it is. I should've been prepared, but it took me by surprise. I turned expecting to see Gramps."

Zeke slid his arms around her back and pulled her to his chest. Her tears covered his shirtfront. His hug consoled her, but she shouldn't let him be this nice. Still, she sniffled into his shirt pocket. "He's only been gone six months. Oh, I know I'm being foolish." Biting her upper lip, she pushed out of his hold. "I need to flip the sandwiches or they'll burn."

Zeke let her go. "It's nothing to apologize for. I lost men in my unit. Two in particular were close friends—I can't tell you how many times I'd hear a laugh or look around the mess tent expecting to see them." His brow furrowed.

"That must have been more than hard. I've only had to deal with the deaths of my grandparents. All four lived long lives. My good friend Lila Jenkins lost her dad in a terrible mining accident when she was twelve. And four years ago her husband was killed in a different type of mine. I can't imagine how haunting that has to be."

Zeke rubbed the back of his neck. "Yeah. The living are left to mourn. Hey, can we talk about something else?"

Myra nodded. "The soup is ready. If you'll pour it into the bowls on the table I'll bring our sandwiches." She didn't look at him, still reeling from how easily she'd been comforted by him. Eric had been right, Zeke was a nice man. She'd felt her nerves tingle. This wasn't good. She needed to watch herself around him. It wouldn't do to lose her focus on getting him to quit the ranch.

"Your pig is acting funny," Zeke said as Myra set a grilled-cheese sandwich on his plate. His chair was closest to Orion's pen. The pig was running back and forth, making snorty noises and banging his nose against the wooden baby gate.

"I wonder if he's looking for Gramps, too. House pigs are super social. And like I told you, Gramps made liberal use of liniment. So Orion knows that scent."

Nothing could have surprised Myra more than to see Zeke lean over the pen, pick up Orion and set him on his lap. He let the pig settle, then as if it was no big deal, went back to eating his soup.

Myra smiled. "Most people would think they had to go wash after touching a pig."

He hiked a shoulder. "Afghan families live, eat and sleep with bigger pigs, goats, chickens and sometimes even milk cows. I got used to it from the times elders invited me to eat with their families. Orion hasn't been outside. Which brings me to one real concern. I hope he doesn't pee on me."

Myra tipped back her head and laughed. "Mini pigs are clean, but they are pigs and still like to root in dirt. Orion uses a litter box I keep on the back porch. It's why he has the doggie door."

"That's a relief. He seems friendly. Guess I won't get a dog as long as you're here. Speaking of which. After Dave gave a bit of insight into the next steps I have to take with those mama cows, I know I need help. A lot of help," he muttered before biting into his sandwich.

"Even I need help with that chore," Myra acknowledged. She pushed aside her bowl. "I've given this arrangement a lot of thought. If we continue to work well together, and unless you hate the solitude of a Montana winter and call it quits, I'll stay until spring. But I don't want any title like manager." She scowled a bit. "I prefer if we call it a friend helping a friend." She almost gagged on the word *friend.*

Zeke set down his sandwich. "Just knowing you'll be here is a huge relief. For the record, I'm not a quitter."

Myra's heart sank and she quickly tucked into her sandwich.

"You don't sound as if you want to consider this a job. Is it crass to talk about money? I have my military pension. But even if I buy all the food and pay utilities, you'll need money for…uh…personal stuff."

"About that. My dad said I should take the revenue from the sale of the yearlings. He says he thought Gramps had sold all of his stock and some land to pay Gram's medical bills before I came to help him. I shouldn't be surprised, I guess. Dad and Gramps were two of a kind when it came to privacy." She crumbled the toasty edge of her sandwich.

Zeke ate, letting Myra talk.

"Something else I didn't know," she said. "In order to clear the deed for you, Dad paid the banknote I planned to retire with the current stock sale. So, here's the thing, Gramps and I operated from a single ranch account. I figured on Hank having the feedlot owner do a direct deposit to that account as usual. All deposits, withdrawals and expenses get logged in the spreadsheet we went over last night. I can share the document online with you so we both see income and outgo. If either of us buy groceries or stuff at the feed store, we post it."

"That's generous of you, Myra. I don't know that I feel right about using that money. The fact your folks signed over this ranch to me was a gift I never expected. I can already see you earned what'll come from this sale."

Talking about her parents handing Zeke the ranch made Myra pissy. She wasn't as generous as her folks. And therein lay the problem. She hopped up and carried her dishes to the sink. "I need to make something clear," she said. "Everything I'm doing to teach you what goes on here, I'm doing because I love the Flying Owl. I can't bear the thought of it going under." She was prepared to say more, but the house phone rang, startling them both. "Dang, I hope it's not my mom. She's been calling to pressure me to move home." Myra hesitated, but went to the old wall phone that rarely got used.

"Hello." She spoke tentatively.

"Myra? It's Tawana."

Myra relaxed. Tawana, a Native American woman, was a close friend and another valuable member of the Artsy Ladies group. Tawana blurted out her sorrow over hearing news about Myra losing the ranch. "I couldn't believe it when Lila told me."

"It's true. But I've made a deal with the new owner to stay on for a while. At least until spring." She peered through lowered eyelashes at Zeke, who'd set Orion back in his pen. He washed his hands at the sink and began putting dishes in the dishwasher. "The good news is I'll be here for the Thanksgiving bazaar. Hey, Tawana, can we talk later? I came in for lunch, but I have to go out again. We have calves to cut so Hank can haul them to market tomorrow."

"Sure. I'm happy to hear you aren't leaving ASAP. Call me when you have time. I worried when I kept getting voice mail on your cell. Oh, wait, I almost forgot…the first batch of snowy owls are back. I've been on the lookout for them. There are five I've seen building nests in Leland Conrad's fir trees."

"Conrad? I know his forest, but I don't know him well. He's kind of a grouch, isn't he? Will he let the owls stay on his property, or will he drive them away?"

"He's not a bad guy. The problem I see is that he is currently trying to sell all of his holdings so he can retire. He's never married. According to Jewell, he's estranged from a nephew he raised. But you don't have time for us to get into his history. I phoned Leland. He's okay with the owls and promises he won't disrupt their nesting. However, if a buyer shows up, he won't make leaving the owls alone part of the deal. That worries me."

"Yes. Maybe Jewell can talk to him. She's persuasive."

"I'll call her. If you have time to ride out there, Myra, they're a sight to behold."

"I may. If we get time I should show them to Zeke."

"Who?" Tawana sounded puzzled.

"Zeke Maxwell. Former Lieutenant Maxwell, the Flying Owl's new owner."

"Oh, right. Okay, I'll let you go. I'm typing up minutes from last night's tribal meeting."

"Say, while I have you on the phone, do you know if anyone's looking for work? After we ship calves tomorrow it's time to take care of the cows. We definitely need some competent extra hands."

"You're in luck. This morning Eddie Four Bear and Aaron Younger stopped by my office to see if I knew of any work. They were helping wean calves on a ranch out by Wolf Point. If you need more guys, Eddie probably knows who else is available."

"We could use three on the chutes. I have Eddie's number. I'll call him. I trust him to pick up vaccine kits from Jewell, too. Save me running into town. Thanks, Tawana."

"Always glad to help our men find work. One more thing… I cut out some new vests last weekend. The beading looks good. I think our customers will really like them."

"They always do. No one ever quibbles over price

for one of your vests. I'll be anxious to see them. Anyway, I've really gotta run. See you."

The two signed off. "That was Tawana White Feather," she told Zeke, who quirked an eyebrow when she faced him. "Sorry to ask her about worker availability without first discussing it with you. But the next part of the process with the cows is a dirty job. It's impossible to do without hiring help, and well worth it."

"I'll leave those decisions to you, Myra. Dave didn't make this part sound fun. So, does this woman you talked to run an employment agency?"

"No. She works in the reservation tribal office. Tawana is a council member and a most talented crafter. She makes leather vests with intricate beadwork. They sell like hotcakes."

"Um. I heard you say I need to see something. Did you mean her vests? They don't sound like something men would wear. I mean, if they're beaded."

"You'll have to see them to judge. Her brother wore one at his wedding and looked sharp. But I wasn't talking about you seeing her vests. I was talking about the snowy owls! Tawana said some of the birds have come back. We were worried they wouldn't return this year."

"Really? How would you know one bird from another?"

"Jewell tagged some of the young ones with neon-pink bands. There are experts who do satellite tracking in other parts of the country, but we couldn't afford GPS transmitters."

"Damn, you guys are really serious about owls."

"You bet. Tawana and others on the reservation are huge advocates of saving the snowy owls."

"Why are they showing up here now? If they fly south for the winter, it's a little late."

"Actually, some go north to the Arctic for the winter, some go as far south as Bermuda. And some don't migrate at all. Our flock seems to like to winter here. Jewell's been studying them the longest. She says they follow the migration of lemmings, which is their main source of food. Frankly we worried that our milder winter last year may have caused them to leave permanently. Tawana's sighting proves some are back."

"Are you pulling my leg? I didn't think lemmings were real. I've always put them in the fake category like going snipe hunting."

"Lemmings are real, you goofus. They're rodents. And snowy owls are good-sized. They can carry off a duck or other waterfowl, too. But it's getting late. Let's go finish our chores. If we have enough daylight left afterward, it'd be a treat to ride out so you can see why so many of us are doing everything possible to save these birds."

"Okay, but I hope you won't hold it against me if I don't get worked up about them. I just don't see the big deal."

Myra didn't say what was on her mind. Not caring about the fate of the snowy owls was strike two against Zeke. Strike one was the fact he fell into owning a ranch she loved. She had little doubt that before she left here there'd be a strike three against him.

The sun shone a bit stronger as the afternoon wore on. Melting snow left the grassy pastures as slick as working on grease. But Myra couldn't find fault with the amount of work Zeke did. She could tell when his weak left side started to bother him a lot, and yet he didn't beg off helping, nor did he shirk in any fashion.

"Did you already tell me why we didn't wean all of the young heifers?" he asked when Myra moved to the gate and declared their job done.

"We hold the sturdiest ones back as breeders. Every year you'll have older cows needing to be sold to a slaughterhouse because they've stopped producing. You rebuild a herd by adding more than you sell. In any cycle you'll weigh the worth, like…do you need the money from the fall sale more than you need to expand your herd?"

"That seems an impossible question for a newbie like me."

"That is a problem with not having grown up on a ranch."

Zeke eyed her as if expecting her to say more. She didn't, instead opening the gate and shooing aside a cow that tried to escape. She gestured for Zeke to follow her out.

"What now?" he asked as he found bare ground to stamp snow and mud off his boots.

"We have an hour or so of daylight left. Not adequate to decide if the alfalfa fields are dry enough to cut. There won't be time to start that for a few days anyway. So I'm going to ride out to have a look at the owls. If you'd rather stay here, that's fine. You may not want to sit a saddle if you still hurt where the cow head butted you. Grab some rest. I'll be back in time to start supper."

"Do you not want me to tag along?"

"It's not that. I've seen you shifting your weight uncomfortably. If you want to go, Ember can use the exercise."

"I do. Lead on. Are the birds on Flying Owl land? I heard you mention to your friend that the owls nest in some other guy's trees."

"Leland Conrad. I don't know him well. I thought he was kind of a recluse. Gramps talked to him at cattle meetings or at the grange hall. Leland never stayed long and he didn't shoot the breeze over potluck tables like other neighbors do. But Tawana said he's not so bad."

They entered the barn and each took the horse they'd ridden the night before.

Once Zeke had saddled Ember, she handed him a set of binoculars and took another set for herself. "These are to better see the owls."

"I figured as much. I'll close the barn door," he said, looping the binoculars' strap over his neck once they led the horses out.

Myra vaulted easily into Cayenne's saddle, then waited for Zeke to mount up.

The horses were frisky, glad to be out and wanting to run.

Zeke held Ember in check, likely because he had no idea which direction they were going.

After they cleared the house and cantered into vast, empty land, Myra let Cayenne move faster.

Zeke did the same to stay abreast of her.

"This is Flying Owl land," she said. "We rotate growing wheat, alfalfa and milo. We reseed our pastures in native grasses every year. Leased pasture on BLM land reseeds itself on the wind. Grass is better for adding weight on cattle. Prairie grass is rich in nutrients. It's also cheaper in time and money than hay."

"At the risk of sounding stupid, why don't you let your pastures reseed on the wind?"

"Zeke, no question is stupid. Running a profitable cattle ranch takes know-how. For us Montanans success hinges on raising healthy calves we can sell for more than it costs to raise them. With our brutal winters, by November cattle have eaten all visible grass. The wind doesn't reseed fast enough for all our needs. That's why we haul hay. You'll do that for four or five months along with supplementary grains bought at the feed store. Right after calving, just before the green grass returns in spring, we feed our stock our richest baled alfalfa. That keeps cows from stripping the new grass down to nubbins." She let out a lengthy sigh.

"I apologize if you've already told me some of that. It sounds familiar. I wonder if I'll ever store in my head all the information that seems to roll off your tongue."

"You asked if there was a book on ranching. I'm sure there is, but ranching in Montana, and even in our corner of the state, will be different from anywhere else. I said I'd make you a list. Actually, I'll see if I can carve out time to write descriptions of what needs doing and when throughout a typical year. It'd be a general guideline."

"That would be much appreciated."

"We're now on BLM land," she said, switching subjects.

"Are we in danger of falling in any of those abandoned mines you spoke of?"

"Not here. I've traveled this route many times. All I know of abandoned mines is from hearing others talk. I believe they're in the foothills. The gold-mine collapse that killed my friend Lila's husband is east of here. That mine operated for years without incident. From what Gramps said, the company followed a vein down the mountain, then an upper tunnel crumpled on top of a new one they'd dug in spokes underneath the played-out section. It caused a huge collapse. They never recovered the bodies of twenty or so men. Lila doesn't talk about it, and if anyone mentions mining she gets up and leaves."

"It sounds like an awful way to die. I worry about my brother mining in developing countries. But I assume in the States there are rules governing mines. Currently Seth's on his second trip to Afghanistan for lapis. I roamed those mountains and went with demolition crews who mapped natural caves. I hated being underground."

Myra slowed and turned Cayenne east. The new pace made it easier for them to talk even as they continued to climb into an area where snow still lay in patches. "Did you get to see your brother while you served in Afghanistan?" she asked.

"Yes. On his first trip. Eric met him, too. The base commander let Seth and another gem hunter stay with us. I hope he calls me when he leaves there to go to Tanzania. Although he may be safer in Afghanistan. Unfortunately, regions where people dig for precious or even semiprecious gems are often dangerous."

"Do gem hunters get shot at? I can't tell you how glad I am that Eric decided not to continue a military career. When he phoned to say you'd saved him during a gun battle with IED explosives involved, my mother was a basket case."

Zeke frowned. "Gemologists do get shot at. According to Seth, many men have died in a quest for diamonds, rubies, emeralds and sapphires."

Myra turned in her saddle. "I've read in our newspaper where what they call summer gem hunters come to Montana searching for sapphires. I think they're found in or around defunct gold mines."

"Is that so? I wonder if Seth knows that," Zeke murmured.

The terrain got steeper and talk fell off. All at once Myra reined in and looked back down the hill to where Zeke had stopped. "What's wrong?" she called. "Did Ember pull up lame? I should have told you to watch out for gopher holes."

"There's no problem. I stopped to look at the mountain shadows. I've gotta say this is truly God's country." Leaning an arm on his saddle horn, Zeke continued to study the light and dark areas where gold from the late-afternoon sun glittered like a crown atop the highest ridges still fringed with snow.

"I've always thought so," Myra said, following his gaze. "I shouldn't be surprised to see deeper snow up here. We should have worn hats and gloves, I guess."

"It's not too cold." Zeke touched his heels to Ember's flanks and joined Myra on the slope. "I get what you meant when you said living here gives you a sense of freedom. That's partly why I left Boston to come see if your father really wanted to give me a house in these wonderful, wide-open spaces."

Myra touched her heels to Cayenne and moved ahead of Zeke.

He trotted his horse up beside her. "In Boston I'd recently seen a TV interview with John Mayer—you know, the songwriter?"

"Kind of a bad boy, right?"

"So went the rumors. Then he dropped out of the LA scene. I'll sort of paraphrase here, but I read this interview when he said he'd moved to Montana where life wasn't all about ego. He said something that resonated with me—how he'd come to realize he wanted one wife in his lifetime, and one set of kids, and neighbors who liked him for himself. Really profound stuff."

"That's why you left Boston?" Myra sounded amused. "Because of John Mayer?"

"I'm making a mess telling this. There's nothing else a man should want in life but what Mayer said in that interview. A lot of my buddies were on second or third marriages. Many had no spare money because they paid so much in child support."

"So military life equates to the fast trackers in LA? Huh. Eric hardly ever talked to me about his time in the service. However, Mom said when he was home on leave, his uniform was a magnet for women."

"I'm still not being clear. My own military career in no way compares to a rock star's life. After opting for a medical discharge, I expected to go back to Boston and nothing would have changed. But the city had gotten bigger, busier, and my friends had moved on. While I don't think I battled ego, I was restless and out of sorts during my time in Boston. That's why the notion of wide-open spaces appealed to me."

"Now, on that score I understand."

"Whoa! What was that?" Zeke asked, ducking from a traveling shadow overhead that was accompanied by a strange noise: *prek-prek, prek-prek.* He stopped his horse.

"That was a full-grown snowy owl," Myra announced. She, too, halted Cayenne. "We were so involved talking I didn't realize how close we'd gotten to the forest." Raising her binoculars, she trained them on the tallest fir in a group that sat at the edge of a denser grove. "The snowy that cruised over our heads lit almost at the top of that middle tree. It was a female. The male's call is harsher, more like *krek-krek.*"

"I'm impressed you know the difference." Zeke lifted his binoculars and spun the dial. "I see a pair," he said excitedly, rocking sideways in his saddle even as the gelding shifted his weight. "Man, their backs blend with the tree bark even though with the field glasses you can see the white face and underbelly."

"Tawana said she counted five. Ah, I've got two in sight. Both in that tree are female. Males are almost pure white. Females have what birders call brown scalloping. The one that flew over us must have been collecting straw or twigs to build a nest. They're night hunters, so it's too early for them to be on the lookout for food."

"I feel foolish for ducking, but that thing is bigger than some of our drones," Zeke said, refocusing his binoculars. "What would you guess their wingspan is?"

"Full-grown, they can span fifty to sixty inches. I only know that from listening to Jewell talk about them. She and Tawana and a few older folks on the reservation are huge advocates. I like seeing owls flying about, though. And I'd hate for their numbers to dwindle. That's what's happening according to the National Wildlife Federation." Even as she finished speaking, another bird left the tree and swooped down less than twenty feet in front of where they sat. The bird picked up a slender tree branch in its beak and soared aloft again.

"Honestly, I didn't expect to be so captivated by them," Zeke said. "They're quite a sight. These owls are the biggest birds I recall seeing in flight—even bigger than the crows in the Afghan cornfields. And when that one lit to get the branch, I managed a good look at its face. I'd swear it smiled."

Myra lowered her binoculars. "Jewell said a lot of people think the dark markings below their beaks and eyes resemble a smile."

"I'm surprised they don't seem to be afraid of us." Zeke again trained his binoculars on the trees.

"They'll be more defensive during nesting season. Adult snowy owls don't have a lot of predators. But they have to guard their eggs against avian thieves, and of course their chicks from foxes, wild dogs and wolves."

Zeke let his binoculars fall the length of the strap. "I see we're losing sunlight. There probably isn't enough light to take a photo with my cell phone if an owl comes as close as that last one did."

"True. And we should go. At this rate it'll be totally dark before we get back to the ranch. Why do you want a picture?"

"To send to Seth and to my mom. She's always regaling us with pictures of parrots in Barbados."

Myra guided Cayenne down the steep slope. As

she passed Zeke, their knees bumped, knocking her foot out of her stirrup.

All at once, nearby—too close for comfort—a timber wolf howled. Then another joined in. Unexpectedly Cayenne reared. With a wild shake of her head, she whistled through her nose and pawed the air, dumping Myra from the saddle.

Losing her grip on the reins, she skid face-first through a wet patch of snow. As she got up on her hands and knees, Cayenne clattered off down the slope.

Zeke lunged for the mare's loose, flying reins, but missed. Another mournful call forced Zeke to keep a tight hold on Ember, then he jumped from his saddle to check on Myra. "Are you hurt?" He knelt close beside her because the fading light made it difficult to see.

"Only my pride," she sputtered, wiping wet snow from her jeans and scrubbing her face. "Did you catch my horse?"

"No. We'd better go after her. Ember is getting antsy and it's too gray to see how near those wolves may be." He helped Myra up.

Myra slipped as she tried to stand.

"Are you sure you're okay?"

"Yes, only a bit shaken. Cayenne's never thrown me before."

"If you're sure you're okay to ride, come on." Zeke nipped her at the waist and boosted her up onto Ember's saddle. "We'll ride double."

"I can sit behind you," Myra said, attempting to swing down again.

"Stay. We've gotta make tracks home and I want to know you're not so woozy you'll fall off." Taking charge, he tightened his grasp of the reins and landed in the saddle behind her.

Myra grabbed the saddle horn to keep from leaning against Zeke, and Ember took off at a trot. Then at Zeke's urging, the nervous gelding moved faster.

Snugged between Zeke's solid thighs and cradled by his arms, Myra relaxed against her will. She'd never ridden double like this before. Somehow her fuzzy mind decided it wasn't a bad way to get down out of the foothills.

"It's really dark now," Zeke said, his breath rustling Myra's hair. "I don't see a moon or stars. Do you think Cayenne will head straight to the ranch?"

"I hope so." Myra turned slightly to look at him. She felt her hair brush his cheek and she froze. She hadn't been this close to a man since moving to Snowy Owl Crossing. At the moment her mind warred with itself. Part of her liked the comfort afforded by Zeke Maxwell's strong arms. Another part of her brain whispered, *But he's the enemy.*

Chapter Five

"The wolves sound more distant," Zeke said. "I had no idea there were any here. Are they a hazard to the herd?"

Myra didn't respond.

He slowed Ember's dash through the dark terrain and shook Myra lightly. "Hey, speak up. Let me know you aren't hurt."

"Sorry, I was back thinking of our conversation about taking photos of the owls before I so unceremoniously got dumped from my horse."

"I'm sure I'll have other opportunities. I hope so, at least. Like I said, Mom always sends me photos of tropical birds."

"I'm surprised you didn't go live with your parents after you got out of the hospital," Myra said. "Seems like you'd be in seventh heaven lying around all day on sandy beaches overrun with bikini babes."

"What, in our short acquaintance, made you form such a low opinion of me?"

She could have said he hadn't seemed to have a problem taking a ranch he hadn't worked for, but

Myra still clung to the hope he'd tire of the hard work and pack it in. And maybe he'd change his mind about fun in the sun during severe Montana winters. "I didn't mean to cast aspersions. I thought that was every guy's dream."

"Can't say I don't admire women in bikinis. But I've never been one to lie around all day doing nothing. And my folks have a one-bedroom bungalow inland from the beach. Honestly, I had enough sun and sand to last me a lifetime in Iraq and Afghanistan."

"Fair enough. I stand corrected. But I still wonder why you ride so well. Boston doesn't strike me as a horse haven. And don't you military guys all travel in Humvees?"

"The one tour I did in Iraq before we pulled out, I was embedded with a friendly nomadic tribe. They liked to make fun of the city guys in my outfit. Once they had their laughs at us, they took us under their wing. Their horses are top-notch."

"Well, that makes sense. Oh, look, there's the ranch." Myra sat upright and the top of her head struck the underside of Zeke's chin.

"Ouch, don't knock me out."

"Sorry. I was trying to see Cayenne."

"I think that's her darker outline by the barn." Zeke pointed over Myra's shoulder.

"That's a relief. I would feel terrible if anything happened to her."

As they approached, the mare lifted her head and

whinnied. For a minute it seemed as if she'd take off running again.

"Let me off to calm her," Myra said. "She's still spooked."

Zeke reined in, swung out of the saddle and reached up to lift Myra down. If not for the hold he maintained on her waist, she'd have fallen again.

"Heavens," she exclaimed. "I hurt my knees more than I thought." She hobbled over to grab Cayenne's bridle then limped on to open the barn door.

"We may both soak up liniment tonight," Zeke joked, following her.

"I hope not. There's a lot of hard work on tap tomorrow."

Zeke stopped her with a hand on her arm. "Let me take care of the horses. You go in and treat your knees. We can do sandwiches or something easy for our meal. No need to fix a full supper."

"I put stew in the Crock-Pot at lunch. All we need to do is make coffee and pop some French bread in the oven for ten minutes or so."

"Great. So what besides shipping calves are we doing tomorrow?" Zeke studied Myra in the brighter light she'd turned on inside the barn.

"I need to call Eddie Four Bear. If he and Aaron Younger can round up a third man, tomorrow afternoon we can vaccinate, spray for parasites and test for pregnancies. Believe me when I tell you that's about the toughest job you'll do outside of calving during wind, rain or a late snowfall." Myra handed over Cayenne's reins and limped off.

In the house, she greeted and fed Orion, washed up and started coffee. Then she went to the bedroom in search of her phone. As she'd guessed, her mother had left a stream of messages, all scolding her for choosing to stay at the ranch rather than apply for teaching jobs. Eric had phoned, too. So after she called Eddie Four Bear and got his promise to pick up vaccinations and bring two helpers to the ranch the next day, she dialed her brother's number just to talk.

"Sis, it's about damn time you called home. What's going on? Mom's in a tizzy because Dad said you're staying at the Flying Owl until spring."

Dropping down on the bed, Myra put her phone on speaker while she rolled up her jeans and inspected her knees. Both had begun to bruise, but she'd had worse injuries getting kicked by a cow. "Eric, it seems to have shocked the family to learn I really love this ranch. I know Zeke Maxwell did a heroic thing risking his life to save yours, but he doesn't know the first damn thing about ranching."

"He'll catch on. And truly, Dad had no idea Gramps still had cows. He and Mom both thought all you were doing was taking care of his cooking and laundry."

"I grew the herd," she snapped. "I assumed when Dad checked the ledgers he'd either let me buy the place or give it to me as my inheritance."

"Holy crap, Myra. Who knew that's what you had

in mind? I guess I made a mess for you suggesting to the folks that they give Zeke the ranch."

"Keep this between us, Eric… I swear if you tell the folks or Zeke I'll hurt you. The reason I'm still here is because I'm betting your city boy will take a hike when ranch life gets tough."

"I don't know, Myra. I saw Zeke in action in some bad spots. He's got guts."

"Well, if you're right, after spring calving I'll lick my wounds and leave." She hated that she'd already seen signs Zeke might buckle down and learn ranching. And darn it all, she had to give him extra points for liking snowy owls.

"What about teaching? You have your degree and credentials."

"I never liked teaching math. Don't tell Mom that, either. If things here fall apart, I don't know what I'll do, but I won't teach. That's Mom's dream."

"Damn, sis, now I feel doubly guilty."

"You didn't know. I should have told Dad at Gramps's funeral, but it didn't seem the time to talk about raising cows when we were all grieving."

"No, you're right. And maybe Zeke's not cut out to raise cattle. I'll tell Dad I talked to you and let him deal with Mom. Stay in touch. And for the record, I'm sorry as hell that I screwed up your plans."

"Stop it, Eric." Myra felt tears punch the back of her eyes. "I can't fault what you did. The guy saved your life."

They said their goodbyes, then Myra dried her

eyes, treated her knees and was in the kitchen setting the table when Zeke came in from the barn.

He went straight to his bedroom.

She put bread in the oven, and as soon as she heard Zeke come out of his room, she dished up their stew. It surprised her how normal she was able to act, given the turmoil in her heart after her confession to Eric.

"Did you reach that Eddie guy?" Zeke asked. He peered into Orion's pen and made appropriate piggy-talk before taking his seat at the table.

Myra retrieved the piping-hot bread and shut off the oven. "I did. He and friends will be here tomorrow. With their help and Hank's, we should have all the calves loaded and off to market by noon."

"Got it. Hey, this stew hits the spot. I didn't realize how hungry I was."

"Thanks. I like meals I can throw in the Crock-Pot. More often than not, I come in too tired and dirty to feel like cooking."

"Speaking of dirty. I need boots I can leave in the barn. I also need work shirts and a lined jacket. Is there a store in town you can recommend?"

"The Tractor Supply Company."

Zeke stopped with his spoon halfway to his mouth. "You said that with a straight face. Is this some kind of a greenhorn initiation? Or did you make it up because I didn't know lemmings were real?"

Myra frowned. "You've lost me."

"Come on. Clothes at a tractor supply store?"

She ladled out more stew. "First of all, that's the

store name. They're in a lot of Western towns. Ranchers and cowboys tend to like one-stop shopping."

Zeke continued to look mistrustful, but he ladled out more stew and let the conversation drop.

It was fine with Myra. It had been a long day.

Once Zeke finished eating, he carried his dishes to the sink and rinsed them. "What time do we start tomorrow? I'm going to go see if I can connect with my brother in whatever time zone he's in, then hit the sack."

"I'll go out early to check fences. The unexpected snow could've driven those wolves into the foothills. We need to be vigilant until we bring the herd down to winter pasture."

"A short answer would do. Is early five, six or when?"

Myra jerked in her chair feeling as if she'd been smacked down by his sharp tone. He needed to know wolf presence in the area could wreak havoc with any herd. "Six," she said. "No formal breakfast. Make do." *There, if he wanted short and sweet, she'd comply. It'd suit her fine if he didn't learn enough to run a ranch.* She watched him take out his phone and leave the kitchen.

Did that shift in his attitude mean he'd decided to flex his owner muscle? She wasn't sure how she'd feel if he started giving her orders as if she were his employee. Perhaps it'd been nothing. Eric used to accuse her of bossiness. But she had been in charge of this ranch for three and half years. If she got on Zeke's nerves this early in their working relationship, it was going to be a long danged time till spring.

Clearing the dishes and setting up for morning coffee, she let her mind float back to how pleasant she'd found it riding double with Zeke. Was that the source of her hurt pride now? Had she read more into the close way he'd held her? Probably it was no more than what he'd said—he didn't want her falling off the horse.

To think of something other than Zeke, she rechecked her tender knees then went out on the back porch to put new litter in Orion's box. He followed. Still too restless for bed, she picked up the pig and carried him into the living room. She hadn't worked on a dollhouse since Zeke's arrival, and she had one ready for shutters. That wouldn't be a noisy task. Another house needed to be roofed, but that entailed hammering.

With Orion yawning on her lap, Myra lost herself in applying dark blue hinged shutters to the windows of a two-story house. She'd set down her tools to admire her handiwork when her cell phone rang. Afraid it might be her mother, she scooped up Orion, switched off the light and escaped to her bedroom before she answered.

"Myra, hi. Jewell here. I was about to hang up."

"Sorry it took me so long to answer. I was in the middle of cleaning up from working on a dollhouse."

"Ooh, can't wait to see the new batch. Listen, I wanted to check with you. Eddie Four Bear stopped by. He said you asked him to pick up vaccine kits. I gave him a hundred. If that's not enough I can drop more off tomorrow. I have a call to make at Ralston's. Lou's buckskin picked up a stone. Dave dug it out, but Lou thinks it's infected. She talked him into paying me to take a look."

Myra chuckled. "We all know how tight that man is with money."

"Yeah. I'm so glad my father was never like that. So, about the vaccine…"

"I only need eighty or so. But extras will keep in the fridge. I could have had a few heifers stray. Some of Hank's and Dave's showed up with my pairs."

"How's it going with you-know-who? Ralston stopped at the café today. He told Lila's mom he'd met Zeke Maxwell and thinks he's a nice guy."

"He's…okay."

"Dave referred to him as the Flying Owl's new owner. Eddie said you made a deal with Maxwell to stay on through spring calving."

"That's right."

"Won't that make it twice as hard to leave? Not that we don't all want you here as long as possible, but I know how you love running the Flying Owl. I'm thinking of you, Myra."

She set Orion in his cage and he burrowed into his favorite quilt. Myra closed the cage door and flopped onto the bed. "It's because I love the ranch. In a weak moment I volunteered to stay and help out. Jewell, the man is a total tenderfoot! At least he knows his way around horses. I offered to ask the bank for a loan to buy him out. He said he wasn't interested. I can only hope he'll change his mind."

"What's he like? Is he a frog or a prince?"

Her friend's question stopped Myra cold. If she said frog she'd be lying. If she said prince that'd be all over town by morning. "What are my other options? I could say he's a rat, but it's not his fault my folks gave him the ranch." She blew out a breath. "Up to now he hasn't shirked, but I know he's had multiple surgeries to rebuild his left shoulder and elbow."

"All the Artsy Ladies want to know is if he's single and hot!"

"He's single, though he could have a girlfriend stashed someplace. He has a twin. A gemologist. Zeke invited him to visit. If he shows up before spring I have to clean my craft stuff out of the third bedroom. But sooner or later I'll have to do that anyway."

"You still haven't said what he looks like. If we're going to find out we'll have to come help you clean that room," Jewell said around a laugh. "Why don't you drag him to the dance next Saturday? It's the last potluck of the year at the grange hall, remember. Unless he's totally gross, that is."

Again sidestepping the question, Myra said, "Did Tawana tell you the snowy owls are back? I took Zeke out to see them this evening."

"I haven't talked to Tawana. And Eddie didn't mention it. Did you see some of my banded ones?"

"Not the one I got the best look at. We counted

three. Two females and a male. There may have been more. They're nesting in Leland Conrad's timber."

"Thanks for the heads-up. The early snowfall in Canada must have driven their food source down. Since I don't have to bring you vaccine, I'll run out there tomorrow. I can get there using my Jeep, right?"

"We rode and angled across BLM land. There's probably a road through Leland's ranch. That'd be quicker."

"Oh, I'm so excited. They need a protected habitat, but I haven't heard back from my inquiry to the government's Natural Resource Committee."

"That's another reason I hate the thought of leaving, Jewell. We've all worked so hard to secure a preserve. I want to see it through."

"Maybe you shouldn't be so helpful to Maxwell. If he flounders, won't he be more likely to chuck it all?"

"I don't see it as helping him so much as making sure the Flying Owl thrives."

"You're in a pickle. I have a call coming in on my emergency line. We'll touch base later. Think about coming to the dance. We ladies will put our heads together and come up with a plan to discourage him from staying."

"I'll see if I can get away. My to-do list is a mile long. Bye, Jewell."

After hanging up, Myra rummaged in her drawer and pulled out a notepad. If she listed all of the chores that had to be done, and roughly which months Zeke would need to plan on doing them, just looking at a list could be enough to convince him to go away.

In his room, Zeke sat on his bed. He had only removed his boots. Seth hadn't answered, so he'd left a message. He had no idea where his brother was or what time zone he was in.

He heard Myra moving around the other part of the house. First in the kitchen, then out on the back porch and later in the living room. He'd gotten up and peeked out his door. Seeing her bent over one of her unfinished dollhouses, he debated going out. Then thought better of it. Until tonight when her horse had gotten away from her and they'd had to ride for several miles together on Ember, Zeke hadn't thought of Myra as a woman. Not in the sense of an attractive one.

First she'd merely been a buddy's sister. Not really a know-it-all, but certainly impatient—with him at least. That was prior to feeling her slender back against his chest, her hips flush between his thighs. But what most messed with his equilibrium had been the apple scent of her hair as it blew into his face. All day they'd both worked like demons to separate calves from their mothers. The sun had only come out a few times to warm the air. But it'd been sweaty work.

Somehow Myra had managed to still smell like a woman.

His last steady girl had broken it off with him while he was in rehab. It surprised him that he hadn't been overly sad to hear she'd found someone else. A dentist. Zeke could picture Stacy with a safe, boring guy. He'd sent her a card saying he was happy for her. And he was. At the time, in his condition, he'd only needed nurses in his life. It helped if they were pretty, but he hadn't grown attached to any one in particular.

Now Myra Odell had gotten under his skin. The discovery shocked him. He didn't view it as altogether good news, either. He had a feeling if her parents had any inclination as to the thoughts running amok in his head, they'd kick his butt off the ranch in short order. And damn it all, he liked it here.

Why, he couldn't say. The work wasn't fun. Cows were dirty. But Myra spoke of ranching in such glowing terms. The notion of calling himself a bona fide rancher one of these days, and having people like Dave Ralston see him as one, was appealing. And how could it hurt to have a woman like Myra at his side—in his corner.

Bolting off his bed, Zeke stripped out of his clothes and hurried into the shower—a cold one. Letting water rain down on his face and aching muscles, his wishful-thinking side argued with his good-guy side—which said he should scrap those libidinous thoughts.

He'd toweled off and burrowed beneath the covers when his cell phone rang. Answering quickly and hoping it hadn't disturbed Myra, he knew it either had to be Eric or Seth. No one else called him these days. Well, his mom, but she was an early-to-bed, early-to-rise person.

"What's up, bro? I just checked into my hotel in Nairobi."

"What are you doing in Kenya?" Zeke sat up.

"A dealer who wants my stash of lapis is here. If I can unload it for a good price, there's also a western bank in town and I can deposit to my Boston account before I hook up with my guide to travel into the hills of Tanzania."

"Now I'll worry this dealer will knock you in the head and steal your stones."

"Nah. I've done business with him before. It's after midnight here. You so rarely call, I figured I should ring you back."

"I just wanted to talk. But we can catch up later. Will you let me know you're still alive when you get to Tanzania?"

His brother laughed. "Has becoming a landowner turned you into a mother hen?"

"Maybe. I met a neighbor who is the fourth generation in his family to run his ranch. And Myra—she's currently running this one—her dad was born in this house. Oh, today she took me out to see snowy owls. They apparently return to nest in the hills year after year."

"Oh yeah?"

"Yeah. Our roots are shallow, Seth. Jeez, I'll let you go. I'm not making sense."

"Stay a minute. You glossed over something I

find interesting. Why is this Myra person running the ranch? I thought you said she was going back to teaching."

Zeke weighed how much he should share with his twin, who often seemed to read his mind. "She handled the ranch for her grandfather when he was ill. She didn't really have a teaching job waiting, and schools are starting soon. I'm not sure how much you know about raising cows. I don't know diddly-squat. I asked her to stay on until I understand more. She agreed to show me the ropes until spring. That's when the next crop of calves are born."

"You two are sharing a house?"

Zeke took a deep breath. Leave it to Seth to hone in on the one thing people might see as an issue. "Yeah. So what? It has three bedrooms. In fact, the house is old and needs updating. Especially the kitchen. I don't have a lot of free time, but I need to put in a new sink and a coat of paint at least. Any chance you can come help soon?"

"Good try at distracting me. Is she pretty?"

"I guess you don't mean the kitchen," Zeke said drily. "Uh, yeah, she's pretty. Not in a glitzy movie-star way, but wholesome."

"Dude, you need lessons in common sense and tact. I've never met a woman who'd be pleased to be described as wholesome. It's like saying she's healthy and sound as a horse."

"Goodbye, Seth. You need sleep. Your thinking is skewed. But remember to let me know you're safe at your next port of call." Zeke quickly disconnected. Setting his phone on the nightstand, he turned out the lamp and slid down in his bed. Mulling over what his brother had said—well, Myra had thick, dark blond hair, golden skin and really expressive amber eyes. Yeah, maybe *wholesome* didn't do her justice. But if he had admitted to Seth how attractive he found her, he'd be letting himself in for constant ribbing. And that he could do without.

THE HOUSE WAS dark and silent in the morning when Myra made her way to the kitchen. She set Orion in his pen and tended to his food before she washed her hands and started the coffee.

It didn't surprise her that she was up before Zeke. He'd taken a late-night call—the ringing of his phone had awakened Orion. She hadn't a clue who might call him so late at night. She hadn't let herself wonder about his friends. *Women or men.*

Myra mixed a handful of blueberries in a cup of yogurt and ate it while the coffee perked. She tossed the cup in the trash and listened for any noise from Zeke's quarters. Hearing none, she poured a thermal mug full of coffee then set down a matching mug for him before heading out.

She had Cayenne saddled when the barn door slid open and in rushed a rumpled Zeke. He was trying to put on his jacket while holding his travel mug between his teeth. "My alarm didn't go off," he said, sounding garbled.

"I thought maybe you decided you didn't want to ride fence."

He shook his head. "Haven't I made clear I want to see all that goes on around here?"

"I guess so. Here, I'll take your cup while you saddle Ember."

Zeke passed her his mug. It didn't take him long to have his horse ready to go. "What's in your saddlebags? Granola bars, I hope," he joked.

"Didn't you eat anything?"

"Nope. So, no breakfast bars?"

"I have wire ties, a staple gun with heavy staples and a hammer. We'll be checking a wire fence stapled to wood posts. Most repairs are simple. Like a staple pulled loose or a broken strand of wire. It's rarely a whole section down."

"Barbed wire?" he asked, closing the barn door before mounting up.

Myra handed him back his coffee. "Gramps installed seven-foot woven wire. Holds in the cattle, keeps out deer and elk. Not a lot of barbed wire used around here. Some use low-voltage electric fences. They're costlier but deter wildlife."

"Do they all keep out wolves?"

She shrugged. "Wolves are clever. If they frighten the cows, the herd can trample a fence for them."

They rode in silence, drinking their coffee as they watched the sun come up and spread peachy fingers of light over the land. With the snow mostly melted, much of the land looked green and pristine.

It took two hours to circle the largest of the ranch's enclosed pastures.

"We rode all that long way and you put in only three staples and wired one broken strand together," Zeke said on the journey home. "Is that usual?"

"I call it successful. It's better not to find places where cows broke out, or predators got in. And we're back in time to meet Hank. That's his big truck rolling in," Myra said, urging Cayenne into a canter.

She greeted the neighbor and introduced Zeke. "If you guys want to pop inside for a drink while you get acquainted, I'll put the horses away."

"I'm for that. I went out without breakfast, so I'm going to buy a microwave," Zeke said, taking the coffee mug Myra handed him. "You want anything?" he asked her.

"No thanks. I'll take water out to where we'll start working with the heifers after Hank has the calves loaded."

The men turned away, chatting. Myra suffered a moment's pang at how quickly Zeke made friends with her neighbors.

They weren't gone long. She'd unsaddled and run a brush over the horses, fed them grain and filled the sprayer, when she heard their voices. She'd packed a cooler with bottled water from the barn fridge and now wheeled it out to the far side of the weaning pen. Already Hank had backed up to the outer gate. He and Zeke were driving calves up the ramp.

Myra walked over with her clipboard.

"I counted sixteen already in," Hank told her.

This was a chore she'd normally done with him, so he knew her routine. It was good when his tally matched the one she took at weaning. Today it did.

With doors and ramp secured, Hank shook hands with Zeke. "Nice to meet you, neighbor," he said as he climbed into his truck. Before he pulled away, a battered red pickup drove in.

It stopped and three young men emerged. One hailed Myra, and he retrieved a carton from the pick-up's bed.

Myra recognized two of the three. "Eddie, this is Zeke Maxwell, new owner here." She rushed over those words that still tasted bitter on her tongue. "Eddie Four Bear and Aaron Younger," she told Zeke.

Eddie wore his black hair long and in one braid that hung to his waist. Aaron's fell straight to his shoulders.

"Myra and Zeke, this is Luke Elkhorn. He's my cousin," Eddie said. "He worked with me and Aaron all spring and summer. He's a good guy."

"Welcome." Myra shook hands with the dark-eyed kid. "We aren't taking you out of school to do this job, are we?" *He looked so young.*

The boy smiled. "I'm nineteen."

"Yeah, he's got a baby face," Aaron teased. And it went that way between the friends until they reached the chutes. For Zeke's and Luke's benefit, Myra went over the process. The other two had assisted her in prior years.

"We talked about who'd do what," Eddie said. "Aaron and me will trade off pregnancy testing and spraying for mites. Luke will pull 'em through the chute and into the open pen if you vaccinate, Myra. Unless Zeke's doing that." He jammed a worn cowboy hat on his head and quirked an eyebrow at Zeke, who held up both arms and backed away.

Myra jumped in. "Zeke is new to ranching. He'll shove heifers into the chute to start. Maybe this afternoon he and Luke can trade off."

Eddie seemed to want to comment but didn't.

Myra motioned to Aaron. "I filled the sprayer. Will you bring it from the barn?"

He left and came back shortly, and Myra pronounced them ready. "Zeke, you've gotta keep heifers moving into the first chute. Cows who have gone through this before may be cantankerous. Twist their tail to make them move, but watch out you don't get kicked."

They each took their stations. She didn't have a lot of time to explain things to Zeke. But it was a self-explanatory process. Zeke shoved a heifer in the chute. Myra vaccinated. It bellowed and the shock drove the cow into chute two, where Aaron doused her with pesticide. Eddie hand-examined the birth canal in chute three, gave Myra a thumbs-up or thumbs-down, then Luke wrestled the unhappy animal into the open pen.

Soon the air filled with grunting, swearing and bawling. Spray churned up mud under everyone's feet, along with plenty of poop mixed with urine. Myra marked her clipboard for each pregnant heifer between readying shots.

They slipped, slid and cursed through lunchtime. By midafternoon they were three-fourths finished. Myra straightened. "Time for another water break."

Zeke left the corral and strode toward the house. Myra watched him as she drank her water.

They were ready to begin again, but Zeke hadn't returned. Then he came out of the house dressed in clean cammo pants and a different shirt. He climbed in his pickup and roared off.

"Where do you s'pose he's goin'?" Eddie asked.

"Was he carrying duffel bags?" Myra murmured.

The others shook their heads. Not having an explanation and shorthanded, they set back to work. Luke took over for Zeke. Aaron and Eddie switched jobs, so Aaron drove finished heifers into the pens. At the end of another hour, tempers were short and they were all hot and splattered with gunk, most of which smelled awful.

Myra's cell rang. She was surprised to see Lila's number. "Hi, Lila. Can I call you later? I'm in the middle of a dirty chore."

"Sure, but I called to tell you we got a look at Zeke Maxwell. He bought a camera, a microwave and wandered around town. Then he bought three pair of boots, some shirts, a hat, a jacket and some paint. Now he's at Cody's Bar on his second beer. Jewell and I popped over. Outside of his looking grim, Jewell said you neglected to say the guy's hotter than a firecracker."

"He's AWOL and left me to pick up the slack," Myra said tartly. "Unless he's leaving town—and it doesn't sound like it if he bought new gear—I guarantee, hot or not, he'll get an earful from me when he wanders back to the Flying Owl. Thanks for the heads-up. Later, Lila, okay?"

Chapter Six

Eddie, who only heard Myra's side of the conversation, spoke flatly. "A couple of owners I worked for refused to get their hands dirty. Not any around Snowy Owl Crossing, but two dudes outside Sheridan, Wyoming."

"Zeke has the option of hiring everything done," Myra said, making a face. "I've deliberately given him scuzzy chores, hoping he'll decide to toss the ranch back in my dad's lap. Or at least sell it to me. When he took off I thought maybe my ploy had worked, but it doesn't sound like it."

"Tawana told us your dad gave away the ranch," Aaron said. "I wish somebody would give me a place like this one. I'd gladly do all the dirty work by my lonesome."

Eddie concurred.

"Yes, but you guys have done most of these type chores since you were kids. Zeke grew up in a city. To be honest, he's not done badly until he skipped out today. And his military record is exemplary, according to my brother, whose life he saved."

"Sounds to me like you can't decide if you want to convince him to give up or not." Eddie paused in his present task of spraying for parasites to point that out to Myra.

She shoved another heifer into the chute, barely avoiding being kicked for her effort. "Maybe I'm conflicted because he got injured carrying Eric out of harm's way."

That seemed to say it all to Myra's helpers. They bent to their tasks and in another hour had completed the unpleasant job.

"Seventy-four heifers are going to have another calf," Myra said with satisfaction after she washed off with the hose and picked up her clipboard.

"That's a prolific bull you have," Aaron noted with a big grin.

Myra nodded. "Gramps chose well with that one. Maybe Zeke won't need to rent a bull to help out. If all the young heifers I kept get with calf, the herd will grow. Hey, guys, you all did a great job. Let's go to the barn and I'll get your pay." She grabbed the cooler handle after each of them took another water bottle.

"There will be growth unless you lose a lot in spring calving," Eddie noted as he rolled the sprayer to the barn. "It could cost Zeke a lot to hire help to handle the calving."

"I did say I'd stay on through spring." Myra opened the barn door. "Of course, that could all change."

"You mean if he flakes off again like he did this afternoon?" Aaron asked.

She shrugged and noticed that Luke hung back, listening but not talking.

Myra went into her office and unlocked her desk. "I need everyone's social security number. Eddie, are you at the same hourly fee as last year?" she asked, taking out a calculator and checkbook.

"Same. Or if you prefer a daily flat fee, Myra, divide it three ways."

"I've always paid hourly. And since we finished in record time and I didn't provide lunch, I'll add a small bonus for each of you." Listing the numbers they gave her, she bent over the checkbook and began to write.

Aaron spoke. "The new owner lets you make that kind of decision?"

She frowned as she tore out the first check and passed it to Eddie. "The bonus is coming out of Zeke's share of the cost."

They laughed and continued to make jokes until Myra handed Luke the last check and the guys got ready to leave. "I like working close to home," Eddie said, pausing as they trooped to the door. "You can give Zeke my phone number in case you take off and he's in need of help."

Aaron poked him in the ribs. "It's because Eddie's got a romance going with Lana Elkhorn. If he runs off to Wyoming next spring, she might find a new boyfriend."

Myra smiled. She'd seen in the past how Aaron and Eddie loved to needle each other. "I'm making Zeke a schedule of ranch jobs and approximate dates. I'll be sure to list all of your phone numbers if you care to leave them. Eddie, I have yours."

Aaron and Luke turned back to the desk and wrote on a notepad Myra set out.

"Tell him about the bonus, too," Luke said, shyly chiming in for the first time. "What I made today pays tuition for a quarter at an online college."

That comment had his buddies ribbing him about being a nerd. Luke took it in stride, Myra noticed as they said goodbye.

Filthy-dirty and tired, she hurriedly put away the checkbook, locked the desk and crossed to the house, anxious to shower off the grime. She shed her boots at the door to be cleaned later. The clothes she had on would take two washings. She wondered what Zeke had done with his things. He had worked long enough to get plenty grungy.

Stepping into a hot shower, she almost purred with joy. Because she'd been splattered from head to toe, she washed her hair first then scrubbed every point on her body that had been exposed. When finished, she wrapped a towel around her head and cleaned the shower stall.

She changed into a sweat suit and heavy socks in case she had to go outside again for any reason, then ran a brush through her hair, electing to let it dry naturally while she started the washer.

Grabbing the net laundry bag, she'd barely stepped into the living room when the front door swung open and Zeke entered carrying some big plastic sacks and two, gallon-size paint cans. He dropped the sacks and shut the door before he noticed Myra.

She scowled at him. "I understand you had a fine time in town, taking photographs, shopping and slugging down two beers at Cody's Bar."

He set the paint down with a thump and aimlessly rubbed the back of his neck. "I'm not used to everyone knowing and blabbing my private business."

"Yes, well, welcome to a small town. Just so you know, ranchers don't usually walk out in the middle of an all-important job. Especially if you're paying help to get it done in one day."

He slowly lifted his hand from his neck and without flinching from her stony gaze, said, "Myra, look—I apologize." Closing his eyes, Zeke ran a thumb and finger over his eyebrows. "You won't understand."

"Try me." She stood her ground.

"Fine! Bawling cows, slippery mud, the awful smell coupled with the noise from metal on metal as cows crashed against the chute—what I started to see wasn't muddy cows, but men covered in blood, like I was back in Afghanistan on a mission going bad."

Myra's jaw dropped. "Heavens, Zeke. Why didn't you say something sooner?"

"I never had a flashback before. I was afraid I was totally losing my grip," he said, avoiding her eyes.

Myra moved forward and curled her fingers around his arm. "I would've understood. We all would have, even though there's no way any of us can half imagine what it must have been like over there."

"I just needed to get away," he mumbled, covering her hand, then as quickly pulling away.

"Did I hurt your injured arm?" she asked, fully withdrawing her touch.

Zeke reconnected, catching both her hands. "No. No. Stay. So…uh…probably everybody in town thinks I'm a bum, huh? Come to think of it…how did anyone know who I was?"

Myra couldn't help feeling guilty. "We don't get many newcomers. When Dad said he'd given you the Flying Owl, I told all of my friends. I wasn't happy, but I'd never deliberately hurt you, Zeke. In fact, have I thrown too much at you too fast? Are you feeling better? Will it happen again?" Feeling herself babble, she took a breath. "I can handle harvesting alfalfa alone if you need time off to see a VA doctor. I'm not sure where the nearest clinic is, but Eric will know."

"Myra, stop. It's okay." Zeke brought her close against him. "The feeling passed before I got to town. I figured since I was there I should make the most of having bailed on you. I bought a microwave and paint for the kitchen. Later, I'll get a new sink and countertops."

"The kitchen?" Myra found it impossible to jump from concern for his well-being to talk of painting the kitchen. Especially when the lazy way he rubbed his thumbs over the backs of her hands sent tingles up her arms—and made her want to hug him. So she did. She slid her arms around his waist. Her head fit snugly under his chin. With an ear pressed to his chest, she was calmed by the steady beat of his heart. Until suddenly it sped, thumping louder. He must be uncomfortable.

Guilt filled her again. "Sorry." She leaned back. "I...uh...hugged Eric every chance I got after he returned. But you're not Eric."

"No," Zeke murmured. "But hugs are fine." He lifted a hand to stroke her damp strands. "Your hair's wet. It still smells like apples. I noticed that before."

"My shampoo." Myra let go. "What did you say about painting the kitchen?" Fully disengaged, she stepped away and rubbed her arms.

Zeke quickly picked up the bags he'd dropped. "I'll go put these new clothes away, then I'll start painting while you work on your dollhouses."

"I've got to put my clothes from today into the wash now. Yours have to be yucky, too. Get them and I'll toss them all in." She couldn't believe she'd gone so swiftly from being wrapped in his arms and feeling almost giddy to talking about mundane things like laundry. What a day.

"I PLANNED TO THROW what I wore today away. It's disgusting to think of the mess they can make in a washer."

"Raising cattle for profit is disgusting work. You can't always be throwing away clothes, Zeke. Gramps installed a commercial-grade washer and dryer for Gram. They do a bang-up job of getting clothes clean."

"I asked you to help me learn ranching, not be

my housekeeper." He left her and the paint cans and headed for his room.

"For Pete's sake, we both live here. Chores overlap. Stop being stubborn."

Zeke paused outside his bedroom. He knew exactly why he was being stubborn. It'd felt all too good touching her and having her arms around him. It'd be way too easy to take things further. He hadn't had a woman in his life for some time. But he wasn't immune, and Myra fit a lot of things on his list of likes. Considering all he owed her folks, taking advantage of their forced proximity was no way to pay back the family's generosity. He'd do well to remember that. "I'll get the clothes if you quit being bossy."

Myra pitched the net bag toward him. "Stuff your things in there while I go feed Orion."

Turning, Zeke watched her stomp into the kitchen, and he felt like a hound dog. *Or should that be horndog?* That was really what drove him to act like a jerk. Maybe he should tell her to leave. How costly would it be to hire Eddie or Aaron on a monthly basis? They'd sounded as if they hired out. On the other hand, they'd acted on Myra's directions. Maybe they'd be good workers, but not effective managers. *Crap!*

Striding back, he yanked up the net bag and almost gagged at the smell. He hurried into his room and found his pants and shirt on the floor of his bathroom, where he'd stripped them off earlier. "Ugh." They made the whole room stink. Doing his best to hold his breath, he opened the bag and dumped his stuff inside. He left the room again and encountered Myra holding Orion in her arms.

Zeke couldn't say how it happened, but suddenly he imagined Myra holding a baby instead. *His baby.* A knot formed in his stomach. He let the bag fall, spun on his heel and retreated to his room, accidentally letting his door slam. Then even as he set to work ripping tags off his new shirts and pants, he couldn't shake the image of Myra as a mother. A wife and mother. *Maybe he did need to see a VA doctor.*

He was in the process of arranging his new boots in the bottom of his closet when he heard the washer start. Two pairs had short heels—better for working, the salesman had informed him. One dressier pair made of black snakeskin had higher, slant heels. That was an impulse purchase, as was a black felt Resistol hat. Looking at it here in his bedroom, it seemed like overkill. Yet when he'd faced a whole wall of hats, some handmade, others duded up with feathers or beaded bands, he'd picked a simple one that felt good on his head. Now he questioned whether people would rib him for playing at being a cowboy. Would he feel awkward wearing all this garb out in public? He grimaced and set the hat on his closet shelf.

As he contemplated returning it for a refund, Myra knocked.

"Zeke?"

Still uneasy about discovering his lusty feelings, Zeke debated several seconds before striding over to open the door.

"I have meat loaf baking. I'm considering making corn bread, unless you'd rather fix your biscuits. They were so tasty."

He brightened. "Do you put creamed corn in your corn bread?"

She nodded.

"Then I vote for that. We had a cook when I attended jumpmaster school at Fort Bragg who made corn bread like that. All the guys in the class wanted to kidnap him when they sent us to another unit."

"Jumpmaster? You parachute out of airplanes?"

"Not recently, but yeah, I've made many jumps."

"Nothing about ranching takes that kind of grit," Myra stated emphatically.

Zeke exited his room and closed the door. "Parachuting is a matter of training. I'm sure you didn't come into this world knowing how to vaccinate cattle. Doing that as many times as you did today, all while avoiding getting hooked by horns, takes guts."

Myra shrugged. "I guess it's a matter of perspective. Okay, getting back to supper, I'll make corn bread tonight if you cook tomorrow night. We've got to start cutting alfalfa, get it baled and stored in the barn ASAP. I heard on the weather network that the temperature's going to dip again. Sounds as if winter's coming early. We need to bring the last of the herd down out of the foothills, too."

It was plain to Zeke that if Myra had ever felt uncomfortable about the hug they'd shared, she'd gotten past it. Perhaps she'd only meant it as a sisterly gesture. Maybe she did place him in a category with Eric. He'd never had a sister, so looking at her that way wasn't an option for him. And just now as their shoulders and hips brushed when they went through the kitchen doorway side by side, Zeke's insides vibrated. He turned and went out to his pickup to bring in the microwave. Plainly he had way more work to do to keep his feelings for her platonic.

Still, dinner was pleasant. They were almost finished and Myra's cell phone rang.

"Hank, hi," she said on answering. "So you're back from selling our stock?" She smiled at Zeke. "That's a good total weight." She jumped up and sorted through some papers stacked on the counter and sat back with a pen. "The cost per pound is four cents less than last year, but with the calf weight up it comes out to approximately the same income." She jotted down a figure and shoved it across the table to Zeke.

It didn't mean much to him and was less than he'd made per year in the military. But Myra seemed pleased, so he smiled back at her.

"I did hear the weather report, Hank. I plan to cut alfalfa tomorrow. So your sons combined today and you rented Dave's baler for tomorrow? I'd better give him a call to arrange our time." It sounded as if she was repeating his half of the conversation for Zeke's benefit. "Sure, Zeke and I can help move bales into your hay shed if you reciprocate." She frowned a bit. "Yeah, I know the October potluck dance at the grange is Saturday night. Jewell reminded me.

No, I didn't mention it to Zeke. We'll see how much work we get done since we're all racing against another snowfall."

They talked awhile longer, then Myra swiped off and set her phone with the pen and paper. She began stacking dishes. "It had better be early to bed tonight."

Zeke grabbed another piece of corn bread before she could make off with the pan. He eyed her as he bit into it.

"Why are you giving me that look? Cutting, baling, moving, stacking should all be self-explanatory," she said. "I'll throw our work clothes in the dryer. They're clean and will be ready to wear tomorrow."

He swallowed and wiped his lips. "What about the potluck dance?"

"Ah...that." She carried dishes to the sink. "The cattlemen's association holds them four times a year. If you've seen any old Western movies with barn dances, it's pretty much like that. Women sit around and talk about fashion, kids and food. Men discuss feed and cattle prices, and football. Everybody eats. Some dance, then everyone goes home."

"You don't sound like a fan."

Myra didn't glance up from loading the dishwasher. "They're okay. It'll be my first without Gramps." Her voice wavered.

Before he could help himself, Zeke was at her side, pulling her into his arms. "Damn, I'm always putting my foot in my mouth. I didn't mean to press and make you sad." He rubbed his hands up and down her tense back until she relaxed.

"It's okay." Her voice was muffled against his shirtfront. "Saturday night will be your chance to meet all of your Snowy Owl Crossing neighbors."

"Is that a problem for you?" He reached between them and with a curled forefinger lifted her chin until they gazed into each other's eyes.

"N-no," she said shakily. "The Flying Owl is yours now. These folks are your neighbors. In a few months they'll no longer be mine."

Zeke noticed again how her voice hitched. Remembering what it'd been like for him to say goodbye to the men in his unit—men who'd been closer to him at times than his twin—he thought he knew what Myra might be feeling. She'd worry that Saturday would be her last gathering with her friends. Bothered by the dull sheen in her normally sparkling eyes, Zeke caught her face in both his hands and he kissed her cool, trembling lips. He didn't stop until he felt them warm under his.

When he eased back, Myra's eyes were no longer dull. They were, however, unfocused, disbelieving. Zeke released her and scrubbed a hand over his face. He wasn't sure disbelief was a good sign.

"What was that for?" she asked huskily, turning aside to grip the edge of the sink with both hands.

Zeke wanted to say he'd been thinking about kissing her since they rode home together on Ember after going to see the snowy owls. Instead, he said, "Nothing," and pinched the bridge of his nose. "I made you sad about your grandfather by asking about Saturday's event. Do you want to slap me?" he asked abruptly, tucking his fingertips into his back pockets.

She whipped around. "No. No. Why would I? I'm not a violent person."

He grinned at that. "Could've fooled me. I've seen you shove a thousand-pound heifer into a chute and stick them with a needle full of gunk that made them holler."

"That's different. It's necessary."

"Okay. I'm going to hit the sack now. I hope you don't change your mind about that slap. I could, probably should, apologize. But…kissing you wasn't a hardship, Myra." Leaving it there, he bent, scratched Orion behind the ears and sauntered from the room.

MYRA CONTINUED TO cling to the sink for some time after she heard his bedroom door close. Heavens, she didn't want to slap him. Far from it. And she was glad he hadn't apologized, but she was sorry he'd kissed her out of sympathy for her grandfather. That sucked.

Yes, she'd felt sad, but her reasons were jumbled. She feared neighbors at the event might view her differently now. While there was pain attached to losing Gramps, there was pain, too, in losing the ranch. Mixed in was more than a little chagrin. What was wrong with her that a great-looking single guy like Zeke felt he had to roll out some excuse for kissing her? Moreover, why did she wish a kiss might happen again?

Myra pulled herself together to phone Dave Ralston and set a date for his baler in exchange for helping him stack hay. Once that was done, she picked up Orion, turned out the kitchen light and went to move the clothes to the dryer. She set items already dry by his door before retreating to her room. Did she seem less womanly for working cattle and running a ranch? Should she be mollified that Zeke said kissing her hadn't been a hardship? What did that mean, anyway? *Dang!*

Before getting ready for bed, she took stock of the clothes in her closet. Normally for potlucks she wore the kind of jeans and shirts she worked in. Clean ones, of course. But she did own a couple of skirts.

"Orion," she announced, setting him down on his comfy quilt. "Saturday night you'll see a new me."

But crawling into bed, she was plagued by second thoughts. *Was she going soft on him?* Her good friends in the Artsy Ladies group would give her a hard time if she dressed up. *Did she care?* Far too late into the night she weighed their probable reactions against wanting Zeke to see her as something more than a rancher.

Chapter Seven

Morning brought gray cloudy skies and blustery north winds.

"Do you think it's going to snow?" Zeke asked Myra. He stood at the kitchen window eating his toast.

"I hope not." She peered over his shoulder. "The fields are dry. If we have to bale wet alfalfa, it'll mold before we need it as feed over the winter. Every rancher in the area will be rushing to finish. Our next few days will be busy running from ranch to ranch."

They tidied up, dressed warmly and went to the barn. Myra drove the combine. Zeke rode shotgun. Talk was limited until Myra noticed Zeke's new jacket.

"I'm glad I bought it," he said. "The wool lining blocks this wind."

Their conversation ended. Myra didn't know what she had expected. After the way they'd parted the previous night, she'd been prepared for some discussion of their relationship. Obviously it weighed heavier on her mind than on his. And she should be the one paying attention to duty. It did still grate on her, how yesterday he'd called her bossy after asking for her expertise and opinions. Then he'd kissed her, of all things.

They lumbered up to the field. Myra stopped the combine and explained to Zeke how they cut swaths up and down the long direction.

"Seems easy enough. Show me how to operate this machine," he said.

She did and it surprised her how quickly he caught on. For the first time since he'd set foot on the ranch, Myra felt as if she wasn't needed. She sat in the jump seat doing nothing as he cut two perfectly straight rows. "It's noticeably colder up here," she said, raising her voice to be heard above the noise of the combine engine.

Zeke made another turn. "I can handle this if you have something else that needs doing."

Myra stiffened, feeling dismissed. But that was foolish. "Let me off. I'll go saddle Cayenne and ride out to bring down the rest of the herd."

"Can you do that alone?"

"Of course."

Taking her at her word, he stopped and helped her down. "If you haven't returned by the time I finish, do I drive to the barn?"

"Do you have your phone?" At his nod, she said, "Program in Dave's number. He'll come over or send someone to pick up the combine. Later, we go help Hank."

Myra thought he'd have more questions, but he added the number she gave him and pocketed his phone again.

A brisk ride up to the herd in an even brisker wind cooled her ire and brought clarity to her situation. She'd been running on the false hope that Zeke Maxwell would fail and she'd reclaim the Flying Owl. While he had walked away from one dirty job, he could easily hire these kinds of things in the future. Calving and branding were chores even she brought in help for. And Zeke had a military pension. A one-man operation didn't require as much funding to stay solvent. That was the truth of it.

Tears leaked from her eyes as she chose a cow to tie a cowbell on so the herd would follow. Myra blinked hard, electing to blame the wind for her tears.

It wasn't hard to circle the herd and start them moving. Dumb as people thought cows were, they knew changing seasons. This mature group knew better food and shelter awaited them if they left the foothills. Because it was a mindless task for Myra, she had time to make plans. Fall, regardless of inclement weather, was when work slowed down on the ranch. She'd finish her dollhouses for the bazaar and in her spare time dust off her teaching résumé. She'd need a job. It couldn't hurt to send out feelers to the school where she had taught four years ago, and to a couple of others.

The very notion hurt, but she needed to think about her future.

With a few decisions now made, she reached the pasture with the herd by noon. The cattle seemed eager to crowd into the large fenced area with access to a stream and plentiful grass. Myra leaned out of the saddle to close and lock the gate after the last straggler. She felt a sense of accomplishment as she always did after completing a job. Shifting upright in the saddle, she rode on to the alfalfa field.

Not expecting to see Zeke done with the cutting so soon, it surprised her to find him with Dave Ralston, offloading the baler. The alfalfa had all been cut.

Myra slid off Cayenne. "Hey, I didn't think we were due to get your baler until tomorrow." She aimed her question at Dave.

"Hank's crew finished early, freeing up Foley's combine. Hank said you're gonna help him load bales and stack them in his shed. Looks like everyone sped up because of that weekend storm."

"I figured on waiting until tomorrow to bale here. But if you have a minute to show Zeke how the baler works, I'll go unsaddle Cayenne, grab a bite and head on over to Hank's. Did you stop for lunch?" she asked Zeke.

He shook his head. "I'm not really hungry."

"Don't skip meals. I'll bring you a sandwich and a thermos of coffee." Swinging into the saddle, she turned toward the house and heard Dave say, "That's why we need a woman around, Zeke, old buddy. They keep us healthy. Yeah, yeah… I know there's other reasons," he added with a laugh.

Not wanting to hear how Zeke might answer, Myra kicked Cayenne into a trot.

Once she stalled the mare and fed her and Ember, Myra went into the house to check on Orion while the coffee brewed. Then she assembled sandwiches and put veggies and a whole chicken into the Crock-Pot for supper. Filling a thermos for Zeke and one for herself, she hurried out to the pickup. It wasn't the first time and wouldn't be the last that she'd eaten her midday meal on the way to another job.

Dave's flatbed and her combine were gone when she again drew abreast of the field. Zeke already had two neat rows of bales strung out behind him. Myra wished she had money to buy a hydraulic bale loader. So far no one in the area had sprung for one. They were costly, but hand loading, unloading and racking heavy bales had caused many a rancher to suffer a heart attack. But what did she care? She was leaving.

She flagged Zeke down. "Take a minute to eat. I'll wolf mine down on the way to the Bar W."

"Dave said since your land is flat I can drive the baler back to the barn when I'm done. He'll pick it up tomorrow. I don't think this will take me more than a couple of hours. What should I do then?"

"The clouds have lifted. It's hard to believe reports of a snowstorm. Still, we need to get our bales inside. If you get through, come to Hank's ranch."

"Okay. Where is the Bar W?"

Myra picked up a stick and drew a rough map in the ground. "This is nice soft dirt. If the weather stays like this tomorrow, I'll take a portable pen out for Orion. He can dig while we load bales. This may be the last clear week before spring."

"No kidding? It's still September."

"Some Montana winters last six months. Or like last year only three. But that's rare. Hey, the day's wasting. Call me if you get lost."

Zeke's sharply arched eyebrow signaled his thoughts on that. He followed up by calling out, "I led men on night patrols from one remote Afghan village to another without losing my way. Around land mines," he added. So Myra tossed him a wave and drove off.

THE BAR W RAN a bigger operation than the Flying Owl. Hank's ranch had grown over time with the help of his sons and their wives. They all had homes on the large property. As Myra drove along their winding lane, she could see the family working in the distance. She parked between barns and rummaged in her center console for gloves and a back belt. Luckily she also had a spare, because she hadn't mentioned using a back brace for work with heavy bales to Zeke. She should have given him one early on when they'd hauled hay to the herd.

Work stopped briefly as she joined the Watson family and their one hired hand. Hank drove the tractor pulling a large trailer between bales that sat a dozen feet apart in long rows that disappeared over a gentle rise.

"Where's Zeke?" Hank asked Myra.

"I left him baling our field. Dave dropped off the baler early. Did you hear we're supposed to have snow by the weekend?"

Hank's youngest son, Mark, straightened and adjusted his Stetson. "This wind is cold enough to bring snow, but there're fewer clouds than when we started at dawn."

Myra passed Mark then Hank's older son, Joe, and went by the hired hand with a brief greeting, indicating she'd load the bale beyond him.

Hand loading required a rhythm. Anyone not familiar with the process might think it was some weird ritual dance. As the trailer lumbered past a helper, a bale was loaded, then that person jogged ahead to the next waiting bale and so on until Hank announced the trailer held enough to take to the shed. One by one each helper grabbed a spot on top of the bales and rode in. At the enclosure they worked in tandem, removing bales and ricking them so air circulated to keep the green-cut hay, alfalfa or milo from molding over a long winter.

They were unloading their second batch of bales when Zeke drove in.

"See, I made it with your sketchy directions," he said, tossing Myra a grin.

She ignored his jab and introduced him to the younger Watsons and to Len Carver, a cowboy who shook Zeke's hand before announcing, "I'll let Zeke take my place. I saw a couple of fences that needed mending."

Joe Watson laughed after the cowboy left. "Len hates doing stuff he considers farmwork. He'll choose tackling anything involving horses or cattle first."

"Give the man a break, Joe," Hank chided. "Len's saved us a lot of stock we would've lost without his experience turning a calf coming breech."

"Is that common?" Zeke asked Myra in a low voice after she had him detour past her pickup for the back belt.

"Not common, but it happens. I've been thinking about spring calving. You may want to hire Eddie and Aaron."

"Aren't you staying through spring?" Zeke unzipped his jacket to Velcro the wide belt around his waist. He'd fallen a few steps behind Myra, so he spoke louder.

Apparently overhearing him, Joe Watson fell back, too. "Yeah, Myra, what gives? We were shocked when Dad told us you were leaving. My wife says the bazaar won't earn half as much for the snowy-owl fund without the draw of your dollhouses."

"That reminds me, Myra," Zeke said as he pulled on his gloves, "three snowy owls swooped right down in front of the baler. They all had something in their talons. What a sight. You'll see where I zigzagged instead of baling in a straight line as I watched them."

"You probably opened up a nest of field mice," Myra said.

"The owls are back early," Joe exclaimed. "Damn,

that generally means a bad winter won't be far behind their arrival."

Zeke turned to Joe. "Will the birds go farther south?"

He shrugged. "Myra, maybe you can answer that. You ladies keep better track of the snowy owls than we men do."

"Jewell tracks them. They don't always follow the same migration path. If we can ensure a safe habitat, we hope over time owl families will return each year and their numbers will increase."

"As long as they stick to hunting rodents and don't start making off with my wife's chickens, I'm fine having their numbers grow," Joe growled. He stopped and lifted a bale next to where his father idled with the trailer.

Myra passed Mark and beckoned to Zeke. "You load this bale when Hank pulls up. I'll go to the next one in line. Watch. You'll see how it's done."

Because Zeke worked behind her, Myra didn't notice as the afternoon wore on how much he favored his left arm and shoulder until Mark quietly called it to her attention. "You maybe ought to advise Zeke to take it easy. He's lifting everything with just his right arm. Being new at this, he could've strained his left shoulder. Unless he takes it easy, he might not be able to help bring in your bales tomorrow."

Myra spun around to assess Zeke. "They're *his* bales now," she said. But Mark was right. Zeke was definitely favoring his left side. "It's an injury from

Afghanistan," she noted, frowning. "Eric said Zeke almost lost his arm rescuing guys in his patrol. He had something like eight or more surgeries. But he's a big boy. Surely he knows his limits."

"So the rumors are true. Your new boss really is a hero. Awesome."

It was awesome. Myra wouldn't take anything away from Zeke's heroic actions. But having Mark refer to Zeke as her new boss felt as if he was jabbing a hot poker in her belly. All of the neighbors seemed only too happy to accept Zeke as one of them. That stung most of all.

She'd worked side by side with these guys for three years. Longer if she counted the summers she'd spent tagging after her grandfather doing these same chores. Suddenly, though, she sensed the circle closing her out. The men were quick to joke and chat with Zeke.

By the time the last bale was stored in Hank's shed and dusk had set in, the men grouped together high-fiving each other for a job well done.

They didn't high-five Myra.

Hank stripped off his gloves and shook hay dust from his shirt. "Sarah Jane phoned to let me know supper's almost ready. Zeke, why don't you stay and eat with us. Meet the boys' wives. And we'll set a time to collect at your place tomorrow."

Zeke swiftly turned to Myra.

Having the grace then to look sheepish, Hank cleared his throat. "Of course the invitation extends to you as well, Myra."

"Thanks, but I have a chicken in the Crock-Pot at home."

"Oh, I didn't know that," Zeke said. "I'll take a rain check, Hank."

Myra cut in. "No need. There's no better cook in Snowy Owl Crossing than Sarah Jane. Maybe Lila's mom, but she cooks for a living. Stay, Zeke, and get acquainted."

He chewed his lower lip, seeming torn. Then because Myra told the men she'd see them in the morning and walked away, Joe Watson said in a tone that carried, "Good, it's settled. I'm starved. Let's go eat."

Myra didn't look back. Her pickup lights, once she'd climbed in the cab and turned them on, outlined the men trudging to the big farmhouse on the knoll above the barn.

She didn't blame Hank for shutting her out. She'd long known that cattle ranching was a good-old-boy network. She had wormed her way into acceptance of her grandfather's standing in the community. But tonight had made it plain that she needed to move on. She headed out on the rural road that would take her home. *To her now-temporary home.*

This was far from the first time she'd driven this road after dark and then had to enter a house empty except for Orion. But now it seemed different. Emptier.

She sighed and turned on the living room light. Tonight the home she loved felt lonelier. But the scent of her Crock-Pot chicken reminded her she was hungry and that she'd put in a long day.

As had been her habit prior to Zeke's arrival, she let Orion loose to root around her feet while she sat at the kitchen table checking local news on her laptop, slowly eating her meal. Snow was still predicted for late Saturday or early Sunday. It looked like a big storm. She hoped she had gauged right on winter feed. It was always a guessing game. *But why should she care?*

Closing her laptop, Myra decided to call Eric. As a rule she spoke with someone in her family every few days. Her dad would be busy moving cattle and harvesting hay, and her mom might still be miffed at her. But unless Eric came home dog tired, it was odd he hadn't phoned her. She pressed his automatic link on her phone. He picked up at once.

"How's life at Rolling Acres?" Myra said by way of greeting.

"Hi, sis. What's up? I talked to Zeke at lunch. He said he was running the baler."

Myra stiffened a tad. "He didn't mention talking to you. He's having supper with the Watsons. How are the folks? And you?"

"Good. Dad told Mom to give you some space. You sound down. What's wrong? Why is Zeke at the Watsons' without you?"

Myra didn't hide her despair. She was always honest with her brother. "Each day that goes by, taking me closer to spring when I said I'd leave, is like adding a stickpin in my already breaking heart, Eric. I'm trying to be glad Zeke is willing to learn what it takes to make a go of the ranch. Yet I still wish he'd fail. I know that's horrible but I can't help it. The other day I had hoped he'd quit. He bugged out in the middle of prepping the heifers. Then he came back and doubled down. I know it's nothing, but he's even taken a real interest in the snowy owls." Emotion choked off anything else she might add.

"Zeke said he suffered a minor flashback to the chaos that happened during our ambush. You know I've had a few. He said that was his first. They're scary, Myra."

"I know. I don't want to wish him ill, Eric."

"Have you considered telling him exactly how you feel?"

"I can't. It's not his fault. Hey, I'm sorry for dumping on you. Do me a favor and tell Mom I'm updating my academic résumé. In fact, I'll get to it as soon as I hang up."

"It's probably for the best. I actually sort of hoped you and Zeke would hit it off. Especially after he told me you're taking him to a potluck dance Saturday night."

"At the grange. Everybody goes. It's not like a date, Eric. I can tell you he thinks I'm bossy. I wonder if he got that from you."

"Ouch. Go tweak your résumé. You may feel a whole lot better if you get away from the ranch and find another job."

Myra didn't tell him her heart would never heal. Clearly no one understood how deep her feelings ran when it came to the Flying Owl. "Listen, we're due for snow and so is your area. Winterize. I'll see you after calving, if not before."

"Right. I love you to pieces, Myra. But I owe Zeke my life. He knocked me away and took the percussion from an IED."

"I'm aware of that. It's why I'm still here helping him. Bye, Eric." Myra hit Disconnect before the tears came.

She jumped up and stored the leftovers from the Crock-Pot, cleaned up and put everything in the dishwasher. Her résumé didn't need much updating. Then because it was too early to call it a night, she carried Orion into the living room. Moving the card table that held an unfinished dollhouse in front of her grandfather's recliner, she tucked Orion in beside her and settled down to assemble the roof. The pig was soon snoring away, which helped lift the gloom from her heart. Orion didn't have a care in the world.

She'd installed the gables and was fitting a faux-brick chimney when her cell phone rang. She didn't recognize the number and almost didn't answer, but the caller didn't hang up so she cautiously said, "Hello."

"Myra, it's Zeke. I…uh…don't know where I am. I thought when I left the Bar W fifteen minutes ago I was retracing the route I took to get there. Somehow I got off the paved road. For as long as I've been on this gravel, I know it's not leading to the ranch. I left the map your dad gave me in the pocket of my other jacket. And I never plugged the address into my GPS. Actually..." He hesitated for a protracted moment. "I don't remember the ranch address."

Myra could have just provided it and let it go. But a little demon nudged her. "Gee," she drawled, "since our lane isn't crisscrossed with land mines, I guess you can't navigate your way home now, Lieutenant Maxwell."

The silence lengthened and Myra blanched, concerned she'd lost him. Then, at last, sounding humble, he said, "I deserve that dig. In my defense, there are no stars out tonight to help with coordinates."

"Sorry, I couldn't resist. Here's the address." She gave it and had him read it back. "If I had to guess, I'd say you turned off on one of the reservation roads. If so, you aren't too far away. You should see the house in ten minutes or so. But if you don't, call me back with some landmarks."

He hung up, and Myra didn't know why, but the very fact the man admitted he deserved her needling left her feeling much friendlier toward him.

Chapter Eight

Myra dislodged Orion, who shook his head and snorted a few times at being awakened. Concerned for Zeke and now wishing she hadn't given in to the petty urge to dig him, she carried her pig to a front window and peered into the night.

She shouldn't have acted so cavalier. Getting lost in this expanse of nothingness wasn't anything to take lightly. Last year a tourist had missed a crossroad at night when a winter storm blew in. It wasn't until the family expecting him to meet them in Canada contacted authorities that they found him way off any beaten path, frozen to death.

Relief swept through her as she saw headlights appear at the lane and bob past the barn. She didn't wait for him to shut off his pickup's engine before she threw open the front door and dashed out.

Zeke bounded up on the porch, his smile speaking for both of them. He swept Myra and Orion into a bear hug, surprising her. And he kissed her, which shocked her.

"I'm an idiot," he professed, walking her backward into the house. Reaching behind him, he shut the door, blocking the wind that rattled the remains of a hanging plant. Tightening his arms again, Zeke gazed into Myra's face. "Do you realize you may be the only rancher in this whole corner of the world with lights on this time of night?"

"Ranchers tend to turn in early," she said. "But how does that make you an idiot?"

He let her go and shrugged out of his jacket. "I didn't fill my gas tank when I was in town the other day. And I discovered I don't have a map or a flashlight in my vehicle. I'm damned lucky my cell phone was charged. Probably luckier there's cell service around here."

"That only happened the year before I came to help Gramps. Some of the big ranchers south of here lobbied to get a tower. This used to be no-man's territory. It's still not very populated."

"Tell me about it." As if noticing she held a yawning Orion, Zeke reached out and rubbed the little pig's head. "We should keep a porch light burning as a beacon to lost travelers."

"That's up to you. But electricity is expensive."

"It was really unnerving being out there in total blackness."

"I'm sure it was. Outside of that, did you have a good time with the Watsons?"

"Yeah. They're a lively bunch. You probably know Joe has a microbrewery in his basement. He took me to see his setup. His mother thinks he could have picked a better hobby, but he claims it keeps him occupied in winter. Sort of like your dollhouses. And Mark has a room at his house filled with model trains. They all thought it was odd when I said my hobby is reading. There wasn't much else to do during downtime in Afghanistan. Unless you count playing basketball or baseball with village kids."

"I don't think it's odd to like reading."

"Thanks. I know you said you had to come home because you had food cooking. I wish you'd been able to stay there for supper."

"Why? Oh, of course, so you'd have been able to follow me home." She laughed.

"That's not why. It was all couples, making me the odd man out."

"Joe and Mark married their high school sweethearts. That's common here. But there are singles around. You'll meet most of them Saturday night at the grange potluck."

"I didn't mean I missed any old company. I would have liked sharing the evening with you." He touched her arm again when he said it.

What was behind his sudden flattery? Myra fought against a flutter in her belly and recalled her recent litany of complaints to Eric. The prime one being how she wished Zeke would opt to leave. Pasting on a false smile, she said, "Probably you're missing the woman you left back east."

Zeke looked surprised. "She found a dentist."

"Pardon me?" Myra frowned in confusion.

"To marry."

"Sorry, I shouldn't have said anything." Myra sidled toward her bedroom.

"Don't be sorry. I'm not. They were better suited." A smile played at the edge of his lips. "Stacy would've freaked out if she'd ever stepped in cow poop. And she wouldn't have owned a goldfish, let alone have a pig for a pet."

"Country life isn't for everyone," Myra said then wondered if Zeke found her amusing because she was in direct contrast to his former girlfriend. She'd been so sure all she needed to do was wait him out and he'd tire of living here. *Maybe not.*

"Speaking of country life," she said. "Mark noticed you had trouble loading today. Is your arm bothering you? We've got more days of gathering bales ahead of us."

Zeke automatically rubbed his left shoulder. "The surgeon suggested I join a fitness club for exercise. Hefting bales should be as good and it's cheaper."

His cheerfulness rattled her. Nodding because she'd run out of things to say, she murmured, "Okay, well, I'm turning in. I set up coffee. First one up in the morning can turn it on." She slipped into her room, not waiting to see what Zeke did.

Sleep didn't come quickly. She was bothered by that kiss and a conscience that nagged her for hanging on to resentment. Zeke was trying. In fact, he'd bent over backward. And some part of her that she couldn't control found him attractive. In ways that went beyond physical. Despite injuries, he pitched in. He joked at his own expense. He admitted to liking books—and snowy owls—and Orion. And he was a great kisser. She kept finding things to add to his positive column. His negative one was shrinking. Thankfully, sleep claimed her before she analyzed too closely where those pros and cons might lead her. She might really fall for the guy.

THE SMELL OF fresh coffee drew Myra out of sleep the next morning. Checking her clock, she saw it was six thirty. She'd forgotten to turn on her alarm. Bounding from bed, she hurriedly dressed, collected Orion and practically ran to the kitchen.

"Gosh, how long have you been up?" she asked, seeing Zeke pull a pan of biscuits from the oven.

"Awhile. At supper the Watsons said if it wasn't foggy they'd be here at eight to help haul bales. Hank said that'd give everyone time to finish morning chores."

Myra lifted the curtain to look outside. "It's cloudy, but no fog. That's good. The bales should still be dry enough to house."

They ate breakfast. "I'll put on a new pot so after chores I can pop back in and fill a thermos," Myra said when Zeke carried his dishes to the sink. "And I'll make sandwiches to serve everyone for lunch if you'll drive the tractor and trailer out to the field."

"I can do that. How long do you think it'll take us to finish? Will it be today?"

"I hope so. Tomorrow we'll give Dave Ralston a hand. His winter-wheat field is near his barn. Even after helping him we should get home in time to shower, change and make it to the potluck by seven. I'm taking a big pasta salad that I'll fix tonight."

Zeke kept nodding.

Myra knew it was a lot to take in, but he didn't ask her to repeat anything. And as cold as it was when they went out to make rounds of the cattle, she thought she may need to change what she'd planned to wear. This might not be skirt weather. Especially not short-skirt weather.

THEY GOT A late start moving bales. While checking on the herd, they discovered a broken section of fence. The bull was out. Zeke went back to the barn for tools while Myra corralled the bull in a smaller pen and phoned Hank. "Hi, it's Myra. We'll be delayed. Our bull got out."

"I'm okay with late. I have a heifer that needs doctoring. I'll tell the boys, too."

Myra and Zeke returned to the house as the Watsons drove in at one thirty.

"Why don't you pack up lunch," Zeke said. "I'll bring the tractor and flatbed by here. We can ride to the field together."

"Sounds good. And we can take Orion out to play in that loose dirt, so let's load his pen and haul everything on the flatbed instead of me driving my pickup."

She had everything waiting on the porch when

Zeke pulled up. He left the tractor idling and shot up the steps to help her carry Orion's things out.

"What's that you've got him wrapped in?" he asked, casting a sidelong glance at the bundle in her arms. "He can't do much rooting in a blanket."

"It's his jacket. More like a cape Jewell knit for him." Myra held Orion up for Zeke to see. "It buttons under his belly in two places. And it washes."

"Huh. He looks like a black-and-white bumblebee with ears."

Myra snuggled the pig and watched Zeke load the pen. "Pay him no mind, Orion. I think you look fashionable. And you can stay warm and have fun."

Laughing, Zeke boosted Myra into the tractor jump seat.

Out at the field the Watsons also poked fun at the pig's jacket.

"Stop, or you'll go hungry," Myra told the boisterous men. Still, once she'd settled Orion, she passed around plastic cups of coffee and wrapped sandwiches. "We can all start work on full bellies," she said.

Not only did they start late, at four, with several rows still to go, the trailer got a flat tire, which had to be repaired.

Pointing to a dusky sky, Myra said, "Hey. If we don't want to make our last run in the dark, we need to get back on task."

Mark shivered and rebuttoned his shearling jacket. "Getting colder, too. We may load out Ralston tomorrow in snow."

His brother took a long gander at the sky. "Not supposed to snow until tomorrow night. I hope everyone going to the potluck has four-wheel drive." Bending, he lifted the first bale in the next row.

They worked steadily to the end of that row and were about to start another when Hank stabbed a finger at the sky. "Will you look at that? Is that a pair of snowies?"

They all stopped and craned their necks, including Zeke, who stilled the tractor.

"It's not dark," Joe said inanely. "I thought they only hunted at night."

Myra scanned the sky and saw the smaller of the two birds dive into the row they'd just left. "Zeke saw them hunting in daylight while he was baling. Maybe they're stocking up because there's a storm coming."

"Could be the same pair," Zeke said, moving the tractor ahead a few feet.

Mark tossed another bale on the trailer and they adjusted their positions. All at once Zeke braked hard, let out a yell and vaulted off the tractor. He leaped over a bale not yet loaded. "The big owl," he shouted. "She's after Orion."

Reacting to his shout, Myra ran after him. She and Zeke reached the makeshift pen inches from a massive bird coming down talons first.

Myra heard Zeke breathing hard and fast. Her heart thundered in her ears amid Orion's frantic squeals. She waved her arms to deflect the owl. The bird kept coming. Up close it didn't look as if it was smiling.

The owl's curved back talons sank into Orion's cape as Zeke grabbed the pig's short front legs. He dodged the flapping wings. The air was a cacophony of screeches, shouts and squeals.

Horrified, Myra saw Zeke and the owl locked in a vicious tug of war. "Lift Orion higher," she yelled. "I'll unbutton his jacket."

Zeke immediately raised his arms, but Myra could tell by his grimace that his once-injured left arm hurt him terribly.

In spite of the determined bird's beating wings tangling in her hair, she ducked and winced, barely avoiding being pecked by the curved beak. Amber eyes she'd once thought beautiful now glowed with menace.

Slow to react to the unfolding scene, Joe and Mark finally joined the fracas. The men waved their Stetsons and made a racket. Grateful, Myra felt the last button slip free of its hole. The force of the release sent Zeke and Orion reeling backward into Mark and Joe. They all sprawled on top of a bale.

The owl issued one last screech. With a forward thrust of her wings, the bird rose above the pen, her only prize Orion's black-and-white knit cloak.

Scraping back her disheveled hair, Myra scrambled to Zeke on her hands and knees. She relieved him of the pig, still squealing because Zeke gripped him so tightly. "Are you all right?" she asked Zeke, her arms and voice shaking. "I'm pretty sure you were in agony while you fought to save Orion." She breathed out a stream of frosty air. "I swear I never dreamed anything like this could happen. Heavens, I can't think straight to properly thank you," she said, cuddling her pet inside her jacket.

"I wish I could've got that on video," Hank said, late crossing the field to join the others. "Unless they see it, nobody will believe what happened. I'll bet no more than two or three minutes passed, but it seemed so much longer."

"Sure did," Zeke said, accepting Joe's hand up from where he lay amid prickly cuttings of alfalfa. He suddenly gripped and rubbed his left elbow, murmuring, "Do you suppose the bird can escape from that knit blanket?"

Myra squinted skyward. "With those talons she'll rip the cloak to shreds."

Mark Watson settled his Stetson again. "In all the years we've lived here, I've never seen a snowy owl that close. Man, Zeke, you leapfrogged over here before I figured out what the hell was going on."

Hank placed a hand on each of his son's shoulders. "We don't want to risk another episode. Myra, you scoot to the house with Piggy. The rest of us will get back to loading bales. That's if Zeke's not too done in to drive the tractor."

"I can do that," Zeke said. "Doubt I can lift a bale. But if you guys load the last two rows, Myra and I can unload in the morning."

"Agreed." Electing to let the men work it out, Myra crooned to Orion on her way to the house. She could tell the fright hadn't left the animal. And her knees still wobbled. Inside the house, she dampened a hand towel and cleaned Orion up before setting him in his kitchen pen. He burrowed under his quilt but poked his nose out when Myra put mixed greens in his metal bowl. "I love the snowy owls," she said, scratching her pet behind his ears. "But I love you more. This was a lesson learned today, and we owe Zeke a ton of thanks for saving you. First Eric, now you," she said, straightening away from the pen.

She remained at the house preparing her pasta salad until she felt Orion had calmed down enough to be left alone.

But before she could go back to the field, the men appeared, all headed toward the barn.

"Is Orion okay?" Zeke called as she came toward him.

"He's fine, thanks to you." She swallowed a lump. "I know some would say he's just a pig. But he's a whole lot more to me."

"I know." Zeke smiled down at her since she'd caught up to his slow-moving tractor. "The little guy is kinda special."

Hearing him say that warmed Myra's heart. But the two of them didn't discuss the incident further that night.

However, the next day when they met at Dave Ralston's to collect his winter hay, Zeke's bravery was a hot topic. He brushed aside the accolades.

Later, as he and Myra returned to the Flying Owl,

Zeke again fussed about how fast information traveled among neighbors.

"Get used to it," Myra advised. "You haven't seen half the gushing. Wait until we get to the potluck. Yikes, is that snow?" she asked, suddenly pointing out the windshield. She drove, but they both leaned forward to peer at the sky.

"Yep," Zeke acknowledged. "We finished at Dave's just in time."

Seeing the fat flakes thicken, Myra mentally scratched any thought of wearing a skirt to the grange hall. Who knew if they'd need to help push friends' or neighbors' vehicles out of snowdrifts?

As if Zeke could hear her thoughts, he asked, "What should a guy wear to this shindig tonight?"

"Dress like a rancher. Didn't you buy new stuff in town?"

"Yeah. I went in for a jacket. A fast-talking salesman sold me fancy boots and a hat. Will people think I'm trying to be cowboy Ken doll?"

Myra sputtered out a laugh. "Sorry, but is there a cowboy Ken doll?"

He shrugged. "I don't know. Seth and I only had G.I. Joe and ninjas."

She spared a glance at him in a cab lit only by green-and-gold dash lights. "Of course you did." His dark buzz cut was growing out, but it accentuated his handsome, rugged features. "Wear the new gear," she said, stopping beside the house.

They went inside through blowing snowflakes and

laughed as they stomped their feet and dusted off each other's hair. "I'll feed Orion then get ready," Myra said. "We should leave in half an hour. I'm allowing extra time because of the snow."

"Gotcha."

Myra heard Zeke's shower running when she passed his room on the way to hers. At her closet she tucked the skirt and blouse she'd put out into a back corner and pulled out her best skinny black jeans. She had a fringed leather jacket—an impulse purchase from last year's bazaar. Until now she'd had nowhere to wear it. But for as many times as she'd attended one of these potlucks without caring what she wore, how dumb was it to be acting all girlie because of Zeke Maxwell?

She did it anyway. She brushed out her ponytail and dressed carefully. The boots she chose had two-inch wedge heels and zipped to her knees. Standing before her mirror, she knew if she indulged in more than her usual lipstick, her friends would tease her unmercifully. Still, she couldn't resist swiping on a light smudge of brown eye shadow. Deep breath and a last fluff of her hair, and out of the room she breezed, then stopped cold.

Zeke paced near the door, turning a black cowboy hat in his hands. He wore black slant-heeled Western boots, pressed blue jeans and a black long-sleeved shirt, open at the throat. It fit him like a glove, showing off his well-honed upper body.

"It's too much, right?" he said. "That's why you're gaping at me."

Myra choked a bit. "I'm thinking no Ken doll I ever remember looked as hot as you."

Zeke definitely blushed.

"Uh… I should have said *fit*," she blurted, charging past him toward the kitchen. "Let me grab my pasta salad from the fridge. Are you driving or am I?" she asked in a rush, trying to cover the compliment.

"I'll drive. And may I say I prefer *hot* over *fit*," he called after her.

She returned carrying a large plastic bowl with a lid. "It was a slip of the tongue. Don't let it go to your head."

Zeke opened the front door and took the bowl. "I can never tell your true feelings about me, because if you give me a compliment it's always backhanded."

They trekked through a dusting of snow to Zeke's pickup. He unlocked the passenger door and steadied Myra as she climbed in, after which he handed her the pasta salad and his hat.

"No comment?" he queried once he was settled behind the wheel.

"Did I take back the praise I heaped on you for saving Orion?"

"No," he admitted, starting the vehicle and turning around.

"Do you mind turning on the heat?"

Reaching out, Zeke twisted a knob, producing a blast of warm air. "Better?"

"Yes, thanks." Myra kept her face turned to the side window.

They fell silent for some fifteen minutes. Then following Myra's directions, Zeke slowed down and got in behind a line of pickups and SUVs. One by one all left the highway to end in a parking lot surrounding a well-lit building. "It's a big Quonset hut," Zeke remarked, shutting off the engine.

"A brilliant design in snow country." Myra passed Zeke his hat and thrust open her door.

"Hold on. I'll come around."

One thing Myra couldn't deny was that Zeke had impeccable manners. He took the bowl for her, then loosely gripped her elbow as she stepped down. And he didn't let go, but rather guided her along the path, which was beginning to get slick from the snow and dropping temperature.

The interior of the building burst with noise—raucous laughter and male, female and children's voices. In the background, sporadic sounds of band members tuning a variety of instruments filled the air.

They'd no more than stepped inside when an older woman whisked the bowl out of Zeke's hands. She bustled to a long table flanking one wall. Across the room, two men, also in Western garb, tapped the first of two beer kegs. Near them and throughout the middle sat smaller tables surrounded by folding chairs.

Zeke barely had time to take it all in when Myra grabbed his hand and pulled him into a good-size coatroom. Shelves above the coats held a plethora of cowboy hats. Bending, Zeke whispered in Myra's ear, "Those pegs on the back wall…are those holstered weapons real?"

"Yes." She hung up her coat. "Many outlying ranchers carry. They've got a greater chance of encountering the wolves we heard in the foothills. Also mountain lions or an occasional rogue moose. You can apply for a permit if you'd like."

He shook his head and shed his outerwear. "I've had quite enough of weapons, thank you."

Myra thought it took a big man to admit that. Again warmth toward him swept through her.

Two older couples entered the coatroom. Myra introduced Zeke, then led him into the great room, where a skinny brown-haired boy ran up and flung his arms around Myra's waist. "Auntie Myra," the kid exclaimed. "Mama sent me to tell you they've got the usual table."

She ruffled the boy's unruly hair. "Zeke, this is Rory Jenkins. His mom is Lila. She works at the café and runs the B and B I told you about."

"Auntie?" Zeke lifted an eyebrow.

"Shh!" Myra touched a finger to her lips. "All of the Artsy Ladies are Rory's aunties." She smiled at the kid.

"Ah. Pleased to meet you." Zeke extended a hand to Rory, who only blinked at Zeke then ran off with a pair of bigger kids.

Myra set off but was startled when she felt Zeke's hand at the small of her back.

Surprised by the possessive sensation of his broad hand, Myra felt heat pooling low in her abdomen. Shaken, she blurted, "You can go find Joe and Mark Watson, or Dave and his son. I'll hunt you up when it's time to go home."

His steps didn't falter. "I've met those guys. I'd like to say hello to your friends." He went with her to where a number of ladies sat around a large table. Chatter ceased as everyone eyed the man all but glued to Myra. She began by introducing Lila's mother, a youngish-looking blonde woman in her late sixties. "You've heard me talk about the crafts and careers of some of the others," she told Zeke. "Tawana, Lila and Jewell, Shelley and Mindy." Myra pointed them out in turn.

The women had all heard about the incident with Orion. They made a big deal about Zeke's part in the rescue. He brushed aside their glowing compliments by singling out Lila and Jewell. "I remember seeing you two at Cody's Bar," he said. "Jewell's a great name for someone with red hair like yours." Smiling, he moved on to acknowledge Shelley and Mindy.

"Shelley teaches ceramics," Myra noted. "Mindy owns the town beauty shop. She makes lovely hair bows and scrunchies that sell like hotcakes at our Thanksgiving bazaar."

Zeke held up his hands in surrender. "I understood fine until you got to scrunchies. I think I'll leave you ladies to your catching up. I saw the Watsons come in." Turning to Myra, he murmured, "Should I come back here to eat with you?"

"You can. Or sometimes the men pick a table so they can discuss cattle futures or the price of tractors and stuff."

He said once more that it was nice to meet everyone, squeezed Myra's shoulder then sauntered off. His gesture caused a flurry of speculation around the table, just as she knew it would. She countered Lila's mother, who said, "That man's a keeper, Myra," by reminding them she was leaving come spring. It cast a pall over the friends until Shelley asked how bazaar projects were going.

As the evening progressed, Myra found herself following Zeke's travels around the hall. He laughed and chatted with most of the local ranchers and their wives. It hurt a little to see how easily he fit in. She longed to be staying. But he hadn't asked her to.

Zeke did eat with a group of men, but wandered back to the women's table when the band struck up their first tune.

It was then Myra learned he loved to dance. And he was good at it. He took a turn around the floor with each of her friends, but spent the rest of the night dancing with her. In his arms she imagined herself a princess. A new feeling for her.

She felt a pang of sorrow when the bandleader announced the last dance. More so because this was her last potluck.

But they collected their coats and her empty dish and said their goodbyes. It was a shock to walk out of the warm hall into a curtain of falling snow.

"Would you like me to drive home?" she asked Zeke. "I know you had a few beers."

"Three over a long evening. But if you want to escort me home and can do it without running off the road in this whiteout, go for it." He handed her the keys.

She reached the main road without incident.

For a few minutes, Zeke seemed tense. "How do you know you're on the road?" he asked.

"See those eight-foot-tall colored poles off to the side?"

Zeke looked.

"Those are snow markers. Every foot up the pole is a different color so you can see how deep the snow is. The top foot is bright red. As long as I've lived here I've never seen it that high. Some old-timers claim they remember when it did."

"Amazing." He leaned back against the seat.

Every time Myra glanced his direction on the slow drive to the ranch, she noticed him smiling. "You seem happy," she finally remarked. "I guess there's no need to ask if you had a good time tonight."

He turned toward her. "I can't tell you when I've enjoyed myself more. I made good friends in the army, but there was always underlying tension. Everybody I've met here is relaxed. For the first time I feel I've found a spot I can call home."

He spoke with such sincerity, Myra didn't doubt he meant the words that struck lances through her heart.

Chapter Nine

A series of storms swept through Snowy Owl Crossing in the next weeks. Weather forecasters advised their listeners to say goodbye to fall and hello to an early winter.

County snowplows maintained the road to and from town, and Zeke helped Myra attach a snow blade to the tractor to clear paths from the barn to all of the holding pens. They also opened a lane to the main road.

"Working together sure makes this easier," she told Zeke. "I did this by myself the last couple of years."

"You mean you didn't call neighbors to help?"

"They would have, but why ask unless it's for something I can't do alone?"

"It's nice to know people are only a phone call away," he said.

"Some winters take more neighbors helping neighbors," Myra responded.

And it seemed she'd no more than made the prediction when needs arose.

In the ensuing weeks, Myra watched Zeke pitch in

anytime a neighboring rancher asked for a hand repairing equipment. It got so friends who'd once called her now phoned Zeke first. Her breath felt constricted as she felt her hold on the Flying Owl lessening.

The simple truth was—in really bad weather ,outdoor activities ground to a halt. Ranchers slogged through essentials like feeding stock twice a day. Otherwise more time was spent indoors.

Myra worked on her dollhouses and kept out of Zeke's way as he moved things around to paint the house. One day he went to town and brought home what he needed to change out the sink and install countertops he'd preordered.

"You're ruining the old-world charm of the house," Myra fretted at supper after he'd shoved the table and chairs aside yet again.

"Ruining?" He glanced up from his plate.

"Yes. There was nothing wrong with how the kitchen looked. I no longer come in this room and picture Gram and Gramps living here." What she meant was that Zeke had put his stamp overtop everything she loved.

"They aren't here any longer," Zeke said quietly. "Fresh paint brightens the rooms. That sink was older than an antique. It was only a matter of time before the pipes rusted through. Then we'd have a flood, which would mean replacing the whole floor. Orion might have drowned," he added, gesturing toward the pen.

His last dire prognostication shut Myra up. She

ate without talking until Zeke broke the silence. "I've heard you rummaging around in the extra bedroom late at night. Are you cutting out a new dollhouse?"

"I'm packing materials. You said your brother might visit. He'll need a bed."

"There's no rush. I talked to Seth at Halloween. He's hunting opals in Australia and plans to winter there, scuba diving with a fellow gem hunter. Our winter is their summer."

"Still, I won't start any new houses. I have ten to sell at the bazaar."

"About those. I looked one over the other day. Have you thought about putting lights in some? If you lit even half, you could sell them for more and it wouldn't cost but pennies to do."

"Lights? Can you show me?"

They cleared the dishes and Zeke brought a dollhouse to the table. "Here, you can add a battery pack and a switch. You have these little lamps already. Run thin wire along the ceiling and add in a micro LED." He showed her how.

"Zeke, that's brilliant. Weather permitting, I'll go buy wiring after feeding stock tomorrow."

"I'll ride along. You can help choose paint for the living room. It's time for that orangutan orange to go."

She scowled. "It makes the room warmer."

"So would gold." He smiled. "Do you have a minute to look at a notebook I started? Joe Watson suggested I list major chores that need doing and when."

"I intended to type something up," Myra said. "All

this bad weather threw me off. But if you write the instructions yourself, they'll probably make more sense later."

He brought out a pocket notebook and Myra had to admit he had neat printing for a man, and he'd absorbed all she'd told him. Things she was sure he hadn't understood. "Looks to me as if you've got everything down. Calving is the next big operation, and you have to experience one season to understand all the steps."

"Believe it or not, cattle ranching is beginning to make sense. I had no idea what to expect when I came here. You're an excellent teacher, Myra. I see why your folks steered you toward a career in education. I actually feel as if I belong now."

She blinked rapidly to hold back a rush of tears. She'd hoped for quite the opposite effect, but was saved any comment because the kitchen lights flickered twice and went out.

"Whoa!" Zeke reached for her and pulled her close. "What now?"

She spoke against his neck. "We give it ten minutes to see if they come back on. If not, we start the generator." She pulled back a bit. "Did you put the LED lantern back after you tore the old sink out?"

"Yes. And I noticed a couple stashed around the house." Zeke let go of her and felt his way along the new countertop. He got out the double mantle lantern and switched it on. "Whew, I'm glad the batteries are good."

"They get replaced every September. That's something you should write in your notebook."

Orion dug under his quilt until he'd covered up, leaving only his snout visible.

"He doesn't like the lantern," Myra said. "I guess because the light is whiter and more intense."

Zeke leaned over the pen and rubbed the pig's ears. "Poor little guy's scared. His heart is beating as fast as when the owl tried to carry him off." He stood up. "Tell me where to access the generator. I'll go start it."

"You know about generators?"

"Oh yeah. That's high on the list of stuff the army teaches."

"It's housed behind the back porch. Take the lantern. You can't miss it. But be careful. It can be cantankerous. Oh, listen to that wind. You'll want your jacket."

"Is there a lantern in the living room? I can bring it back to you so you have a light while I go outside."

"It's in the pocket under the window seat. I'll just get Orion and come with you. We may be without power for some time. That means no TV, no radio, no microwave or dishwasher. The unit isn't strong enough to light the whole house. So depending on what caused the outage, we may be early to bed, late to rise for days."

"Sounds like we need a bigger generator," Zeke grumped.

"Gramps put it on his Christmas wish list every year. Santa never delivered."

"Funny." Zeke held the light aloft while Myra juggled Orion and retrieved the second lantern. "Speaking of Christmas…are you planning to spend the holiday with your folks?"

She straightened, shooting him a look. "No. The last few years I've stayed here with Gramps and mailed their gifts to them. Are you inviting someone to visit you so that you want me gone? A lady, perhaps?"

"Didn't we have this discussion? My last girlfriend married someone else. I ask because Eric said your mom would love if you were home for the holiday. I thought if you'd be gone a week or two, I'd hire Eddie Four Bear to help feed our stock."

"You don't need help with that. Your money is better spent on chores you can't do alone."

Zeke donned his jacket and hat, picked up his lantern and walked out.

Myra shifted back to thinking he wasn't ready to run a ranch. She would leave for a week if she thought it'd hasten him into reaching the same conclusion. But if he had the wherewithal to hire Eddie, she should probably give up. Except she'd committed to staying through spring, and going home would give her mom ample opportunity to guilt her back into teaching. Not that she wasn't considering it. She'd updated her résumé but hadn't sent it out. She listened to her heart, which still disputed Zeke calling the ranch *his* home. Yet as hard as it was to accept, she needed to separate herself from the Flying Owl and find a teaching job.

ZEKE STEPPED OFF the enclosed porch and was hit with a blast of icy wind. It served him right for acting churlish in there. But dammit, he was doing everything he could to impress Myra. When it came to the ranch it seemed nothing he did was enough. Somewhere around the time of the potluck dance he'd stopped thinking about her leaving, but as yet he hadn't had the nerve to bring it up. Really, he hadn't fully figured out in his own mind how that would work—what it meant. At odd times it popped into his head that he could offer her a business partnership. At others, when they talked and laughed over meals, or went around the ranch, he imagined a totally different relationship. Often at night he pictured her sharing his bed. *Yeah, he definitely needed to start showing her how he felt. See if she had any thoughts along those lines.*

But what were those lines? he wondered as he shone the light over the generator. *Love? Marriage? Kids?* He wanted all of that in due time. Myra, though, was hard to read. What if she scoffed at his feelings? Or what if she just up and left? As independent as she was, why did she need him? Not to start this damned generator, apparently.

One good look at it and he saw that to supply electricity to a house this size it would have to be twice as big. He wondered why Myra's grandfather had muddled along with something so ineffective.

If she hadn't been joking about the man asking Santa for a new unit, then money must have been the issue. He hadn't studied the spreadsheet since the first day she'd showed it to him, but if the ranch didn't earn enough for upkeep, or for the owner to take a few days off, or hire help, why pour heart, soul and endless hours into the place? Anyone could see it was what Myra did.

He started the generator, happy to hear it chug to life without coughing or wheezing.

Returning to the house, Zeke had geared up to launch a serious talk with Myra, only to discover she'd fallen asleep with Orion in the recliner. Funny how sleep softened her. Unable to resist because they looked so cute, he got his camera and snapped a photo, then decided he may as well call it a night.

THE POWER OUTAGE lasted five days, causing undue hardship on some neighbors and businesses in town. Myra and Zeke split up many days, each dashing off to assist a neighbor. The dairy farmers were forced to milk cows by hand, as the electric milking machines required too much power for most generators.

The night the power was restored, Zeke volunteered to cook. For the whole week they'd cooked on a hibachi he'd set up on the porch.

"Ow," Zeke yelped in the middle of rolling out the biscuit dough. "My fingers are cracked from milking so many darned cows."

"Hey, you did it, though. You learned the rhythm. Something Eric never got the hang of."

"Really? He must have never pulled goat duty in Afghanistan."

"Did you keep goats on base?" Myra asked, looking up from threading electrical wire through one of her dollhouses as Zeke had shown her.

"At our more remote sites. Village elders tended to cooperate better if we passed around skins of warm goat's milk first."

"Some of the Afghan terrain I've seen in news clips reminds me of here. Empty, wild, yet beautiful."

"It's hard for me to compare the two." Zeke slid the pan of biscuits into the oven then stirred the noodles he had boiling. "There, I was always looking over my shoulder for snipers or checking paths for mines."

Myra spliced wire to a hanging lamp. "Do you think it'll ever be safe?"

"There's always hope. Hey, some little girl is going to be ecstatic with that dollhouse."

Looking satisfied, Myra said, "I hope parents can afford the higher asking price for the lighted houses. Extra money will be welcome. We plan to request an appointment with the federal Natural Resource Committee in Washington so we can discuss the owls in person. We haven't had any luck in three years of petitioning our state house for a snowy-owl refuge. Our group could buy land, but it wouldn't be a recognized preserve. If we can't post it as a refuge it's pointless. And there's a matter of yearly taxes we'd have to pay. We voted to set aside funds to send Jewell and Tawana to DC. So we're all trying to earn more at this year's bazaar."

"It's next weekend, right?" Zeke put the coffee scoop back in the can and turned on the maker. "Do you think I can do my Christmas shopping for my family there?"

Myra tried the dollhouse lights before setting aside her tools. "I heard you ask your mom the other day for gift suggestions. What does she want?"

"She said to save my money. Their beach condo is small."

"Hmm. Maybe crafts made in snowbound rural Montana won't go well in sunny Barbados."

"And Seth's in equally sunny Australia. Although he's there temporarily. I can always buy him travel items."

"You mentioned photographing the snowy owls for your mom. We don't have professional photofinishing here, but you could ask Carl Meyer at the newspaper to print one of your shots to frame."

"What a good idea. I'll take my camera out tomorrow if it doesn't snow."

THE NEXT DAY after they finished feeding the stock, Zeke removed his gloves and tucked them in a back pocket. "If you can get by without me for a while, I'll saddle Ember and ride into the foothills to see if I can scare up an owl to photograph."

"Go ahead. I'm going in to put on a pot of chili for tonight. Then I'll take a load of dollhouses into town while the weather is good. I talked to Lila last night. She said the grange hall is ready for crafters to start setting up."

"Do you need me to help load and unload them?"

"I've always done it alone. I'll take half of them today. Saturday of the sale, if you like, we can ride together and haul the other half. Driving one vehicle makes sense since parking is at a premium."

"I know you've always done things by yourself. But I'm here and I want to help."

Myra cast him a quick glance. "Are you accusing me of stepping on your toes?"

"No, but at first you readily explained everything. Lately, I have to see you tackling something and barge in to offer assistance."

"I told you winter's the time to catch up on small chores. You've insisted on painting and spiffing up the house in spite of the fumes, so if I see something that needs doing outside, I do it. Frankly, half the time I forget you're here."

"Well, thanks a heap. So glad you find me forgettable," Zeke said testily.

Myra huffed out an exasperated growl and stomped toward the house.

Left to grumble alone, Zeke went into the barn and saddled Ember. Not only hadn't he found a good time to bring up to Myra his earlier thoughts about their relationship, it seemed to him as winter dragged on and the holidays approached, she went out of her way to put more space between them.

It was hard to stay irritated riding through a cold, crisp day. Snow sparkled in areas touched by the sun. White peaks rose in the background. Lower down, evergreen trees stood out against the patchwork like lonely sentinels. But they reminded Zeke he felt lonely. Throughout his years in the army he'd almost never spent time alone. Myra thrived on solitude. She also didn't like change—that was evident in her unhappiness over his sprucing up the ranch. Yet she embraced his suggestion of adding lights to her dollhouses. And after he'd seen how the Watsons had strung canvas between trees to shelter part of their stock, she'd seemed pleased when he'd done the same here with a little help from Joe and Mark.

Maybe he was misreading her. Perhaps she thought he should do more on his own.

He went over their earlier exchange. He could have worded his part of their back-and-forth better.

Just as he vowed to make more of an effort to show Myra he could be a real asset, he saw a trio of snowy owls skimming an open field. Reining in Ember, he lifted his camera. For ten minutes or more the birds flew between the field and a nest situated high in a tall pine. Two of the owls wore pink bands. Zeke couldn't wait to tell Myra so she could relay the information to Jewell.

Before the birds flew farther afield, Zeke scrolled back through several of his photos. Excited to see how clear some of the shots were, he turned and rode home. *Home. It had a good ring.*

Myra's pickup was gone. Zeke was disappointed until he recalled her plan to take a load of dollhouses to the grange hall. Then he decided if he hurried he might take advantage of her being in town. He didn't know Carl from the newspaper, but if he could find Myra in Snowy Owl Crossing, she could introduce him. And help him pick out a nice frame for his mom. Unsaddling Ember, he returned the horse to his stall.

Damn—there he went relying on her again.

It wasn't until he was under way that he hit on another idea. He knew Jewell well enough. So rather than track down Myra and expect her to tell her friend about the banded birds, Zeke could find the vet and tell her himself. Maybe if he showed her his photos, he could ask her help in meeting Carl and picking frames. Satisfied he'd solved two issues with one simple solution, he drove straight to Jewell's clinic.

Chapter Ten

Myra backed her pickup close to the side door of the grange hall. She went inside to find help to unload her dollhouses. If she'd waited for Zeke to return from his ride as he'd suggested, he'd be here to help her. Instead, she'd been bent on proving she didn't need assistance from anyone.

She didn't know why she'd acted so snarkily to him. Actually, she did know. Day by day she felt her hold on the Flying Owl slipping away. Zeke took over more and more ranch chores. He had become a reliable part of the larger ranching community. She saw he wasn't going to leave. Nor should he. He fit in.

Once the power had been restored, she had sent out résumés to principals she knew in Billings and Bozeman. She had scrolled through school websites in Great Falls, but they were her last choice. Great Falls and Helena were too big-city. She'd always considered herself a country girl. She *was* a country girl.

Stepping farther inside the hall, she saw it had been transformed by rows of booths all decorated for the fall bazaar. Classes at the local elementary school had decorated with brown-and-orange crepe paper. Stapled around booth openings were turkeys, pilgrims, cornucopias and hundreds of faux oak leaves cut from construction paper.

In past years Myra hadn't given much thought to booth decorations. Looking around today, it hit her hard knowing this was her last year to exhibit. She would never have children of her own here, running around on sale day showing off their own and classmates' decorations. Discovering how deeply she longed to have a child struck out of nowhere. She'd attended friends' weddings—had even been a bridesmaid. Never had she felt anxious that love, marriage, babies and life on the ranch would drift out of her reach.

"Myra, are you all right? Why are you just standing there?" Lila Jenkins stepped out from a booth.

Giving herself a mental shake, Myra waved. "I guess I was taking it all in. The kids who decorated outdid themselves this year. Did Rory's class do your booth?"

"Mine and some others." Lila crossed the room. "You requested shelves, so the committee assigned you a corner booth. Have you brought dollhouses today?"

Myra nodded. "Five. Wait until you see the addition Zeke suggested. Battery-operated lighting. There wasn't time to refit all of them. But they'll sell for more, so it's good to try a few, I guess."

"The committee ran ads in more newspapers this

year. My quilts and your dollhouses were featured because we always sell out."

"Maybe they should have said in the ads this will be my last year." Myra teared up.

Lila hugged her friend. "Don't say that. The Artsy Ladies are praying for a miracle. Come on, let's bring in your houses and I'll help you arrange them. Then if you have time for coffee we can stop by the café. This morning Mom said she hadn't seen you in ages."

Myra swallowed back the pain that accompanied her declaration about this being her last year. "Did the café close during the power outage?"

"We were open thanks to Mom installing a new generator. There weren't a lot of customers, though. Since school was closed, Rory bussed tables. That freed me up to finish handwork on my last couple of kid quilts. Rory wants the one I made with baseballs all over it. Did I tell you he's gone crazy over baseball? Matt and Lori Barnes's son Kemper plays for Little League. Rory so wants to join. But the fees are expensive. And games are in Wolf Point. Getting him to and from would be hard since I'm doing my best to hang on to the bed-and-breakfast and work part-time for Mom."

The women chatted as they went out to Myra's pickup. "I don't know much about Little League. Do they practice a lot?"

"Daily," Lila said, taking the dollhouse Myra handed her. "They practice at our park, but the field isn't right for league games." The women carried houses in, and after settling them, Lila added, "The games also coincide with fishing season."

"Oh no. Fishermen are your best customers." Myra led the way out to get more houses. "Rory's young. Maybe the B and B will pick up to the point you can hire help. Then next year he can join a team."

"He's ten the day before Christmas. Matt Barnes said players really need to get involved in the sport by then, or they lose valuable instruction."

Myra commiserated as they set the last house. Then she said, "Hey, before we go, let me show you the lights." She flicked on one battery pack. Light shone through the windows.

"That is so cool. You must be getting along better with Zeke if he took that kind of interest in your dollhouses."

"He's okay. But I'm sorry he is who he is." Myra shut off the lights. "Let's go. I don't want to talk about Zeke."

Lila nodded. "You head over. I picked up the grange key from Harv Bell, so I need to run it by his office. Tell Mom I'm on my way."

They parted and Myra drove down Main Street and parked beyond the café. She hurried back and went in. "Hi, Doreen," she called when Lila's mother emerged from the kitchen. She relayed Lila's message. "Doesn't look like you're so busy that she and I can't have coffee."

"And a cupcake. I'm trying out new recipes. Rory's

class is going to sell them at the bazaar. Today I have a batch of lemon and a batch of applesauce."

"Applesauce sounds perfect," Myra said, taking the full mug Doreen Mercer passed her. "I'll take that back booth by the window," she announced as Lila breezed in.

Lila brought her mug and two cupcakes over. She stood by while Myra shed her jacket. "Golly, will you look at that," Lila exclaimed, bending nearer the window. "Isn't that your guy, Zeke, walking across the street with Jewell?"

"Can't be," Myra exclaimed, whirling to peer in the direction Lila pointed. "For one thing, he's not my guy. But Zeke went riding." She pressed her nose to the window and was shocked to see that Lila was right. Zeke and Jewell walked side by side, talking, gesturing and, by the look of them, both having a great time.

Emptiness clawed at Myra's stomach, but she did her best to act normally when she again faced Lila. Still, she barely managed a careless shrug. "He must have gotten back early." She deliberately took a bite of her cupcake and drank her coffee without retaining much of what Lila said. Her mind kept seeing Zeke and Jewell looking so happy together. Although why was that surprising? Jewell was gorgeous, smart and athletic. At the potluck Zeke had remarked on her red hair. So, had he kissed her, too? Myra recalled his kisses. And she could still feel the warmth of his proprietary hand on her back as she introduced him around at the potluck.

"Myra, Mom has asked you three times if you liked the applesauce cupcake."

Jerking her head up, Myra realized she'd been lost in memories. "Sorry, it was really good. I guess I have a lot on my mind. Stuff I need to do between now and calving season so I'll be ready to leave. Last week I put out feelers on teaching jobs."

Lila reached across the table and clutched Myra's hand. "No! Why can't you continue working for Zeke like you're doing now?"

"I can't." Myra's throat was too tight to say more. But she probably wouldn't have admitted how jumbled her feelings were. Seeing Zeke with Jewell made her realize how much she'd come to care for him. Maybe more than she cared to own the ranch, and that was scary.

"I hate to eat and run, but with Zeke in town I need to get back and feed the stock. According to the almanac, this is only a short hiatus between storms."

Lila and Doreen said they'd see her again at the bazaar.

As she drove to the ranch, Myra couldn't shake how much Zeke and Jewell looked like a couple.

Two hours later, she had fed the stock and was parking the tractor when Zeke drove in. He stepped from his pickup and called, "Why didn't you wait for me to help? I went by the grange hall and saw the booths. It's quite a production. Your dollhouses look nice."

Myra shrugged and crawled off the tractor to close up the barn.

Zeke fell in step on the way to the house. "When do you want to eat? I bought paint for my bathroom. If there's time I may give it one coat before supper."

"I've got chili in the Crock-Pot. There's French bread to toast. You can eat anytime you wish. I have things to do and plan to eat in my room."

"O…kay." Zeke slowed then turned back.

Presumably to get his paint.

Myra ran into him again when she returned her empty chili bowl to the kitchen. He sat eating at the table. "We should drive separately to the bazaar," she announced.

"Didn't you say parking was a problem?" Zeke frowned at her.

"It can be. But the Artsy Ladies always clean up. And I may want to join them afterward."

"Is something wrong, Myra? You seem out of sorts."

"Nothing's wrong. Did you get your photographs?"

Zeke scooted his chair aside to give her room to pick up Orion. "I did," he said, but didn't elaborate.

And Myra noticed he didn't offer to show her the pictures.

"I brought in the mail," he said. "You have two envelopes from schools. Did you send out résumés?"

"Where is it?" Myra demanded.

"On the credenza by the door."

Myra rushed out of the kitchen. She snatched up the mail and went directly to her bedroom. She had thought any response would come via email. Her heart beat faster as she set Orion in his night cage and sat on her bed to open the first letter. Maybe one or both schools had midyear openings. If so, her tenure at the ranch could end ASAP, and Zeke would hire Eddie and Aaron to help with calving.

The first note came from her former principal's secretary, pointing out that her certification had expired. If she took courses over the summer and reapplied, they'd consider her. The second letter was similar, suggesting she take the courses online. *How could she have forgotten to renew her certification?*

This was so far from what she'd expected she sat with her body numb and her mind racing. At last she folded the letters and put them in a dresser drawer. The thought of returning to school was repugnant. Should she even consider going back to teaching? Shouldn't a teacher—a good one—be excited to learn? Now her situation seemed dire. She couldn't stay at the ranch Zeke owned. And if he and Jewell got cozy, Myra couldn't fathom them being okay with having her sharing this house with Zeke much longer.

She slept fitfully that night. And the snowstorm that blew in overnight didn't help her disposition. They were back to hand feeding cows each morning and evening. That meant working too closely with Zeke.

It was still snowing on Saturday. Myra and her

friends worried the weather would keep people away from the bazaar.

But it didn't.

"Perhaps because winter seems never-ending," Tawana said. "People just needed to get out and shop for Christmas."

"I need gifts for my dad, my brother and Zeke. It's probably cheesy to buy the same for all three, but I think they'd all like those belts you made with eagle beadwork in patches along the leather." Myra handed over her credit card.

"Zeke was here earlier. He bought a beaded vest for his brother."

"Really?" Myra tucked her card away. "When I first mentioned your beaded leather vests to him, he sounded totally uninterested."

"He was in buying mode. I saw him at Jewell's stall for quite a while. Maybe buying some of her knit scarves for his sisters?"

Myra felt herself scowl. "He only has a twin brother. And his mom lives where it's sunny all the time." She didn't mention that Zeke may have tarried with Jewell for a totally different reason. But the stark reminder stole away the joy Myra usually had for the bazaar. It didn't even help to have so many moms rave over her lighted dollhouses. She gave Zeke credit, but all the same it hurt to sell her final house, knowing it would be the last one she'd ever sell here in Snowy Owl Crossing.

After the crowd thinned out, Jewell was noticeably absent from their cleanup crew. And Zeke wasn't helping the men break down the booths. Rather than looking for him, she reluctantly stayed to help count their earnings.

"We made enough to more than fund Tawana and Jewell's trip to DC," Shelley announced once they'd all met up at the café. "Next year's profits will be gravy."

Everyone high-fived. Everyone but Myra. Lila slipped an arm around her shoulders. "No matter where you are, can't you still come back for the bazaar?"

"Definitely," Tawana vouched. "But we hope it works out for you to stay. Even if the worst happens, we'll keep in touch. You'll want to know what's happening with the owls, Myra. This morning Jewell said our snowy population is up a bit. She plans to band more chicks next week. If we can get an appointment with the federal committee, and they authorize a preserve, you'll have to come to the dedication."

"I can't help feeling out of sorts," Myra said. "I'm not good company. I think I'll go on home and start wrapping Christmas gifts. Maybe that will cheer me up. Anyway, my bad mood shouldn't drag you guys down." Before the other ladies could say more, Myra put on her jacket and hat, and left the café.

Again she beat Zeke to the ranch. The gloomy way she felt, she considered retreating to her bedroom to brood. But they needed to eat. And as long as she remained, chores needed doing.

She assembled a casserole she could pop in the oven to bake while they made the evening round of feeding. *They*, provided Zeke came home. He didn't have to. He was a big boy. Nothing was stopping him from spending the night with Jewell. If they fell in love she ought to be happy for her friend. *Then why was it so hard?*

Myra heard the front door open, and for a split second her heart lifted. She recognized Zeke's footfalls. He didn't call out to her, but went straight to his room.

She put the casserole in the oven, but rather than be caught hanging out in the kitchen, she grabbed her outdoor gear and hurried to the barn to load hay bales. Hard work eased her frustration. By the time Zeke came to find her she was almost her normal self.

"Something smelled good in the kitchen," he said, entering the barn as he pulled on his gloves.

"A casserole my gram used to make. I hope it tastes like hers."

"Hey, I saw a lot of people carrying out your dollhouses."

"Your lights were the big hit."

"Next year maybe I can make some basic wood furniture to go with."

Myra plopped a bale close enough to Zeke to cause him to jump back. "I don't know who will construct the houses since I won't be here."

He fell silent and bent to the task of arranging bales.

They got through their rounds with minimal talk.

Only after they were back inside eating supper did Zeke again broach the subject of Christmas. "You haven't mentioned putting up Christmas lights or a tree."

Myra set down a forkful of casserole. "We used to. Everything is stored in the barn. Last year after Gramps died, I had too much to do to decorate."

"Point me to it. I'll decorate," he said. "I did my shopping at the bazaar, so I only need to wrap and mail packages to my family."

"Same for me," Myra admitted. "So you found something suitable for your folks and your brother?"

"I did."

Myra waited for him to say what he found, but he dug into his meal, and when he finished, rinsed his dishes and retired to his room.

THE NEXT DAY he followed through on his promise to decorate. Myra could have helped, but she fought too many conflicting emotions. After the bazaar, time always seemed to speed up. Everyone was ready to say goodbye to Old Man Winter, when spring rains would wash away the snow and bring new grass and baby calves. But for her, looking ahead spelled the end of her life on the ranch. And she honestly had no idea what she was going to do.

Zeke's decorations inside and out left the house looking cheerier.

In the days that led up to Christmas, all of Myra's family phoned trying to talk her into joining them for the holidays. Her mother said, "Honey, we miss you. Come home. I spruced up your room with new bedding in the lavender shades you love."

"I appreciate that, but we've been slammed with snowstorm after snowstorm. The day I mailed your packages was the last day the road to town was open. The room will keep until March. We should be finished calving by then."

"Sweetheart, Eric told us your teaching credentials lapsed. We're sorry that happened while you were helping Gramps out. Can I help?"

"No, but thanks, Mom. Listen, I'll phone you on Christmas." Myra hung up because tears gummed up her throat.

Zeke, who'd been painting moldings, had listened unabashedly to Myra's end of the conversation. Noticing how she clutched the phone and wiped her eyes, he set down his brush and paint can. Crossing the room, he pulled her out of the chair and into his arms. "What's wrong? If you're homesick, I'll get along. I talked to Eddie about helping with calving like you suggested. He said he's available any time I need him." Zeke rubbed his chin over Myra's hair. "I hate seeing you so distraught."

"Don't hold me, Zeke, or I'll totally fall apart." She wedged a space between them.

Zeke might not have let go, if his phone hadn't rung. He wanted to get to the bottom of her woebegone attitude. He'd noticed a change before the bazaar that seemed worse after.

Dashing a kiss over her forehead, he flashed an apologetic look as he dug out his cell phone. "Seth! Hey, bro. Ah, you got my package? Yeah, yours came. It's lucky. Would you believe we have five feet of snow?"

"Wow, it's eighty-five here."

"Sure, rub it in. Eighty-five sounds like an impossible dream." Zeke turned to include Myra in his smile and saw her closing the door to her bedroom.

"Will your snow be gone by April?" Seth asked. "I'll wind down my opal hunt by then. If I book a flight now I can manage a couple of weeks to see your ranch before heading to a little spot in India showing promising rubies."

"Great, that'll be great. Myra cleared her crafts out of the third bedroom, and it's next on my agenda to paint. Your timing is typical. You'll have missed helping me update the house."

"Will your housemate still be there in April? I thought you said she'd be leaving in the spring."

"Well, ah…here's the thing," Zeke said, lowering his voice and moving away from Myra's bedroom door. "Don't come unglued, but if I had my way, Seth, she'd stay."

"What? You devil, you. Are you implying the *M* word?"

"*M* as in *maybe*. I'm not doing a good job of making my feelings known. I can't read how she feels about me. Since we share a house, work and all meals, I'm reluctant to romance her too much. It could easily get out of hand. Then if she didn't want to commit I'd feel like a heel and it could drive her away. I mean, look at all I owe her family."

Seth cleared his throat. "I'm not a good person to give advice in the love game, Zeke. Women always see me as a rolling stone."

"We're something, huh? My travelin' days are over. I love it here. This is exactly where I see myself living for the next forty or fifty years."

Myra's bedroom door opened and she sped past where he stood talking to Seth. He wondered how much of his conversation she'd heard. Should he hope she caught the last part? Everyone around knew how deeply she loved the ranch, but he doubted she had any idea he'd developed the same care for the place. What he hesitated to tell her was how big a part she played in what he liked about work and life here.

"Hey, Seth, I need to get back to painting. I'll give you a holler after we open our gifts, okay? If you're not off surfing, that is. Make your reservations and I'll tell Myra you're coming."

IN THE KITCHEN, Myra picked up Orion and hugged him close. She guessed it was fortuitous she'd come out when she did. Her mother used to say eavesdroppers always got their ears full. But Zeke hadn't exactly been trying to cloak what he was saying to his twin. All her wishful thinking that he'd quit and sell her the ranch was dashed for good. She felt calmer on the outside than on the inside, she knew as she went to the fridge for Orion's lettuce.

Instead of clinging to hope, she should've left the day her dad informed her they'd given the Flying Owl to Eric's savior. Now her affection for the ranch was all mixed up with her confusing affection for Zeke.

She only had a few months left to get through. Hard, though, when she wished for more than Zeke meant by that casual kiss he'd brushed across her forehead right as his brother called. Considering his comment to Seth about the ranch being his forever home, Zeke probably couldn't wait for spring calving to pass so she'd leave the place totally to him.

She sighed and set Orion down to eat his lettuce.

Chapter Eleven

Christmas morning brought the heaviest snowfall yet. Myra had managed to get into town Christmas Eve to attend a candlelight service. Zeke had declined to go. When she left the church, it was bitterly cold and the sky was thick with clouds. No one expected it to snow another two feet during the night, though.

"Jeez," Zeke exclaimed in the morning when they stepped out to go feed the cows. "Merry Christmas… not! Do you think we can get to the barn and on out to the pens?" He waded through snow up to his waist, breaking trail for Myra.

"Luckily the plow is still on the tractor. After we load the hay, if you plow a track, I'll toss bunches over the fence. I think the worst of the storm has passed. At least there are far fewer clouds than when I drove home last night."

"How was the service? I probably should have gone, but I promised my folks a group call with Seth, and we're all in different time zones."

"Did you open your gifts last night?"

"The ones from them. I didn't open the one from you."

"I saw you'd put two under the tree for me," she said. "You shouldn't have when I only bought you one thing. Eric gave me earmuffs. My folks sent a check they designated for an online class to renew my teaching credentials." She wrinkled her nose.

At the barn, Zeke unlocked the door and pulled it back. "Eric said something about your certificate being out of date. But once you said you'd rather work on a ranch than teach. Did you change your mind?"

Myra hooked the trailer on the back of the tractor and began loading bales. "I feel like my life is in flux."

Zeke found the long-handled hook and pulled down bales from the next tall stack. Then he and Myra fell silent while they filled the trailer.

The feeding process took much longer than normal due to the deep snow. They'd returned the equipment to the barn when Zeke said, "Will all of the heifers make it to springtime to have their babies? A half dozen or so look ready to pop now."

"Hey, you're paying attention. We'll need to watch closely during January. None should drop calves until February. We count back to when I put the bull in the heifers' pasture."

Zeke's grin was sheepish. "I'll jot that down in my notebook. I wondered how you were so sure calves arrive at a predetermined period."

They stomped the snow off their boots and entered the warm house. "Sometimes I suspect a bull gets randy through the fence. I've had a couple of mid-January calves."

"You talk so matter-of-factly about the birthing stuff. Dave Ralston offered some insight into how messy it can be. He said his wife and his daughter-in-law both help with their calving. I guess it surprises me that women, uh, get so involved."

Removing two mugs from the cupboard and filling them with hot coffee, Myra also dispatched an eye-roll. "Calves are the lifeblood on a ranch. So Ma, Pa, grandparents and kids help make sure they get a safe start. As for women being involved, who do you think birth children?"

Zeke accepted his mug. "Women, of course. But does seeing the process so up close and personal year after year dampen a woman's enthusiasm to have babies?"

"Not that I've seen. Birth is actually rather amazing, Zeke." Myra put a premade pan of cinnamon rolls in the toaster oven and turned it on.

"So, you want kids?" he asked casually.

"Sure, but I have to find a husband first," she responded drily as she checked the rolls.

"Are you hunting?" Zeke set out plates and forks.

"What kind of question is that? Are *you* hunting for a wife?" She pulled on oven mitts, removed the steaming pan and smacked it down on the table atop a hot pad.

"Well, yeah," he admitted, eyeing her as he sat down.

"Silly me, I should've known," she muttered, picturing him laughing with Jewell. "Hold out your plate," she ordered, slipping a spatula under a big roll. Her remark or maybe her testy tone effectively ended what she judged a pointless conversation.

But as she nibbled at her roll, Myra wondered if Jewell knew Zeke was that serious. At the candlelight service Jewell had only talked about the snowy owls.

"Wanna go open presents?" Zeke asked after they finished eating.

"Sure. But I wish you hadn't bought me two gifts. I didn't get you anything elaborate," she said, clearly fretting.

"Are you always such a worrywart?" Bending, Zeke plugged in the tree lights.

"I never considered myself a worrier. Everyone thinks I'm practical. For sure you're into the commercial aspects of Christmas. You bought more lights."

"Maybe it comes from spending so many years on military bases, missing home at the holidays."

"I never thought of that. Sorry… I didn't even plan a traditional meal."

"It's okay," Zeke said, handing her a package. "Maybe next year."

Knowing she wouldn't be here next year made this exchange of gifts more awkward. "Here, open yours, too." She passed him a gaily wrapped box, realizing he must have wrapped the one he'd handed her. It wasn't in a box, so she could tell immediately it was a picture frame. She tore open the overly taped paper, expecting to see a snowy owl the way Zeke had planned to send his mother. The picture in the lovely frame brought instant tears to her eyes. It was a snapshot of her in her grandfather's chair. She'd fallen asleep while working on a dollhouse. Orion dozed in the crook of her arm. His pink ears touched her chin.

"Why are you crying?" Zeke asked, leaning over to frown at the item. "I thought it came out good."

"It's wonderful," she blubbered, hugging it to her breast.

Zeke smiled and lightly brushed her tears away. Sitting back, he opened his gift. "Hey, this belt is great. I saw them in Tawana's booth and intended to buy one when I went back for Seth's vest. She'd sold all the belts. Thanks." He leaned in again and kissed her cheek. "You have one more gift," he said, setting a soft package in her lap.

Flustered by the intimacy of the moment, Myra quickly ripped into it, figuring to find gloves. Once again Zeke had shocked her. "Ooh, you got Orion a new cape."

"I had Jewell knit it to replace the one the owl made off with. I tried to explain what I wanted when I went over to her booth. This one's woven tighter and closes with Velcro to make it easier to remove if another owl grabs Orion." Zeke gazed expectantly at Myra.

His easy mention of Jewell combined with all the thought he'd put into these gifts left Myra weepy. She burst into tears and didn't want Zeke to console her.

"Myra, honey, what's wrong? Do you hate it? I don't understand."

Getting up, she held the gifts close. "They're too perfect. I…I need to be alone." And she fled to her bedroom, where she sobbed out her sorrow. She wouldn't take Orion out to the fields for another alfalfa harvest, because they'd be gone. Where, she had no idea. The truth of it was that Zeke didn't need her. He had Jewell. The warm way he spoke of her help with the gift drove Myra's pain deeper.

But once she emptied out all her tears, it also served as a catalyst for her to buck up and prepare for her ultimate separation from the ranch, from Zeke and from all of her friends in Snowy Owl Crossing. When she finally left her room, she was able to present to Zeke a new, coolly detached woman.

CHRISTMAS WAS A turning point in the weather, too. Where for months they'd been plagued with ice and snow, rains came to melt the snow and turn everything into mud.

Zeke sensed Myra withdrawing, but he wasn't able to put his finger on why. She still did more than her fair share of chores inside and out. She continued to explain the work that needed to be done in terms he was able to jot down in his notebook. But her usual warmth was missing. And the sparkle he loved. It was as if the long winter had sucked joy out of her. He was afraid to bring it up, afraid he'd make her cry again.

EMERGING FROM THE third week in January where Zeke felt he and Myra were drifting further apart instead of growing closer as he'd envisioned before Christmas, he finally had to ask her. "Myra, you seem preoccupied. What's wrong?"

"I'm busy bringing heavies to the corral by the barn so when calving starts in earnest we'll be ready for any event. Up to now you've seen three calves born, and they were normal. You're about to get baptism by fire."

"Uh. Okay. I assume heavies are the heifers about to give birth."

"Bingo. Give the man a Kewpie doll." Tightening Cayenne's cinch, she rode off.

Zeke wasn't sure if he should get Ember and follow. But he wasn't imagining Myra's frostiness.

Deciding his frustration had gone on long enough, he thought he'd ask Eric what was going on. Myra spoke often with her brother. Perhaps their folks were having some problems at Rolling Acres and she didn't feel right sharing that news. Pulling out his phone, he put distance between himself and the barn, lest Myra return unexpectedly.

"Eric? Hi, it's Zeke. Sorry to bother you on a busy workday, but we haven't touched base in a while. Since we're about to be buried in calving, I assume you are, as well."

"Yeah. It's been a wild January. We're up to our ears in mud. Myra said you are, too. She also said you're turning into a real rancher, Zeke."

"Really? She hasn't been that forthright with me. In fact, that's why I'm calling." Zeke quickly laid out his observations and concerns. He finished and Eric didn't speak.

"Hey, buddy, did I lose you?"

"No. Zeke, listen. You didn't hear this from me, okay? Myra made me promise not to say a word, but you sound as if you care about her."

"I do. I care a lot. Is she ill? Tell me. I want to help."

"She's sick at heart. She wanted the Flying Owl. It rocked her world when our folks signed the ranch over to you. Myra hoped you'd give up and go away, and I think she figured you'd sell to her. I wish I loved this place as much as she loves that one. She knows now it'll never belong to her. If you want my advice, leave her alone to grieve. She promised you she'd stay through calving and she will. Oh, hey, Dad's calling me. I've gotta dash. Keep what I told you between us or she'll wring my neck. Bye."

Zeke found himself holding a dead phone, staring into space. He felt as if he'd been kicked in the gut. Eric's words had landed with more force than when he'd been kicked by the heifer. Now, at least, he had an answer. How had he been so blind? Myra would never fall for him as long as he stood between her and her greater desire to own the ranch. Worse, she didn't need him. She'd handled the Flying Owl fine before he showed up. And she could do it again.

He went to the house for coffee and saw Orion rooting around in his pen. Zeke picked him up. Dang, but he'd let this little fellow become his pet, too. Scratching between Orion's ears, Zeke set him down again. He was the interloper in this household.

In rehab he'd met and gotten to be friends with a colonel who'd lost a leg. Stewart Redding was a former Montana lawyer who went home to rebuild his private practice. Zeke had his number. Stewart said if Zeke ever needed legal advice, to call. He didn't need advice; he needed someone to regift the ranch to Myra.

Before he could have regrets, he phoned the colonel.

Making such an exchange would be far simpler than Zeke imagined. He needed to fax a copy of his deed to Stew along with his address. In two or three weeks, Redding would return the new deed to him by mail. That meant he could stay and help out through calving, and be out of Myra's hair for good soon after.

Zeke worried that he'd have too much time on his hands to reflect and be miserable. The next day he drove to town and went to the library to fax off the deed. A day later, calving hit with a vengeance.

"I don't know where you got off to yesterday," Myra finally snapped after the birth of two healthy calves. "Added to a seven-day-a-week schedule feeding stock, this is a twenty-four-hour-a-day process. I'll take nights because I've done it before and know what problems can crop up. I'll know if the temperature drops to where a cow needs to birth in the barn instead of in the corral. I suggest you call and ask Eddie Four Bear or Aaron Younger to work alongside you six to eight hours a day for the next few weeks. They're both old hands at this."

"You're saying you haven't taught me enough?"

"You've done great so far, and to date no cow has abandoned her offspring. You haven't had to watch me pull a stuck calf or turn one. But…I plan to leave the day after the last calf drops, so you may want to dicker a price with the guys to help you ear tag babies. That needs to happen ASAP. And after that, the branding. Then you'll move the herd up into the foothills to the leased pasture."

Zeke opened his mouth to beg her to stay. A look on her face stopped him, so he dug out his cell phone. A few minutes later he garnered Myra's attention. "Eddie and Aaron have jobs until March. Eddie says Luke Elkhorn took a semester off to earn money for tuition. Whaddya think? Eddie vouches for Luke."

"It's your call, Zeke," Myra said, going back to a cow pacing with her tail stuck straight out behind her, a sure indication she was in active labor.

FOR THE FIRST three weeks of February, Zeke and Myra passed one another without speaking, usually in the kitchen, where one stumbled awake as the other dumped a thermos and yawned off to bed. A few times they both fed Orion, which he loved.

Zeke made a point to check the mail every day. It wasn't hard since Myra caught her sleep then. His package came from the lawyer on a day he and Luke were kept busier than they'd ever been. Luke had to teach him how to turn a breech calf, then he went home.

Zeke tossed the envelope on his bedroom dresser and piled the remainder of the mail on the kitchen counter. Myra had left him a note saying she'd sent a check for grass seed, and he'd need to pick it up from the feed store.

He asked about it next time he saw her.

"Don't worry about it. You won't seed pens until after you move the herd. And there's still a possibility of a late storm. In fact, the almanac predicts falling temps and maybe a norther by the end of next week. I hope it holds off until then. At that point we should only have a few stragglers to birth. Things are going exceedingly well. You haven't lost a single calf. Better, there are no orphans."

"Luke said the same."

"Yeah, but this morning at dawn I went out to bury some of the clutter that built up from calving. I saw two wolves slinking around, so I set out smudge pots along the pen perimeter. If we burn them a few nights, the wolves will likely give up."

"I had no idea. Are you safe riding out there alone at night?" Zeke circled his fingers around Myra's wrist to keep her from dashing away.

"I'm fine. If you run into wildlife, clap your hands and shout." She freed her arm and left the room, saying she was asleep on her feet.

Thursday of the following week, shortly after daybreak they met again in the kitchen. Zeke asked about the wolves and noted Luke had replenished the fire-pots.

"I only saw wolves that one time. You probably noticed the herd gathers in the center of the enclosures. All of them except new heifers know when the pots are lit it's time to circle the wagons, so to speak."

"Ah, I'll keep that in mind. Say, Jewell phoned last night to see if we needed her to check any calves. She was at Hank's ranch. He had a sick cow and she brought antibiotics. If we need her, you should give her a shout-out. Tomorrow she and Tawana are going to band owl chicks. But she'd drop by here on her way back to her clinic."

Myra stifled a yawn. "I don't need her for the cows. But give her a call. You probably want to see her."

"Why would I want to see her?" Zeke straightened from dumping used coffee grounds into the garbage can. "Luke said our calves are all healthy. One cow wandered off from her calf, but Luke and I scrammed her back, and she recognized her baby."

"I assumed you two haven't gotten together since you went to town two or three weeks ago. That's a long time to not see your girlfriend." Myra rinsed her thermos, set it upside down on a paper towel to drain and headed off.

"Wait." Zeke scratched his head. "I haven't seen Jewell since I ordered Orion's cape at the bazaar. Uh, well, she did introduce me to Carl Meyer at the newspaper. You mentioned him. Jewell wanted to see my photos of the snowy owls. She asked to buy a few, so I traded her for the knitting."

Myra studied Zeke through sleepy eyes. "Christmas Day you said—" Breaking off, she covered a huge yawn then rubbed the center of her forehead. "Never mind. My brain isn't awake. Let's leave it this way. Unless something drastic happens during your shift today, we don't need Jewell's medical expertise. And if all goes well and we wind down calving by the weekend and I'm out of here, I plan to stop in town and tell everyone goodbye."

"We need to talk first, Myra," Zeke said, starting after her.

She held up a hand. "We'll have to carve out a time later. I know the money from the fall sale is in the ranch account and we haven't resolved a split." She backed through the door. "Truly, Zeke, my brain is mush, and I'm dead on my feet."

He pursed his lips to one side then waved her away. "What I have to talk about is important. Let's wait till we're both awake."

The next morning Zeke rose early, determined to give Myra the deed and tell her of his own plans to leave. Prior to retiring for the night, he'd looked the papers over to be sure everything was in order. He packed most of his clothes in the duffels he'd arrived with. He, not Myra, would be gone by the weekend.

Standing at the kitchen window, he was surprised

to see there'd been a massive shift in weather since he went to bed. Angry black clouds occluded the sky. Obviously the temperature had dropped, because Orion objected to going out on the porch through his doggie door. He'd push his snout out, squeal and return to hide under his quilt.

Aware the pig needed to use his litter box, Zeke picked him up and carried him out. Wind blew sleet into the screened room. Orion took care of business and darted back inside, leaving Zeke alone and shivering.

He dashed back in and had to push hard to shut the outer door. As he turned to the coffeemaker, he noticed a paper on the fridge. It was a note addressed to him.

Zeke, it's 4:00 a.m. The storm I told you the almanac predicted has hit. I went to bring in the last pregnant heifer but I found a portion of fence down and maybe twenty head of stock had wandered out. I saddled Cayenne and drove them all back in and repaired the fence. But the pregnant heifer is still loose somewhere. It's five now. A bit lighter, but colder. I'm afraid freezing rain will cover her tracks. I'm going after her. Heading northeast. Like I said, she's our last to deliver. I'm determined we'll have a perfect record. Myra.

Zeke held the note for a minute. The kitchen clock said almost six o'clock, meaning she'd been gone an hour. Unless she'd returned with the heifer and had her in the barn awaiting the delivery.

Darn the Montana weather. He hadn't needed his heavy jacket the past few days and last night he'd packed it. He debated about fixing coffee to take to Myra. If she was in the cold barn she could use a hot drink. On the other hand—well, he didn't want to think about the other hand.

Hurrying into his room, he unpacked his winter jacket and found his heavy gloves. This day called for a hat with earflaps. The one Myra first loaned him still sat on a shelf above the coatrack. Once suited up for the cold, Zeke battled wind-driven ice to reach the barn.

One look around and he knew Myra hadn't returned. Cayenne's stall was empty. Given the changed weather, he needed to make the early feed run. They'd removed the snowplow from the tractor several weeks ago, but because they still supplemented feeding, the trailer remained hooked up.

Zeke began loading bales, telling himself Myra would be back before he finished rounds. Since coming here, he'd been getting stronger, but he soon discovered that to fill the trailer by himself took a hefty toll on his left arm. Picking up the last bale left him in pain. Perhaps the frigid weather had something to do with his hurting again.

Still no Myra.

The drive out to the big pasture was slow going.

He had to stop the tractor, break open bales and pitch hay into the enclosure at intervals.

It wasn't until he fed and checked on cow-calf pairs in the three smaller corrals that he realized how much time had lapsed. His watch said 9:00 a.m. Four hours had gone by. There was still no sign of Myra.

He returned the equipment to the barn and stood in the doorway gazing toward the northeast. He'd seen her boot tracks at a section of newly repaired fence. In spite of the sleet, a lot of areas remained muddy. Zeke rubbed his aching arm, trying to decide what to do. Now he wished he hadn't let Luke take the day off.

Then all at once he saw Cayenne plodding toward him.

But hold on. Plodding wasn't right. Limping was more like it.

Zeke ran out to meet the horse and saw she was riderless. She had gashes across her knees. Blood dripped down her legs. The saddle sat askew and she kept stepping on one loose rein.

Terror smacked Zeke even as he led the mare into the barn. Obviously something bad had happened to Myra. His mind immediately went to a wolf attack. But would wolves only leave banged-up knees? Had Cayenne stumbled and fallen?

He removed the saddle when he heard a vehicle pull up. Hoping someone was bringing Myra home, Zeke dropped the saddle and ran outside. Jewell emerged from her pickup.

"Hey, Zeke, Tawana and I had to abandon our plan

to band owls today. It's too slick to get up to where they nest." Then she stared at him. "You look awful. Sorry, that's a horrible thing to say by way of greeting, but is something wrong?"

Zeke clasped her arm and yanked her into the barn, showing her Cayenne. He dispensed a short version of Myra's note, then said the horse had come in bloodied and alone.

"So Myra's out in this storm someplace without a way to get home? We need to call around and organize a search party. Usually it takes an hour or so to gather one."

Zeke clapped a palm over her phone. "You take care of Cayenne. I'll saddle Ember and go find her. If I don't pick up her tracks, I'll call you."

"Zeke, that's foolish. Do you have any idea where to look?"

"Her note said she headed northeast. I saw her tracks by the fence. Now I have Cayenne's tracks, which are fresher. I did this kind of thing in the military," he said, cinching the saddle tight before adding a bridle.

"Okay," Jewell said. "But northeast from here are a lot of deep ravines. Take a blanket and water in case she's injured. I'll treat Cayenne until you get back or call. Come to think of it, why hasn't Myra phoned home?"

Zeke frowned as he tied lariats around a blanket bedroll. "Don't dredge up trouble. She's going to be fine," he said harshly, swinging into the saddle.

Jewell placed a hand on the bridle for a moment. "You love her, don't you, Zeke?"

He didn't respond.

"If I'm right, why are you letting her leave? Luke told Tawana that Myra will be gone for good this weekend."

"She's not going anywhere," he stated firmly. "Turn loose, Jewell, so I can bring her home where she belongs."

Offering a self-satisfied smile and a double thumbs-up, Jewell stepped aside and let Zeke leave the barn.

Chapter Twelve

Zeke galloped to where Myra had repaired the fence. The tracks were clear. He turned northeast, but sleet soon hampered his ability to see well. Then Cayenne's tracks intersected larger, deeper ones. This could be where Myra picked up the trail of the pregnant heifer.

Pausing at intervals, he called her name. Ice crystals stung his face as wind drove her name back down his throat. Everything remained eerily quiet.

All at once the terrain got rocky. Tracks disappeared. Farther uphill were scattered trees, but dropping away on his left side were the ravines Jewell warned about. A knot formed in Zeke's belly. He had ridden roughly two miles up a vertical incline without finding Myra. By then he was hoarse from yelling for her.

Reaching a fork in the trail, he dismounted. No tracks. Had he lost them? Had he taken a wrong turn? He remounted, panic gripping his throat.

Suddenly a low-flying snowy owl swooped directly over him sounding the *krek-krek* Myra said was an alarm. Since the bird flew down from the left fork,

Zeke judged it a sign. For all he knew, worse danger lay ahead. Regardless, he urged Ember forward.

Evergreens dotting the granite-pocked slope offered some relief from the diminishing sleet. Zeke had his head tucked into his chest to ward off wind when Ember rounded an abrupt corner and kicked rocks over a precipice. The stones rattled down a shear drop-off, causing Zeke to rein in fast.

Sitting to still his racing heart, he spotted a lone heifer. She wasn't pregnant, which stole hope that this was the heavy Myra mentioned in her note. The silly cow languished out in the weather, bawling at nothing Zeke could see.

Passing by, he looked her over but didn't see any injuries. However, she bore the Flying Owl brand. He renewed his hoarse shouts for Myra.

His first call echoed back from the ravine. A second one resulted in a responding thin cry—or so he thought. A muffled "help" merged with a louder bawl from the heifer, who plodded closer to the rim.

Zeke vaulted from his saddle again. Looping Ember's reins around a spindly pine, he cupped his hands at his mouth and at the cliff he yelled Myra's name. This time he heard an unmistakable response directly below a crumbled area that had fallen away.

His heart thundered as he dropped and lay on his belly. Leaning out as far as he dared, he spotted Myra huddled on a narrow outcrop some ten feet below. Sheltered in her arms was a newborn calf. At first a burst of joy stole his voice.

"Zeke, is it really you?" she shouted. "Thank heaven you saw my note."

"Cayenne came home with bloody knees," he managed to say.

"Oh no, is she badly hurt?"

"Jewell stopped by just as she limped in. She'll be fine."

"Good. The heifer delivered, but didn't accept her baby. I thought she'd follow if I carried her calf. I tried to mount Cayenne, but she stumbled. It was hailing and windy. I didn't realize we were so near the edge."

"Let's see what I can do to get you out of this mess."

"It's a really steep slope. I tried grabbing a bush to climb up, but the granite is as slick as glass."

"I have ropes. If I tie them together they'll reach you." He scooted back, stood up and unwound two lariats he'd tied around the bedroll. His major worry was that his bad left arm lacked the strength to pull her and the calf up.

"Is there a way to send the calf up separately?" he called, looking around to see what he might use for added leverage.

"No. She's just a baby."

"Okay, look, I'll make a loop in one end of this rope and snake it down to you. I'll wrap it around a pine. It's scraggly, but far enough back from the unstable shelf I think it'll hold. You're going to have to climb some if you can, Myra. I hurt my left arm feeding stock earlier. My only power is from my right side."

"Zeke, I'm sorry. Can Jewell round up some guys to help?"

"I didn't get her number. But she wondered why you didn't phone me."

"I dropped my cell trying to get it out of my pocket without losing my grip on the calf. This protrusion isn't very wide."

He heard her concern, which reopened a hole in his stomach. But he'd been in worse fixes in Afghanistan. He would make this rescue. "I'm sending down the rope. Hook it around your waist. When it's tight, hang on and I'll pull."

"Ready," she called a few seconds later, her voice wobbly.

Zeke gritted his teeth and forced his injured left arm to help with a hand-over-hand tug-of-war. At least it felt like a tug-of-war. He braced his feet against the skinny tree, praying it would hold. It was slow going. A strand of the rope frayed and split. In spite of the cold, he began to sweat.

After what seemed an interminable amount of time, he saw Myra's hat peek over the rim and his heart kicked. He wound the thinning rope around his body for added support, gave a giant yank, and like a cork popping out of a bottle, Myra and the calf exploded from the ravine and flattened Zeke.

For a time they all lay panting atop chilly, muddy pine needles.

The heifer plodded up and began licking her calf. Myra set the babe on its feet and threw herself at Zeke, pressing kisses all over his face. "You did it," she babbled. "You saved us. Saving Odells must be your lot in life. You've now rescued both of my parents' kids from sure death. What in the world can they give you this time to show their appreciation? What can I give you?"

Zeke scooted upright and kept kissing Myra. He finally took a breath and held her head still. "This is a helluva time to start this conversation. Seriously, Myra, the only thing you can give me…all that I want is—" he hesitated and brushed a tattered glove over her eyebrows "—is you. I might have lost you today without ever telling you I love you."

Myra stared at him with saucer eyes. "Zeke, when you fell backward did you hit your head on a rock? You're talking nutty. I'm leaving, remember?"

"My head's fine and you're not going anywhere," he said gruffly. He tried to hold her, but was forced to let her wiggle away. Distributing his weight on his good arm, he got up. "This isn't something to settle here. We need to get the cow, calf and us home. Can Ember carry our combined weight?"

"Probably. Let me mount, then hand me the calf. Keep Ember well back from the brink when you climb aboard."

"Definitely. Do you know Jewell's number? We should call and tell her you're okay and she can go home. You and I have business to settle." Zeke passed her his phone.

Taking it, Myra punched in numbers. "Jewell, it's Myra. I got the new calf and Zeke's bringing us home. Is Cayenne okay?" She listened a moment. "Ah, good. No, you don't need to wait if you have another call. Bye." She returned Zeke's phone and swung into the saddle. "Wrap the calf in that bedroll I see on the ground."

He did and handed the bundle to her over the mother's protests. Ember danced around, making Zeke's mounting difficult. He finally managed and the heifer lumbered along beside them. Zeke held Myra close. It felt good. It felt right.

The gelding stepped out briskly. In the improved weather they soon reached the juncture where the two paths merged.

"How did you know which trail to take?" Myra turned slightly toward Zeke.

"I heard a snowy owl. It flew down from the left fork. I took it as a sign—a good omen. I've developed a real liking for snowy owls."

"I'm lucky. The right-hand trail is wider. It leads to the summer pasture. Had you taken it you'd never have found us."

"I wouldn't have quit looking. I meant what I said back there. I love you, Myra." He felt her stiffen. "I haven't known how to tell you."

"What about Jewell?"

"What about her? This isn't the first time you've

mentioned her like she means something to me. I barely know Jewell."

"Lila and I saw you two laughing and talking as you walked along Main Street. And at the bazaar you two went off together."

"I told you she made Orion's cape in exchange for a photo of the owls. That's all it was."

"It doesn't matter. I'm all packed. I'm going home to Rolling Acres later today."

"If anyone leaves the Flying Owl, it'll be me. But I'm not going far. I intended to have this talk in the warmth of the house, but as we're in it now I'll go ahead and tell you I've deeded the ranch to you."

"What?" Myra whirled so fast she almost dropped the calf, who cried and caused the heifer to trot up and bawl her disapproval. "Why, when you've proven yourself in so many ways? Plus, I heard you tell your brother how much you love living here."

"Don't you know you're the biggest part of that? Maybe I should have guessed how much you wanted the ranch. I didn't. Not until I asked Eric if he had any idea why you were so down in the dumps. I swear I had no idea the ranch caused a divide between us that widened day by day."

"I'll kill him. I told Eric not to share that with you or our folks. I confided in him at a low point. I was hurt that the folks didn't discuss it with me. On the other hand I never told them how I felt. I'm so ashamed you found out."

"Don't be. I wormed it out of Eric. Just know it means everything to me to see you happy. Look, we're home." He pointed at the barn. "Let's get the cow and calf in where it's warm. Are you okay to feed them while I take care of Ember?" Myra nodded. "Then we'll go to the house and I'll get you the deed I had drawn up." Reining in, he got off and lifted Myra and the calf down.

"I won't take it, Zeke. How can you possibly love me knowing I wanted you to go away from the beginning? I shoved crappy jobs at you hoping you'd fail."

He leaned over and kissed her lips. Drawing back slowly, he said, "It's the crazy kind of love that got hold of me and won't let go. But in case you think it's all about the ranch, I swear if you sold everything and moved to Timbuktu I'd follow you."

She touched a finger to her mouth, then did the same to his before she tightened her hold on the calf and led the heifer into the barn's interior.

Zeke took care of Ember, checked Cayenne and fed them both. He and Myra completed their chores at the same time.

As they trekked to the house, he casually slipped an arm around her waist and was pleased she didn't shove him away.

"I know you hate what I did to the house," he said, helping her off with her jacket after they went inside.

"It's more that I didn't want to like it. I love the improvements."

Smiling, he guided her to the kitchen, where he'd left the deed. Seating her at the table, he handed her the documents. "Read it all, including the fine print. I'll make some coffee to warm you up."

Myra pushed the packet aside. "This isn't the answer, Zeke. If I accepted this I'd never be happy here. Guilt would eat me up. Undo it."

"Why?"

She clasped her hands. "I'd see you no matter where I turned. Chores went so much easier when we did them together. I'd miss you," she admitted, her voice quivery.

"You'd really miss me?"

"Yes. Do I have to say I've fallen for you, too? I thought you could tell I was eaten up with jealousy thinking you and Jewell were an item."

"Then what does it matter whose name is on the deed? I don't want to get the cart before the horse, but can you picture the Flying Owl belonging to Mr. and Mrs. Maxwell?"

"You want to give it to your parents?"

"No!" Zeke pulled Myra out of her chair and into his arms. "Oh, I see that smile. You're teasing. I get it now. You need me to say, Myra, honey, will you marry me?"

She snuggled against him. "Well, that way we could put the ranch in a trust so it'd be there for the next generation. Be there in the future for our family."

"That crossed my mind a few times, too. I was so afraid you'd turn me down. I was afraid you'd think I wanted you to stay only for the sake of saving the ranch."

Myra clutched the front of Zeke's shirt. "We both almost foolishly let the ranch stand in the way of our love."

"So you'll marry me?"

"Yes." She rose on tiptoe and kissed him.

"How soon?" he asked when they both finally had to breathe. "Seth wants to visit in April. I'd like him to be my best man. Maybe my folks can come. How's April for ranchers? Will your family be able to leave Rolling Acres for a day?"

"May would be better. We'd have calves' tagged and branded, and stock moved to summer pasture. But maybe your brother can't stay that long."

"He'll stay awhile. Didn't you tell me once that people found sapphires in old gold mines around here? On the other hand, I don't want him underfoot. Especially if we're not going away for a honeymoon." Zeke tightened his arms around Myra.

She looped hers around his waist. "Lila runs a B and B. Can we rent your brother a room there?"

"I like how you think. A May wedding, then." They kissed until Orion turned over his empty bowl with a bang and broke them apart.

Laughing, they fed him together.

"You said you only wanted me to be happy," Myra murmured. "Knowing we'll spend all our days and nights together in a place we both love does that."

"For me, too. Let's start calling family and friends to spread our good news."

Myra threw her arms around Zeke's neck. "Growing up I dreamed of an Old West–style wedding. I'd love to put planning ours in the capable hands of the Artsy Ladies."

"Perfect," Zeke agreed, lifting her off her feet.

Epilogue

May in the Crossing brought intermittent blue skies and rain that carpeted the hills in green. May also brought snowy-owl chicks, which Jewell banded in orange to make counting next winter easier. And May brought Myra and Zeke's wedding.

She had requested her mother sew her an ivory satin dress with mutton sleeves. Online she ordered a big-brimmed hat with a pink plume to match a ribbon belt and new cowgirl boots. A nosegay of baby roses rounded out her Old West look. Her matron of honor, Lila, wore a burgundy dress with a bustle. Jewell, Tawana, Shelley and Mindy were rays of sunshine in jonquil yellow.

Zeke and his attendants resembled old-time gamblers in gray pin-striped pants, white shirts, black satin vests, string ties and black elastic armbands.

They held the ceremony at Myra's church. A reception catered by Lila's mom would follow immediately at the grange hall so guests could spread out, talk, laugh, eat, dance and get to know Zeke's family and friends.

Once the church filled, a pianist began to play, and a hush fell over the crowd as Lila started down the aisle on the arm of Zeke's brother, Seth, blond haired and green eyed in contrast to his twin's dark hair and hazel eyes.

Jewell accompanied Myra's brother. Three of Zeke's former military buddies, one using a cane, escorted her other best friends to the front of the church, where the minister and Zeke emerged from a side room. He adjusted his string tie and fidgeted until Seth grinned and nudged him with the ring box—a tanzanite-and-diamond band Seth had helped Zeke pick out.

Myra absorbed everything as she waited with her dad at the back of the sanctuary.

"Honey, you're positively glowing today," he said.

"I'm happier than I've ever been, Daddy."

"The old home place never looked so good, and Zeke's quick to give you all the credit."

"Not true. He remodeled inside the house."

"He meant how you handled stock growth. I'm late saying this, Myra, but I couldn't be more proud of how you revived that ranch. I felt awful for giving it to Zeke after discovering it should have rightfully been yours."

Smiling, Myra slid her arm through his. "But see how well it turned out."

"You have a big heart, girl. You so pleased your mother by asking her to sew your wedding dress. She was afraid you'd never forgive her for nagging you to return to teaching."

Myra straightened his boutonniere. "I should've spoken up. Listen, there's our music. Are you ready to give me away?"

"With my record, should I give anything again?" He paused at the satin runner, his eyes questioning.

"Daddy, I love Zeke. And he loves me. I've never been so sure of anything than I am that marrying him is right."

"I see that by looking at you both," he said and moved them onto a trail of rose petals that led down the aisle to where Zeke greeted Myra with open arms.

* * * * *

The Lawman's Christmas Proposal

Barbara White Daille

MILLS & BOON®

Barbara White Daille and her husband still inhabit their own special corner of the wild, wild Southwest, where the summers are long and hot and the lizards and scorpions roam.

Barbara loves looking back at the short stories and two books she wrote in grade school and realising that—except for the scorpions—she's doing exactly what she planned. She has now hit double digits with published novels and still has a file drawer full of stories to be written.

As always, Barbara hopes you will enjoy reading her books! She would love to have you drop by her website for a visit, barbarawhitedaille.com.

Dear Reader,

One of the many things I love about the writing home I've found here is I'm able to share my favourite kind of stories with you. Small towns and families. Softhearted yet strong heroines. Sexy and even stronger heroes. Quirky but sometimes interfering characters. When I settle down to write—or to read—a book, those story elements are at the top of my list. I hope they're favourites for you, too.

The Lawman's Christmas Proposal has all of the above, along with Grandpa Jed up to his matchmaking tricks again and the entire town joining in on some holiday fun. Enjoy this visit to Cowboy Creek!

I always love to hear from you, so please feel free to get in touch through my website, barbarawhitedaille.com, or mailing address, PO Box 504 Gilbert, AZ 85299. You can also find me on Facebook and Twitter.

All my best to you.

Until we meet again,

Barbara White Daille

DEDICATION

To all my readers,
thank you for your support,
and Happy Holidays—no matter
which ones you celebrate!

And of course, to my number one reader, Rich.

Prologue

"Don't look now, but here comes trouble," Jedediah Garland said to his old friend Paz.

He had driven her into town to pick up a food order for the Hitching Post, the hotel he owned and where she worked as his cook. On the way, they had made a quick stop for coffee at SugarPie's, Cowboy Creek's popular sandwich shop. As usual at this early hour, they found the place filled to capacity.

The woman approaching their table owned SugarPie's, which consisted of both the shop and the adjacent bakery.

Paz looked over her shoulder, then turned back. "Why do you say trouble, Jed? Sugar is smiling."

"That she is. And that smile's telling me she's got something more than today's menu on her mind. Haven't you?" he asked as the woman came to a halt beside their table. He gestured to an empty chair. "Take a seat, and let's hear whatever load of gossip you've got for us this morning."

Sugar grinned at him. She plopped into a pink-cushioned chair beside Paz, who scooted her chair over to allow the sturdy businesswoman a little more elbow room.

"Now, Jed," Sugar said in her soft Southern drawl, "how did you ever know I had something to say?"

He shrugged. "That not-so-sugar-sweet smile on your face is a dead giveaway." He crossed his arms over his chest. "Let's have it."

"Well…" After a quick look around the crowded shop, she leaned forward and said, "Lyle stopped in this morning."

Jed nodded, knowing she meant Lyle Weston, Cowboy Creek's sheriff.

"Is there something wrong?" Paz asked.

Sugar shook her head. "No. Well…there is and there isn't. Mitch is home."

Attention caught, Jed leaned forward. "Home? You mean to stay?"

Sugar shrugged. "Lyle doesn't know for sure himself. But he'll settle for having the boy here till the holidays."

No wonder the woman had been grinning like a fool. Mitch was the sheriff's oldest son, now an officer with the Los Angeles Police Department. While Lyle was fit to bust with pride over all the boy's commendations, no one in town liked the idea of him living so far away.

Trouble was, nobody knew what had been to blame for Mitch's departure. And at the moment, Jed didn't know what had led to the boy's return.

One of the waitresses signaled to Sugar from over near the kitchen. She hustled away, leaving Jed and Paz staring at each other.

"Oh, Jed," Paz said in a low voice. "I know that look. You're at it again."

His grin must have rivaled Sugar's, and no doubt Paz had accurately read his mind.

A self-proclaimed matchmaker, he'd had some success bringing two of his granddaughters together with the men meant for them. "Well, why not?" he demanded. "The Christmas season's almost upon us—and isn't that the time for miracles? Besides, no sense putting myself out to pasture when I'm on a winning streak on the track. *And* when I've got one granddaughter still unattached."

"But, Jed…you can't think Andi is ready for a relationship yet."

"I don't think she knows what she's ready for." He looked down at his coffee cup rather than meet Paz's eyes. He couldn't admit she had a point.

As her gaze caught his again, the tears in her eyes told him he didn't have to confess a thing. She was as much a part of his family as Tina, the granddaughter they shared and who was now happy and settled, thanks to their efforts.

Paz knew as well as he did that the entire family feared his widowed granddaughter, Andi, would never be happy again.

Chapter One

Two days later

With the finesse of a well-trained pickpocket, Mitch Weston snagged a carrot from the vegetable tray his mother was preparing. Of course, a skilled pickpocket wouldn't have been dumb enough to flash the stolen goods—at least, not until he put them up for sale on some street corner.

Mitch, on the other hand, chomped down on the carrot in full view of his mom.

"You don't eat enough," Nancy said.

"I do," he countered. "But I'm betting while I'm here, you're going to do your best to fatten me up."

In the two days he'd been home again, this was the first chance they'd had to talk alone, and he instinctively knew the direction she would take any private conversation between them.

With a long oak table large enough to fit the family, the kitchen didn't offer much room to hide. With his four younger brothers and sisters living at home, there wasn't much privacy in the entire house. And with the way he had been feeling lately, he'd rather have solitary confinement.

"Your father mentioned he'll try to be home early tonight for a change," Nancy said. "But you know how hard it is to get him away from the office. About as difficult as it is to get you back here for a visit."

His mom hadn't intended it, he knew, but her gentle nudging only reminded him he shouldn't be here now. It wasn't that he didn't love his family. He just didn't enjoy coming back to his hometown. And this time, he didn't want to think about the circumstances that had brought about his return. The disaster that had left him lying on a cold concrete floor next to his partner's body.

"I hope you won't have to rush off too soon."

He had missed Thanksgiving by just a few days, and already both she and his dad had hinted they hoped he'd stick around for Christmas. He hadn't had the heart to disillusion them. Hell, he didn't have a reason. Yet.

This enforced time away from the job could end in an instant. Before the holidays, he had appointments scheduled with both the surgeon who had patched up his knee and the department shrink who thought his mind needed some patching, too. Good reports from them would put him right back where he belonged.

Bending down, he kissed her temple. "Let's not get into my visits again right now, Mom, okay?"

"Your lack of visits, you mean." She shot him a glance from eyes the same shade of blue he'd inherited from her. Since he'd gotten his height from his dad, she had to reach up to rest her hand on his shoulder. "I'm worried about you, sweetheart. We're *all* worried about you."

"Don't be." Unable to handle seeing her tears, he turned to grab a stalk of celery he had no taste for. "I'll be fine in no time, just as soon as the last of the stitches dissolve."

Yeah, he'd be all fixed up and ready to get back to work.

Nancy returned to chopping vegetables. "You had a call while you were out to SugarPie's for coffee."

He tensed. "From the department?"

She shook her head. "No, from Jed Garland. He heard you were back in town and wants you to get in touch."

He nodded. As with most of the guys from his high school, he had once worked as a wrangler on Garland Ranch. He hadn't seen his old boss for a while…the same length of time he'd been away from his family. The look in Nancy's eyes said she'd just had a similar thought. That, and knowing why he'd returned now, added fresh layers of guilt.

"I'm surprised it took him this long to find out I'm back in town," he said. "He's usually right on top of everything that happens in Cowboy Creek. A regular old gossip, that's Jed."

To his relief, his mother laughed. "Gossip and more. He's in the matchmaking business now."

"What?"

"They've restored the Hitching Post's banquet hall and reopened the honeymoon cabins. Tina and Cole were married from the chapel in June. They're planning to hold the first guest wedding there around Christmas."

"Jed, a matchmaker," he said with a laugh. "Who'd have believed it? Then again, he's always had a knack with people." His former boss had always been there for him, too, especially in those days right out of school when Mitch felt he couldn't talk to his dad. "I should stop by and check in with him."

"You certainly should. He's eager to see you." She set the vegetable platter in the refrigerator. "And when I saw Paz at the L-G Store yesterday, I promised her some of the surplus I'd canned from my garden last fall. Just give me a few minutes to box up a few jars, and you can take them along with you."

Fighting yet more guilt about his need for space from his family, he nodded. He knew how much they all loved him, but he had to have a break from seeing them tiptoeing through the house and talking in hushed voices, as if they were attending a wake.

Yet why wouldn't they act that way in his company?

Thanks to him, a damned good cop was dead.

LATER THAT AFTERNOON, a warm one even for the tail end of November in New Mexico, Mitch parked near the barn on Garland Ranch. He found Jed Garland standing in the sunshine near the corral. As he loped across the yard toward his former boss, Jed smiled.

Since he'd last seen him, the other man's face had developed a few more wrinkles, and his hair had turned completely white. But he still had the same piercing blue eyes and the firmest handshake around.

"Good to see you again, boy." Jed's fingers kept his trapped for another long beat before he let go.

Mitch nodded. "You're looking good yourself. So is the Hitching Post. I see you've made some changes around here."

"Yep. Got the signpost redone and the whole place painted."

"Yeah, my mom said you're in the wedding business again."

"That we are." Jed's guileless expression put Mitch on alert. "We'll be all set whenever you're ready for our services."

"For a wedding?" Laughing, he shook his head. "Thanks, but I'm not the type to settle down."

"That's not what you once said about staying in Cowboy Creek, though, is it? You'd always planned to follow in your dad and granddad's footsteps and join the sheriff's department—yet you went and became a big-city policeman."

"Yeah. I'm a big-time LA cop." Mitch said the words with a hint of bitterness backed by the knowledge of how drastically his plans had changed.

Jed nodded as if he'd read his mind, something he'd always been good at. Mitch found the trait much more disconcerting right this minute than he ever had years ago.

Probably because now he had things to hide.

"With your family's connection to the sheriff's department, I reckon it was a given you'd get involved in law enforcement even after you left town."

He nodded. "Upholding the family tradition." As he'd always known he would.

"Yep. Much as you liked horses and ranching, you never had a doubt about what you wanted to do."

"No." He still hadn't, but his decision now had repercussions he couldn't bring himself to confess to his parents or Jed. His long-held certainty, his downright arrogance that he could handle anything, had let him down when he'd needed it most. Clamping his jaws together, he hooked his biker boot on the lowest fence rung and stared across the corral.

"Let me say, son, I'm sorry about your troubles." Jed's clap on his shoulder hadn't lost any of its strength, either. "I can understand if you're finding your recuperation painful in more ways than one."

His vocal cords seized up, overpowered by the lump in his throat. Looked as though his former boss was still here for him.

Jed Garland was one mighty smart man, but he couldn't know about *all* his doubts. No one could.

Jed rested his forearms on the fence and linked his fingers together. "I'm sure you realize a man doesn't reach success without some failure along the way."

"Yeah," he said harshly, "but *my* failure resulted in someone dying."

"And in your line of work, you think that makes you stand out from the crowd?"

He shot a glance toward the other man. "You've been talking to my dad."

"'Course I have." Jed sighed. "I'm not saying what happened wasn't a tragedy. I'm not saying it's something you can ever shake off. But you're too good a cop—too good a man—not to get past this."

Looking away again, Mitch gripped the rail and squinted into the lowering sun. The bright light made his eyes water.

"Meanwhile," Jed said, "it's good you've come home."

"Temporarily." He hoped he sounded convincing. He lived and breathed law enforcement, had done ever since he was a kid watching his dad and grandpa pinning their badges to their uniforms. There was nothing else he wanted to do with his life. Nothing else he could do.

"You'll have to hang around till Pete and Cole get in from the northern pastures. And Paz will have my hide if I don't get you to stop in to see her. While you're here, you can say hello to the girls."

"The girls?" He gripped the rail even harder.

"Yeah. Tina started off handling the contractors for the upgrades to the Hitching Post, but Jane's been helping out since she moved in a few months ago. And now we've got a wedding booked, Andi's here to pitch in, too."

Jed's three granddaughters.

Tina had grown up on the ranch and become the bookkeeper for the hotel. Jane was a well-respected photojournalist, originally based in New York. And Andi…

Andi was the reason he'd left Cowboy Creek.

"If I have to look at one more fabric swatch today, I may scream."

At her cousin's pronouncement, Andi Price forced a laugh.

The hotel and its dude ranch activities had always been a big draw for the guests, but their grandfather had recently decided to reopen the banquet hall with a focus on catering wedding receptions.

So far, the one wedding they had scheduled a few months earlier had been canceled, and the business was getting off to a slow start.

"What have *you* got to scream about?" she said to Jane, only half teasing. "I'm the one dealing with the bride-to-be."

"Otherwise known as Bridezilla. Sorry, cuz."

"Don't be." She sighed. "It's the truth. I should have known better than to agree to cater a wedding for the friend of a woman I barely know."

"Yeah. Especially one who wants everything wrapped up in a bow—within a month."

"I thought I was helping Grandpa and you and Tina."

"You are. In Grandpa's words, he's tickled we've got another wedding booked."

"I know." And she couldn't let him down.

The wedding receptions had always been their late grandmother's passion. They all knew Jed was determined to see that part of the business flourish again. As Jane had once said, it only made sense to capitalize on a hotel called the Hitching Post.

"Good thing Tina's around to help," Andi said. "But what would we both do without you?" Jane's career as a photojournalist gave her a good eye for envisioning just about anything. "You know you're the one with the talent for color and line."

"You're not doing badly with those yourself. And the designs you've come up with for the banquet hall are pure genius."

"Thanks. I've attended a lot of receptions and formal dinners since I got married." Thoughts of all the events she had attended once she'd become part of the affluent Price family now blended with other memories she tried not to dwell on. "Knowledge of fancy napkin folds comes with the territory," she attempted to say lightly.

"You're doing a lot more than arranging napkins." Jane tossed a sample book onto the pile with all the others. "But, though I hate to say this, there's an area where you're not doing such a great job."

"Really?" She frowned and looked at everything they had spread out on the tabletop. "What's that?"

"I wish I knew." Jane shook her head. "You've changed since you were here at the end of the summer. There's something bothering you. Don't ask me what, because I have no idea, but I think you ought to let me in on it. We didn't spend all those vacations and holidays together here for nothing, you know."

While their grandfather and cousin had always lived in Cowboy Creek, Jane and Andi had met up at the family ranch only on school breaks. Neither of them had ever stayed at Garland Ranch longer than a summer vacation—until now. Jane had returned only a few months ago to live here permanently.

Andi had come back to help get the new venture off the ground with this Christmas wedding—and for other reasons she tried to shove aside with her bittersweet memories. "Nothing's wrong. I just…felt the kids and I needed a change of scenery. When Grandpa asked me to handle this wedding while you and Tina focused on the business end of things, it seemed like the perfect time for a visit."

Jane's gray eyes narrowed. "Sorry, but I'm not buying that. It might be hard to handle the heat in Fountain Hills, Arizona, but the scenery there is even better than it is here."

"I don't live in Fountain Hills anymore," she said quietly.

"Oh. When you'd told me the other day you and the kids had moved to an apartment, you didn't mention it was in another town." Jane touched her wrist. "Andi, if there's anything I can do, any way I can give you a hand with something, just say the word. I've got some savings built up. I know Grandpa and my dad would help you out in a heartbeat. You know that, too. And wouldn't your mother-in-law be willing to pitch in?"

"It's not money."

Truthfully, it *was* money that worried her—not enough money and not enough life insurance to pay the mortgage. Grant had insisted they could afford the too-big house in their upscale area not far from his mother. With his salary included, they had gotten by. Without it, she had been forced to sell the home where both her children had lived since they'd been born. But she couldn't tell her mother-in-law Grant hadn't provided for his family.

Just as she couldn't reveal to anyone what Grant's real job had been. How did you explain to a man's family that he worked undercover for the CIA?

But now she could tell Jane the truth. Or part of it. "It's not money so much as the need to get some space from Grant's family."

"Things have gotten that bad between you?"

"No." Andi's eyes misted. "They're great." They just didn't know he had told them the same cover story she had told her family, that he worked for a computer company with customers and suppliers all over the world. "Ginnie's always been a fabulous mother-in-law, and everyone else in his family is wonderful. Except…he's been gone for over a year, and they all act as if he's just away on business and will walk in the door again any day now."

She glanced at Jane again. "I loved Grant, you know that. *They* know that. But I've managed to accept that he's gone. I've had to, for Trey and Missy." Her children had given her the strength she'd needed to survive her loss, and now she needed to stay strong for them. "Ginnie and the rest of Grant's family still haven't come to terms with his death. They need—*I* need—to let go and move on. I know that sounds awful—"

"Not awful at all. It's a sad fact of life."

"It's beyond sad. But I just can't keep living in the past. For the kids' sake, I have to think about what comes next." Her two-year-old son and infant daughter were too young to really feel the loss of their daddy, especially when Grant's work assignments often had him out of touch for a month or two at a time. But as they got older, they would realize their loss. It was her responsibility to make sure they never lacked for anything else.

So far, she was doing a poor job.

"Then it's good you're here," Jane said. "You've got the break from Grant's family, and you can plan for the future."

She nodded. Still, despite how determined she might have sounded to Jane, she worried. Her sales assistant job at a clothing store barely covered the rent on her new apartment. She'd had to take the position. With only a year of college behind her, she had left school to get married. Relocating to Arizona, planning a wedding, buying a house and getting swept up in the Price family's social whirl had made her put school off for a while.

After she had gotten pregnant, she had tabled the idea of school indefinitely. Then she had gotten pregnant again…and Grant had died.

The end result was, she had no employable skills to speak of. The only bright spot was having a best friend with a night job who had volunteered to watch the kids while she worked during the day.

The sound of raised voices came from the hotel lobby. Andi jumped to change the subject. "That's Grandpa, and he sounds excited."

They heard a woman's laugh.

"And that's Tina," Jane said. "I wonder what's going on."

They didn't have to wait long to find out. Their cousin Tina entered the dining room. Smiling, she said, "You'll never guess who Grandpa's bringing along here with him."

She was right, at least as far as Andi was concerned.

When Jed Garland walked into the room accompanied by a tall, broad-shouldered man with a noticeable limp, her heart skipped a few critical beats. The man locked gazes with her, and her heart leaped. Never in a million years would she have forgotten those deep blue eyes or that crooked grin or the thick black hair worn just bad-boy long. Never in a million centuries would she have expected—or wished—to run into Mitch Weston again.

She could only hope that since they had last seen each other, he had forgotten all about her.

Or had learned the value of forgiveness.

Chapter Two

All through the conversation in the dining room, Mitch managed to keep his smile in place. He hadn't wanted to come in here and see Jed's granddaughters, but the man had insisted.

No. Truth was, he hadn't wanted to see Andi again.

Thankfully, his undercover work had prepared him well for slipping into different roles. He'd never had more of a need to hide his true self than he did now. His first glance at blonde, beautiful Andi today had rocked him just the way she had years ago.

Also thankfully, he'd heeded the surgeon's caution to wear his knee brace. Otherwise, he'd swear his legs would have gone out right from under him.

"How long will you be around?" Jed asked.

Instinctively, he knew the man meant how long would he be in Cowboy Creek, a topic he didn't want to get into. He forced a grin and pretended to misunderstand. "Surely you're not inviting me for supper without clearing it with Paz first."

"Of course you'll join us."

He shook his head. "You think you have to worry about Paz skinning your hide? If I didn't show up at home tonight, my mom would have me stuffed and mounted. It's the first time the whole family's sitting down together for a meal since I've gotten back." He shrugged. "Well, it'll be the whole family if my dad manages to make it home."

"He's a good one for sticking to duties," Jed said.

"And," Tina put in, "the day he retires, Cowboy Creek will lose a good sheriff."

"Which probably won't be any time soon." Mitch laughed, happy he'd detoured around the conversational land mine. "Like my grandpa, he always said he would never take off the badge." And like his dad, he wouldn't be keen on retiring, either. He didn't like even being away from the job this long. "Well, I need to head back to town."

"Don't forget that box you said your mama sent along," Jed reminded him.

"Yeah, her garden tomatoes. I'll get them out of the truck now." He moved slowly, giving his healing knee a chance to loosen up, rather than let them all see him hobbling from the room like an old man.

"I can go out with you," Tina volunteered.

"Hold on," Jed said. "I need to talk to you and Jane for a bit." He turned to Andi. "Why don't you go along with Mitch and retrieve that box for Paz? She's eager to see what she can use from it for supper."

Andi nodded. As they left the room, he caught her profile from the corner of his eye. When he and Jed had walked into the dining room, before she'd had time to raise her defenses, he'd seen the sparkle in her blue eyes and the smile on those full pink lips he'd always remembered.

Now, with her gaze frozen and her mouth pressed into a flat, determined line, she looked as if he were marching her to face a firing squad.

She didn't have that far wrong. He planned to fire a

few shots at her. Verbal ones. Questions he'd spent years asking himself.

And he didn't intend to let her go free until he got the answers.

"ALL RIGHT, ABUELO, let's hear it."

Jed frowned. The sound of Mitch's and Andi's footsteps had barely faded from the dining room.

His youngest granddaughter, Tina, sat back in her chair and stared him down. "What's so important I couldn't take a few minutes to give Mitch a hand?"

"I wanted to go over some of those estimates for the last of the cabins again."

Jane laughed. "You're in trouble if you want me here for anything involving numbers. Didn't you always say I'm the artistic one in the family?"

Tina shook her head. "It's not that, Jane. Grandpa's up to his tricks again. I know the signs. So should you." The smile that tugged at her lips gave the lie to her stern expression. "Isn't that right, Abuelo?"

He shrugged. "Yeah, I pulled a few tricks on you both. But I don't hear either of you complaining."

"We aren't," Jane said. "In fact, you know we're glad you're two for two in the matchmaking stakes."

He beamed at her.

"We're very glad," Tina agreed. "Andi's a different story. We all want to see her happy again. But trying to match her up with someone she barely knows may not be the best idea. At least, not right now."

"Huh-uh, cuz," Jane said, "as Grandpa would say, you haven't come close to hitting the mark there. You didn't hang out much with us when Andi and I used to visit. But one summer, I spent plenty of time at the barn because that's where she chose to go. And trust me, it wasn't all due to her love of riding horses."

"Really?" Tina's gaze flew from Jane to him and back again.

Barely able to believe this unexpected good fortune, he grinned. Maybe this wouldn't be his toughest match, after all. "You're saying Andi had a hankering for Mitch?"

"I am," Jane confirmed. "A major crush."

"Really," Tina said, thoughtfully this time. "And you think…"

"Yes, I think. Big-time."

"I think, too." But he wasn't yet ready to share the rest of his thoughts on the matter. "And I do more than just let an idea sit in my head. I plan."

"And you scheme," Tina said.

"Yes," Jane said, "and you force people into situations where they can't avoid each other."

"Darn straight, I do. Why wouldn't I? If I didn't, we'd all still be waiting for the two of you to get together with Cole and Pete."

Jane laughed. "So now you're determined to have a try at Andi and Mitch?"

"Darn straight," he repeated.

"Well, you won't get any argument from me, Grandpa. I go along with that."

They both turned to look at Tina.

Quiet, levelheaded, by-the-books accountant Tina looked back at them, meeting their gazes with a frown. "You really think we ought to be pushing Andi into something like this?"

"Not pushing," he said. "Assisting. If there's still interest there, why shouldn't we add a spark to it?"

"Like Grandpa did with you," Jane said softly.

His granddaughters exchanged a glance.

Finally, Tina smiled. "Well, I can't argue with that. All right. You can count me in, too."

"That's my girls," he said.

MITCH AND ANDI left the hotel through the lobby and went down the porch steps, and still, as she walked along beside him, Andi said nothing.

Apprehension showed in the tiny lines around her eyes. Why wouldn't she feel uneasy? She knew as well as he did they had unfinished business to discuss.

He remembered another day they had spent together when she hadn't said a word. When they strolled down to the creek hand in hand, accompanied only by the sounds of crickets chirping. When his heart had thumped so hard he worried she could hear that, too.

Now his heart revved only in anger. Jaw clamped tight, he strode toward the parking area behind the hotel as quickly and steadily as his leg would allow.

"Been a long time," he said as mildly as he could. A half-dozen years had passed since he'd last seen Andi. "I hear a lot has happened in your life."

She nodded. "I'm a mom now, with two children, a boy and a girl."

Her voice sounded strained, yet he couldn't mistake the pride in it. He didn't want to acknowledge even to himself how her statement made his anger rise.

When they were teens, he hadn't thought too far into the future. He had simply known he would be settled down in Cowboy Creek and wearing a gold sheriff's badge. He had also somehow known he would one day be the father of her kids.

Wrong, yet again.

He noticed she hadn't mentioned her husband. In letters, his mom filled him in on all the happenings in

Cowboy Creek. No one knew about his relationship with Andi, but as he had worked with Jed, Nancy put special emphasis on everything concerning Garland Ranch. She had told him about Andi's becoming a widow, losing her husband when he was killed in a car accident while traveling for his job.

"I was sorry to hear what happened," he said.

"Thanks."

She crossed her arms as if the sun had gone behind a cloud and left her chilled. Or as if she needed a comforting hug. He swallowed hard, feeling a small part of his anger slip away. Somehow, he managed to keep from wrapping his arms around her.

He could see the effect the loss had on her. While she was still as beautiful as ever, her face now looked stretched taut. Grief left her with nothing to soften her cheekbones or to fill the hollows beneath them.

Her eyes held a deep sadness. Tiny lines creased the skin in the outside corners. Those lines made him want to touch her. To stroke away her tension.

Instead, he reached into the truck for the box Nancy had sent along with him for the Hitching Post. The action gave him something else to do with his hands. It gave him time to pull himself together. Maybe, if he tried hard enough, that beat of time would let him swallow his remaining anger. For now.

He balanced the box on the truck's hood and turned back to her. "I'm glad Jed sent you out here. It keeps me from having to track you down."

He could see her nerves take hold in the way she brushed her hair away from her temple. The movement distracted him, again making him want to reach out to her. Unfortunately, the urge wasn't strong enough to derail his thoughts for long.

He had all the sympathy in the world for her…but that still couldn't give him answers. "What happened that summer, Andi? You were here one day and gone the next, and that was it. No note, no letter, nothing."

She didn't respond.

"You owe me an explanation, at least," he said harshly. "You walked away from me as if I'd never existed. I thought we had something good going." *Something good?* Hell of an understatement. "I guess, no matter what you'd said then, *thought* is the key word here."

Over near the corral, a horse neighed and one ranch hand called out to another. Andi's silence went on long enough to make him wonder if she would ever answer. But he'd had plenty of practice at holding on, waiting for a witness to make a statement or a perp to make a confession.

Which would she do?

"My mom got sick," she said finally.

"And when she got better, you couldn't get in touch?"

"She didn't get better. She had breast cancer, and she wasn't a survivor. Grandpa didn't tell you?"

He sucked in a breath. "I'd heard from my mom…after your mom passed away. But I didn't know she'd gotten sick back then. Or that it was why you'd left."

"She wouldn't let us tell anyone here, because she didn't want Grandpa to worry."

"Jed didn't know?"

"Not right away. And once Mom got sicker, she didn't want anyone around her except my dad and me. She held out for a long time, and we were grateful for every minute we had left with her. That's why I didn't come back here to visit until…until after she was gone."

Now he couldn't keep from touching her. He rested his hand on her arm, feeling the warmth of her skin and the way her muscle tightened beneath his fingers. "I'm sorry."

She nodded, then grabbed the carton from the hood and rushed away, but not quickly enough to keep him from seeing the tears in her eyes.

He'd gotten answers to his questions, discovered his anger had slipped away, but didn't know what he could find to replace it.

He curled his fingers, trying to hang on to the warmth he would swear he still felt from her skin.

HER ARMS TREMBLING, Andi carried the carton Mitch had given her into the Hitching Post's kitchen. She wasn't shaky from the weight of the box but from seeing him again. And she wasn't ready to consider what had brought on the reaction.

As Andi set the carton down, Paz crossed the room to investigate. "Ah, very nice," she murmured with a born chef's appreciation.

Jane merely leaned forward from her seat at the table to peer into the box. "All those healthy vegetables. They look heavy. I'm surprised Mitch didn't volunteer to carry the box for you."

Andi heard the teasing in her cousin's tone, but couldn't summon the energy to match it. She said simply, "He had to get home."

She wasn't about to tell anyone how abruptly she had turned and walked away. At the porch, she had risked a look over her shoulder and saw him climbing into his truck. Seeing the way he eased into position told her how much he must have been hurting.

She didn't want to think of him in pain.

She didn't want to think of him at all.

"That's good, right, Andi?" Jane said loudly.

She started. "What?"

Paz smiled at her. "I said, tomorrow, I will make my vegetable soup."

"That's great. Sorry, I was daydreaming..." Andi looked toward the door. "I need to check on the kids."

"They're fine," Jane said. "Grandpa has them all in the sitting room."

"Then that's where I'm headed."

"I'll go with you. Unless you need some help, Paz? And if you do, I volunteer Andi." Jane laughed.

"Oh, no, you don't," Paz said, attempting to sound stern. "Pete loves my spicy vegetable soup, and this is your chance to learn how to make it."

At the look on her cousin's face, Andi laughed.

Smiling, she left the two women and went down the hall leading from the kitchen to the hotel's lobby. She could hear voices coming from the sitting room.

Her son gave a high-pitched screech of uncontained laughter. At the sound, tears welled in her eyes. Back home again after their last visit to Cowboy Creek, Trey had reverted to being quiet and withdrawn. The change in him had started not long after Grant's death, and it broke her heart to think that maybe he, like Jane, had sensed changes in her she had hoped no one could see. She hadn't been able to hide her stress, and all her worries kept her distracted. That had to stop, especially if it was already affecting her children.

Coming back to the ranch for the holidays and to oversee the wedding had been the right decision. Being with Tina's son, Robbie, and Pete's kids was good for Trey.

But being around Mitch wasn't good for *her*.

Thank goodness he had turned down Jed's invitation to join them for dinner. Before that, she had noticed how quickly he deflected the question about him staying. She was certain he knew as well as she did Grandpa had meant his visit to Cowboy Creek.

In any case, his answer might not have mattered. He had a long drive between his parents' house in town and Garland Ranch. Judging by the trouble he'd had climbing into his truck, today's trip to the hotel could very well be his last while he was here.

In the sitting room, she found Jed in his favorite chair, holding Missy on his lap. "You'll be spoiling her, Grandpa," she scolded gently.

"Then she'll be spoiled," he said with a grin. "I'm taking every chance I can get to hold her. She's been away too long. You all have."

As she took a seat on one of the chairs near them, she forced a smile. Jed hadn't made any secret of the fact that he wanted her and the kids to move to the ranch permanently.

She wanted only to prove she could take care of her family on her own.

Trey crossed the room to them, thumping his chest with one hand. "Look, Mommy. Look what I got."

Rachel, Pete's five-year-old, followed in his footsteps. "It's Robbie's badge. Robbie let me play with it and I shared it with Trey."

"That's very nice of you, Rachel. And that's a very nice badge, sweetheart." She tapped the plastic star-shaped pin and touched her son's cheek.

"I'm the chef."

"You mean sheriff," Rachel corrected. She turned to Andi. "He means sheriff. Grandpa Jed said Mitch has a badge, too. Didn't you, Grandpa Jed?"

"I sure did."

Yes, Mitch had a badge. And a gun and an injury and a dangerous job. Grant's position had the potential for danger, too. They'd both known it. But Mitch's could expose him to risk every day of his life.

"Mitch is going to show me his badge," Rachel announced.

"Well," Andi said, "I think he must have forgotten. He's gone home already."

"But he's coming back tomorrow."

She froze. The clock on the wall chimed, saving her from having to reply for a moment. When it stopped, she looked from Rachel to Jed. "Mitch is coming here tomorrow?"

"Yeah," Robbie put in. "Grandpa says so."

Nodding, Jed patted the phone on the end table beside his chair. "Just spoke to Nancy, and she confirmed he's got nothing on his schedule. I told her I want him to come by and talk with me for a bit. And I want to make sure he catches up with Pete."

She fisted her hands in her lap. She didn't want to see Mitch again.

Watching him in the dining room surrounded by her family had been bad enough. It allowed her too much time to resurrect the many sweet memories she had buried long ago.

But to her dismay, standing outside with him had been so much worse. Being with him had forced her to see what she didn't want to admit.

Time and distance and even marriage to a man she loved with all her heart hadn't destroyed her feelings for Mitch.

Chapter Three

"Did living in LA turn you off your mom's good cooking?"

At his dad's question, Mitch started. He looked up to find everyone at the table sitting with their eyes trained on him. The combined stares of his parents, two brothers and two sisters added up to way more attention than he needed.

"Are you kidding?" He forked up a chunk of onion, chewed and swallowed it. "I'm just trying to draw out the pleasure. You always did tell me I ate too fast."

"You both do that," Nancy said.

"Hazard of the profession," his dad agreed.

Mitch nodded and tried to ignore the elephant in the room. Since he'd been home, he'd had plenty of hugs and kisses from the girls and lots of slaps on the back from the boys. He couldn't deny his family's happiness at having him here again. He just hated to see them all suffering on his behalf.

Everybody wanted to comfort him for his loss, he knew, but no one wanted to be the first to bring it up. His dad insisted on acting as though nothing much had happened. Even his mom hadn't cornered him yet, as he'd expected.

And he didn't want to think about recent events at all.

He glanced down at his plate. The roast Nancy had made for supper, always his favorite, tasted dry as dust. It wasn't Mom's good cooking that had him distracted, though. It was the vision of a slim woman with long blond hair and sad eyes.

"Your mom said you were out to Jed's place this afternoon." His dad passed him the meat platter. "How's everything at Garland Ranch?"

"And how's Daffodil?" his younger sister Laurie asked. Daffodil was an old mare living out her days at the ranch.

"I didn't go near the corral," he had to confess.

Like the typical teen she was, Laurie rolled her eyes. She loved anything that walked on four legs, but especially horses.

"You need to drop by the office," his dad said, "and say hello to the boys."

He nodded. He knew most of the men in Cowboy Creek's sheriff's department. Heck, he'd grown up with them. Considering what had happened, seeing them didn't rank high on his list. Then again, stopping by the office gave him something to do.

It might help keep his mind off Andi and his decision not to visit the ranch again.

"Oh, Mitch," Nancy said. "I forgot to tell you. You hadn't made it home yet when Jed called. He wants you to go back out to the ranch tomorrow. He seems to have something important on his mind."

Again, he had to appreciate the work that had trained him to keep his reactions hidden. He also suddenly found a lot more to like in his dad's idea. "Thanks for passing the message along. I'll probably be a while at the department tomorrow. But I'll get out there again one of these days." On another trip back home. When Andi wasn't there.

"From what your mom says, maybe you ought to make the trip a priority," his dad suggested.

"I can go with you after school," Laurie offered. "I can see Daffodil and then go for a ride."

"And," his mother said, "I told Jed I'd send along some more vegetables for Paz."

His brothers volunteered to help her box up the canning jars.

As he considered the conversation, Mitch sat back in his chair and shifted his leg to make himself more comfortable.

Nothing had been mentioned about what had brought him home. No furtive looks had been exchanged between anyone at the table. Yet somehow, he felt certain every member of his family had given the elephant in the room a strong, steady push in the right direction.

At least, from their perspective.

LATE THE NEXT AFTERNOON, accompanied by nonstop chatter from Laurie, Mitch drove up the road to Garland Ranch for the second time in two days.

She went on about her classes and friends and riding and the holiday open house Jed held every year at the hotel. He hadn't made it back for one of those parties since he'd left town to go to school. Maybe he'd be gone for this one.

He thought again about his family ganging up on him over today's trip. *Something* had made them all suddenly think the return to Garland Ranch would do him good.

Sure, they wanted him to relax and unwind and go back to being the son and brother they'd always known. That wasn't going to happen, no matter how much they tried. He would never be the man he was before the incident. The incident…

He'd trained himself to use that cop-speak every time he thought about the day. To put a professional spin on an event leaving more than one man dead. To keep from obsessing over the knowledge his partner's death was personal and a memory he would always carry with him.

He ran his hand over his face, then opened the window all the way, hoping the fresh air would chase away the images filling his mind.

"Hey," Laurie yelped. "It's December. You want me to catch pneumonia and miss the party?"

"You'd go to that open house if you had both legs and one arm in a cast."

"Sure would." She laughed.

He thought again of his family's efforts to get him out to the ranch. Their methods had sent up a red flag. Something wasn't right about their determination.

"You do much riding out at Jed's?" he asked.

"Not as much anymore," she admitted.

"Mom says you spend weekends there, though."

To his surprise, her cheeks turned red. "Well, I go to see Daffodil. She's old, you know."

"Yeah. She had been getting up there even when I worked the ranch. She always thought she should be treated like a queen."

"Jed said she earned that right. And Eddie… I mean, Pete thinks she likes when I visit."

"Sounds like Eddie-I-mean-Pete knows a thing or two about horses."

Laughing, she smacked his arm, the way she had done a hundred times before. It surprised him to realize he'd missed that, along with roughhousing with the boys.

"All right," she said, "I meant Eddie. He takes care of the stables."

Just the job he'd had the first time he'd seen Andi. The luckiest day of his life till then.

It looked as though his little sister might have the same kind of good fortune. Maybe hers would last. "Am I going to have to play biggest brother and give the guy a warning about being good to my sister?"

"Show him your gun. That'll work even better."

His hands clamped onto the steering wheel so tightly, he could barely make the turn into the drive. The flash of memory that hit made him wince.

PTSD, the psychiatrist assigned to him after the shooting had labeled it, the body giving way as remembered trauma took control. According to the shrink, the stress showed up in different ways.

Yeah, he'd dealt with that, right after the…incident. It had eased up a lot since then. He was fine. Fine, except for those nights he woke up in a sweat. And those times he paced his apartment to outrun the demons chasing him.

And, so it seemed, when he heard his baby sister joke about his weapon.

He parked near the corral on Garland Ranch and shot a glance at the woman who stood outside the fence, her back to them. Andi. He thought of all the drugs the shrink had offered him and he had refused. Seeing Andi again made him feel better than any drug ever could.

With one boot planted on the lowest rail, she watched a blond-haired little boy on a small Shetland. Her son, Trey, he had no doubt.

"That's him," Laurie said, as if she'd read his mind. But one glance told him *her* mind was on the teenager leading the horse. He'd wager he knew who that was, too.

By the time he had eased out of the truck and made his way around it, Laurie had left him far behind.

Either Andi had no interest in newcomers or she hadn't recognized Laurie as his sister, because she hadn't moved from her spot near the rail. He had time to notice the fall of blond hair around her shoulders and the way her jeans hugged her curves. He even had time to remember how it had felt to hold those curves. By the time she turned to look his way, he'd broken into a sweat brought on by the memories. *That* was the kind of healing meds he needed.

Dragging his shirtsleeve across his brow, he took a deep breath. Then he moved forward, cursing his knee brace and every halting step she had to see.

She clung to the top rail the way he'd gripped the steering wheel. Her gaze shot toward the barn.

"Eddie and Laurie are with the boy. Your son?"

She nodded.

"Tell me about your kids."

The light in her face told him he'd said the right thing. The same light he once saw when she looked at him.

"Trey is two, almost three."

"Ah. The terrible twos?" When her eyes widened in surprise, he shrugged. "I remember my brothers and sisters going through them."

"Well, I'll admit my son has had his moments." A smile lit her face even more. "It's been good for Trey to be here on the ranch and around Tina's son, Robbie, and Pete's two kids. You remember Pete Brannigan?"

He nodded. "Jed said he's ranch manager now. And he did mention the kids."

"Yes. He has a girl and boy of his own. All three of the kids are just old enough not to take any interest yet in my daughter, Missy."

"She's…?"

"Six months."

"Yeah, she's young." He did the math. By rights, he and Andi could have started a family of their own before either of her kids had been born. But she had left him, and they had lost their chance.

The sudden faraway look in her eyes prompted him into speech. "Jed tells me you're staying at the hotel."

"Temporarily," she shot back.

He winced at the echo of his response when Jed had mentioned his coming home. Hopefully, he hadn't sounded as defensive. Looked as if Andi didn't plan to stay around Cowboy Creek. Neither did he.

"I'm only here through the holidays," she added.

"This is just a short visit for me, too."

"And then you'll go back to Los Angeles."

She sounded as if what he did concerned her. He couldn't trust that he'd read her right. But he would bet good money she hadn't forgotten their summer.

He would never forget that day he'd looked across the barn to find the hottest girl he'd ever seen standing in the doorway, a blonde angel in a T-shirt, jeans and riding boots. He'd fallen head over heels and would have sworn she'd done the same.

Every day, once his work at the ranch was done, they had spent as much time together as they could. Until that one day she had just up and left without saying a word.

But here they were.

He had the feeling she was about to repeat history and walk off. "I belong in LA," he said, half to remind himself and half to keep her with him, as pathetic as both of those felt for him to admit. "I'm with the police department."

"That's a dangerous job. A tough one for you, and just as hard on your wife and kids."

As she ought to have seen by her own husband's death,

in the right—or wrong—circumstances, any job had its risks. He shook his head. "I don't have a wife. Or any family there. It's just me."

Alone at home. On his own on the job.

And now standing here beside the girl who'd started him down that road.

He couldn't stop himself from reaching up to gently stroke the fine, lined skin near her eye.

"I'm not wearing well," she said with a forced laugh.

"We've all gotten older." But maybe not wiser. He cupped her cheek with his palm. The warmth spreading through his hand more than made up for the risk he'd taken in touching her. For a brief moment, she tilted her head, resting against his hand. Her reaction closed the gap left by all the years they had lost. It finally chased away all his resentment.

Her eyes misted. She turned away. "I'm sorry about not contacting you. Everything was just too much for me. I had to focus on my mom."

She looked toward the barn, as if planning to head over there. He didn't want her to leave.

"That's a big load for an eighteen-year-old to handle," he said.

"For anyone to handle, believe me." She sighed. "Sometimes, life doesn't seem fair."

"That's because it isn't. We all get the luck of the draw—and sometimes it's bad luck."

Just what he'd heard from everyone back in LA.

After a quick nod, Andi walked away.

He leaned against the rail, easing the pressure on his knee, and watched her go. That summer afternoon years ago, he'd had no idea he wouldn't see her again. Would the same thing happen now? Was he simply destined to have bad luck when it came to her?

Though he could parrot the words his buddies on the force had told him, that didn't mean he wanted to accept their verdict about the situation.

And though everything in him said he should keep his distance from Andi, that didn't mean he had the strength to heed his own warning.

Chapter Four

As she crossed the yard to the barn, Andi could almost feel Mitch's gaze on her back. She could definitely still feel the warmth filling her from the touch of his hand against her cheek. In that one all-too-brief moment, she had changed into a teen again, and he had become the boy she loved. In his eyes in that moment, she saw the boy who loved her, too.

But their teenagers-in-lust days were long over.

Resolutely, she focused on the group standing in the barn doorway and kept moving toward them, away from Mitch and his warm hands and his crooked smile and his unfamiliar stiff-legged walk.

When she approached the group, her son gave her the wide grin that always reminded her so much of his daddy. "Mommy, I rided Bingo."

"I saw you," she said. "You did a great job."

"He did," Eddie, the stable hand, agreed. "I'll be happy to give him another practice run anytime."

"I'm sure Trey would love that."

"Yeah, Mommy, wanna ride horse. Bi-i-ig horse."

"Don't you worry, mister," Eddie said, "we'll get you up on Bingo again tomorrow. How's that?"

"Yay!" Trey clapped his hands. No sign of the terrible twos now, as Mitch had mentioned.

With a smile, she watched Eddie ruffle her son's hair. She didn't need a policeman's skills to note that the tall, quiet teen grew much more talkative every time Mitch's sister Laurie arrived at the ranch. Whenever she saw the two of them together, the pair made her think of Mitch and herself.

With luck, this couple's summer romance would end more happily than her and Mitch's had done.

When he came to stand beside her, she turned to Trey. "Come on, sweetie, we need to go back to the hotel."

"I don't wanna! Wanna see Daff now."

"So do I," Laurie said quietly over his head. "Is it okay if I take him with me for just a few minutes?"

"I'll go and keep an eye on things," Eddie said.

His tone made it evident he considered himself responsible for everything on the ranch. Just the way Mitch had when she'd met him.

The trio entered the barn.

She went to take a seat on one of the stools the cowhands had left a few yards from the doorway. She hoped Mitch would get the hint, would follow the rest of them in to the stalls or turn and go to the hotel.

But no, he was ambling her way, moving slowly. Maybe to control his limp?

She tried not to stare. Not to let her emotions show in her expression. As a teenager, he had been a star athlete, she knew. Football quarterback. Pitcher for Cowboy Creek's baseball team. Whatever had happened to him on the job, it would devastate him if he couldn't return to being just as active.

He took the stool beside hers, his leg stretched out before him. He sat so close, she could count the stitches running down the leg of his jeans. "Seems like Jed's training up another hand to join the crew."

"Grandpa's good at that."

"Yeah," he agreed. "And I should know."

"You needed to be trained?"

"Sure did. I might have bummed a ride or two on a friend's horse when I was a kid, which meant I could handle myself in the saddle, but that was about it."

"Why did Grandpa take you on in the first place?"

He raised a brow. "This is a dude ranch. Considering all the charm and good looks I had back then, you really have to ask that question?"

Of course, she didn't have to ask. She remembered. He'd had plenty of charm and tons of good looks, and the years hadn't taken any of that away. Not that she would ever admit it to him. "You don't need either of those to groom a horse."

"Ha," he said with a laugh. "You never saw me trying to charm Daffodil on one of her cranky days. But Jed probably thought I'd make a good candidate for working with the hotel guests. Growing up in a family of seven, I learned how to get along with people. Like that kid in there." He jerked his thumb toward the barn doorway. "That one's a real talker."

"When your sister's around."

"Is that so? Well, I seem to remember girls having that effect on me. Especially you." He'd lowered his voice to a husky murmur.

She wrapped her arms around her waist and fought an urge to run.

"Tina was always the quietest cousin," he said, "but you were on the quiet side, too. At first, I couldn't get you to say two words in a row to me. Maybe it's because you were an only child."

No, because she was a tongue-tied teenager who

blushed every time he looked at her. A tendency she didn't seem to have outgrown.

"If not for you wanting to ride," he said, "I'd bet I never would have met you."

If he only knew. On previous vacations here, she had always enjoyed riding. Her interest had skyrocketed the summer she had discovered the new stable hand with the tousled black hair, stripped to the waist of his low-riding jeans, pitching hay into a stall. Suddenly, along with riding, she had felt the urge for twice-daily visits to Daffodil. She had dragged poor Jane, who couldn't have cared less about horses, along with her for company. And camouflage.

"You're still quiet," he said.

She shrugged. "I guess we don't have much to say to each other, do we? We never did much together, except…"

"Except hang out at the barn and sneak away to make out every chance we got?"

Her cheeks burned. "We were kids, Mitch—"

"We're grown-ups now."

"—and that's all in the past. We don't need this trip down memory lane."

"Why not? They're fond memories, aren't they?"

She heard bitterness in his tone but read something else in his face. Something she couldn't afford to see. Instead, she gazed past the corral in the direction of the creek. Another thing she couldn't afford to envision. "Fond memories? Even the final ones?"

From the corner of her eye, she saw his hand clench on his thigh. Why was she reminding him about the way things had ended?

Because she knew they couldn't start anything between them again.

"I'd better go check on Trey."

He laid his hand on her arm. "Maybe I'll give you a second chance for walking away without a word."

"Thanks. But maybe I don't want one." She pulled her arm free.

"I don't need to ask if you still feel something for me, Andi. Your reaction when I touched you a few minutes ago already gave me the answer."

She shook her head. "That was just another quick trip down memory lane."

"Yeah? And don't your memories match mine?" He leaned toward her.

It took more effort than she wanted to look away from him. "Nothing matches anymore, Mitch."

"That sounds like a woman at the end of her rope. What's wrong?"

The question made her jump, but she forced herself to turn to him again. "Nothing's wrong."

"You know, one of the first things they teach rookies is to notice a perp's expression. Always watch the ones who won't look you in the eye—but pay equal attention to the ones who stare you down."

"I told you, nothing's wrong. When I said nothing matches, I just meant we don't have anything in common anymore." She rose from the stool. If he caught her eye again, he would trap her in that lie.

A few hurried steps past him took her into the barn, where she hoped the cool shade would ease the flush in her cheeks. What she would need to cool the rest of her, she didn't know.

Yes, she had lied. She and Mitch had plenty in common. A mutual interest in each other. Leftover lust from their summer together. And somehow, a spark that survived despite the fact she had left him without a word.

STUNNED BY HIS close encounter with Andi, Mitch stayed in place on the stool.

He'd been so wrapped up in the idea of seeing her again today, he had spent most of the morning exercising his leg on a slow walk through town, made only a brief trip to the sheriff's office after lunch and found himself sitting outside the school waiting to pick up his sister the minute the final bell rang.

Now he had arrived at the ranch, things hadn't gone nearly the way he'd planned.

A black stallion trotted into the stable yard. Mitch recognized the cowboy astride the horse—Pete Brannigan, his former wrangling buddy and now the manager of Garland Ranch. By the time Pete dismounted, Mitch had risen to his feet.

The other man approached him, leading his mount. "Jed told me you were back in town. Been a heck of a long time, Mitch."

"Yeah, it has."

As they shook hands, Eddie came to lead the horse away. Mitch noted Laurie walking beside the boy. He tried not to notice Andi and her son emerging from the barn. She nodded at Pete before turning away.

The foreman eyed him. "I'm glad you stopped by. If you've got time, how about you give me a chance to shower, then come on over for a brew?" Pete lived in the manager's house on the property, barely the length of a couple of baseball fields from the corral.

"Sure. Jed wanted us to get together. We might as well kick back while you tell me what that's about."

"Not a clue," Pete said. "I saw him around noontime,

but he didn't say a word. You'll have to find out from him for us both. Hey, Andi," he called.

She turned back to face them. Mitch saw how carefully she kept from looking his way. No matter what she said, there was something not right. He'd have to prove that to himself…to make up for the last time he hadn't followed his instincts.

"The boss was looking for this former cowboy earlier. Take Mitch along to the Hitching Post and help him track down Jed, will you?"

When she nodded, Pete strode into the barn.

At a much slower pace, Mitch walked to catch up with Andi and her boy. One look at her brittle smile and suddenly rigid shoulders told him how she felt about having him join them. She couldn't have cared that much about escorting him to the hotel. Maybe she was afraid of giving herself away.

No matter how quickly she'd backed off from him and run into the barn, it had been too late. He'd already seen the truth in her widened eyes and reddening cheeks, just as he had in her reaction to his touch over at the corral. She wanted him just as much as she had years ago. But something was bothering her. Holding her back. Something she didn't want to share with him, and maybe with anyone.

"You cowboy?" her son asked.

The kid must have remembered Pete calling him a former cowboy. He shook his head. "No, I'm a cop."

"What's a cop?"

"A policeman. You know, like a sheriff. With a uniform and a badge."

"A badge? *Mine.*"

Andi took his hand. "You borrowed Robbie's badge, Trey, remember?"

"Mine," the kid repeated.

Mine, Mitch had once thought when it came to the kid's mother.

Wishing something so didn't make it happen. He'd first learned that years earlier with Andi's abrupt departure. He'd had his latest lesson only a few weeks ago during an undercover op shot to hell.

Feeling he had failed in both instances didn't sit well with him at all. He couldn't save his partner, but he sure could try to find out what troubled Andi.

"JED IS OUT by the honeymoon cabins, I think," Paz told them. "Tina wanted to show him something the workmen had done."

Sagging in relief, Andi rested one hip against the kitchen table. With her son's short legs, the walk back to the hotel had seemed to last forever. She and Mitch had discovered both the sitting room and Tina's office empty. Now, thanks to Paz, she could send Mitch off on his own.

"Looks like you're busy in here," he said.

Paz nodded. Cooling racks filled with cakes and cookies had taken over almost every flat surface. The kitchen smelled of cinnamon and cloves. "It's never too early to start my Christmas baking."

"Cookie, Paz," Trey demanded.

"What do you say?" Andi prompted him.

"Please."

Smiling, Paz took a cookie from one of the racks.

"Let's go track down Jed," Mitch said.

Andi frowned. "You can do that on your own. I'll stay here with Trey."

"I think I've forgotten how to get to the cabins."

She glanced at him, then away again. After what he had said about cops, she didn't know which was worse from his perspective, locking gazes with him or refusing to look his way at all. She knew what was better for her. Looking. Staring. Getting her fill.

Better for her, but much too risky.

"That's fine, Andi," Paz said. "You leave Trey with me and go right along with Mitch."

"Great," he said, halfway across the room without waiting for her answer.

Grimly, she followed him out to the porch and down the steps. He took his time, favoring his bad leg. Despite her irritation with him, she had to bite her lip to keep from asking how much he hurt.

She was so wrapped up in concern for him, she hadn't realized he'd reached the bottom step. He turned back, catching her off guard. Instinctively, she bit down harder, then winced from her own pain.

"It is that bad?" he asked. "Seeing how I hobble down steps like a two-year-old who's just learned to walk?"

"You handled those steps quite a bit better than my two-year-old does," she said matter-of-factly. Still, knowing how Mitch must feel made her eyes mist.

"Those tears for me?"

"Of course they're not." While she had stopped a couple of steps up, he stood on the ground, putting them at eye level. This time, she was determined not to look away, no matter how his cop's training would interpret her stare. No matter how shaky her reaction to his blue eyes left her feeling. "I accidentally bit my lip and it hurts. Not as much as your knee must, though, I'm sure."

"I don't need your pity, Andi."

"That wasn't pity. It was a not-very-smooth attempt to find out what happened."

"Why? So you can fix it?"

"I never said—"

"You didn't have to. There's nothing wrong with me a few weeks of rest won't cure. And maybe this."

Before she could blink, he had cupped the back of her head as gently as he had cupped her cheek, urging her toward him. Once his mouth met hers, she had nothing but the memories of another time and another place and all the feelings that came with them.

For this one long, heart-stopping, teenager-in-lust-again moment, she loved Mitch Weston as desperately as she had the last day they had been together. She kissed him as desperately, too, without a thought for her tender lip or her obligations or anything but how she'd always felt when Mitch held her. He was broader now, sturdier, more muscled…and an even better kisser.

Reluctantly, she pulled herself together, resting her hands on his wide shoulders to anchor herself. No, to prepare herself. Finally, she pushed away.

Her legs trembling, she went down the rest of the steps, fighting the urge to raise her hand to her mouth. To touch the warmth he had left against her lips. To hold back the words she would not and couldn't afford to say.

With unsteady hands, she smoothed her hair as she attempted to catch her breath. "Are you crazy? It's broad daylight and we're out here in the open and anyone could have seen us. I told you I don't want to fix you." *Liar.* "So just what was *that* supposed to prove?"

"I thought it might help speed the healing."

"Of my lip?"

"No, my knee." His chest rose, as if he were struggling with his breathing, too. He gave her a crooked smile. "All right, that was also to prove you haven't forgotten me any more than I've forgotten you."

"Maybe I haven't. They say you never forget your—"

first love "—first kiss. But I've had other kisses since then."

He whistled. "That's cold, Andi."

"That's the truth."

"All of it?"

She stiffened. "What do you mean?"

"C'mon, don't play dumb with me." His laugh sounded strained. "You kissed me back just now."

"Like I had a choice?"

"We always have choices." For a moment, his face hardened and his eyes looked bleak.

"I don't think so. Not always." He was remembering their past. Good. She wouldn't have to lay things out for him. And hopefully, once she had finished here, she would never again have to face a sneak attack on her pitifully weak defenses. "When I left you that summer, it wasn't my decision. But I *am* making the choice to walk away now."

Chapter Five

So much for the shy little Andi he had once known. The girl he'd had to coax out of her shell had grown into a strong woman whose still-quiet manner hid one heck of a sucker punch. He could use her as the bad cop to his good cop during an interrogation. He could even admire her skill—if not for the fact that she'd used it against him… and then walked away.

He had changed from the day he first met her, too, in more ways than he wanted to deal with at the moment. But despite everything, he still had a few skills of his own, including his bulldog tenacity when it came to getting to the truth of a matter.

He glanced after Andi, whose hip-swaying departure just about wiped her words from his memory bank. It definitely overrode any annoyance he'd felt at getting sucker punched.

Besides, he'd faced a hell of a lot worse and was still standing. He wasn't about to let her knock him down. Or to let her get away.

He followed her across the Hitching Post's backyard toward the cabins a few hundred yards ahead. "Looks like Jed's had the honeymoon havens fixed up, along with the rest of the place."

"Yes," she said shortly, not looking at him. "I'm surprised you noticed the improvements, considering you didn't seem to recall much about the cabins."

He laughed. She had seen through his ruse. No big deal. He'd never hoped to get away with claiming he didn't know the location of the site—not when they'd once spent a rainy afternoon making out in one of those honeymoon havens.

In two strides, he caught up to her. "I recall plenty. But you want to help jog the rest of my memories?" When her cheeks turned pink, making her eyes look even more blue, he couldn't hold back a smug smile. Yeah, she remembered that day, too.

Up ahead, Jed and his granddaughter Tina came around the side of one of the cabins. Jed hailed them with a wave.

They met halfway, in the shade of a few pines that would protect the cabins from the sun of a long New Mexico summer.

"How's everything?" Andi asked Jed.

"Looking just fine."

"The contractors only finished up the remaining cabins this past week," Tina explained.

Mitch nodded. "My mom said you've all done a lot of renovations inside the hotel, too."

"We sure have," Jed said. "You'll have to get Andi to take you on the grand tour."

He sensed more than saw her stiffen beside him.

"Of course," she said too politely. "But right now I've got to get back and take care of business."

"Right," Tina said. "We need to get our order ready for the wedding favors. I'll go back with you."

Again, he felt rather than saw Andi's reaction—relief as she instantly turned away. He went to follow her, then paused, recalling why they had come out this way to begin with. "I got word you wanted me to stop by again," he said to Jed.

The older man nodded. "Yeah. Let's sit. You girls go on ahead. Your old grandpa can't keep up."

"Oh, you—" Andi cut herself off, but Mitch had picked up on her tone. She'd held back a teasing response—because of *him*?

"Okay, Abuelo," Tina said. "See you both later."

As the women left, Jed gestured to a wooden bench on the porch of the nearest cabin.

He nodded. Though he hadn't been on his feet for that long, he felt grateful for the chance to sit again.

No matter what Andi had begun to say about Jed's ability to get around, he had to admit, at the moment, the older man's healthy stride would put his to shame. It wasn't pain that drove him to the bench but the stiffness that locked up his knee from time to time. Sitting was the worst danged thing he could do for it, but he'd rather have the opportunity to get limbered up again before he had to cross the yard with Jed. With luck, he would manage a few stretches stealthily enough to keep his former boss from noticing.

He gave thanks Andi had left. Her denial hadn't carried much weight, not when her eyes had filled with pity, something he refused to accept from anyone and especially not from her.

After they took their seats on the bench, he watched the women cross the yard, Tina's dark, waist-length braid contrasting sharply with Andi's flowing blond waves. No doubt in his mind which sight he preferred. The thought of running his hands through Andi's hair made more than just his bad knee suddenly ache from stiffness. Made him realize how hot he'd gotten over the girl who'd left him behind.

More than anything, his reactions made him see staying close to her might be more of a challenge than he had anticipated.

"Nice view, isn't it?"

Startled, he turned to stare at Jed. He'd forgotten he had company on this bench.

Jed waved his hand. "A pleasant view of the ranch for any honeymooners who stay out here instead of in the hotel."

"Yeah…it's nice scenery." Especially over near the hotel, where the women were climbing the porch steps. "So, you wanted to see me again."

"I do." Jed ran his hand over his pure white hair.

An unmistakable tell. Mom had been right. Something was up with Jed. And the familiar gesture told Mitch his former boss was about to clue him in. "What's up?"

"Your mama says your time is pretty much your own, and I could use your help."

"Anything I can do, you know I will."

Jed smiled. "I figured that. Well, you know we tend to get busy here around the holidays."

"I remember." The dude ranch had always been popular with folks wanting a break from colder climates.

"Now we've got Christmas *and* a wedding to prepare for, both coming up in less than a month. My girls are doing most of the work on their own, and they could use an extra pair of hands."

Mitch nodded slowly.

"Normally, I'd get a couple of the boys in here to give them some assistance. But we're shorthanded, and Pete's up to his eyeballs in work as it is. If you could manage to spend some time around here, you'd be doing us all a favor."

Mitch nodded again. Compared to some of Jed's plans,

this one sounded harmless. And he had meant it when he said he would do anything to help Jed.

To tell the truth, he would be doing himself a few favors, too.

He could avoid his family's hushed voices and averted gazes.

He could bypass some trips to the sheriff's department in town. No matter how often his dad encouraged him to drop in, he knew how all those visits would make him look. He'd seem no better than an old retired cop who took his vacations anywhere from Maine to Alaska but spent those days hanging out with the local law.

Most of all…best of all…he would have a reason to hang around the ranch. A chance to be near Andi and to find out what was up with her.

If she wouldn't tell her family what was worrying her, she'd have to tell someone. She needed *an outlet*, as his department-assigned shrink would say. Considering her decision to walk away from him, getting her alone had presented a problem. Jed had just handed him the solution.

With all those perks attached to the request, how could he turn the man down?

He couldn't appear too eager, though. "Sure," he said casually. "I'll be happy to lend a hand. For whatever time I'm in town."

"WHAT DO YOU think of this design?" Andi turned the pattern book on Tina's desk to show her cousins the photo she was indicating.

With the waitress on duty ready to set the tables for dinner, they'd had to move all their samples from the dining room into Tina's small office off the lobby. It didn't matter to her where they worked, as long as she kept busy enough to keep her mind off Mitch…and that kiss that had made her lose control.

Her face burning, she glanced quickly at her cousins. Luckily, Jane and Tina had both switched their attention to the pattern book.

Jane looked at the fabric swatch in the photo. "I like the other one better."

"I like this one. Then Tina gets to choose."

"Oh, no, I don't," their cousin said. "You two are the experts."

"We need a tiebreaker."

"And if Tina doesn't want to be on the spot," Jane said, "she shouldn't be. Shay's in the kitchen. Don't you think we should get her in on this? She's got a good eye, too."

"Great idea," Tina said.

Shay, who was a frequent visitor to the Hitching Post, was dropping off an order of ice cream. Though Paz made the desserts for the hotel dining room, they had contracted SugarPie's to provide the wedding cakes and pastries for the receptions. But when it came to ice cream, they relied on the Big Dipper, the shop not far from SugarPie's in the heart of Cowboy Creek's small business district.

As Tina left the office to track down the other woman, Andi caught Jane looking at her with a thoughtful expression.

"I see Mitch is back again," Jane said. "And he appeared just when you happened to be at the corral."

She snapped her head up. "That was a coincidence."

"On your part or his?"

"What does that mean?"

"It seems *way* too coincidental he showed up at the same time you were standing there waiting."

"I wasn't *waiting*. I was checking on Trey." She caught Jane's grin and realized her cousin was teasing. She also knew she had overreacted. Forcing a smile, she added, "So…you suspect Eddie and Laurie of synchronizing the clocks on their cell phones?"

"No, actually, that hadn't occurred to me." Jane's tone turned serious again. "Maybe fate stepped in, leading Mitch here at just the right time."

"No. It was Grandpa wanting to see him. And Laurie asking him to bring her to the ranch for a ride." Hoping to close the subject, she glanced at the pattern book again. "There's no need to wait for Shay. I don't know why you're digging your heels in over this. Now, look. This morning, you agreed with me this pattern's a better match for the tableware."

"Yeah, and I've always agreed that you and Mitch made a good match."

"*Jane.* Please."

"Now, you look," Jane said quietly. "You can't hide anything from me. I know how you felt that summer you were seeing him. And I heard you crying the night before you left the ranch. You cared a lot. So did he. You two really had a chance together."

A chance she had blown back then, and that circumstances now put out of her reach. "That was a long time ago." Her children's births and husband's death ago.

"And here you are, in town at the same time."

"Just another coincidence."

"I won't argue that. But my point is, how likely is it this will happen again soon?"

Focusing on the pattern book kept her from meeting Jane's eyes. It couldn't help close her ears to Jane's softly spoken words.

"Maybe you both need to take this second chance."

Shay walked into the office, saving Andi from a response.

"Shay," Jane said, "you're still planning to waitress for us the night of the wedding?"

"Oh, yes, I'll be here. I'm looking forward to it."

Still shaken by Jane's statement, Andi fought to focus on the other woman. "How's your gran?" They all knew Shay's elderly grandmother had been having some health issues.

"Not too bad. I'm on my way to pick her up now. But Tina said you wanted to show me something?"

"Yes, if you have a few minutes." She indicated the two samples. "Which one?"

"This one's a better match," Shay said immediately, pointing.

"Perfect," Jane said. "You've got a good eye, too."

Shay had chosen the same pattern Jane had so suddenly been unable to make up her mind about.

"I always did like interior decorating," Shay said. "Well, if that's all you need, I'd better get going."

After she had left the room, Andi frowned and turned to Jane. "'Perfect'?" she repeated. "That was another rapid turnaround on your part, wasn't it?" When her cousin shrugged, she added, "You set me up. You gave Tina a reason to leave the room just to give yourself a chance to question me about Mitch."

Jane shrugged. "Possibly. But that's one thing I haven't changed my mind about. You and Mitch. Remember what I said?"

Maybe you both need to take this second chance.

"Oh, I didn't forget. But it's not going to happen."

AS PETE HANDED him an uncapped bottle of beer, Mitch nodded his thanks and set it down on the coffee table in the other man's living room.

Outside, the sun was hanging low, filtering through the curtains. On the other side of the room, a handful of kids played a game with blocks, toy cars and a plastic runway that seemed to involve a lot of rules.

He nodded toward a blonde five-year-old. Pete's daughter. "Rachel seems to have taken charge over Tina's and Andi's boys."

"She does that often," Pete admitted ruefully. "But I'm getting her to learn the value of sharing. I think."

He looked at Pete's son, playing happily by himself in a playpen nearby. Pete said the boy was just two, while Andi's son would soon turn three.

He'd been gone long before any of the kids had been born. Long before Andi had become a wife and mom.

He took a swig of beer, then, forcing a laugh, shook his head. "Have you got enough kids around here to keep Jed happy?"

"Ha. Not even close. At least, not close and permanent, which is the way he would like. I know he wants Andi to settle down here with her two."

"And she doesn't go along with that?"

"Doesn't seem to. According to her, she's here for the holidays and to help get the bridal business off the ground, then she's headed back home."

"Home being…"

"Arizona. Fountain Hills, Scottsdale, somewhere around there."

"Nice area, so I've heard. And steep, if you're talking Fountain Hills."

"I gather you mean money more than the elevation. That's what I hear, too. But her husband comes from money. It'll be hard for her without him, of course, but I reckon she'll be all right financially."

He nodded. Between the man's background and his responsibility to a wife and kids, Andi's husband would have been prepared to take care of his family. Mitch took a long swallow from his bottle. "It was a shock, hearing he'd gotten killed."

"Yeah." Pete shrugged. "I don't know all the details. I'm not sure anyone does."

Another family crisis Andi had kept from the rest of her family and friends. Her mother's illness. Now her husband's death. How much more would she try to handle on her own?

He knew what she was going through, knew what grief could do. He'd fought his way through it. And he wouldn't leave her to fight alone.

"What was it the boss wanted us to talk about?" Pete asked.

He shrugged. "He just thought the two of us would want to catch up. I'm glad I managed to run into you this afternoon. You can't have too much free time if you're shorthanded."

His beer halfway to his mouth, Pete paused. "What are you talking about?"

"What *Jed* and I talked about. He said you were short a few cowhands."

At that, Pete grinned and shook his head. "Your old buddy's on the payroll now, and you know he's worth any three wranglers."

Mitch and his best friend, Cole, now Tina's husband, had gone through school together. Cole had always been a hard worker and had done nothing but ranch work since they'd graduated.

The other man frowned and watched the kids play. After a few minutes, he turned back. "Did he say something about work not getting done around here?"

"No, nothing like that."

"What else did he say?"

"That you're snowed under. He asked if I'd help the

women out over at the hotel, give them a hand with moving furniture in the banquet hall, put up some of the Christmas decorations."

After a moment, Pete said, "The boys would normally help, but we've got plenty going on around the ranch to keep them busy. That's just like Jed to put another able-bodied man to work."

"He never did miss a chance to do that." He gave a rueful laugh, trying to hide the suspicions that had begun to gnaw at him.

Yeah, Jed never had liked seeing any of his boys sitting idle. But he had always been one to take care of his cowhands just as well as he cared for his family. The boss would lend a helping hand to former employees no matter how much time had passed since they'd worked on Garland Ranch.

Damn.

He should have realized it sooner.

True to form, his old boss wanted to help *him*. To give him a reason to feel useful.

Pride ought to make him turn down Jed's request, but doing that would also mean walking away from time with Andi.

He could see her now as clearly as he'd seen her earlier, standing in the sunshine out by the corral.

I'm not wearing well, she had said when he touched the fine lines near the corner of her eye. Others would have pointed out lines on their faces as proof of their troubles. Andi had just given him a laugh. One that didn't ring true.

Those small crinkles gave her face character and charm. More than that, they added maturity he didn't recognize and strength he hadn't expected. Both would make it harder to get close to her.

But he had been trained to handle tough situations.

Chapter Six

During a busy morning spent with Tina and Jane, Andi had managed to keep her thoughts away from Mitch.

After lunch, Tina closed herself in her office to take care of the hotel bookkeeping. Jane took Robbie and Trey over to Pete's house to visit his kids and Sharon, their nanny.

Alone, Andi went into the quiet banquet hall hoping to distract herself with preparations for the wedding. She wasn't there long before she heard heavy footsteps she recognized. The sound instantly made her heart beat faster.

Groaning, she shook her head and bent over one of the cardboard cartons she had set on a folding table.

As foolish as it was, she had been almost disappointed yesterday when her path hadn't crossed with Mitch's again after he had gotten together with Pete. At dinner, Jed had mentioned seeing Mitch driving away from the ranch.

By this morning, though, she had come to her senses and acknowledged the best thing for them both would be never to see each other again.

She should have known that wouldn't happen.

She shouldn't feel this excited right now.

As Mitch strode through the doorway, she crossed

her arms, rested her hips against the table and gave in to the pleasure of seeing him. In tight black T-shirt, jeans and black biker boots, he looked taller and tougher and sexier than ever before. That T-shirt and his black hair made his eyes startling blue.

"Jed and Paz told me I would find you here."

She frowned. "Is everything okay? Do they need me to take Missy off their hands?"

"No, they're feeding her Paz's Christmas cookies, and they said that's keeping her out of trouble. They also said your kids won't ever want to go home."

Just what Jed was hoping for, she knew.

"What can I do for you?" she asked. When he grinned, she crossed her arms more tightly. "I'm very busy."

"That's why I'm here. Jed figured he'd keep *me* out of trouble by giving me a job."

She stood straighter. "I don't need a helper, thank you."

"Too late. I'm on board. What do you want me to do?"

She turned away and rummaged through a carton of ornaments. "Nothing. I've got everything under control." The words made her think again of her reaction to his kiss. Of her *loss* of control.

"Andi, walking away yesterday didn't make me go away. Pretending to be busy here doesn't mean I'll disappear. Why don't you tell me what's bothering you?"

"At the moment, you are."

"Well, that's a start."

She shot a look over her shoulder and found him smiling down at her. He was so close, she could have taken a step back and found herself in his arms. Instead, she shifted aside. "Really, Mitch, I don't need your assistance."

"Jed seems to think you do. You and Tina and Jane. And I made a promise. So that's that."

She sighed. He had made a promise. And once Grandpa made up his mind about something, that was that. As she had no choice in the matter, she might as well give in gracefully. “Fine. And I’m not pretending to be busy.” She pointed to one carton. “That’s what I’ve got on my mind right now. Decorations for the wedding. Our client requested Christmas lights. You can get started with those.”

She had hoped having him work at a distance would keep him from distracting her, but she could still hear everything he said to her. Worse…or maybe better…she could see every move he made. Who knew hanging a string of lights required so much physical activity? His shoulders flexed, his biceps bulged, and she didn’t even want to think about what happened to the strong muscles in his thighs as he climbed up and down the ladder.

Good thing she had acquired a helper, because she wasn’t getting much work done herself.

It was a relief to hear sneakered feet pounding down the hallway. Robbie and Trey ran into the room. Naturally, Trey, who loved to climb, headed straight toward the ladder.

“Me, too! Me, too!” He reached out to Mitch, who climbed down and swung him onto his shoulder.

He wouldn’t… “That’s not a good—” Before she could finish her sentence, Mitch had plopped Trey onto a chair.

“You, too, Robbie,” he said. “Come and watch.”

Jane entered the room and came to stand beside Andi.

When both boys were seated, Mitch waved his hand in front of the window. “Okay, ready for some magic?” He inserted a plug in the nearby socket. All over the room, white fairy lights sparkled to life.

“Like stars, Mitch!” Robbie exclaimed.

“Mitch!” Trey echoed.

"Not bad at all," Jane called. In a lower voice she said to Andi, "You really ought to give that man a chance, cuz. Every woman can use a little magic in her life."

"WELL, HERE YOU ARE," Jed said from the head of the dining room table. "Just in time to join us for supper."

Andi finished settling Trey in his booster seat and reached for her utensils. As she turned to smile at the guest who had entered the room, her fingers froze around the napkin-wrapped bundle of tableware. Her smile froze, too.

Who said history didn't repeat itself?

Mitch strode through the doorway.

She had spent a very long afternoon with him in that banquet hall. Jane and the boys had stayed, and Tina had eventually joined them. Mitch had talked easily with her cousins, had given Robbie and Trey "important work" to do, and had never missed an opportunity to chat with her every time she stood still.

The last thing she needed was to deal with him again, especially in front of all her family at the dinner table.

Unfortunately, she had no say in this matter, either. Worse, when Jed directed Mitch to the empty chair beside hers, she had nowhere else to go.

He eased into his seat, then greeted her with a cool, brisk nod that made her think yet again of yesterday's anything-but-cool kiss.

"I couldn't turn down an invitation for one of Paz's home-cooked meals," he told Jed. "But don't let my mom know I said that."

"No worries, son. Your secret's safe with us."

"You have a secret?" Robbie asked.

"A secret?" Trey echoed.

"Don't we all," Mitch said.

He didn't look her way, but she felt certain he had meant the comment for her.

Rattled, she turned to the boys. "Grandpa was only teasing. There are no secrets."

"No secrets?" Robbie's eyes widened in alarm. "But Trey—"

"Not now, sweetie," Tina said quickly. "We'll talk about that later."

The Hitching Post served supper family-style, and as bowls and platters were passed, conversation turned to "have some vegetables" and "please pass the rolls."

Everyone had jumped into action to cover the slip Robbie almost made about her son's upcoming birthday parties. A slip that would have been *her* fault because she had been so distracted by Mitch.

As if he'd read her mind, he suddenly leaned closer. She tensed, until she realized he only intended to hold the heavy meat platter for her. Under cover of the voices and clanking cutlery around them, he murmured, "I wasn't teasing."

"About your mom?" she asked, pretending not to understand.

"About people keeping secrets."

"I guess you're in a good place to know." She nodded her thanks, and silently, he passed the platter along.

"It's nice to have you back here at the ranch again, Mitch," Tina said.

"It's great to be here, though I don't want to feel I'm wearing out my welcome."

This time, she refused to check whether or not he had glanced in her direction.

"No way that'll happen," Jed said. "We appreciate you giving us a hand."

Some of us appreciate it.

"And once the girls get this wedding stuff squared away," he added, "we need to start decorating around the hotel."

"We'll have lots of work for you to do," Tina said with a smile.

"No problem. As long as you leave me time to catch up with Jed."

"Hey, what about the rest of us?" Cole asked. "Including your best friend? I hear you talked to Pete yesterday, then forgot about tracking me down."

"We'll get together. And just to set the record straight, I don't forget people."

That sounded like a threat.

Swallowing a sigh, Andi concentrated on feeding Missy. If she insisted on reading hidden meanings into everything he said, this would be one never-ending, uncomfortable meal.

"How long are you staying in town?" Jane asked.

Andi didn't miss the way her cousin's gaze flickered from Mitch to her and back again. She also couldn't miss the fact that he sat there without saying a word. As much as she wanted to know the answer herself, she didn't like seeing him put on the spot. "I'll bet he'll stay at least long enough for the guys to have a reunion at the Cantina," she said with a laugh.

He looked at her gravely. "A reunion that's long overdue."

"I'll say," Cole agreed. "I'm holding you to it. In fact, I'll check and see if Pete and some of the other boys can make it this week. At least that way, we'll know for sure you'll be around."

"What about our open house?" Tina asked. "You'll be here through the holidays, won't you?"

"Don't know yet," Mitch said simply.

"Your daddy would like you to make this visit permanent," Jed said.

"And your mama," Paz said.

Mitch laughed. "Yeah, I'm sure they would. But my… life's in LA."

"You have a sweetheart there?" Paz asked, sounding almost dismayed.

Heart thudding, Andi kept her gaze on her plate. This time, she wouldn't jump in to save him. Yet she wasn't at all sure she wanted to know his answer.

A ridiculous reaction altogether. Considering how eager he'd been to kiss her, he couldn't have a girlfriend in LA…could he?

"No," he said. "No sweetheart."

Just the answer she wanted.

"No plans in that direction yet, either," he continued. "As I've already told Jed, there's no point in trying to get me to book the hall for a wedding. You might say I'm already married. To my job."

Just the answer she needed.

No matter how much she hated hearing him say it.

FROM HIS YEARS working on the ranch, Mitch knew the routines at the Hitching Post. After supper, the Garland family would move to the sitting room to spend time with their guests.

Preferring not to make a spectacle of himself limping along, he waited till most of the crowd left the dining room. He was just as interested in hanging back to let Andi take her seat first so he could grab one right beside her.

She sure hadn't liked seeing him walk into the room tonight or take the chair at her side. Her refusal to look his way during supper confirmed it. Her constant fiddling with knife and fork and water glass proved how nervous she felt. All those reactions had only made him more determined to get her to feel comfortable with him again.

He had thought she might grab the chance to wander away.

Instead, in the sitting room, she settled herself and Missy in an overstuffed chair close to the fireplace.

So much for sitting beside her. He took a seat on a nearby couch. "Looks like you haven't done much renovation in this room."

"We didn't change anything," she said, "besides some fresh paint. It's always cozy and welcoming in here."

That it was, from the overstuffed chairs and couches covered with Paz's bright handmade afghans to the old rocker pulled up close to the hearth. On the wall across from him, a clock gave a slow, steady *tick-tock*. Over in one corner of the room, Robbie and Trey galloped toy horses across a low wooden table.

Trey must have caught his glance. He waved. "Look! Horse. Bi-i-ig horse, Mitch."

"I see that. Just like the one you ride."

"Yeah." Trey laughed, then turned back to Robbie.

Jed came to take Andi's daughter from her. Mitch saw the smile she gave her grandfather. It lit her face, reminding him of the smiles she'd once sent his way.

Holding the baby in one arm, the older man took a seat beside him on the couch.

"Later on, Jed, when your hands aren't so full, maybe you and I could get together about what else I can do for you around here."

Jed waved his free hand. "Aw, relax. You're a guest here tonight. Besides, this is family time." He turned slightly to show off the baby. "Cute little thing, isn't she?"

"She is. I remember Laurie being that small. Heck, I can remember all my brothers and sisters at that stage."

"And I bet you never let 'em forget it."

He laughed. "I do like to remind them, the boys especially, of all the times I saw them running around in diapers."

"Changed those diapers, too, I'd reckon, knowing Lyle."

"Yeah, that was one of the drawbacks of being the oldest. Dad put me through my paces, no matter how much I protested."

"Good training for you. You'll make a good daddy, then. Won't he, Andi?"

She started, as if her thoughts had been far away from the sitting room. Still, she didn't miss a beat. "As you said, Grandpa, we know his father. I'd imagine Sheriff Weston has Mitch well-trained for almost anything."

She'd stressed those final two words. Why, he couldn't tell. When she raised her chin, he couldn't read that, either. Defiance? Determination? Challenge?

Was she thinking about yesterday, when he had kissed her?

He had told her the kiss was to show her neither of them had forgotten their past. *Yeah, right.* That had been the handiest excuse he could grab on to to explain his heat-of-the-moment response.

The truth was, after seeing the pity in her eyes, he had acted out of pure gut instinct, kissing her to prove he was well on the way to being himself again. And he had succeeded.

Just in case she had started to think he was hinting about the future, at supper tonight, he had made it clear he didn't have any plans to settle down. But at this point, he couldn't swear whether he'd meant the announcement as a caution to her or reassurance for himself.

All he knew was, he'd need to try like heck to avoid any potentially hot moments.

Chapter Seven

"Nice hideaway."

Startled by the familiar voice, Andi jumped. Her sharp scissors almost punctured the package she was attempting to open. She set aside the order of candy-covered almonds destined for wedding favors. Mitch stood there leaning against the door frame. She glared at him. "This isn't a hideaway. And was it necessary for you to sneak up on me like that?"

"I didn't sneak. You should be more aware of what's going on around you."

He had a point, considering she had sat there so deep in contemplation, she hadn't heard his approach. Worse, though she had left the sitting room intending to put space between them, she hadn't been able to escape her thoughts.

"I didn't read you as someone antisocial enough to go off and leave her family," he said.

"I didn't leave them. They're in good hands. Literally, in my daughter's case."

When he and Grandpa had gotten involved in conversation, she had checked to make sure Grandpa hadn't wanted to turn Missy over to her. Not much chance of that. Experience had taught her Jed wouldn't give up any opportunity to cuddle his only great-granddaughter.

A quick look across the room had shown Trey engrossed in playing with Robbie and his toy horses.

It was safe for her to slip quietly from the sitting room without anyone noticing. Or so she had thought.

When Mitch closed the door to the suite, she felt both a rush of annoyance and a shiver of anticipation. She didn't know which upset her more. But she shouldn't have *any* feelings when it came to him.

"Speaking of your family," he said, "what was all that at the supper table about secrets?"

"Robbie almost spilled the beans about Trey's surprise birthday parties."

"Parties, as in more than one?"

"Yes. The kids and I are going back home to celebrate with my mother-in-law and the rest of her family on Trey's actual birthday. After that, we'll have my family party here at the hotel. But that can't be why you're up here now. What can I do for you?" she asked as levelly as she could.

He glanced around him. "I also didn't read you as someone who'd hide away in a hotel bridal suite. Unless, of course, you were waiting for your groom."

The thought of Mitch playing that role made her entire body overheat. Flustered, she snapped, "I told you, this isn't a hideaway. Jane and Tina and I are organizing for the wedding, and we decided we needed a better temporary workstation than Tina's small office downstairs. Besides, we figured one of the suites would give us more privacy."

"It does that."

"Obviously not as much as we thought. How did you know where to find me?"

"I'm a cop, remember?"

"How could I forget? But that doesn't answer my question."

"Tina gave me the heads-up you might have come here."

"Tina?" It was bad enough Jane had already begun pushing her in a direction she didn't want to go. But why would her quiet younger cousin have gotten involved? Tina didn't know anything about her summer with Mitch. "Is she on her way up here?"

"No. And it sounded like she and Jane were finished working for the night. I guess you're an overachiever."

"Officially, I'm the hotel's interim wedding planner while they look for someone to hire permanently. Grandpa's already upset we had our first wedding party cancel a couple of months ago. And it was a wedding I'd booked. So I've got to make sure this one's a big success."

He crossed the room to sit on the king-size bed within arm's reach of the desk chair. Immediately, she rose. She couldn't have changed seats at supper, but she had managed to slip away from the sitting room. And she could certainly leave the suite now.

He stretched his leg in front of him and sucked in a breath through clenched teeth. Concern froze her in place. "Are you okay?"

"Fine."

"What happened, Mitch?"

"I sat too long, and it stiffened up on me."

"That's not what I meant, and you know it." Concern gave way to frustration. "You question me like you're a cop—"

"I *am* a cop."

"Yes, I know. But I don't like being treated like a suspect. And I don't like when you want to know things about me, yet never give back anything yourself."

"It seems to me we've got a lot more history to discuss than my bum knee."

"You mean the fact we hadn't forgotten each other, don't you? We *should* forget those memories. We're better off letting them stay in the past."

"That's not what I'm getting at this time."

He rested his hand on her forearm. Despite her frustration, she couldn't ignore the pleasurable chill his touch sent through her.

"I think you've got something else on your mind. Other worries. Other memories, maybe. And we've already seen how they can come back to haunt us."

Haunt was the right word. Meeting Mitch again had instantly reignited their teenage passion. Their first love. But his injury and his claim of being married to his job in Los Angeles were both painful reminders of what she *had* to put behind her. She had to make it clear to him, once and for all, that she'd gotten over their past.

"I've made other memories that take the place of ours." *More lies.* Though she had found a new life, nothing could take the place of those memories she had created with Mitch. But she couldn't tell him that. "I've had two children. I lost my husband—"

"I know that."

"No, you don't. Not all of it."

"That's just my point."

He took her hand. Her mind warned her to pull free, but as he tugged gently, her emotions refused to listen. She sank to the bed beside him, making sure to keep space between them and still, she fought to keep from sliding closer.

"That summer, we talked about everything, Andi. All I want is for you to talk to me now the way you did then. Tell me what happened. After that, you'll be able to put those memories away in some neat, little box—like a Christmas present. Or like that package over there." He gestured to the desk.

She took another unsteady breath.

Obviously, he did a better job than she did of tuning in to the surroundings. She hadn't thought he had even noticed the package.

She shook her head. "I lost my husband. He went to work one day and never came home. That's all." She had the right to keep her story to herself, the way he guarded his. It had to be related to his injury and why he had come home. She tugged her hand free. "You need to leave, Mitch. I respect what you and everyone in law enforcement do. But there's no way I'll get close to someone in such a dangerous job."

"We're already close. We're friends. Don't think about what I do. Think of me as the boy you once knew."

"You're not a boy, you're a man—"

"Glad you noticed." He gave her a crooked smile.

"—and I'm a woman—"

"No argument there."

"—with responsibilities." Why did her voice have to shake? "*Lots* of responsibilities," she ended firmly.

"And I respect you for that. But there's no way I'm going to walk away when I think you need to talk. And I hope you'll tell me the truth."

"I don't—"

"Yeah, you don't lie. I've heard that before, a million times, from people who couldn't make an honest confession if I dictated it to them. But never from you. And I know you want to set a good example for your kids. Then be responsible now," he said, "and give me straight answers."

Sighing, she shook her head. "You won't give up, will you?"

"You don't want me to, do you? Because you know talking to me might help."

He wrapped his arm around her shoulders, his touch gentle, almost brotherly, yet her heart pounded even as her breathing seemed to shut down.

When she turned to look at him, he reached up to brush her hair away from her face. Their eyes met. Their gazes held. They were so close, and in an instant she was standing outside at the corral again. Just as she had then, she instinctively tilted her head, nestling her cheek against his palm.

Did he move closer, or did she? She couldn't have said. All she knew was they met somewhere in the middle, and when he lowered his mouth to hers, she returned his kiss as eagerly as she always had that one summer.

No matter what she had said, they weren't a man and a woman now, not in her mind. They were a boy and a girl again. A couple of teens in love, making out in the hayloft or beside a summer-swollen creek or inside a honeymoon cabin not far from the hotel.

Just a couple of teens on their own…

But not alone. Not when she could hear footsteps in the hallway.

Backing away, she brushed at her lips with one hand and smoothed her hair with the other. They had never been discovered during any of their make-out sessions. How ironic to be caught now.

The sound of footsteps, many footsteps, thudded on the wooden floorboards. They grew louder as what sounded like an army of people approached the suite… reached the doorway…

And passed by.

She let out a sigh of relief.

"I didn't mean for that to happen—" he began.

"Neither did I—" Then why wasn't she sorry? "—but we both know it can't happen again. Mitch, you have to leave."

"Now?" He frowned and leaned back, using his elbows to prop himself up on the bed.

She fought the urge to throw herself on him just as the teenage Andi would have done. Judging by the way his jeans tented in front, that could be both a very satisfying and a very stupid move. She had no time in her life for either.

Instead, she returned to sit at the desk.

"Things were just getting interesting," he protested.

She could hear the forced amusement in his voice. He was trying to laugh this off, to make less of it, probably in an attempt to leave her feeling better about this mistake…about this *kiss* that never should have happened.

"Maybe things were getting interesting for you," she said as lightly as she could manage. "But I'm not interested, thank you." *Liar.* She was intrigued. Fascinated. Ready for more. But she shouldn't be.

She reached for the package and the scissors, hanging on to them tightly as if they would help fend off Mitch's advances…not that he was making any at the moment.

She risked a look over her shoulder.

He raised a brow.

Again she struggled, this time to swallow all the questions she could barely hold back. How could they have reached this moment of mutual temporary insanity? Worse, how could she have given in to it? And how could he sit there looking at her so coolly when she was burning up inside and out?

"Not interested, huh? You could have fooled me."

If only she could have tricked herself. But that was impossible when her reactions were so easy to define. She wasn't simply recalling a teen's faraway memories. She was feeling here-and-now emotions without having a clue how to handle them. No, she might not be able to fool herself, but she certainly was acting like a fool.

"Mitch. We can't continue this conversation here. We can't *be* here. We're lucky the people who passed by weren't headed for this suite. Please, go—before anyone else comes along."

Slowly, he rose to his feet. Deliberately, she knew, he adjusted his jeans. "You can feel sorry for me and my limp all you want at the moment, because it won't be my knee making me hobble out of here."

Feel *sorry* for him? No, sympathy certainly wasn't on her long list of emotions. Clutching the scissors so tightly her fingers went numb, she watched him walk slowly across the room.

At the doorway, he turned back. "I'm leaving for now," he said, "but that doesn't mean we've wrapped things up."

"COFFEE'S UP," DEPUTY HERNANDEZ announced.

"Sounds good."

Mitch propped his leg on a desk in the outer office of Cowboy Creek's sheriff's department and lost himself in the memory of last night.

Once Tina had filled him in on Andi's possible whereabouts, he'd gone up to the suite only to talk. Even taking her hand and putting his arm around her had been meant as reassuring gestures, nothing more. His aim was to find out what was bothering her. To help her, not to come on to her like the oversexed adolescent he'd once been.

But touching her cheek had done him in. Watching her tilt her head as if seeking more of that touch had made him lose control. Before he had known what was happening, he had gotten so carried away, he'd pushed aside thoughts of his goal. Hell, he'd forgotten he had one.

She seemed to have that effect on him.

He had to forget about that, too. Had to put his teenage hormones on hold if he was ever going to help her. But besides frustrating him to death, what good would that do? She would never open up to him with all of her family and the hotel guests within earshot. The way she had insisted he leave the suite—in his condition, no less—had proven that.

"Here you go." Paco set the foam cup on the desk beside Mitch. "Black okay with you?"

He nodded at the coffee cup. "Black's fine. Back home, we don't have the luxury of making it light. Or sweet." He grinned at Paco. "Depending on whose turn it was to stock the kitchen supply cabinet, we're lucky to find a few packets of fake sugar wedged into a crack in the shelf."

"Same here," Paco said. He took the chair behind the desk. "I guess you big-city cops aren't so different from us, huh?"

Mitch nodded in the spirit of solidarity. The desk phone rang, and as the deputy answered the call, he glanced around the office again.

Not much had changed in here for years.

Growing up, he had made plenty of visits to the office with his dad. In those days, this room had seemed so much bigger, so much more exciting than it did now. Maybe he'd outgrown it. Or more likely, he'd grown used to a different place.

Still, the office looked familiar. Comfortable. All law enforcement offices might feel the same way. He wouldn't know, as he'd gone straight from school to the LAPD.

Paco hung up the phone. "Routine call. Miz Greta's cat is on the loose again."

They both laughed.

"I'll bet you see more action in LA."

"Sometimes, sometimes not. We get our share of animal rescue calls."

"And break-ins and shootings and drug busts." Paco sounded almost envious.

"Yeah, those, too. There's a lot to be said for peace and quiet, though."

"We get plenty of that."

"I'll tell you one thing we don't get, at least in my area. That's cattle rustlers."

"Yeah, I'll bet. We still run into them, but not too often. Your dad got a reputation for clamping down on that around here—" Paco laughed "—after he drop-kicked the last wannabe rustler in the creek."

"I never heard that one." What else had he missed that a flying visit and a few-times-a-year phone call didn't cover? "That was a while ago?"

"Years," Paco said firmly. "And we haven't had a problem in that line since. Your dad's a good man."

A while later, once he'd left the office and started a slow walk up Canyon Road toward home, Mitch thought of that comment again.

Lately, he hadn't lived up to his old man's high standards. His former boss was telling stories to help him save face. He'd let himself down again last night by losing his ability to keep his hands off Andi.

At the moment, he didn't have much going for him. The one thing he had to hang on to was his determination to follow his instincts.

If he couldn't trust himself to do that, he wasn't worthy of wearing a badge.

Chapter Eight

"Well, we're making progress," Jane announced.

Andi looked up from the pile of red netting she was cutting into rectangles. "We are?"

Tina sat at the desk in the honeymoon suite going through their wedding checklist.

Jane knelt on the floor poring over photos she had taken of sample place settings they had designed for this first wedding. "Sure," she said. "We've moved on from picking out fabric patterns to finalizing settings and party favors—now that Bridezilla has finally started making some decisions."

Andi rolled her eyes. "Her name's Sandra. You've got to stop calling her that, Jane. When she gets here for the wedding, I'm liable to open my mouth and say the wrong thing."

"Not you, sweet cousin," Jane mocked.

"Don't squabble, girls," Tina said. "And look at the bright side. We're on budget and a week ahead of schedule."

"Spoken like a true accountant."

Andi glared at Jane, then turned to Tina. "That's true. Double kudos to you." She hoped her smile didn't look as strained as it felt. During the past few days, instead of progress, she had felt only pressure from every direction.

Jed had so many hopes riding on relaunching the Hitching Post's bridal business. This wedding had to be a success, to generate word-of-mouth referrals and bring in new reservations. It had—as Grandpa had often said lately—to go off without a hitch.

Mitch had shown up at the hotel every day this week and without a murmur of protest had helped with anything they requested. He had repositioned tables and chairs in the banquet hall, brought down boxes of Christmas decorations from the attic and strung lights in the lobby and sitting room.

He had also kept the conversation rolling, had kept the kids occupied once they started getting underfoot, and had even managed to keep Jed from trying to climb a ladder to hang some of the decorations.

He had somehow done all this without once being out of her line of sight…or maybe she had just spent too much time watching him.

Yesterday, Jane had jokingly told him he could have Sundays off, yet he had returned this morning for brunch.

Each day he had acted as if nothing had ever happened between them, while she still dreamed of the kiss they had shared on this very bed. The kiss she wanted to repeat.

I'm leaving for now, Mitch had said before walking out of this room that night, *but that doesn't mean we've wrapped things up.*

His parting words only added to her stress.

He kept insisting she talk to him, that she had something bothering her. And she did. But their kiss and her response had only added to her list of worries.

She even felt pressure from her own son. Maybe because of their conversation about their "badges," Trey seemed to have latched on to Mitch. He had insisted on carrying his booster seat over to the chair on the opposite side of Mitch's. When they had all moved to the sitting room, he trailed after the man like one of Robbie's miniature cars on a string. And the latest new words in his vocabulary? *"Mitch... Mitch... Mitch."*

Her son's growing attachment worried her more than anything else could.

Beside her on the mattress, her cell phone buzzed with the special ringtone she had set for their client's messages.

"Now, if only Bridezilla would stop texting you every three minutes," Jane said, "we could get everything wrapped up."

Andi glared. "Would you *please* not call her that?"

Tina closed her laptop. "Why don't we quit? It's almost dinnertime." On Sundays, the Hitching Post offered only two meals, brunch and a midafternoon Sunday dinner. "I need to see if Abuela needs help. Cole mentioned taking all the kids into town for ice cream after dinner. I think we should go along, too."

"Ice cream?" Jane said. "It's December."

Tina laughed. "The kids don't care about that. And you're not in New York, anymore, remember? It's not nearly as cold here."

"True. Then count me in."

Andi nodded. "It *is* a good idea. I'll be with you in a minute. I just need to check my phone." She hesitated. With everything else bothering her, she didn't need an argument with Jane on her conscience. "The text was from…the woman we will now refer to as you-know-who."

To her relief, Jane and Tina laughed.

As she watched them both leave the room, she cradled the cell phone in her hands. Nothing would excuse the way she had responded to her cousin, but she had to admit she knew the cause.

Since her encounter with Mitch in this very room, her nerves had felt as tight as a high-tension wire. At Jane's comment, the wire had snapped. Her cousin had been right when she'd mentioned wrapping things up. Right in more ways than she knew.

That's what *she* needed to do—with Mitch. To wrap things up between them once and for all.

She couldn't get involved with him.

For her children's sake, she needed to let go and move on.

Yet the worst of the pressure she'd felt these past few days had come from inside her.

Seeing Mitch here provided a constant reminder that she had once loved him. That she still couldn't resist him. And that, instead of wrapping up their relationship, she wanted to pick up from where they had left off.

MITCH STOOD NEAR the Big Dipper's front counter patiently waiting his turn to pay for his ice cream cone. With Andi right in front of him, he was in no rush to move the line along.

Earlier that morning, though he was off duty according to Jane, he had made the trip out to the Hitching Post. He didn't want to admit it, but he was hoping for more time alone with Andi. Not for a repeat of the night he had found her upstairs in the suite, but for the chance to talk.

After brunch, when she had left the sitting room and hadn't returned, Jed mentioned she had gone upstairs again. She was in the middle of wedding preparations. With Jane and Andi.

After a final cup of coffee, he had wandered by the suite, where she'd made a point of indicating how busy they all were. His certainty she was avoiding him had been confirmed both by the look on her face when she'd seen him waiting in the Big Dipper and by the way she was attempting to ignore him now.

And after what had happened between them the other night, maybe she had the right idea.

So far, she'd given him only a glance, quick and colder than the double scoop of rocky road he planned to order.

"Didn't expect to see me here, did you?" he asked over her shoulder. Their eyes met in the mirrored panel on the wall behind the cash register. Hers still looked a frosty blue.

"I'll bet you didn't expect to be here," she countered.

He laughed. "You win. Cole must have told you. At first, when he called to get together here in town, I thought he meant the Cantina. Then he mentioned taking the kids to the Big Dipper." And *then* he'd said Tina and Jane and Andi were also coming along. Suddenly, an afternoon at the ice cream parlor sounded even better than a night out with the boys. "I figured I'd take him up on the invitation."

"Why?"

"Why?" He sure couldn't tell her the truth, that despite all the warnings he'd given himself, he'd wanted to see her again. "Because I like ice cream."

When it was her turn to order at the counter, he said, "I've got this." Once he'd ordered, he reached around her to take his cone from Shay, the clerk. His arm brushed Andi's shoulder, and he thought again of the way he had held her that night. He handed Shay a twenty. "Keep the change."

"Better check to make sure it's not counterfeit," Andi said.

He leaned around her to meet her eyes. "Hey, I work on the right side of the law, remember?"

"How could I ever forget?"

She grabbed a handful of napkins from the dispenser, and they moved away from the counter.

The folks of Cowboy Creek had turned out in force tonight. The place was packed. Cole and the rest of their group sat around a couple of tables.

"No seats in our corner," he said, attempting to hide a smile. Much as he liked Jed's clan, he didn't at all mind this chance to get Andi to himself. Maybe to finally get her to open up to him.

"It looks like there aren't any seats anywhere," she said, scanning the room.

"Guess we'll have to go out front."

She waved to the group in the corner and pointed to the door. They all smiled and waved back.

He trailed her outside to a table. Fortunately, it was on the sidewalk opposite the side of the shop where her family sat. At least he wouldn't have the Garland clan sharing a play-by-play of the action.

He took a seat beside her and gestured at her cone. "What is that, anyway, plain old vanilla?"

She nodded.

"A poor choice compared to mine."

"You think so?" She shrugged. "I don't much care for that bumpy stuff you're eating."

"You mean rocky road."

"'Bumpy stuff,'" she repeated. "That's what Robbie calls it, so of course Trey calls it that, too."

"Nice kids," he said. "I'll bet you're happy they're getting so much time together now you've come for a visit. Trey's happy, I can tell you that. He definitely looks up to Robbie."

She froze with her ice cream halfway to her mouth.

Slowly, she lowered her hand again and began fiddling with the paper wrapped around the cone.

"What's the matter?" he asked quietly.

She shrugged again. "Just thinking."

He thought, too, back to what he had said. Maybe this would be the opening he'd been waiting for. "I'll bet your son looked up to his dad. Most boys do. How is he dealing with what happened to your husband?"

"He's fine." The chill he'd heard in her voice earlier had returned. "He's too young to be aware of things."

"What will you tell him when he asks where his dad is?"

"I don't know. I'll face that when it happens."

"Well, you're right. He *is* young." Young enough to forget, something he wished he could say about himself. "That's a point in his favor."

"Favor?" She shot a glance at him, then looked past him into the distance.

Her level stare told him she wasn't noticing the sun-drenched sidewalk, the strolling pedestrians or the Sunday drivers coasting along Canyon Road.

He could feel her shutting down. Slipping away. He wanted her back. "Kids Trey's age can easily mix up reality with what they see on the cartoons. Plus they're resilient. They bounce back from things that hit adults like a ton of bricks. That's all I meant. Sorry for sounding too blunt."

"That comes with being a cop, doesn't it? Because you're used to dealing with tragedy."

"Not as much as people think. For sure, not as much as they see on TV."

"But you face it more than most people do."

He gripped the cone in his hand. How had she managed to spin the questions back his way? "Yeah, we all see our share of life's worst moments."

"How bad was yours?"

He shook his head. "Nothing we need to discuss. Let's just stick to the first topic. We were talking about your boy."

"No, you were leading up to talking about my husband, and I was avoiding falling into your trap."

"Trap?"

"Another one of your interrogations."

"I wasn't interrogating you, Andi."

"It felt that way," she said sadly. "Tonight and the other times you've asked questions. You want to find out what happened in my past. What happened with Grant. But when I ask about your past, about how you got hurt, you change the subject."

She had kept her voice pitched low, and still he felt uneasy. He wasn't used to being on the receiving end of a grilling. He wasn't ready to talk about what had gone down in LA.

He spotted a trash can a few feet from them. Leaning over, he sent his ice cream cone into the kill zone. "This isn't the place or time to get into that."

"Then where is the place? And when will it be time?"

He shrugged and said simply, "I don't know." Because *nowhere* and *never* wouldn't satisfy her.

Chapter Nine

Mitch tipped back his bottle and took what should have been a cold, refreshing slug of beer. Cold, yeah, the Cantina had that covered. He couldn't blame them for the drink not measuring up to the rest.

At this point, nothing could refresh him. He was as worn-out as the oily rag he used to clean his firearms.

To hell with the dangerous job Andi liked to throw up to him. To hell and back with the bullet he'd taken in his knee. His relationship with her was going to do him in.

From just a few yards away, a jukebox blared. In the booth opposite him, Pete Brannigan looked at his watch. They were waiting for Cole and a couple of their other friends to show up. "They ought to be getting here soon. I bet it'll be good to see some of the guys from school. Cole said you might even make it out to the ranch for Jed's party."

"I don't know about that." Who knew where he'd be a couple of weeks down the road. Between now and then, he had the follow-up appointments with the surgeon and the department shrink. He had a lot riding on those appointments. Too much. Right now, he couldn't risk thinking about the outcome.

He didn't want to think about where things might stand with Andi by that time, either.

He took another slug of beer and thought again about his lack of progress with Andi. He'd tried to talk with her—despite her accusation about his questions. Half the time he'd said anything remotely personal about her, she had switched the conversation to something else. The other half of the time, she'd tried to get him to open up.

Talk about interrogation. She had a damned good technique herself.

He looked up to find Pete frowning at him. "You're not drinking tequila," Pete said, "so I don't guess you've swallowed a worm. But you sure look like it. What's up?"

He shrugged. "Thinking about some things I've been working on. I've hit a brick wall."

The other man shook his head sympathetically. "That's rough."

"Yeah." He sat back, ready for some diversion from his thoughts. He had seen the front door open and Cole enter the bar. If anyone could distract him, his best friend could. He lifted his bottle in greeting.

Pete rose. "My shout."

As he walked away, Cole slid into the vacant seat and said, "I'm late. Got out of the shower and found Robbie sitting on the edge of the bed, waiting for a heart-to-heart. Maybe you need one, too. You've been walking around lately looking like a bear with a thorn in his butt. Pete will be back with the beers soon, so let's not waste time. What's up?"

"Nothing." He scowled. First Pete picking up on his mood, and now Cole. He could kiss his undercover work goodbye if he didn't do a better job at hiding his thoughts.

Another problem he could attribute to Andi.

"You ought to settle down, have a kid or two." Cole grinned. "It could help your disposition."

"There's nothing wrong with my disposition. But,

what—you've been a daddy less than a year, and already you've found it's the cure for everything?"

"Close to it." Cole suddenly sobered. "Being a family man gives you a new perspective."

So does watching your partner die.

"And," Cole went on, "I know where you can find a ready-made family."

Andi and her kids.

"She's leaving tomorrow, going home for a couple of days, but then she'll be back. You couldn't do any better, Mitch. Andi's one in a million. And those kids of hers would only sweeten the deal."

At the thought of Trey and his *"Bi-i-ig horse, Mitch!"* he had trouble holding back a smile. He gulped his beer to ease the sudden tightness in his throat. A family didn't fit his lifestyle. Besides, Andi wouldn't smile at him two days in a row. She would hardly settle down with him. "Not interested, thanks. Why would I want a wife and kids when I'd never be around to spend time with them?"

"My thought, too. But I finally saw the light."

He shrugged. "The only thing I see is Pete coming back with our beers."

AT GARLAND RANCH the next morning, Mitch parked his truck near the corral in the spot he'd begun to think of as his.

Across the yard, he saw Cole sitting on the Hitching Post's porch rail, more than likely watching for him.

Later on last evening, he had turned over what Cole had said to him about Andi. Especially the part about her leaving town. In a phone call afterward, he had asked a few pointed questions. With luck, by now his best friend had gotten some answers.

Now he walked up to the other man, who clapped him

on the shoulder. "About time. C'mon, let's go inside. I told Tina you called last night because you wanted to stop in for breakfast."

"*Breakfast?* That's the best reason you could come up with?"

"What's wrong with it? You've been around here for almost every meal lately, anyhow." Cole laughed and headed up to the porch. "Tina and Jane think you and Andi ought to get together."

Mitch stumbled, almost missing the next step.

For a split second, he thought his leg would let him down—literally. But he managed to grab the rail and continue up the steps a couple of beats behind Cole, who appeared not to have noticed.

"Did they volunteer that all on their own, or did you ask them?"

On the porch, Cole came to a halt and hung his head in mock shame. "They grilled Pete and me about what went on at the Cantina last night."

"And you coughed up."

"I didn't say anything about whipping your butt at the pool table."

"Well, thanks for that."

"You *ought* to be thankful, old friend. I could have ruined your reputation."

Got that taken care of.

"And I didn't say anything about our heart-to-heart or the way you blasted my suggestion. But I've got a feeling you didn't mind the idea as much as you tried to let on."

"What does that mean?"

"It means I don't think you're completely rejecting the idea of getting together with Andi. How could I, after your phone call?"

"And you've coughed that up to the women *and* Pete?"

"Not a single word. But I still managed to get the info you wanted."

"Where is it?"

"Right here." From his pocket, Cole pulled out a slip of paper and handed it over.

He nodded his thanks. "Save me a seat in the dining room. I'll be there in a few minutes. First, I've got to make a call."

"I'll bet you do." Laughing, Cole walked away.

Mitch he took a deep breath and went over to the porch swing.

He had no delusions about a relationship with Andi. But he still had a goal to reach. Wasn't that why he'd called Cole last night and why he'd come here to have things out with Andi this morning?

He thumbed open the folded sheet of paper and stared down at the details of her flights to and from Phoenix.

Then he pulled his cell phone from his pocket. He was taking a risk—a big one—but what did that matter? This might be the only chance he would ever have to be completely alone with Andi.

"I'LL BE LEAVING soon for the airport."

Andi laughed. "Not too soon," she said into her cell phone. Cara, her best friend forever—and now also her kids' babysitter—would pick the three of them up in Phoenix for the drive to her mother-in-law's in Fountain Hills. She was looking forward to staying with Cara tonight, sharing girl talk and catching up. "I know it's a short flight, but we haven't even left the Hitching Post yet."

"I just can't wait to see you and the kids again. It's been a long couple of weeks."

That was an understatement.

"Are you done packing yet?"

She looked down at the small pile of clothing on the bed and laughed again. "Almost. It's just for one night. It's not like I have that much to bring with me. Two bags and the kids' car seats, that's it."

"You'll have a lot more with you after Trey's party, I'll bet."

"I'm sure I will. Ginnie and the rest of Grant's family have always been so generous with gifts for the kids." Her mother-in-law had asked especially to have Trey's party at her house on his actual birthday. "I won't bring my package for Trey, since I'd just have to carry it back here again. I'll give it to him at my family's party tomorrow night."

"You're still okay with leaving the kids at her house and coming to stay with me?"

Cara knew all her worries about Grant's family, but they both also knew Ginnie was a wonderful grandmother. "Of course I'm okay with it. We're overdue for some BFF time. And I'm glad Ginnie wants to keep Trey and Missy overnight."

When they finished the call, she dropped the cell phone onto the bed near her purse.

At the time Ginnie had asked to keep the kids the night of Trey's birthday, Andi had been grateful for the chance to work some overtime at the dress shop.

Now, here she was staying in Cowboy Creek and grateful for the opportunity to leave, even if only for a day. It would give her some breathing space, some time to be on her own without worrying about running into Mitch.

A knock sounded on the door. "Come on in," she called, folding up the sweatshirt Trey might need for the airplane.

She heard the door open and close again immediately. Frowning, she turned.

Mitch stood leaning against the door.

She clutched the sweatshirt in an automatic reflex triggered half by happiness at seeing him and half by apprehension. "What are you doing here so early?"

"I came for breakfast—"

"The dining room's downstairs." When he grinned and headed toward her, her heart gave an extra little beat.

"Very funny. As I was saying, I came for breakfast and was surprised you weren't there."

"I'm packing."

He looked past her. "Yeah, I can see that."

"How did you know where I was?"

"You were the only one not at the breakfast table, so I deduced I might find you here. Trey told me the other day which room he was staying in."

She turned back to the bed. "Well, I don't know that entertaining you in our hotel room is such a good idea."

"Did you plan to entertain me?"

"Oh, you're very amusing, too, aren't you?"

"Believe it or not, I can be, in the right circumstances." He stood behind her just as he had at the ice cream parlor. Now, just as then, a tingling awareness ran through her. "But we haven't had the right circumstances for much of anything."

"We managed," she said drily, crossing her arms and turning to face him. She hadn't realized he had taken another step toward her. Her forearms brushed his chest, and she would have sworn an electrical charge passed through her.

She didn't lose her balance. She wasn't a bit unsteady on her feet. And still, instinct or memory or familiarity made her reach out to him just as he reached for her.

Every sense seemed heightened, more alert. The warmth of his hands on her shoulders made her melt like a scoop of softened ice cream. The heat of his mouth on hers made her hot all over. She tugged on his T-shirt, wanting him closer. Wanting more. This was no boy-and-girl kiss, no revival of old memories. This was forging new memories. This was taking a risk.

This was crazy.

She backed away, or as far away as she could with the bed planted behind her. "Mitch, we can't—"

"I know. We can't do this here. We can't talk in the suite upstairs. We can't avoid all the hotel guests and we can't get any space from your family. But I know where we can do all that."

"Where?" she blurted.

"Arizona."

"What?" She couldn't have heard his response. She darn well wouldn't give away how breathless the suggestion had left her. "We can't."

"Why not? We need to talk."

"Talk?" Her senses were still reeling. But she felt sure talk wasn't the only thing on Mitch's agenda. She tried to ignore her shiver of pleasure at the thought, to forget about what he might have meant and focus on what he had actually said. The idea of conversation—of *talking*—with Mitch made her pause.

If they were completely alone with no fear of anyone breaking in on them, would he finally open up and tell her what had happened to him?

If they were completely alone—

"We need some time together."

He seemed to have read her mind, although considering the jumbled state of her emotions, she wouldn't have been surprised to learn her expression had given her away.

She swallowed hard. They stood so close, she had nowhere else to look—nowhere else she *wanted* to look—but into his clear blue eyes. Obviously, he did plan more than just conversation. She couldn't deny how much she wanted that, too.

But once they had crossed that line, would she be able to cross back again?

"Andi, we need the right place to talk, and that danged sure isn't here."

"I'm leaving for the airport in just a few minutes."

"I know that. So am I."

Her jaw dropped. "You're riding with us?"

He shook his head. "No. At breakfast, Jed mentioned someone needed to give you a lift. I volunteered to take you to the airport. And then, if you're willing, I'd like to go with you to Phoenix."

Her heartbeat went into triple time. She had to force herself to protest. "I'm only going overnight."

"And you're leaving the kids at your mother-in-law's for a sleepover."

She swallowed a gasp. "How do you know?"

"Jed mentioned that, too."

There was no way now she could mistake what he was asking, what he wanted. Something much riskier than their kiss. They might have only this one chance…

"One night," he murmured. "Before we say goodbye once and for all."

Her breath caught at the thought of never seeing him again. She already had too many sad memories, too many things she couldn't go back in time to change. But she could fix this. She could end things between them on a better note than she had before. She could finally satisfy the need—*her* need—to make up for walking away from him.

He lifted his hand to her cheek.

As always, she tilted her head and nestled against his palm. "One night," she whispered.

And one chance that could lead to something more.

Chapter Ten

From the driver's seat of their rental car, Mitch could look into the rearview mirror and see both Trey and Missy strapped into their seats. A better view than the one to his right, where Andi sat staring through the front windshield without seeing a thing, he'd bet.

"Look, Mitch," Trey yelled from the rear seat, pointing to the designs carved into the highway's retaining wall. "Bi-i-ig lizards!"

"I see them, buddy. There are lots of them, aren't there?"

"Yeah. Bi-i-ig lizards. And bi-i-ig trees."

On their ride to Fountain Hills, the kid pointed out the planes banking toward them, the palm trees in the distance and every single lizard they passed. Trey's chatter helped fill the silence from Andi's corner of the car.

When she had finally agreed to let him accompany her on this trip, he couldn't help the rush of satisfaction that thrummed through him. Sealing the deal with another kiss had left him certain she wanted him along, too.

But at the car rental counter waiting for their vehicle, she voiced her concerns about how her in-laws were going to take his presence. Then the attendant had presented their paperwork, and they hadn't had time to finish the discussion.

She had most likely spent the ride to her mother-in-law's trying to come up with a plan.

Their midafternoon arrival spared them from heavy traffic. "What happened to that Phoenix rush hour I've heard people complain about?"

"We didn't miss it by much," she said. "Turn at that next corner, after the big saguaro."

"Bi-i-ig cactus," Trey yelled.

Mitch grinned, and Andi smiled.

He coasted along a wide curved drive and stopped the rental in front of a three-story stucco building the size of a small castle.

A concrete walkway led to a towering, metal-girded double door sporting Christmas wreaths larger than the tires on his truck. The door could easily have been plucked from an abandoned castle on the moors. A moat and drawbridge wouldn't have looked out of place, either.

No doubt about it, Andi's husband's family had some bucks.

He released Trey from his car seat, then went to the trunk to collect the bag Andi had said held the kids' overnight clothes.

By the time she had taken the baby into her arms and joined him near the trunk of the car, she was more than ready to talk.

"How are we going to explain my bringing you along with me?" She had kept her voice low for the kids' sake, he was sure.

"You having second thoughts?" he asked. Better to find out now, to regroup if necessary.

Her steady gaze gave him the answer before she replied. "No, I'm not."

"Good. No worries, then," he said in the calm, measured tone that often came in handy on the job. Andi had called her mother-in-law from the airport and asked to bring a guest. "I'm an old friend of your family's from Cowboy Creek who's at loose ends for the evening. And who, regretting that he's missed too many of his own family parties, jumped on the chance to help celebrate Jed's great-grandson's birthday." He smiled. "Nobody will blink an eye at that, since every word is true."

To his surprise, it was, right down to the added cover he'd tossed in about his family, something he'd have to think about another time.

The only thing he hadn't mentioned was his plans for after the party.

She seemed satisfied with his answer, judging by her small smile.

Over at the castle, the huge front door opened without so much as an ominous creak. A woman stood on the doorstep. Slim, late sixties, with silver-shot dark hair and a gleaming smile, she held her arms wide for the little boy who barreled toward her.

"Nana! Nana!"

At the sound of her son's voice, Andi turned and waved, then looked back at him. "All right." She hiked the diaper bag up on her shoulder. "Let's get this show on the road."

For a long moment he froze, hearing the echo of his partner's voice.

He hoped like hell this undercover op would end on a better note than his previous one had.

ANDI SIPPED HER after-dinner cocktail and tried to fight off feelings of both desire and despair.

At that overly dramatic thought, she almost choked on her drink. But melodrama or not, she *was* struggling with heightened emotions.

Surreptitiously, she glanced over the rim of her cocktail glass at Mitch, who sat at his ease on one of Ginnie's many pale leather couches. He caught her glance—he never did miss much—and smiled at her.

Her heart gave an extra throb, reacting like that of a love-struck teenager. That was just her problem. Exactly her predicament. She and Mitch couldn't have a future together, but her yearning to relive the past—to finish what they'd started as teenagers—was overwhelming. Wasn't that one of the reasons she had agreed to let him come along on this trip?

"Trey seems happy with his gifts," Ginnie said.

Across the room, Grant's family had gathered as Trey and some of Grant's nieces and nephews played with her son's new toys.

Andi smiled at her mother-in-law. Despite the risk to her flowing cocktail dress, Ginnie held Missy in her lap, helping her guide a half-gummed teething biscuit to her mouth.

"Oh, he's thrilled," Andi assured her. "You know I'll need to take most of the toys with us tomorrow. He won't want to be parted from them."

Ginnie had always been a loving mother and grandmother as well as a gracious hostess. She had been both that morning when Andi had made the last-minute call just before they left for the airport. First, Ginnie had asked eagerly about Trey and Missy. Then as Mitch had so calmly reminded her outside the house, Ginnie had readily agreed to include Andi's family friend on her party guest list.

She winced thinking about the other call she had made. Or rather, the text message she had sent to her best friend. She had told Cara only that she had had a change in plans—nothing to worry about—and would be in touch within the week.

"It's so nice you were able to join us this evening," Ginnie said to Mitch.

"I'm very glad you were willing to have me," he replied.

Who *wouldn't* want to have Mitch Weston? She certainly did.

Andi stared down at her glass. She ought to be ashamed of herself for a thought like that. Considering she sat here in her mother-in-law's house celebrating her son's birthday, she ought to be thinking instead of Grant. But she wasn't ashamed. She had put her life with Grant where it should be, in a special, treasured place never to be forgotten but one she would never be able to visit again.

If only she could get her in-laws to do the same.

She was happy to see the family again and had enjoyed dinner and birthday cake and Trey's excitement at his celebration, but she wished it were time for her to go.

Or did she?

She glanced at Mitch again.

In an upstairs bedroom, he had changed into dress clothes, a long-sleeved shirt with cuffs fastened with unadorned silver links and slacks as dark as his polished belt and shoes. Nothing flashy about him, nothing ostentatious. Nothing to show he was pretending to be someone he wasn't.

Well…someone he was, but tailored to match his role, one he carried off as if he'd been born to it. He had fit in with the Price family as well as he'd always fit with her own.

For all she knew, like Grant, Mitch spent a good part of his time doing undercover work, getting plenty of practice in taking on different roles for his job.

For all she knew, which was so little.

"Andi told me about the accident," he was saying. "I'm sorry for your loss."

She gripped her glass. He had to mean Grant. How had he managed to steer the conversation in that direction? And what had she missed?

"Thank you," Ginnie said quietly. "There's not a day that goes by that we don't think of him. I love seeing Trey here again. He reminds me so much of Grant at that age." She brushed her chin against Missy's curls.

Andi's eyes blurred.

Mitch nodded. "As I said, I don't get back to Cowboy Creek as often as I like, but I know her granddad is having the time of his life with the kids around."

Andi blinked and took a breath. Where was he headed now? Was she wrong to feel suspicious? "We'll be back here in Arizona again soon."

He laughed, but looked at Ginnie. "And I know Jed won't be happy to learn that. You know," he went on, "they're doing some reconstruction at the hotel and opening up the banquet hall again."

She wasn't wrong at all. He was fishing for details, trying to learn things he hadn't heard from her. Trying to *get* information from Ginnie by *giving* her information.

"I hear Andi's got a job there waiting," he said, "any time she wants to take it."

She started, almost spilling her drink. "I've told Grandpa thanks but no thanks," she informed him. "I've got a job in Scottsdale." She turned to her mother-in-law. "Ginnie, I think we'll say goodbye. I know you want to spend time with the kids before they go to bed. Should I clean my daughter up and get her into some fresh pajamas?"

"No, you shall not." Laughing, Ginnie hugged Missy.

"I refuse to miss any part of being a nana, including changing messy babies."

Andi's heart sank. She had tried to be strong for the kids and for Ginnie's benefit, too. She didn't deliberately keep them apart—or she hadn't until she'd made the decision to go to Cowboy Creek. But grabbing overtime every chance she could meant her free time was limited. Ginnie knew that, yet her mother-in-law often gently hinted she didn't see enough of the kids.

She set her glass on the cocktail table and reached for her purse.

Maybe she was reading too much into too little with Ginnie tonight.

Maybe she was wrong to wonder if Mitch had played a role with her, too, making it so easy for her to agree to this time alone. Most of all, maybe she was wrong to believe he'd given his word that they would talk only as a way of getting information she had been so reluctant to share.

By the time they left Andi's mother-in-law's house, it was full dark. It was also a typical December night in Arizona, dry and clear and a few shades warmer than at home in Cowboy Creek.

Mitch left the windows open as he drove through the neighborhood of widely spaced homes fully decked out for the holidays. Eventually their travels took them toward the outskirts of Scottsdale.

Neither of them had spoken much since they'd left the house. The silence felt companionable to him, but they had come here for a number of reasons, most of all, to talk. To give him the chance to help her.

"Want to go for a nightcap before we find our room?" he asked.

"Yes. There's a restaurant and bar not far from the hotel." As she had on their way to Ginnie's, she gave him concise directions.

"Trey did have a ball tonight, didn't he?" he asked.

"Yes. Ginnie spoils him, and so does the rest of the family."

"Looks like nobody's hurting for it."

"What does that mean?"

He looked at her in the flickering light from oncoming headlamps. "It means it looks like they can afford to buy your kid a toy or two."

"Oh. Yes, they can."

Silence again. By the time they'd gotten to the restaurant she'd mentioned, he'd had enough of the quiet. He parked the rental at the far end of the lot, just outside a pool of light from the streetlamp. When he turned off the ignition, she reached for her door handle.

He placed a hand on her arm. Her skin cooled his palm. "Was it cold for you with the windows down?"

"A little. But it felt good."

He slid his hand down to her wrist, trying to warm her. "You feel good."

"Mitch."

She shifted as if planning to back off. He slid his fingers down to twine with hers, loosely, letting her know she could pull away any time she wanted to. Looked as though she didn't want to, as her hand stayed in his. He swallowed a sigh of relief. "What is it? Having those second thoughts now? Is that what's got you uncomfortable?"

"No, that's not it. Not all of it." She stared through the windshield at the restaurant, a square, squat, fake-adobe building not unlike the Cantina. After a minute, she turned to him. Her eyes glinted in the dark. "Why were you talking to Ginnie about Grant?"

He shrugged. "Paying my respects to a woman who lost her son."

"That's it?"

"Yeah. Why should there be any other reason?"

"I don't know. Why did you bring up the Hitching Post and all that about my having a job there?"

"Because you do." He rubbed his thumb across her knuckles. "You know Jed would keep you on the ranch in a heartbeat if he could."

"You shouldn't have said anything to Ginnie. You don't know anything about my relationship with her."

"Because you won't say anything to me about it. But you can now." He turned in his seat, being careful of his knee near the steering column, and reached across with his free hand to tuck a strand of her hair behind her ear. "That's what we came here for, isn't it? To talk."

"In a *parking lot*?"

The astonishment in her voice made him laugh. "Yeah, you're right. We came here to talk—and for more than that, and we both know it. But not in a parking lot. Now we're here, though, no sense missing out on an experience we've never had together."

He let his fingers slide down another strand of her hair, let his knuckles brush the front of her sky blue shirt. The deep breath making that shirt rise and fall, the touch of her breast against his hand—both sent a hair-trigger response through him. His fingers tightened reflexively around hers. He had no idea what drove her, but she gripped his hand in return.

Swallowing a groan, he leaned down to plant his mouth on hers. She tasted good. Very good. But after traveling all this way, waiting all this time, wanting her from the minute he'd seen her standing in the barn doorway years ago, he refused to settle for a taste. He slid forward just as she inched toward him, enough to bring them together. Not full frontal contact, but satisfying enough to pull a few more triggers.

Damn, if he didn't have the raging hormones of a teenager right now. He'd summon the matching stamina, too, because he planned on making this a long night.

Chapter Eleven

Andi slid onto her side of the restaurant booth and put her bag on the seat beside her.

"All fixed up?" Mitch said teasingly. "Let me see."

She laughed as she swatted his hand away from her face. "I'm fine. But my lips may never go back to normal size."

"You should thank me, then. You won't need any of those injections women get to plump theirs up."

"Are you saying I needed them *before*—"

"Before we nearly got arrested for indecent exposure?"

"Mitch!" They sat in a corner booth of the restaurant, Mitch with his back to the wall. She glanced at the table closest to them and beyond that at the row of stools at the bar. No one seemed to be listening, but she leaned forward, anyway, to set the record straight.

Yes, they'd gotten carried away in the car, and yes, Mitch had gotten her blouse unbuttoned and her bra unhooked, and yes, she had loved every minute. Every touch. But that was as far as they'd gone. "We did *not* get arrested. We didn't even come close."

"True. Where *is* the law in this town, anyway? Asleep at the wheel?" He smiled. "We sure weren't. Although I have to admit to a crick in my hip from maneuvering around the steering column."

She laughed. "Stop. Please."

He did stop, probably only because the waitress came up to their booth. After she had left with their order, he reached across the tabletop and linked his fingers with hers, the way he had in the car.

"All right, then. Let's talk."

Instinctively, she began to pull away. He didn't move. Of course, he wouldn't argue. The decision to back off would be hers.

Those words sounded so final…so familiar… The day she had met him near the corral, to shield herself, she had made her awful declaration about choosing to walk away. Years ago, her choice or not, she had walked away and left, too. And she had never reached out to him again.

Now she tightened her grip on his fingers.

Recalling the thoughts she'd had about him at Ginnie's made her feel guiltier than ever.

They sat there just holding hands until the waitress arrived with their drinks, accompanied by catcalls from a couple of men over near the bar. Mitch glanced in that direction, then focused on her again.

She took a sip of her drink. A Virgin Mary this time. No more after-dinner cocktails. She wanted to have a clear head, although to tell the truth, she still felt a little light-headed—in the most wonderful kind of way—from their session in the front seat of the car. Her first time making out in a parking lot. With the first boy she had ever loved.

She hoped this would be a night of many firsts.

The thought of what he might start in their room left her hot all over. She would let him make the first move there. But here… Maybe if she opened up about her past, he would follow and tell her about his.

"My relationship with my mother-in-law," she said

slowly. "You wanted to know. She's always been so good to me, even when I first met her. She could never take my own mother's place, but really, the timing between when my mother died and I met Grant was so close, Ginnie just naturally—eventually—became like a second mother to me." She paused, then added, "With Grant, the timing for everything was so close."

"You mean kids?"

"No." She shook her head. "We were already married before I got pregnant with Trey. With the timing, I meant Grant and I got married very soon after we met. The proverbial whirlwind courtship, a short engagement and then the baby surprise while we were still newlyweds. We were so happy about Trey. And everything…everything helped so much to take my mind off my mom, too."

She took a quick sip of her drink to ease her dry throat. "We were still in college when we met and got married, but I quit school before graduation because I was already pregnant by then. It was a high-risk pregnancy, and I was sick for the first two trimesters, then on bed rest for the third."

Mitch took her hand again and squeezed her fingers gently. She nodded in thanks for his silent sympathy. She could have stopped talking, could have turned the focus of the conversation to him, but she wanted to go on. To tell him everything.

"My father-in-law passed away not too long after we were married. Ginnie was alone in that big house and encouraged us to move in with her. We did, for a while. And we stayed close, buying a house in Fountain Hills, which is why I didn't move away right after…after Grant was killed."

He sandwiched her hand between his. She could read

the questions in his eyes, but he didn't ask them. His restraint made it easier for her to go on.

"Everyone, including Grant's family, believed his job involved selling high-end computer systems to customers all over the world, which is why he traveled so much. That's what we wanted them all to think."

Across the room, raucous shouts rose over the rest of the voices in the room.

He looked that way again. His momentary distraction and the noise gave her the chance to take a deep breath and let it out in a gust of air.

She was taking a chance now with Mitch. Taking a risk. But she trusted him.

When he looked back, she said, "Very few people know this. Grant was with the CIA."

His fingers pressed hers tightly for a moment. "On an op when he was killed?"

She swallowed hard. "Yes. I was pregnant with Missy. He never got to see her." Her voice broke. "Never even got to see her ultrasound."

"I'm sorry."

After another deep breath, she nodded in acknowledgment again. "I've come to terms with losing him, Mitch. I loved Grant, but I accept that he's gone. Only, sometimes…like remembering he never saw Missy, and knowing he missed Trey's birthday party, and realizing he won't ever share a Christmas with the kids…" Her voice broke. She forced herself to continue. "Times like those still hit me out of the blue."

"That's understandable." His voice sounded gruff, gravelly. But his hands around hers were gentle, his thumb stroking hers a tender caress.

She sighed. "You know, my mom was there for most

of my life—and for all of my childhood and teen years. But Trey and Missy won't ever know their daddy."

"That's not true. They *will* know him. Through pictures and conversations and your memories." His eyes were dark and shining. He leaned forward and said earnestly, "People die, Andi, but that doesn't mean they're forgotten. You won't let that happen. Neither will Ginnie."

His compassion helped ease her tension at telling this story so few people knew. At the same time, seeing how much he cared raised feelings she couldn't…wouldn't… deny. Feelings he deserved to know.

"Mitch, I—"

A loud crash from the other side of the room startled her into silence. They both turned to look just as a man sprawled on the floor beside a toppled bar stool scrambled to his feet with both arms swinging. A second man spun him around, pinning his hands behind his back. From an adjacent bar stool, a restaurant patron threw a punch at the attacker. Yet another man grabbed the patron and put him in a similar armlock, but his captive quickly bent at the waist and lifted him from the floor.

Mitch rose from his seat.

"Mitch—no!" A sudden flash of him in danger made her grab his wrist. She'd lost her husband. She couldn't lose Mitch, too.

"I'm just going to check things out."

"No!" Knowing she was overreacting, she took a quick calming breath. "Why do you need to get involved? Whatever's going on doesn't concern us."

"Those guys over there need a hand."

So much for just checking things out. "You could get hurt again. Think about your knee."

Mitch loosened her hold on his arm and lightly pressed

her hand flat beneath his on the tabletop. "I can't be a bystander, Andi. This is what I do."

He kissed her forehead, then was gone.

"I DON'T UNDERSTAND."

Mitch didn't need to hear Andi's words. In the halo of light from the lamp nearest their rental car, he saw her confusion.

"Why do you need to go to the police station?"

"I told you," he said evenly, "to make a report."

"But what is there to say? All you did was walk outside with those guys for a few minutes and then come right back in to our booth."

No. That wasn't all he'd done.

His first look at the intoxicated pair at the bar had put his senses on alert. Not for danger or serious trouble at that point, just the usual scan for any signs indicating a rowdy conversation would become a drunken brawl.

A later glance had told him the situation could get far worse.

By the time the bar stool toppled, he had known the setup was much more complicated than it looked on the surface.

And when the apparent onlookers joined the fray, he had gone to lend assistance to a pair of his fellow officers.

"Come on," he said, "let's get inside." He held the passenger door of the rental open until she entered the car.

As he walked around to the driver's door, he thought of what they had done in this car just a short while ago. Then he locked the memory into a separate compartment in his mind and focused on what he would do now.

Once he'd left the key in the ignition, he turned to her. "I walked outside to talk to two of those guys," he clarified, "because they were undercover narcs involved in an op gone wrong." He tried not to wince as he said those all-too-familiar words.

She sucked in a breath. He waited. "You couldn't know they were cops," she said finally.

"I could. As soon as I saw them in action."

She shook her head, puzzled. "I still don't understand why you'd need to make a statement. You walked over there after everything had ended. You didn't *see* anything."

He took her hand and held it between his palms. "I did see."

She frowned. "You barely glanced over at the bar the entire time we were in there."

"Andi, I'm a well-trained cop." Her fingers twitched against his. "We're taught to register in a glance more than most people see after a long, steady look. Before the narcs arrived, I saw an exchange go down and a guy leave the bar. Could have been money that changed hands, could have been drugs, could have been the key to a bus station locker containing a murder weapon."

"And it could have been a business card."

"Yeah, that, too. But it wasn't. It was drugs."

"Then you could have been taking your life in your hands by going over there."

She sounded full of concern for him…

Or distraught over yet another situation hitting her out of the blue. A situation hitting too close to home and family.

He released her hand and cranked the car's engine. "Taking risks is part of the job."

Taking hits.

Taking bullets.

Taking lives.

"I told you," he said flatly, "this is what I do."

"WHAT DID YOU say to that?"

Startled, Andi wrapped her arms more tightly around her upraised knees and stared at Cara.

She had almost forgotten she was sitting on her best friend's couch wrapped in her best friend's afghan. It wasn't so much warmth as comfort she was seeking from the crocheted wool and from the cup of tea on the table in front of her and from explaining the events of the evening to Cara. The events that had finally, sadly proven to her how dedicated Mitch was to his job.

She'd had to volunteer *something* to justify her late text and even later appearance on Cara's doorstep. And once she had begun, the words had poured out, just like the water Cara was pouring to reheat her tea.

"There wasn't much I could say to him after that," she admitted. "I could tell his mind wasn't on our conversation. He wanted to get to the police station to fill out his report. So since it was on his way, I just asked him to drop me off at the hotel."

He seemed distracted yet reluctant to go, until she reminded him the sooner he left, the sooner he could return.

At the time, it had seemed the right thing to say.

Alone in the room, she had felt the walls closing in.

"And then I texted you," she told Cara, forcing a smile. "I'm just glad you were here and didn't decide to go into work tonight, after all."

"I wasn't about to give up a night off. But you know I looked forward to it a lot more when you were planning to stay."

"Sorry. I must seem like a Ping-Pong ball, bouncing back and forth with our plans."

Cara shook her head. "No, not a Ping-Pong ball so much. More like a woman who can't make up her mind. Are you going to regret this?" she asked softly.

"Spending the night here with you? How could I? You bought the cupcakes, didn't you?"

"*And* the ice cream."

Truthfully, she didn't want to think about cake or ice cream. They only reminded her about the party tonight and her conversation with Mitch at the Big Dipper. Maybe if she hadn't pushed for the *where* and *when* of their talk about what had happened in Los Angeles, she wouldn't be sitting here now.

As it turned out, she had done all the talking. And she might never hear Mitch's story.

"Andi, you know what I meant. You waited a long time for tonight."

Cara had known about her crush on Mitch from the beginning. Her first letter to Cara from Garland Ranch that summer had been filled with details about Grandpa's new stable hand.

"I don't know what I'll regret." She glanced away and sighed. "No, that's not true. I do know I'll wish I'd had tonight with Mitch."

She couldn't worry about regrets.

"Everything doesn't have to be over with him," Cara said, "just because your plans for this trip didn't work out."

"Yes, it does. I can't have a relationship with him. Missy and Trey have already lost one father to a dangerous career. I can't risk having them lose another one."

"Nothing may ever happen to Mitch."

"He's already been injured. And I told you what he said—this is what he does." Her chest tightened at the memory of how finally he'd said those words. "Seeing him in action tonight, and then later hearing how he had kept track of what was going on—while I didn't have a clue—just proved it to me. Mitch may be lucky and never get hurt again. But he's all cop, all the time, and he always will be."

Alone in the hotel room, she'd had to face that truth.

Now she tried to deny the truth she had been about to share with him at the restaurant.

Mitch's compassion had eased her tension the way nothing else could have. His understanding set off feelings she couldn't deny. Out in the parking lot, she had reacted like a crazy, hormone-driven teen, but no matter what she tried to tell herself, it wasn't adolescent lust pushing her to make out with him. It wasn't fond memories or unfulfilled dreams.

She loved Mitch, more now than she ever had. She loved that he helped at the Hitching Post without a word of complaint. Loved the way he talked with Trey and Robbie and included them in everything he did. Loved how he held her gently and kissed her till her head spun and, yes, how he never stopped trying to find out what worried her.

She loved everything about Mitch.

Just as she had begun to tell him, the fight had broken out, he had run into battle, and she had lost the chance to share her feelings.

But she had to be grateful for that fight. It had saved her from herself. Her feelings for Mitch had almost caused her to make one of the biggest mistakes of her life—putting her own desires ahead of her children's needs.

Chapter Twelve

After a nod at the clerk, Mitch made his way through the hotel lobby.

He'd spent more time than he'd expected to at the station. First had come his official questioning, then an off-the-books session. Some officers wouldn't have opened up or taken the help, but the narcs he'd worked with tonight were a couple of good men who didn't mind an assist from an out-of-town cop.

After that, they'd stood around shooting the bull. But tonight, the usual lure of sharing war stories couldn't keep him from edging toward the door after only a few minutes.

His thoughts had been with Andi, and that's exactly where he wanted to be now.

A stay in a fleabag motel would have done him just fine, but no way would that have been right for her. He hoped while he'd been gone she had taken advantage of the hotel's amenities.

He hoped she was ready for an eventful night.

As he punched the elevator button for their floor, his hand shook. Fatigue, possibly. Eagerness, for sure. He spent the ride up envisioning her in a plush hotel towel and nothing else, smelling like fancy soap and looking like his long-ago dreams come true.

When he reached out with his key, he had no doubt what made his hand shake.

The door swung open silently. The room was spotless and spacious, with oversize Southwestern-style furniture and a king-size bed.

An empty bed. With the covers still tucked up around the pillows.

He thought of towels and soap and muscle-soothing hot water. His gaze went to the open doorway on the far side of the room, but though his mind had already registered the dark bathroom beyond it, his subconscious had also picked up something along the way. Something he'd have noted immediately if his cop sense hadn't been dulled by dreams of satisfying a few other senses.

A stiff paper rectangle sat propped up on the dresser. A sheet of notepaper, folded in half and turned the color of whipped butter by the glow from the adjacent lamp. At least she hadn't left him in the dark. So to speak.

He stared at the notepaper, considering.

If he hadn't spent so much time at the station tonight… if he hadn't heeded the feeling in his gut at the restaurant…if he hadn't insisted on coming along on this trip…

Hell.

If he hadn't let things ride years ago instead of finding out why Andi had gone away.

The reminder pushed him across the room to snatch up the note. His hand shook just as it had in the elevator and outside the door. Not from fatigue or eagerness or the need he had finally admitted to himself, but from dread.

His instincts were talking again, telling him history had come back to bite him. He looked down at the handwritten note. Simple. Short. Sweet. No greeting. No goodbye.

I'll stay with a friend and pick up the kids tomorrow.

History *had* repeated itself—with a twist. The girl he'd once loved, now his one-night lover, had left him.

He crumpled the note in his fist.

THE NEXT MORNING, Mitch dropped off the rental car and made his way to the departure gate.

He'd had to drive a ways, but he'd found a greasy spoon for breakfast to make up for the fancy hotel with the big, lonely bed. The sight of the oil slick on his platter didn't diminish his appetite. After twenty-four-hour stakeouts, he'd seen and eaten worse.

He probably should have waited to buy breakfast here at the airport. As he now saw, he could have spent time with more pleasant company than his own.

He slid his overnight bag beneath a plastic table with enough chairs attached to make a quad.

"Mitch! Look!" Trey exclaimed, grinning. He was playing with a couple of the toy ponies he'd gotten as birthday gifts. "Little horses, like Robbie's!"

He grinned back at the kid and reached across the tabletop to give him a high five. Then he looked over at Andi, who sat staring at the paper-wrapped sandwich in front of her.

"Is this seat taken?" Not waiting for a reply, he planted his rear in the seat beside hers. His left knee twinged from the punishing workout he'd put himself through that morning. A small twinge, and he'd felt no backlash from it till now. A good sign of progress.

Too bad he hadn't had such luck with Andi.

His right thigh brushed her leg, reminding him of all he had missed. "I see you made it here on time. No sleeping in after a night of girl talk?"

"Who said my friend was female?"

"Very funny." This time, his grin felt forced.

After that Dear John note of hers, this lighthearted exchange sounded unreal.

She was putting up a front for the sake of the kids, especially her son, who was old enough to pick up on their words along with tone and facial expressions. He didn't blame her for that. It was the same reason he hadn't pushed her for answers the second he'd taken his seat. That, and the fact that she would just refuse to reply, leaving him unsatisfied…again.

"Jed mentioned you'd initially planned to stay with your best friend, the kids' babysitter…Cara."

"Grandpa has a lot to answer for," she mumbled.

"He also has a lot of answers. Which is more than I can say." He lowered his voice. "You planning on telling me why you left me high and dry and damned frustrated last night?"

Silently, she focused on the sandwich in front of her. He had called it right. He would have to approach her from another angle. "We had use of the rental all day. I'd have gone with you to pick up the kids."

"That's okay. I wanted to spend some time with my mother-in-law."

"Didn't she miss me when you showed up alone?"

Her brows rose. "Why would she? You were just there for the party since you had time on your hands."

"Yeah. And I had a lot more of it later on." He shot a glance at Trey, who appeared zeroed in on the ponies. Still, he lowered his voice. "What happened?"

"We chatted while the kids ate breakfast, and then I called a taxi to bring us here."

"You know that's not what I meant."

Her chin went up the way it had that one day at the Hitching Post. Then, he couldn't tell defiance from determination from challenge. Now, he had a bad feeling she'd just given him a shot of all three.

"Last night was a mistake," she said quietly.

Fool that he was, he couldn't keep his pulse from jumping. "You mean leaving?"

"I mean considering it at all."

"Quite a change in tune, isn't it?"

She turned away to spoon something for Missy, baby food or applesauce maybe. He cared only because it took his mind off the conversation. But a split second later, his thoughts went where they were bound to go. To where they'd been all night. To what might have been.

In the time they had spent in that restaurant, she had told him what he'd wanted to know—what had her so worried. A story she had kept from so many people, but not him. She had trusted him with the truth. Then why had she run off?

"Would it have made a difference if I'd gone up to the room with you?"

He saw her chest rise, heard her breath catch. He felt his own breath lodge in his throat until she shook her head. "Not enough to make it matter in the long run, Mitch."

She had told him how much she had been devastated by her husband's death. Yet she had said she'd come to accept her loss, and he had seen the truth of that in her manner. In her eyes. Still, he felt certain she was holding something back, trying to handle it on her own. And despite the way she'd walked off on him, he still wanted to help her.

Maybe, no matter what she claimed, she hadn't gotten over her loss yet. He could understand that.

Or maybe he couldn't trust his instincts about her.

Maybe he'd never be able to depend on his instincts again.

LATER THAT DAY, Mitch found himself wandering toward Cowboy Creek's sheriff's office, something he had sworn he wouldn't make a habit.

But in all honesty, he needed the visit to distract himself from an image he couldn't erase from his mind. He kept seeing Andi and the kids in the airport taxi she'd insisted on hiring rather than let him drive them to the hotel.

How would we explain that? she had asked.

Even as he'd opened his mouth, she had added, *I don't want to have to tell another cover story, especially one involving the kids.*

That kicker kept him silent, and finally, he'd agreed to let her go.

The bad taste *that* phrase left in his mouth had him yanking open the office door.

"Well, look what the wind blew in," Paco said with a grin. "Ready for a cup?"

"I'll pass, thanks."

"Sheriff's in his office."

Nodding, he went past the desk to the door in the rear of the room. He hadn't expected to run into his dad until suppertime.

When he entered the office, Lyle glanced up from the spreadsheet he was perusing. His eyes over the rims of his half glasses were as clear and alert as ever, but his hair was mostly gray now.

"Coffee?" his dad asked.

"What, are you trying to give it away? Paco just offered, and I turned him down. I think I'll get a cup of the real stuff over at SugarPie's."

"Good thinking. Don't overdo it on the bakery goods, though. I hear we're eating early tonight." Lyle propped his crossed feet on the edge of the desk and sat back with his hands behind his head. The wooden captain's chair creaked in a handful of places.

"Sounds like my old bones cracking, doesn't it?"

"Not that I've ever heard." He took a seat in one of the visitor's chairs. "How's the arthritis?"

"Good days outweigh the bad. How's the knee?"

Mitch shifted and felt the reminder of too much exercise that morning. "Doing okay. The good days are adding up."

"Nice to hear. Mine are going in the opposite direction. I won't be sorry a few months from now when I turn in my badge."

He looked again at Lyle's graying hair. Retirement had to come for his dad sometime. He'd always known that. He just hadn't realized it would happen this soon. "You'll miss it."

"Well, sure. Just the way your granddad did when he left."

"Leaving his legacy behind him."

Lyle smiled. "Just as I'm doing, son."

Mitch swallowed hard. He propped his ankle on his good knee to take the strain off the bad one. To have an excuse not to look across the desk.

Both his dad and granddad had been proud to have another member of the family in law enforcement. When he had packed to leave for the job, they had each taken him aside. He'd gotten invaluable tips from two lifetimes of experience. And, above all, he'd gotten the advice to "go with your gut."

Advice that had served him well—until a poor judgment call left him wounded and his partner dead.

He tapped his knee brace and looked at his dad again. "You'll be missed."

"I'm sure I will, for a while. But someone will come

up the ranks to replace me, and later someone to replace him. That's part of a legacy, too, always having officers ready to protect and serve."

He nodded, knowing that as well as his dad did. He'd heard that call even before his dad and granddad had shared it with him years ago. It was what had made him want to follow in their footsteps.

"Of course," Lyle said, "with all that shifting around in the department, we could end up being shorthanded around here."

He nodded, but said nothing. First Jed, claiming a shortage of wranglers on the ranch, and now his dad, hinting at a similar situation in the department.

At least *some* folks wanted him around.

Chapter Thirteen

Mitch escaped from the glaring afternoon sun into the dimmer interior of SugarPie's. At this time of day, the sandwich shop was nearly deserted, except for one lone white-haired diner.

Mitch couldn't have left if he'd wanted to. Jed Garland's eagle eyes had already spotted him, and Jed's hand was raised high, waving to the waitress.

"I just got here," Jed told him. "Paz and Tina are finishing up an order at the L-G." He gestured toward a chair. "Have a cup and help me kill some time."

Mitch took one of the pink-cushioned chairs opposite Jed.

"How was your trip?"

He froze. Just how much did the man know?

"Nancy said you had to go away overnight, too. How'd your knee hold up with the traveling?"

Slowly, he relaxed. "The trip was fine, and the knee's improving every day." He wished he could say the same about his interactions with Andi.

The waitress, Cole's sister Layne, came to take their order.

"And how are you doing, girl?" Jed asked, reaching for her hand.

She smiled. "Fine, Jed. Just tired, but that's not news lately."

"I'd think not. Between that little boy of yours and the new baby, I'd be worn-out, too. I told Tina to let you know we've got plenty of room at the Hitching Post if you need to come stay awhile."

"She did tell me, thanks." After a warm smile for Jed, she took their order for coffee and went back to the kitchen.

Jed turned to him. "Missed you at the hotel yesterday, Mitch. We're getting kinda used to seeing your face out there again."

He didn't know what Jed knew or surmised or would make up out of whole cloth about his absence. Thanks to his years working with the man, he did know for sure the heights Jed was capable of going to for his family. And the breadth of his concern for extended family such as Layne.

He'd always admired Jed's kindness to others.

He only hoped his efforts at the Hitching Post had paid back some of his old boss's many favors. Because his days of playing assistant were over. "I don't guess I'll be around as much out at the ranch."

Jed's white eyebrows shot up. "Why's that?"

"They can use a hand over at the sheriff's office temporarily, and since I've done about all I can do at the hotel, I told them I'd swing by."

"You'll be back to help with the Christmas tree?"

He'd forgotten about that. Jed sat frowning so intently, Mitch didn't have the heart to give him an outright no. He looked down at his coffee mug. "With that crew at the ranch, you'll have plenty of hands to set up the tree. And I'd be no good at the rest of it. I'd break more ornaments than I got hung."

"That's a tradition in the family," Jed said, chuckling. "And speaking of family, Andi and the kids are back home. We're having a party tonight for Trey. You're invited."

"Thanks, but my mom's going all out for supper." Not a word of lie there. She'd insisted on making a big meal to welcome him home after his overnight trip. Because he *had* skirted the truth about that, and because she'd gone to so much trouble, it would take a stronger man than he was to miss the meal.

But this man could get used to having a home-cooked supper every night. Too bad he didn't plan to stick around.

He wouldn't even consider moving back home.

Jed might succeed in getting Andi to stay in Cowboy Creek permanently, and how would he handle that? How could he risk seeing her but not being able to have her?

ANDI SET HER cell phone on the bed beside her and picked up her notebook again.

"Let me guess," Jane said. "You-know-who."

"Yes." She had had several texts from Sandra at the airport this morning, then another round this afternoon. She looked at her cousin, who sat at the desk in the suite checking place cards against Tina's printout. "I can understand the bride stressing out as the wedding gets closer, but having her make so many last-minute changes is hard on all of us."

"They wouldn't be, if you'd put your foot down and remind her a non-family-owned reception hall wouldn't provide this type of hand-holding."

"*You* should be the one in this position, Jane. I won't say I'm a pushover, but I do want the wedding to be what the bride wants it to be."

"Like yours was?"

"Yes." She smiled. Planning her wedding had been one of the happiest times of her life, right up there with the ceremony itself and the birth of her children.

"You're such a romantic," Jane teased. "A believer in true love, and a fan of happy endings."

Sadly, the first two didn't always lead to the last. "I'd say you were all of those yourself."

Jane laughed. "You're right. I guess it's why I went along with Grandpa's plans for the hotel in the first place. Besides wanting to help him, of course—which I know is why you're in this, too."

"Yes." Though Jane also knew her other reason for coming to Cowboy Creek, Andi didn't want to get into it again now. She picked up the notepad sitting beside her phone. A few weeks ago, she couldn't have realized what her decision to stay at the hotel would lead to. But along with being a hopeless romantic and wanting to help Jed achieve his dream, she had had the overwhelming need to get away. To put some space between her little family and her many in-laws.

That reason needed to say hidden. How could she share all her feelings with Jane—or anyone else? She would sound ungrateful…would *feel* ungrateful…for all her mother-in-law had done for her and the kids.

At the party last night, she had felt more guilt than ever about leaving town with Trey and Missy to come to Cowboy Creek in the first place.

Long afterward, as she had tried falling asleep at Cara's, she had felt guilty about the way she had left Mitch to spend the night alone.

"You haven't said much about the party," Jane said.

Startled by the connection to her own thoughts, Andi jumped, then stared down at the line she'd just slashed across the notebook. She imagined Mitch coming into the hotel room and finding that cold, emotionless note she had left for him. But she hadn't known what else to say.

"The party was great. Trey loved all his gifts, and I had to bring a huge carry-on home with us."

"So I heard. You should have let one of us pick you up at the airport instead of taking a taxi home."

"I didn't want to bother anyone to make that trip."

"Oh-h-h," Jane said, teasingly again, "and you didn't mind bothering Mitch?"

"He—" *Drove home alone.* Swallowing the words along with a sigh of relief at her catch, she said, "He didn't pick us up." He *had* offered several times this morning to drive them home, but she had preferred to be on her own with the kids.

"According to Grandpa, Mitch took you to the airport. I just found out this morning. You never mentioned that to me, either."

"It was a last-minute arrangement. Like Sandra with the additions to the seating chart."

"Yes, but much more fun. I'm glad you're giving the man a chance."

"I'm not!"

Jane's eyebrows shot up.

Andi flushed. But she had only spoken the truth. Besides, after their conversation at the airport this morning, she doubted she would ever see much of Mitch again.

JED STOOD SURVEYING the dining room, where Jane and Tina were busy transforming its "simple, Southwestern charm"—according to the new website Jane had put together—into something out of a science-fiction movie. Stars and planets and spaceships hung from every light fixture, and crepe-paper creatures climbed the walls.

"Looking fine," he said. Their guests might not like

the disruption to the dude ranch atmosphere, but nothing was too good for one of his great-grandkids.

"They do look great," Tina agreed. "Robbie will want the same thing for his next birthday. We'll leave them up for a day or so before we decorate for Christmas." She handed a balloon to Jane, who stood on a stepladder in the center of the room.

"Thanks." Jane tied the balloon to the light fixture above the family's table and reached for the next one. "You know, Grandpa, I was just talking to Andi."

"Yeah? And…?"

"I hate to say it, but I don't think this plan of ours is working."

He shot a look over his shoulder at the doorway. "Careful. She might come walking right in."

"No, it's okay, Abuelo," Tina said. "She's staying up in her room with Missy and the boys so Trey won't see the decorations before time."

He waited till Jane had climbed down from the ladder. "What's going on, then?"

"That's the problem. I don't think anything is." She gathered up the packaging from the balloons. "She's not talking to me. Yet. But I get the feeling things didn't go well on their trip to the airport."

He swallowed a smile. Though he hadn't shared the news with the girls, his idea to have Mitch see Andi off on her flight had paid off in more ways than even he had anticipated. And this afternoon at SugarPie's, the boy had looked downright exhausted from what had to be lack of sleep—which he figured meant a promising sign of progress.

Mitch had gotten a little gun-shy about returning to the ranch. That didn't worry him any. He knew the boy would do what he'd agreed to and help them with the Christmas tree.

"Andi hasn't said much to me, either," Tina said. "We tried chatting upstairs, but with the boys running around the room, we didn't get very far. And truthfully, I don't think she minded at all when I said I had to go down to help Abuela with supper."

"Something's got to give, if Andi won't," Jane said.

Tina nodded. "I never thought I'd say this, but we may need to do something drastic."

"Hold off a bit on that," he said.

Both girls stared at him.

"Oh, don't you worry," he assured them. "Your old granddaddy's got a few tricks up his sleeve yet."

He chuckled, liking the thought he could still surprise them. Taking Tina and Jane into his confidence had worked well for him. But there were some things a man just had to do on his own.

Nobody in Cowboy Creek would have a clue what else he had in store for Mitch and Andi.

"GREAT MEAL, MOM," Mitch said to Nancy.

He sat back in his chair in the dining room and looked at all the empty plates. The rest of their family had already left the house, and he and Laurie were the only two still sitting at the table with their parents.

"I'm glad you enjoyed it, Mitch. And that *you* won't have to eat warmed-up leftovers again, Lyle."

Considering his dad could rarely make it home at this hour, the early suppertime tonight was odd. On the other hand, it had been so long since Mitch had been around here on a regular basis, he wasn't sure of the family schedules anymore.

He had more of a handle on what went on with the

Garland family, who lived by the clock when it came to mealtimes for the Hitching Post's guests.

He wished he had more of a handle on what had gone through Andi's head yesterday. Last night. This morning. He could come up with all the reasons in the world why she had changed her mind about sharing his bed, but he would never know the right reasons if he didn't get the answers from her.

A chance he didn't plan to have, since he didn't intend to go near her again.

"What's on the menu for dessert?" he asked.

"Nothing, I'm afraid," Nancy said serenely.

Another surprise. In his day, the Weston family had never skipped dessert after their main meal. Obviously, his day around here had come and gone.

Nancy poked Lyle in the ribs.

"Oh, yeah," his dad said, slapping his stomach. "I've got to cut back on all those sweets."

Now, *that* was something he'd never heard before. In fact, Lyle always joked that he would never get a reputation as a lawman who liked his doughnuts—because he liked anything with sugar on or in it.

Mitch gave a mental shrug and turned to Nancy. "Well, if we're all done, I think you ought to sit and relax and let Laurie load up the dishwasher."

"Or *you* could do it," she said. "Couldn't he, Daddy?"

"I don't see why not. This is an equal opportunity household."

Mitch shook his head. "Next time you're around, kid, remind me to give up my right to free speech."

"Never mind." She gave him her best devious-little-sister smile. "I'll help you out this one time, if you'll help me."

"With what?"

"Giving me a ride to Garland Ranch for Trey's birthday party. I have a present for him. And you could get some dessert." Before he could respond, she had grabbed a few dishes and rushed to the kitchen.

"I think I'll help before it runs too late," Nancy said. "Jed told me they would wait on the cake until you got there."

"'You'?"

"Well..." Her smile looked almost as conniving as his sister's. "Laurie and whoever she got to take her to the party."

Frowning, he carefully reviewed the evidence.

Early dinner with his dad home, but no dessert.

Laurie dropping her request and running.

Laurie's and Nancy's smiles.

And, topping the list, Jed holding up his family's party.

All proof enough to him that *his* family had joined Jed Garland as coconspirators in one of those matchmaking schemes his mom had mentioned.

A scheme that appeared to involve *him*.

Seeing how Jed had encouraged him to drive Andi to the airport, he shouldn't have been surprised. Knowing his former boss's unwavering concern for family and for employees old and new, he should have figured out before now what Jed was up to.

Leading him into a trap. Tightening a noose around his neck. Attempting to rope him into the Garland clan the way he had Cole and Pete.

And all a complete waste of effort, as the overnight trip with Andi proved Jed's scheme wouldn't stand a chance.

Chapter Fourteen

The dining room was filled and overflowing into the hallway. At the moment, people were mingling and carrying glasses of birthday punch. There would be enough seating for them all, but with so many guests, Andi regretted she hadn't suggested using the banquet hall just to give everyone a little more elbow room.

Most of the ranch hands who worked with the guests were in attendance, including Eddie. The poor kid kept looking toward the doorway as though judging how easily he could make a run for it.

She smiled sympathetically. He would be happier if Laurie were here. The thought made her think about Mitch. Pushing him out of her mind, she went over to Tina. "Where's our other cousin?"

"She and Pete had to run to town. They should be back here any minute."

"Okay. I'm going to fill up another pitcher of punch."

"Great. I'll make another pass with the appetizers."

Slipping through the doorway and between chatting guests, Andi made her way down the hall toward the lobby. Ahead of her, she heard the rumble of a man's deep voice and then female laughter. With luck, that was Jane and Pete.

Smiling, she rounded the corner into the lobby. When

she saw the couple crossing toward her from the front door, she nearly skidded to a halt.

Not Jane and Pete. Mitch and Laurie.

Laurie's bright smile almost rivaled the shiny ribbons on the gift she carried. "Hi, Andi! Has the party started?"

"It sure has." She forced a smile. "In the dining room. You know the way. And I think you'll find someone there who will be very happy to see you."

Laurie giggled and took off.

Andi couldn't have described anything about Laurie other than her smile and the beribboned box. But she took in every inch of Mitch, from his thick, wavy hair to his button-down blue shirt to the polished belt buckle and black biker boots. After a long moment, she realized she was staring—and probably giving him the wrong idea.

Still, she couldn't keep from meeting his eyes.

"Trey, I presume," he said.

"What?"

"The someone who will be happy to see Laurie."

"Oh. Yes, of course, Trey, too. But I meant Eddie."

He nodded. "I can understand that. In his shoes, I'd be just as glad. In my own shoes, I'm not complaining."

He moved forward.

She rested one palm on the flat, steady surface of the registration desk. As Mitch reached for her hand, she couldn't help wanting to link her fingers with his as they had done last night at the restaurant. The memory made her hesitate just long enough for him to brush her wrist with his fingertips before she moved her hand out of reach. "Mitch, don't."

"What? Don't touch? Don't stare, the way you just did? Don't darken your door again?" He smiled without humor. "I'll oblige you with the first two. As for the last, I'm invited to this party—sort of, since I was Laurie's ride."

"It's down the hall."

He nodded. "Maybe we should wait a few minutes. With the expression you're wearing, it's going to be obvious you're not in a party mood. Look, let's just forget last night and move on."

She flinched. Hadn't she been telling herself that, trying to do that with so many things for so long? She hadn't known it would include moving on from Mitch again. "That's a good idea," she agreed. "You go your way, I'll go mine. I'm headed to the kitchen."

"That won't help matters. Walking around each other's as much a dead giveaway as your expression. Act normal."

"Normal?"

"Yeah. Smile."

Rolling her eyes, she forced her lips to curve.

"There you go. Now hold that, no matter what. No matter if someone surprises you." He reached out again, putting his hand over hers, warming her skin. "No matter if someone attempts to catch you off guard." He slid his hand along her forearm, sending a wave of heat through her entire body.

"What is this," she asked, trying to keep her voice from shaking, "a lesson you learned in the police academy?"

"Exactly. If you don't want to blow your cover, don't let anything throw you."

He moved a step nearer. How could she find him closer than she wanted and yet still too far away?

The front door swung open. This time, for certain, she recognized Jane's husky laugh.

Quickly, she stepped away from Mitch and pasted her

act-normal smile on her face—just in time to watch her mother-in-law enter the lobby.

THE PARTY WAS winding down. Trey had torn open his gifts. Tina was topping off the guests' glasses with the last of the punch. The cake platter sat empty but for a few crumbs and a smudge of frosting.

Jed, in his usual place at the head of the long dining room table, had insisted on seating the guests earlier. Odd for a kid's birthday party, at least in Mitch's opinion. Heck, he didn't care. He had made the first cut and wound up sitting next to Andi.

Now he shifted his chair closer to hers, trying to lend her moral support without a word or a touch.

She would never make it on an undercover op. In the lobby, in the space of an instant, he had seen her expression go from cardboard happiness to stunned surprise to genuine delight. She had added that delight to her voice when she'd greeted her mother-in-law. But he'd spent too much time watching faces and listening to voices not to pick up a disconnect.

He was tuning in to another one now, from the head of the long dining room table.

"I brought along the rest of Trey's gifts from last night," Ginnie was saying. She laughed. "But I can see they won't be missed."

"He was as happy to see you as the gifts," Jed said. "We're glad you've come to the party, too."

"Very glad." Andi smiled.

In the lobby, Trey's grandma had given him a smile, too, and a big hello, but nothing beyond that. Nothing to indicate they'd sat down to dinner together in her home less than twenty-four hours earlier. It seemed almost as if she didn't want folks to know they had already met.

There were disconnects and undercurrents and events going on around here that he couldn't figure out. He'd swear they all revolved around Andi, and not only because he had every one of his senses hyper-focused on her.

To his mind, her mother-in-law's showing up unexpectedly was a hefty coincidence. And he didn't believe in coincidences.

Jed's taking the woman under his wing, so to speak, and ushering her to the seat right beside his might be nothing more than a host catering to one of his guests. Or it might be another of Jed's schemes.

Folks began to get up from their seats and mill around the room. Andi went over to talk with Tina.

From one corner, Cole lifted a beer in salute, and Mitch wandered that way, stopping only to snag a bottle from the ice bucket on the drinks table.

"I see you grabbed yourself one of the best seats in the house," Cole said with a grin.

He shrugged. "I sat where the man directed me."

"He sure planned that well." Pete laughed.

Mitch looked from him to Cole and back again. He recognized a setup when he saw one. They were about to spill the details of Jed's latest scheme. After Cole's speech about the benefits of marriage, he wouldn't put it past his own best friend to be in on the deal with Jed. Well, playing along was always a good way to get information. He spoke in a lowered tone under cover of the conversations around them. "What are you two talking about?"

The other men exchanged a glance. Obviously, they had planned some fun at his expense.

"Matchmaking," Pete said in a low voice.

"What?" He shook his head. "No way."

Pete laughed. "Believe what you want, buddy, but I'll

bet my Christmas bonus Grandpa Jed is fixing to get you hitched."

Mitch looked at Cole, who nodded emphatically. "He's unstoppable. The man got us, but good. First me, then Pete."

"And he didn't try to hide what he was doing?"

"Sure he did. At least, with me. I was able to head Pete off, just the way we're doing for you now. But he was too hardheaded to listen, and look where it got him. He and Jane are set to tie the knot soon, too." He shrugged. "If not for you being too tied up with the job these past few months to stay in touch, you would have known all this already."

If not for his undercover op, he'd have been here in Cowboy Creek, standing up for his best friend when he'd married Tina.

"All I've got to say," Cole added, "is that the boss has one granddaughter left, and trust me, he's itching to get her married off, too."

"Not to me. You two can put that idea right out of your minds. He knows I'm not his man."

He wasn't Andi's man, either. Through both her words and her actions, she had made that plain.

Fine by him. He didn't want a relationship with the woman, just the chance to help her.

FEELING AS IF he had a target pinned to his back, Mitch stood for a while longer with Pete and Cole.

He saw Andi and Tina round up their kids to get them to bed.

Despite the way he had shrugged off his buddies' ideas, he knew Cole and Pete were right. Jed saw him as a contender in his matchmaking stakes. He still had his suspicions about Cole's involvement. And though he couldn't be sure about Pete, he'd begun to have second thoughts about him, too. About everyone.

He wondered if he was the last person in Cowboy Creek to know.

Why hadn't he caught on before tonight to what the old man was up to? Were his instincts entirely shot to hell?

His skill at watching other people's backs had surely taken a beating. He didn't have great faith in his ability to watch his own.

A short while later, Tina came back alone.

Laurie and Eddie had drifted over to a love seat in the corner of the dining room, where they looked to be settled in for the night.

In another corner, Jed and Ginnie sat at a table for two. They had their heads together as if they were old friends, which, for all he knew, was exactly the case.

The rest of the family and guests all seemed good to hang on for a while.

He finished his conversation with Cole and Pete and left the room. As he climbed the stairs to the second floor of the hotel, he noted with satisfaction that his knee hadn't stiffened up a bit. Progress.

Now he hoped to make some headway with Andi.

He tapped his knuckles softly on the door, expecting that the kids would be asleep inside. Andi opened the door just as quietly.

She looked surprised to see him. She also looked resigned. "Why did I have the feeling I would see you again tonight?"

"Wishful thinking?"

She shook her head.

"I want to talk."

"I'll bet. But I can't stand out here in the hallway 'talking' with you."

"Let me in, then."

Her eyes narrowed.

"Come on, do you really think I'd try to pull a fast one with your kids in the room? All I want to do is talk." He smiled. "You owe me for not blowing your cover when your mother-in-law showed up."

He saw her wince.

"Look," he said, "I know something's wrong. Something more than just being surprised to find me here tonight. More than you had time to tell me last night. And I know it somehow involves your mother-in-law. What else? Something connected to Jed? To someone else in your family? Is that what brought you back here?"

"I came here for just the reason I told you, to help Grandpa get the bridal business up and running again."

"That's not all of it." Her distress only confirmed what his gut had already told him. She was hiding something. "Talk to me."

He could see her indecision, and his need to find out, to comfort her, to protect her from whatever was bothering her outweighed the thought of any more strain between them.

He smoothed a strand of her hair away from her face. He wanted to stroke the fine lines near her eyes, wanted to lean down and kiss her, but he flat-out refused to give in to the urge. That wasn't why he'd come upstairs to find her, and for once he was not going to lose sight of his goal. He tipped her chin up to get a look at her eyes. They seemed unfocused. "I don't like seeing you this upset."

"I'm not upset."

"The hell you're not," he said evenly, keeping his voice low. "Andi, I'm not going until you give me some answers."

Again, he waited. Why did she have to make helping her so darned hard?

Finally, she sighed. "The kids are asleep."

"We'll talk quietly."

She opened the door wide. He stepped inside without making a sound.

Trey was sprawled across a corner of the king-size bed. Missy lay asleep in a nearby crib.

When Andi took a seat on the small couch off to one side of the room, he joined her. "I know you didn't expect me here tonight," he said. "But why were you so surprised to see your mother-in-law?"

After a quick glance at the kids, she looked back at him for a long moment. Finally she said, "I didn't know she was coming to the party, either."

"She invited herself?"

"I don't know."

"You were all right at her house last night. Why are you so uptight now she's here? Maybe Jed or Tina invited her as a surprise for you and Trey."

"I don't know," she said again, looking away.

He rested his hand on her shoulder until she turned back to face him. "I'm not leaving," he reminded her. He couldn't condemn himself for that. If he didn't push, she wouldn't talk, and it looked as if talking was exactly what she needed.

"All right," she said finally. "You remember I told you about staying close to Grant's family after we were married."

He nodded. "I remember."

"And I'm still close. I love Ginnie. You met her—you know she's a wonderful woman, and she's fabulous with the kids."

"And…"

"And I…I almost told you this last night. But it makes me feel so disloyal even to have these feelings. I just…had to get away from her. From the entire family." She blinked rapidly a few times. "They won't let go of Grant. They won't move on. They won't…they talk *about* him when I'm around, but they don't talk *to* me. It's as if they think I can't hear. Or as if he's the one who's still living, and I'm the one who died." She swallowed hard.

He kept his hands by his sides, not wanting to do anything that would send her into silence again.

"You were right, Mitch. The kids and I—all of his family—will always have Grant in photos and stories and memories. I would never keep that from them, but I can't act like their father's not gone. And I can't—" Her voice broke.

"Can't what?"

She took a deep breath. "I can't tell Ginnie the rest. That Grant left me in financial trouble. It would break her heart to know he didn't provide for the kids."

He frowned. "He had no insurance?"

"He had some, through work. Not enough for our outstanding debts, as it turns out. He always said, why would a man under thirty be worried about life insurance?"

"But you have two kids."

"I know. He thought he had plenty of time to worry about it later. We both did. He's not the only one at fault. But I've lost our house. I told Ginnie I wanted to move to a smaller place, closer to Trey's preschool." Her eyes shimmered. "I'm not sharing this to get your sympathy or your pity, but so you see why I needed some distance from her. I don't want to make up stories. Or tell outright lies. But if she can't even accept the fact that Grant's dead, how would she deal with hearing all this? And more?"

"More?"

She raised her hands palm-up in a gesture of hopelessness. "I need to take care of my kids in my own way. The best way I can. I need to stand on my own. And I can't say that to Ginnie, either. She would think she was losing the kids. So when Grandpa asked me to help with this wedding, I jumped at the chance to come. To get some space. To give all of us a breather. And, hopefully, to give Ginnie and her family time to grieve and accept and move on, the way I have."

He wrapped his arm around her and held her against him, her head tucked beneath his chin. She felt right there, as though she was made to fit there. As though she was where she belonged.

He felt her breath brush his collarbone as she exhaled in a rush. When she shifted restlessly, he took his arm from her shoulders. He felt lucky—grateful—to be sitting beside her. Though their night away had already triggered his need to have her, she had refused to let him get even this close. But he wasn't about to take advantage of her distress to push her into anything she didn't want.

Still, *he* refused to walk away without doing something to protect her from any more hurt.

"Let me help." He linked his fingers with hers.

Her hand jerked, yet she didn't pull away. He'd take that as a good omen. "You don't want anything from me, Andi. At least take my help with this. If you want to move *on*, then you need something—or someone—to move *to*." Hadn't his shrink tried to get that into his head? He'd resisted the idea, but he would recommend it to anyone if only it would convince Andi.

"Trust me," he said. "I know. You need something to let your mother-in-law know you're ready." It was his turn to take a deep breath. "Let's tell her we've gotten engaged."

Chapter Fifteen

Mitch had just proposed.

Andi couldn't stop the wave of pleasure that washed through her. She couldn't deny her overwhelming yearning for that proposal to be true.

But she had no right to think about Mitch and marriage and pleasure all in the same breath, and she certainly had no intentions of going along with his crazy idea.

As if he'd read her mind, he released her hand and held his up in a pacifying gesture. "Hear me out. I'm talking about a temporary engagement. For a very limited time."

Her heart thudded in disappointment despite the cautions she'd just given herself. Despite the fact that, no matter how much she might wish for it, their engagement could never be real.

She couldn't consider his suggestion. But she had to know what he was thinking, how he could ever believe he could get her to go along with him.

Most of all, though she hated to admit it, she had to find out if his reasoning might not be as crazy as it seemed. "A fake engagement," she said carefully.

"Yes. You said you want your in-laws, especially your mother-in-law, to let you and the kids move on."

She nodded.

"You want your independence."

"Yes."

"And when all is said and done, you're doing this to protect your kids."

"Of course."

"Then let me help. Take what I'm offering, no strings attached."

She shook her head. There was nothing she could say. "You haven't convinced me."

He exhaled heavily. "Then, Andi," he said in a low tone, "consider this. Maybe they're protecting you."

She frowned. *"What?"*

"You said you've accepted that Grant's gone. But if you haven't told them that, if you don't talk about what happened, it may look as if you haven't come to terms with anything at all." He paused, then went on. "Maybe your in-laws are…walking on eggshells around you. Talking around you, not to you, because they know you won't take it in. Because they want to help you but don't know how."

"No."

"Think about it," he urged. "Maybe that's what Ginnie needs. For you to take the first step."

"But…an engagement? That's an enormous step. She wouldn't believe it."

"Yes, she would. After you'd asked to bring me to dinner at her house last night, and now after she's seen me here at Trey's party tonight, she'd believe it. And I think she'd be relieved you've made a move."

She shook her head again, not in denial this time but in confusion. She didn't want to accept what he was saying, but in some way his arguments made sense. What if he was right? What if *she* was the one holding everyone back?

"It would only be temporary," he reminded her. "We'll

play our roles, Ginnie will go back home, relieved, and after a few days, we can call things off."

"What about my family?" she asked.

He smiled. "We won't have trouble convincing them. You have to know Jed's already doing his best to bring the two of us together."

She couldn't hold back a soft groan. "I didn't know." She had been too wrapped up in Mitch this past week to notice much of anything. "But after his success with Tina and Jane, I should have realized."

"Right. And I've got a feeling Jed's mustering plenty of reinforcements. If we want to bring that to a halt, getting engaged will do it. Then, once we call off the engagement, they'll all know they gave it a good, hard try but will have to concede defeat."

She sighed. He had solutions at his fingertips, answers to ease her every concern, stories written in the space of seconds to fit any circumstance. What a wonderful undercover cop he must be.

But how could she go along with his plan?

She looked across the room at Trey, sleeping with his new space alien on the pillow beside him, then at Missy with her tiny hand fisted near her cheek.

What if, in the long run, she was making everything worse for them instead of better?

She looked sideways at Mitch. "A temporary engagement," she said slowly.

He nodded.

"Absolutely not for real?"

"That's correct."

"Betrothed *without* benefits."

"Copy that."

"I'm serious, Mitch." She kept her voice low, but stress

made her sound hoarse. "If you've come up with this idea just as a way to—"

"Don't say it. Don't even think it. I'm in this for you and the kids."

Blindsided, she sagged back against the couch. That little kicker had hit her like nothing else could. Except Mitch himself.

She took a deep breath and let it out slowly. "All right," she said. "You've sold me on the idea."

He'd convinced her his crazy plan would give her a way to show Grant's family that life could—and had to—go on after their loss. His plan would make her family back off, too.

If only she could stop thinking about her own crazy idea, one she was a fool even to consider. One she couldn't let go. The idea that this "temporary engagement" for "a limited time" might lead to something permanent.

"THE HOUSE IS locked up tight, and the family and hotel guests are all tucked in their beds." Jed turned to the fine-looking woman on the couch beside him. "I've been waiting all night to have you to myself. Now, let's get down to business."

Ginnie Price laughed. "I thought you'd never ask."

"That idea of mine of sending Mitch with Andi to the airport turned out to be pure gold, didn't it?"

"It certainly did."

He'd felt sure something would come of getting those two together in close confines. Nancy's phone call later that morning, reporting in about Mitch's sudden overnight trip, had confirmed his hunch. Ginnie's phone call today had come out of the blue but had him tickled pink.

He'd been just as tickled when she had agreed with him that Andi and Mitch made a perfect pair.

He wasn't quite as sure about her idea of coming out to the ranch, but he had to admit the birthday party for Trey gave her the perfect excuse.

"I was so surprised when Andi called," she said. "And I was very pleased to meet Mitch. We all had a lovely night. She didn't say a word about him when she came to pick up Missy and Trey this morning, though, and I didn't push her."

"You never let on we talked?"

"Of course not. You should have seen the surprise on their faces when I walked in tonight." She smiled. "I think I had them very confused, but as you and I discussed, I didn't acknowledge I'd spent the evening with Mitch yesterday."

"Good. Let's keep that up. I'll be the gung-ho granddaddy, you be the voice of doubt. Then they won't suspect we're in cahoots."

She nodded. "Of course, I wanted the two of us to have a chance to speak to each other first."

"And to plan."

"And to plan. Although judging by the way Mitch disappeared not long after Andi went upstairs with the kids, it seems they might have plans of their own."

"Then, it can't hurt to help them along."

"No, it certainly can't. I'll try to get Andi alone for a chat tomorrow."

"I'll get Mitch out here again somehow, kicking and screaming, if need be."

She laughed. "Let's hope it doesn't come to that."

MITCH TUGGED ON his shirt collar, smoothing it into place. Then he ran his hand over his hair, smoothing that, too. He'd played plenty of roles over his years in the LAPD.

He shouldn't be this uncomfortable over posing as a love-struck fiancé in a bogus engagement.

"They ought to be here any minute," Andi said.

Last night, they had decided to break their news to Ginnie and Jed before they told the rest of the family. Andi had asked them both to meet her here in Jed's den this morning.

She sat quietly on the couch on the other side of the room, looking as cool and collected as if she made announcements like this every day of the week.

"I didn't bring you a ring," he told her.

That shattered her composure. She sat more upright and looked away. "A ring's not necessary. We can always say you wanted me to choose my own."

"Where's the romance in that?"

She stared at him. "There *is* no romance here, Mitch. You said this is all fake, remember?"

He took a seat beside her. "I remember. And you remember what else I said—when you're undercover, your best bet is to do what's normal in the circumstances." He reached for her hand and found it cold. She'd had him fooled with her unruffled facade. Maybe she would be better than he'd thought at handling a covert op. "Nervous?" he asked.

"Normal," she said. "Bride-to-be jitters are expected."

He laughed. "And grooms-to-be are very good at calming those jitters." With his free hand, he tucked a strand of hair behind her ear. Then he did what any normal groom-to-be would have done. He lifted her chin and leaned down.

He intended to give her a kiss as cool as her previous composure, as light as their conversation and as swift as it necessarily had to be, considering they were about to have company. But the first touch of her lips against his sent him straight to hot and heavy. And slow. Slow enough to notice he wasn't the only one doing the kissing.

It took them both a while to notice the sound of Jed clearing his throat to get their attention.

With a gasp, Andi tore herself away from him. When she rose, he did, too, slipping his arm around her to make sure she didn't go far.

Jed grinned, Ginnie looked at them with a puzzled expression, and Mitch suddenly wished Andi's impending announcement could be the real deal.

"Well," Jed said, "we're right on time for this meeting, but I'm guessing you two would rather put it off for a while."

"Yes," Andi said. "I mean, no, we don't need to postpone the meeting, and yes, you're on time. We have some news," she added brightly, "and we wanted to share it with you first. Mitch asked me… Mitch and I…" She laughed without a trace of nerves this time, with nothing but a show of bride-to-be happiness. "We're engaged."

Jed responded with a back slap that almost made Mitch stagger. Ginnie's hug was much more low-key, but whatever her thoughts, she put on a decent show.

Jed swept them out of his den and down the hall to the dining room, where the family had already assembled for breakfast.

At Andi's announcement, Cole grinned at Mitch, as if saying he had known all along his best friend didn't stand a chance of escaping matchmaker Jed.

Mitch gave his best groom-to-be grin.

"You two need to celebrate, big-time," Cole said.

"You need to celebrate in style," Tina agreed.

"Heck," Jed said, "you two need some privacy."

When the laughter at his pronouncement finally faded away, Ginnie said quietly, "Jed's right. I think a trip to

Santa Fe would be just the thing to…to give you some time to think about things. My treat."

"Oh, we couldn't—" Andi began.

"I think you should," Ginnie said stubbornly. "You're making a big decision here. You need to make sure—" She cut herself off, then she added, "I'll get on the phone after breakfast."

ALONE IN THE bridal suite a short while later, Andi sat at the desk and watched Jane, overcome with laughter, plop onto the bed.

"Wow. When I said you two should take a chance, I had no idea you'd come up with a scheme like this one."

"It was Mitch's idea," she blurted.

"Then that proves my point. He's still interested."

"It only proves he wants to help me out of a bad situation."

"Because…he's still interested."

"*Jane.* This is serious."

"So am I."

Feeling a sudden chill, Andi rubbed her arms. She didn't have the power to warm herself the way Mitch had with just a touch. And she was rapidly losing the will to keep thinking of this as just a farce. "I went along with him. I let him convince me. But I hadn't thought everything through."

"What's to think about?"

"For one thing, everybody in the family now believes we're really engaged."

"And all of Cowboy Creek will know in no time."

She stared. "What do you mean?"

"Tina and Paz plan to go into town to shop either today or tomorrow. If they make a stop for coffee…" Jane didn't need to finish the sentence.

Andi groaned. "Once the word hits SugarPie's, it will be all over town. What am I going to do?"

"You could get Tina aside and tell her the truth. You'd have to let Paz in on it, too. And Grandpa. But that's still no guarantee Sugar won't hear about it."

"This just gets worse." She slumped into the chair. "And then with Ginnie talking about a *trip*…"

"You'll have to tell Mitch's family, too. You might as well just stay engaged."

"Thanks." She glared. "I brought you up here to talk because I thought you might be able to help."

"I *am* helping. Don't you see how right this could be?"

"No. Not when it's all wrong."

"I don't know why—"

At the sound of footsteps in the hallway, Andi waved to cut Jane off. She reached for the notepad on the desk, hoping that whoever was approaching the suite would think she and Jane were busy working.

Her mother-in-law appeared in the doorway and gave them a small smile. *A smile.* Andi couldn't understand Ginnie's reactions. She had expected her to be upset, or tearful, or at the very least, resigned. Between Ginnie's odd insistence at first on their need to talk things over, now this tentative acceptance, and Mitch's suggestion that had started all this, she didn't know what to think of anything anymore.

"I have news," Ginnie said. "I know you didn't want to be away for long. I found an inn right in Santa Fe and arranged a one-night stay."

"Oh-h-h…" Andi couldn't catch her breath.

"That's great," Jane said. "Wait till Mitch hears. Right, Andi?"

"Oh-h, yes. But you shouldn't have." *Really* shouldn't have.

"If I hadn't, your grandfather would have."

Was that why she had gone along? To play the gracious mother-in-law bestowing gifts? But she had never acted that way before.

Confused, Andi nodded. "Thank you. I'm sure we'll love our stay. I'll see about it right after the wedding—"

"Oh, no," Ginnie said. "I was able to get a reservation for tomorrow night."

"EVERYTHING'S A MESS," Andi hissed to Mitch, her voice louder than she had anticipated in the empty banquet hall.

All morning, she and Jane and Tina had trained the Hitching Post's crew of waitresses who would serve at the wedding.

After lunch, the three of them had gone over new arrangements to accommodate the bride's revised seating chart and other changes. When Mitch appeared in the doorway, Jane and Tina had left.

This was the first time all day she and Mitch had had more than a few moments alone.

He came close, too close, and smoothed her hair as if she were a horse he was trying to calm. His touch had just the opposite effect, making her excited and bitterly disappointed at the same time.

Events were moving much too quickly, and in just a few hours, her determination to see this farce through had begun to buckle under the strain.

"Ginnie did make a reservation for us." Quickly, she explained. "We can't accept."

"We've got to, Andi. The whole point of this is to convince her you're making changes in your life."

"But we'd be taking her gift under false pretenses."

"You should have expected something like this."

"I didn't. I thought she would wish us well and then leave and that would be it until I could go back home after the holidays to talk with her. I didn't think beyond that point."

"This idea will work," he assured her, "if you can just calm down and see it through."

"I thought I could, but it seems too dishonest—it *is* too dishonest. You might be comfortable with all this role-playing, but I'm not."

"All the more reason for us to go to Santa Fe. It will give you a break."

"I can't leave tomorrow. I've got too much still to do for this wedding, and it's only a week away."

"Tina said you're ahead of schedule."

"Anything could come up between now and then."

"And if it does, at the rate you're going, you won't be in any shape to handle it."

He took her hand, the way he had this morning just before he'd kissed her. Warmth flowed through her from the memory, from the heat of his fingers against hers, from the sudden slow burn of desire.

Why was she arguing against their trip when all she wanted was to be with him?

The yearning triggered by that question alone told her what she didn't want to acknowledge. They might as well end this farce now, because a "temporary engagement" to Mitch for "a limited time" would never be enough for her. And no matter what she longed for, they couldn't have more than that.

"Look," he said, "I won't say anything to my family yet, and by the time we get back, this will all be over. But we've got to go through with it for now to convince Ginnie."

"I don't know. She seems to be accepting our news, but something doesn't feel right to me."

"Even more reason to keep up the pretense until she leaves. So we'll stay the night in Santa Fe, you'll get a break from the role-playing, and then once she's gone tomorrow, we'll come back home and tell your family the engagement is off."

"How will we explain to everyone else who might have found out?"

"We don't need to explain. It's none of their business."

"Mitch, you've been gone from Cowboy Creek way too long if you think we can get away with that."

He shrugged. "Then we'll say we had an argument and discovered we're incompatible."

"Due to irreconcilable differences?"

"That'll work. We'll admit our quick engagement was too quick, we didn't know enough about each other, and we've now realized it's better for us to go our separate ways."

She tried to ignore the tightness in her chest. He'd come up with that scenario so easily, tossing it out as though it was only another one of his many cover stories—which, she had to remind herself—was exactly what he meant it to be. "And when Ginnie finds out, then what?"

"Then you'll have made your point. Her reaction to our engagement shows she'll be ready to accept that."

She couldn't keep from worrying there was something wrong about Ginnie's apparent acceptance. Maybe she was only hiding her pain. Maybe she believed refusing to accept their "engagement" would put her grandchildren out of her reach.

But Ginnie had already booked the room, which meant they couldn't back out.

And once again, she couldn't fault Mitch's arguments. They made sense. This would prove she was ready to move on.

Except for the fact that she wasn't ready to move on from him.

Chapter Sixteen

They arrived in Santa Fe in midmorning the next day, too soon after breakfast to have lunch and too early to check into their room. Mitch would have been happy to find an air-conditioned restaurant or bar and an even cooler drink, but Andi wanted to walk. She felt the need to unwind from the added stress of the past couple of days, he'd bet. She might also be wondering—as he was—how many beds they would find in the room they would share tonight. Sure, they had agreed to be "betrothed without benefits." But they hadn't let Ginnie in on the news, and she had made the reservation.

He tried not to think that far ahead.

They spent a few hours exploring the streets of Santa Fe and going in and out of shops to avoid the heat. Well, he wanted to avoid the heat. Andi went to window-shop.

He thought about her financial situation and knew it was on her mind, too, especially as they walked the aisles of a store filled with wood carvings. Twice, she looked back with regret at a small wooden donkey wearing a cockeyed sombrero.

A moment later, she exclaimed over—and bought—a couple of parrots with colorful tail feathers, claiming they'd look good in a niche in the dining room wall of the Hitching Post. "Tina gave me a budget for the hotel. These can go on the expenses."

In a shop filled with Southwestern pottery and kitchenware, she let herself go wild.

"For the banquet hall," she said, holding up napkins and a tablecloth in some rough material the color of dry earth.

"For a wedding?"

"Why not? Considering the dude ranch setting, some brides might prefer Southwestern style instead of our more traditional place settings. We… I mean, Grandpa and Tina and Jane can provide both." She'd corrected herself, as if making it clear her visit to Cowboy Creek was only temporary. "And they'll cater other events, too, not just weddings." Her eyes gleamed. "If I buy in bulk, maybe I can convince the owners to give me a good discount."

"Now you're talking. Tina will be proud."

She laughed. The sound made his heart thump extra-hard. Her smile was the first genuinely carefree expression he'd seen on her face in days.

"And look at this!"

He looked. She held up a small brown rectangle with a large hole through the center. "What is it? A bracelet?"

"No, it's a napkin ring. Terra-cotta. *Perfect* for these napkins."

"Napkin rings and wooden parrots. You're not too hard to please, are you?"

"I think I am. I have very high standards."

"Oh, yeah?" That let him out. She fingered through the napkin rings, trying to find ones she could accept. Smiling, he shook his head. "You know, you really ought to stick around the Hitching Post. Jed could use your expertise."

"He's got Jane and Tina. He doesn't need me."

I need you.

He rubbed his chin and swallowed hard. The dryness of his throat made him wish they had stopped in for one of those cold drinks he'd wanted.

She turned back to the napkin rings, and he went back to watching her.

Wanting her.

But like a fool, he had promised her no strings attached to this engagement. And so he'd sworn to himself he wouldn't touch her. That he would sleep on the couch or on the floor or in the bathtub if he had to, but he wouldn't go near her—provided she even stayed in the room.

All those promises had seemed like good ideas…at the time.

"Looks like you're going to be here awhile," he said. "I'll probably cramp your style while you're chewing down the prices."

She laughed again, and his heart thumped in response.

He had to think for a moment to recall what he'd planned to say. "I'm going to take a walk."

"Okay. If I'm done first I'll wait outside for you."

"I won't be long." Just long enough to cool down some. Outside, it was still a balmy December in New Mexico, but the temperature couldn't come close to his own body heat right now.

He couldn't resist reaching up to touch her hair, to skim his fingers down her cheek and brush his thumb near the corner of her mouth, still curved from her smile.

He didn't bother to fight the urge to kiss her. Seeing how nervous she was whenever he got close, he wouldn't put it past her to walk away from him yet again tonight. To leave him alone in the room.

Or try to.

As teens, they'd had an attraction that wouldn't quit. They still had, and neither of them could deny it. He didn't know about Andi, but he wasn't about to give up on them now. Forget those promises he'd made. Tonight, if he had his way, they damned sure were going to have the one thing they had never shared.

He took his time, kissing her thoroughly, putting the seal on his silent vow.

WHEN MITCH HELD up the small pitcher of iced tea the waiter had left at their table, Andi nodded.

On the patio of the restaurant at their inn, a clay fireplace banished the December chill. They sat far from the streetlights in a corner filled with shadows. The darkness around them was broken by a tall vine-covered trellis threaded with small white lights. An ornate black metal candleholder with four squat candles illuminated their table.

Shadows danced against Mitch's shirt, highlighting every move he made. The white broadcloth made his hair look as black as midnight. She fought the urge to reach up to run her fingers through it.

They ate silently for a few minutes. She sipped her iced tea and toyed with the last few strands of cheese left from her Mexican lasagna.

She had hoped the time here would bring them closer, and it had. They had talked all afternoon. They had talked all this evening. Light and inconsequential conversation that still helped them to pick up where they had left off years ago, to reminisce about the past, to catch up on events they had missed in each other's lives.

No, they hadn't covered some of the most pressing topics, such as Mitch's injury and the answer to what they would do for the rest of the night. But she still had hopes.

"Did you enjoy your meal?" he asked.

"Yes." She had enjoyed the meal and the company and the sense of anticipation about what would happen next.

She had also enjoyed his kiss. In fact, she had spent a large part of the evening analyzing it—or rather, trying to guess what his unexpected act at the store that afternoon really meant.

So many contradictions.

It was perfectly appropriate for a newly engaged man to give his beloved a kiss that rocked her to her toes. But their engagement was a fake. His kiss was lingering enough to satisfy her completely, yet it made her crave more. And it came with the feeling of a promise she knew he would never make.

"Good food," he said, "but not as tasty as my mom's cooking. Or Paz's."

"Very true. Living alone in LA, you must miss home cooking."

He shrugged. "As often as I work double shifts or undercover, I'm eating on the run no matter what. But yeah, I miss that. I miss a lot of things." The flicker of candlelight reflected in his eyes made her breath catch. "Are you interested in any dessert?"

Was she interested…?

Now his every question, every word, every action seemed to hold a double meaning.

She could order dessert to postpone the pleasure of discovering whatever would happen next.

She could tell him the truth. It wasn't dessert she was interested in, but him.

She could take his question at face value and give him a straight answer.

"I think I'll pass," she said.

After he had signed their bill, he took her arm. Warmth from his hand tingled her skin. On their walk across the flagstone patio, the slight unevenness of the stones made her arm brush his side. The friction stimulated more heat.

"You feel like taking a walk?" he asked.

She felt like doing much more than that.

"A short one, if that's okay with you," she said politely. "And then I'd like to go up to the room and call home. It's too late for me to talk with Trey, but I can check in and see how the kids are doing."

"That sounds good." He opened the gate leading to the sidewalk.

The street was well lit, with merchants still open for business, trying to bring in customers in this last week before Christmas. She should have been back at the Hitching Post, helping with her own family's business. But she couldn't regret this time with Mitch.

In silence, they walked to the end of the block and turned back. When he released her arm, she immediately felt the evening chill and a wave of disappointment. A second later, she realized he had only wanted to step around her to walk on the outside, closer to the street. The chivalrous gesture made her smile to herself. When he took her arm again, as if he didn't want to let her go, the chill turned into a tremble of increasing anticipation.

If this kept up, she wouldn't be able to make the trip all the way to their room. She searched for something to calm herself.

"I know you're close to your family. Being away from them, you must miss out on a lot more than just home cooking." His shrug told her nothing. "Why did you ever leave Cowboy Creek to begin with?"

"You."

She gasped. Turning to look at him made her stumble. He reached out to prevent her from falling. The warmth and weight of his arm around her waist almost made her melt on the spot. For a second, his arm tightened, as if he wanted to pull her close. Instead, he released her and took a step back.

She stared at him. "You left home because of *me*?"

He nodded. "Once you were gone, it seemed like a good time for me to go, too."

A simple explanation. She had set an example for him, that was all. Why did she feel a twinge of disappointment?

Back at the inn, he escorted her into the reception area, where earlier the Southwestern decor made her think fondly of the Hitching Post. Now she thought of the last trip she had taken through a hotel lobby and her solitary ride on the elevator.

They went down a long hall papered in a floral pattern that made her feel they were walking down the aisle of the Hitching Post's chapel.

He unlocked the door to their room and ushered her inside. The bed, a king-size four-poster of knotty pine with black accents, dominated the room. The linens were bold turquoise, edged and shot through with silver. Other than the rest of the bedroom suite and a couple of chairs on either side of a small, square table, the bed was the only piece of furniture in the room. The only place they would have to sleep.

"If you don't mind," he said, just as politely as she had spoken earlier, "since you're going to be on the phone, I'll jump in the shower first."

"That's fine."

They were on their best behavior, acting like brand-new roommates rather than former sweethearts turned potential lovers. Maybe that bed would be only for sleeping, after all.

He grabbed his overnight bag and closed the bathroom door behind him. She waited for the sound of running water before taking a deep breath and sinking onto the foot of the bed. Showering—his, then hers—would put them so many steps closer to the rest of the night.

He had told her this engagement would be no strings attached. But they already had strings, past and present, tying them to each other.

They had missed what seemed like two lifetimes in between.

He had faced a tragedy in his life he wouldn't talk about.

She'd had a life of her own, a husband, children.

She had loved Grant, truly and completely. Nothing could ever change that.

But she had loved Mitch before then. And she loved him now.

The day had fulfilled her hopes of bringing them closer. Whether it was close enough for Mitch to trust her, she didn't know. Whether it offered enough for him to want her in his life, for him to decide she and her children meant more than anything to him, she didn't know, either.

Maybe they *would* be more than roommates. But maybe that would be only for tonight, and she would have only the memories of this one time to hold close to her heart.

THE INN HAD provided fluffy white toweling robes, his and hers. Mitch's still hung on the back of the door. She took the other robe and slipped into it.

He had come from the steamy bathroom with his hair

slicked wet and a pair of thin cotton sweats riding low on his hips. She had mumbled something and made her own trip to the shower.

Those low-riding sweats reminded her of the first time she had seen him in worn jeans, pitching hay in the barn. His hips were still slim, but the rest of him had bulked up and filled out.

She stared at the door, then closed her robe and made a secure bow of the long tie around her waist. She didn't have the nerve to leave the bathroom wearing only the nightgown she'd brought with her, but she knew this time, she would stay the night.

She had left Mitch on the ranch years ago, left him alone at their hotel in Scottsdale. Whatever happened, she wasn't leaving him now.

Whatever happened, she was going for her one-and-only time.

He had turned the covers of the bed down to the foot and lay half propped against a couple of the pillows. Cans of soda from the room's mini-refrigerator sat on the night-stands on either side of the bed, and a magazine she had seen on the table lay spread open on his lap.

She piled her pillows together.

"Before you get into bed," he said, "I left you something over on the table."

"You did?" A brown paper sack with the top rolled together sat in the center of the wooden square. "What is it?"

"Go find out."

She crossed the room and opened the sack. Smiling, she pulled out the wooden donkey she had seen in the shop that afternoon. He now wore a big red Christmas bow around his neck. "You shouldn't have."

"I had to. I saw you look back after we walked away."

"And when I was still in the kitchen shop, you went to get him?"

"Yeah."

She stared down at the donkey. "I'll bet he was sad I left him there."

"Very."

She looked again at Mitch. "I'm sorry about that. Truly sorry. And I'm so glad he's here now."

"I'm sure he is, too."

"Thank you."

He smiled. "My pleasure."

She set her gift on the nightstand and climbed onto the bed. As she propped up her pillows, the robe shifted. She eased it closed again, hoping he hadn't noticed. Not yet. She wanted him more than she ever had before. It was too soon for that, too.

He hadn't said another word. She took a breath and let it out slowly. "You were right that day by the corral, Mitch, when you said I'd want to have a memory of us. I do, to go along with all the other good memories we shared."

"Like that jackrabbit?"

"Oh. *Him*." She laughed, feeling her cheeks heat. One day toward dusk, when he had finished his work in the barn, they had slipped away. They had gone to "their" spot near the creek, where a couple of large, flat rocks made a perfect place for them to sit and talk. They had been doing just that when a stray rabbit bounded out of the underbrush near them, scaring her nearly half to death.

"Yeah, *him*," he agreed. "I don't know where we'd ever have gotten if he hadn't come along."

"You mean I have the jackrabbit to thank for our first kiss?"

"You sure do. Well, that and the fact you'd jumped straight into my arms."

Even the memory was enough to make her feel like an awkward teen again. Something she did *not* want to experience tonight. Struggling to think of what to say, she cleared her throat and looked away.

"There's a drink for you over there." He gestured to the can on the nightstand beside her. "I thought you might like a nightcap, compliments of the house. They've only got soda and iced tea here. For anything stronger, I can take a trip down to the restaurant again."

"You'd have to get dressed."

"I wouldn't mind, if you had a taste for something else."

"I *would* mind. And I *do* have a taste for something else."

She shifted on her pillows to face him.

He sat without moving a muscle, as if he wasn't sure what was going on or what he was supposed to do. His reaction made her think of her own indecision a moment ago. She smiled.

His gaze drifted from her face to the front of her robe, then back again. He shook his head. She realized his hesitation hadn't come from indecision but out of concern for her. "Whatever this is, Andi, it's not necessary. I told you this trip was just for show."

"Then show me."

"What?" he asked hoarsely. "How much I want you?"

She nodded.

He took the magazine from his lap and tossed it onto his nightstand.

She looked down at his thin cotton sweats. "I guess that proves your point."

He laughed, but shook his head again. "Are you sure?"

"Are you crazy? How much more obvious do I need to make this?"

"I don't know. But I don't guess I can expect another jackrabbit to come by and move things along." He reached across the bed for the tie at her waist and undid the bow. Her robe fell open. The sound of his sharp breath and the look in his blue eyes made her glad she had left her nightgown hanging on the bathroom door.

He slid his hand inside the robe, his rough thumb brushing her breast with just enough friction to make her own breath catch.

"You know how long I've waited for this," he said.

"As long as I have."

"But tomorrow—"

"Mitch." Through the robe, she touched his hand. "We're not talking about tomorrow. In fact, we don't need to talk at all tonight."

"That would be fine. But here's the thing." He smiled. "If I get started…not talking with you, I won't want to stop."

"Show me."

He moved closer and kissed her, long and hard, and then he showed her what she'd missed for all these years.

ANDI WOKE TO lamplight shining directly into her eyes. At first, they had been too busy to think of turning the lamp off. Later, they had drifted to sleep in its glow.

Mitch lay pressed against her back with the heavy warmth of his arm around her. When she stirred, he shifted away, easing her onto her back. Before she could move, he rose to one elbow and dipped his head, kissing her with a familiar thoroughness but more gently than he had all night. That gentleness made her want him all over again.

As if he'd read her mind, he kissed and caressed her until she was ready for him. And as they made love, his tenderness made this time seem bittersweet.

Afterward, she closed her suddenly damp eyes and turned onto her side. He moved to lie against her again, his hand curved around her lower belly. When he stroked her there, she felt an answering response even lower down.

"You do know it's still the middle of the night," he murmured.

She nodded. "I saw the clock."

"Restless?"

"I guess so. Or maybe just a mother's instinct, being always on the alert for noises that shouldn't be there."

"Yeah. Kind of like being a cop."

Just the words she needed to break her heart. "I'm sorry if I woke you. Have you been up for a while?"

"Give me a break, woman, I've been up quite a few times already." His laugh ruffled her hair. "And I'm having a great middle of the night. You can take that to court." She stiffened. His arm tightened just a bit, and she couldn't tell if it was in reaction to her movement or not. He kissed her bare shoulder. "I'm getting a good night's rest, too."

She forced a laugh. "Maybe that's not such a compliment."

"It's a darned good one." He rolled her onto her back again. "Actually, since coming back to Cowboy Creek, I've slept better than I have in…a long time."

"Getting out of the city is doing you good." In the lamplight, she saw his eyes narrow for a moment, then he gave her a smile that didn't seem any more natural than her laugh.

"It's not the city I needed to get away from." He sounded grim.

"I'm here if you want to talk about it."

"I'd rather talk about you. You're the one helping me sleep at night."

"Me?" Something else he attributed to her, just as he had made her departure his reason for leaving Cowboy Creek. "And how do I do that?" The question was out before she had thought about how teasing it might sound, but his thinned lips and tight jaw made her see this wasn't a light topic.

"Let's just say I'd rather dream about you than have nightmares any night. But we were talking about you." He brushed his thumb across her stomach. "You've got scars. From the kids."

"Yes." She half sat up to push her pillows behind her, then dragged the sheet up to her shoulders. "I told you I had trouble carrying Trey. Bed rest got me through the final trimester, but I wasn't able to deliver him naturally. Or Missy."

Through the sheet, he rested his hand on her stomach again. "You don't have to hide."

"I'm not. I had a chill." No…she'd had a chill last night. She had seen his scars for the first time. The glow from the bedside lamp had revealed a corrugated pink mass scoring the skin over and all around his knee. The sight had made her shiver. Now it made her frozen inside.

She hesitated, but couldn't go on. He had his secrets. She'd had hers.

She still had one. But not for long. She had one more truth to tell him that she couldn't keep to herself. "Tonight has been…wonderful."

He gave a low laugh. "As I said, I'm having a good time myself."

"Worth waiting for?"

"Without a doubt." He kissed her hand.

She reached up to touch his cheek. Dark stubble prickled her fingers. “I like you kissing me and touching me. But making love… When we were teens, I didn’t know what I was missing.”

“Me, either. But I thought about it a lot.”

“I thought about it, too. I dreamed about you, especially after I went away. I loved you, Mitch. I still love you, even more now than I did then.”

His eyes darkened. She could see his throat working hard, hear his swallow. After a long moment, he said, “Enough to take me as I am?”

When she said nothing, he rested her hand on his chest. She could feel his heart thumping against her palm.

Hadn’t she known he would ask the one question she didn’t want to answer? Closing her eyes, she turned her head away.

As he pressed her hand beneath his, she heard him sigh.

Chapter Seventeen

They left Santa Fe even earlier than they had intended, and the ride home to Cowboy Creek felt longer than usual in the quiet. It gave Andi too much time to think about the man beside her and the question he had asked. The one she couldn't bear to answer.

Up ahead, she could see the final turnoff to the road leading to the Hitching Post. In just minutes, they would call off their engagement, as planned.

Admitting their romance couldn't be real, that she had no hope left for a chance with Mitch, made her feel empty inside. The feeling only confirmed what she had known from the minute she had seen him again. She had always loved him.

But now, she needed to walk away.

When they reached the hotel and he began to turn his truck toward the parking area, she said, "Just drop me off in front, please."

He kept driving. "I'm not letting you go in to break the news to your family on your own."

"It's all right—"

"Not by me, it isn't."

"I can handle it, Mitch."

"It was my idea that got you into this," he said stubbornly. "Besides, I'm going to have to face your family sometime. I might as well do it now." He parked the truck and took her overnight bag from the rear seat.

She hesitated, wanting to tell him again to go. To assure him he didn't need to take on her guilt. But he had already come around to open her door.

Sighing, she gathered up her collection from yesterday's shopping expedition. All the items she had bought for the reception hall…the parrots for the dining room… the gift he had given her—the wooden donkey with the sombrero and big red bow, a whimsical little reminder of a trip that hadn't lived up to its promise.

She would always regret this morning.

But she could never forget last night.

Her only bright spot in this very dark day was her son's greeting. When they went into the lobby, she saw him and Robbie in the sitting room. She set her bags on the registration desk.

The minute he spotted her, he broke into a huge grin and ran to throw his arms around her in a tight hug. "I missed you, Mommy!"

"I missed you, too." She kissed the top of his head, then gave Robbie a hug. "And Missy. Where is she?"

"At Rachel's house," Robbie said. "With Jane."

She didn't have to ask where Grandpa Jed might be. He rose from one of the couches in the sitting room and stood beaming at them. The boys ran back to where she could see they had spread a few of Trey's birthday toys on the floor. She followed, taking the rocker near the fireplace.

Mitch settled onto a couch across from Jed.

"Where's Tina?" Andi asked.

"She drove Paz to town for an order."

She swallowed a sigh of relief. That took care of the

rest of her family. For now. "And our guests are out at the corral for their riding lessons?"

"Yep." He was still standing, which puzzled her. In fact, he had started toward the door. "I'll just run up and tell your mother-in-law you're home."

She gasped. *Mother-in-law?*

Before she could question him, he was gone.

She turned to Mitch in dismay. "Oh, no. Ginnie was supposed to be on her way home this morning. Now what do we do?"

"We go to plan B," he said. "Until we find out what's going on, we keep everything status quo. But my gut's telling me we can forget the breakup idea until you talk to her after the holidays."

"But—"

"It's probably better to draw things out, anyway. When the time's right, we'll tell people we gave the relationship a good, honest try, and it just didn't work out. Till then, we can play the loving couple. "

"I can't." *Not after last night.*

He shrugged. "Take your pick, Andi," he said in a low, harsh tone. "Get everybody in an uproar just before the wedding and go right back where you started as far as your mother-in-law is concerned. Or wait till things settle down. You're lucky enough to have not one but two backup plans."

Now hearing nothing but bitterness, she swallowed hard. She couldn't understand why he would choose to continue the farce. But she knew she didn't have a choice.

ONCE MITCH LEFT, Andi fled upstairs for a while to be alone. To think.

Only a few minutes later, Jane tapped on the door, holding Missy in her arms.

It was the sight she needed to restore her. "Hey, sweetie. Let Mommy hold you." She reached for Missy and gave her a kiss.

"She needs a change," Jane said.

"You ought to be practicing those skills," she said with a shaky laugh as she pulled a diaper from the bag on the desk.

"I have other things on my mind." Jane plopped onto the edge of the bed. "Such as wondering what's the matter with you."

"There's nothing wrong with me."

"Right. That's why you look ready to bawl like a baby Missy's age any minute."

Andi finished diapering her daughter and cuddled her close.

What was wrong? The trip with Mitch. The finality of knowing they would never be together. Their arrival home to find they had to prolong their "engagement."

All that was too much for her. And Jane was too sharp-eyed not to notice.

"I missed my babies," she said honestly. "And we've still got so much to do to prep for the wedding." She *had* received several texts with new requests from the bride yesterday.

"I don't buy it," Jane said flatly. "Yes, of course, I know you missed the kids. I even believe you'd worry about Sandra. Who *did* happen to call this morning with an emergency since she couldn't reach you on your cell."

"I forgot to turn it on earlier," Andi said.

"I can imagine you were too busy."

Ignoring her cousin's smile, she said, "But that's almost a relief she called here. I can't imagine how she would feel if she couldn't get through to someone. What did she need?"

"Don't worry about that right now. Tina and I took care of it. And don't try to distract me. Andi, *nothing* should make you come home looking this upset after a trip with Mitch—especially considering the way you feel about him. Now, what's going on?"

She sighed. Reluctantly, she confessed the rest of the plans she and Mitch had made for continuing their act. "I just don't want to talk with Ginnie about Grant until the timing is better. She'll have so much to take in. And now, on top of that, I'll have to explain why Mitch and I pretended to be engaged. Once I'm back home again, I'll sit down with her. But until then, we're stuck in this fake engagement."

"I wish you luck with that one, cuz. It's not going to be easy."

"No, it isn't." Not easy having to be around Mitch, to play his beloved bride-to-be, to have him touch her, look into her eyes, say sweet nothings as if he really loved her… She took a deep breath but couldn't keep her voice from shaking. "We thought she'd be gone. She was *supposed* to be gone."

Her cousin's sudden interest in arranging the strands of her silver necklace against her shirt made Andi's stomach clench. She sank to the bed and stared at Jane, who still hadn't looked up. "All right," she asked, sure she didn't want to know, "now it's your turn. What's going on?"

"Grandpa didn't tell you?"

"No. *You* tell me."

This time, Jane sighed. "Grandpa invited Ginnie to stay for the open house."

MITCH'S DAY STARTED early the next morning, with a stop at the sheriff's office for coffee with Paco and a couple of the other deputies. He hung around long enough to keep from showing up at the Hitching Post at the crack of dawn. To delay having to face Andi. He felt sure she wouldn't be giving him the warm welcome a genuine fiancé could expect.

And he was right.

As arranged, he met Cole in the hotel lobby.

"You ready to play lumberjack?" Cole asked.

"Hell, no. I'm just along to keep you from getting lost."

Cole laughed.

In the hallway behind Cole, Mitch saw Andi round the corner from the direction of the dining room. She glanced toward them, then fled up the stairway. Mentally, he shrugged off her action. Cole hadn't heard her approach, and with none of her family around, they had no need to stay in character.

But the vision of her running away from him stayed in his mind all morning.

It was nearly noon when he and Cole returned to the hotel with the freshly cut Christmas tree. At that point, Mitch had thought he was done. He hadn't counted on Jed's roping him in to help Cole set up the tree in the sitting room. He hadn't counted on Tina and Jane's insistence that the tree be turned to every possible angle so they could choose the one they liked best.

Pete's daughter, Rachel, and the boys sat cross-legged on the floor, adding their two cents' worth.

Of course, none of them could agree.

Through all this, Andi sat on the couch, holding Missy in her lap and not saying much at all. She hadn't come near him, which must have made him look like a rejected suitor to anyone watching. And everyone was.

Maybe he should have gone along with her about ditching the engagement plan. Should have just walked away. But if he'd done that, he could never have forgiven himself. Andi wouldn't admit it, but she needed his help. For her sake, he had to go through with this farce.

Thinking of it like just another undercover op—a successful op—would get the job done.

When Tina appealed to Andi about the tree, she shook her head. "Oh, no, I'm staying out of this."

"What's that saying about too many cooks?" Mitch asked. The women promptly hushed him into silence.

From time to time, Trey would clap his hands and yell, "Bi-i-ig tree!"

Mitch couldn't hold back a grin…until the time he looked across the room and caught Andi staring at him. As soon as she saw he had noticed, she glanced away. Her cheeks turned pink. Good. She looked like a blushing bride-to-be.

After a last turn of the tree, and Tina and Jane's assurance the position was perfect, he went to take a seat beside Andi. From the corner of his eye, he saw her stiffen. *That* didn't fit her role. He wrapped his arm around her and leaned close. "Remember," he murmured, "do what's natural."

That went for them both, didn't it?

He brushed his cheek against hers and kissed those tiny lines near her eye.

Missy lifted her arms to him. He shook his head. "Not now, baby. After messing with that tree, my hands need a good washing."

Cole looked down at his hands. "So do mine."

"You both look like you could use an introduction to the shower," Jed said.

"Good idea," Cole agreed. "I'll use ours upstairs."

Tina nodded. "Mitch, Andi can show you to the one in the family wing. And Cole can lend you a clean shirt."

"No, that's fine. I can head home and get cleaned up there."

"Nothing doing," Jed said. "After lunch, we've got a busy afternoon scheduled. You don't think you can set that tree up and then leave the hard part to everyone else, do you?"

"Decorating, you mean? That's the fun part," Mitch corrected. "I always supervised my brothers and sisters when it came time to doing the tree at home." How many tree-trimming parties had he missed over the years? And who had taken his place since he'd left?

"I thought you told me you tend to drop ornaments," Jed said drily.

Mitch gave him a sheepish grin. When they had talked at SugarPie's, he felt sure the old man had seen right through that excuse.

"Mitch," Robbie said, "we gots cowboy boots to put on the tree! And cowboy hats!"

"Hats," Trey echoed, clapping again.

Mitch smiled. Suddenly, he had the urge to stay, no matter how Andi would feel about it. One way or another, he'd soften her up to the idea. And, again for her sake, he'd get her loosened up in front of her family. He'd consider it a badge of honor to coax a genuine smile out of her.

"I've got a change of clothes out in the truck," he said.

"Well, that's settled, then." Jed grinned. "We sure wouldn't want you to miss out on any family fun."

"We don't plan to miss a thing. Do we, Andi?" He glanced at her.

"Of course we don't. And we'll count on you and Cole to put all the decorations on the highest branches." She gave him a glowing smile. He tightened his arm around her.

He could see the effort she'd made, and the smile

looked damned good. Genuine and loving, as if she'd really meant it just for him.

This close, he'd wager only he could see that the sincerity didn't reach her eyes.

He ought to be angry she wasn't doing a better job of playing her role. He definitely was done with her pretending she didn't need him to play his. No problem—he had a few solutions for that.

Deliberately, he trailed his fingers down her back and curved his hand around her hip. The smile stayed in place, but he heard her sharp intake of breath.

Yeah. As he'd said to himself about her once before, he knew how to handle a challenge.

ANDI DIDN'T KNOW how she was going to make it through another minute of being around Mitch. She had had as much as she could take of seeing his smile, of hearing his laugh. He had done a lot of both during lunch in the dining room, then even more since they had spent the afternoon in the sitting room decorating the tree.

"Cole," he said now, "you call yourself a wrangler? I could've done a better job of roping and tying that garland to the tree, and I haven't worked this ranch in years."

He sat on the couch with Missy on his knee and the boys and Rachel close by on the floor near his feet. All afternoon, he had talked with them and teased them and treated them as if they were his own kids.

She'd had enough of keeping up pretenses in front of her family. But he continued playing his role. He had brought her into conversations, too, when she would rather have been quiet. He had taken every chance available to put his arm around her. He had smiled at her like a man in love.

It all made her heart hurt.

Her mother-in-law had left the hotel for a visit of her own to friends in Santa Fe. That provided a reprieve, but not a long one. She would be back in a couple of days.

And there was still her family to deal with. Other than Jane, she couldn't share the truth with the rest of them. She was having a hard enough time pretending everything was happy and normal. She couldn't drag them all into this farce, too.

She rose from her chair. "I'll bring some more punch." She was only halfway through the doorway into the lobby when laughter broke out behind her and she felt a hand on her arm. She turned to find Mitch smiling at her. Because he knew he had to. The thought left her misty-eyed.

He still held Missy, who had curled her fingers in his hair.

With his free hand, he pointed upward. She didn't need to look to know exactly what she would find. She stood directly beneath the sprig of mistletoe Jed had hung from the door frame.

"Oh, boy," Rachel said, laughing. "Grandpa Jed told me what that means."

She knew what it meant, too. But she couldn't stand here and kiss Mitch in front of all her family. She might be playing a role for them, but his mouth on hers would be all too real.

"I think I caught you," he murmured.

A long, long time ago.

"Yes," she said with an exaggerated sigh, "I think you did. Well, never let it be said I passed up a great opportunity." She smiled, leaned forward and kissed her daughter's cheek.

He scowled.

She laughed along with everyone else, then darted away and across the lobby.

"Hey, Mitch," Cole called, "who's the better wrangler now? At least I held on to that garland, which is more than you can say about your girl."

"We'll see about that."

She heard Mitch's boots thundering across the lobby's wooden floor. She was halfway down the hall to the kitchen when he caught up with her and swung her to face him.

"Hey, you forgot something."

"Oh, no, I didn't." She matched his teasing tone, saying the words loudly enough for those in the sitting room to hear. Then she lowered her voice. "We're alone now. You can drop the act."

"Who's acting?" he said huskily. "At Christmastime, nobody ignores the mistletoe and gets away with it."

"I didn't ignore it."

He grinned. "All right, then—nobody ignores *me*." Taking her by the hand, he led her the few feet to Jed's den and closed the door behind them. Then he turned and wrapped his arms around her.

Everywhere his body touched hers, she felt the heat, as if a string of Christmas lights draped between them had sparked to life. Those lights definitely twinkled brightly as he lowered his head to steal the kiss she had refused to give him. She wanted to refuse him now, but he had his mouth on hers and his fingers threaded through her hair, holding her close and steady, just the way she liked him to kiss her.

Just what she didn't need.

She pulled herself away and backed off, still feeling the tingle everywhere they had touched.

He ran his hand through his hair and looked as dismayed as she felt.

"Well," she said, exhaling heavily, "I don't think our agreement calls for kissing in private."

Mitch exhaled just as heavily and watched as Andi moved to lean against Jed's desk. She shook her head, making all that blond hair he'd just run his hands through tumble around her shoulders. His hands and his mouth and his body ached to get back to where they'd left off.

"I think we'd better call a halt to this playacting," she said. "I can't keep doing it anymore."

"We can take a break from it for a few days."

"Take a break? How is that going to work?"

"I could try not talking to you, the way you've done all day with me."

"So that's what this is all about?" She gestured between them. "Male pride? I wouldn't talk to you and then I wouldn't kiss you, and this is how you get your feelings across?"

"I don't do feelings. And *this is all about* what it's been all along. Helping you cut the cord to your in-laws."

She had the grace to blush. It did nothing to ease his irritation. "Look. I'll admit we do need a break. I'll find a reason to stay in town tomorrow, and then I'll be leaving for LA."

"Leaving?"

She sounded startled. He wished she sounded sad, then wished he hadn't had any reaction at all. "I've got a visit lined up with the surgeon who operated on my knee. If all goes well, I should be declared fit for duty again soon."

"I hope you get a good report."

Now he heard only politeness in her tone. He had known she wouldn't feel overjoyed at this news. The fact that he didn't mean more to her made him want to walk away without another word.

And still, he couldn't leave without trying to do what he could to help.

"I hope the report is good, too," he said seriously. "I've had some bad things happen on the job, Andi. Seen some bad things go down. They only reinforced what I've always known—there are no guarantees in life. That doesn't mean folks stop living. I don't think you get the point that life goes on."

"Of course I do. That's exactly what losing Grant taught me."

"No," he insisted. "I'm not talking about becoming independent—which is what you've claimed all along to want."

"Because it is. That's why we agreed to this fake engagement. So I could show Ginnie how I felt."

"No," he said again. "You told me that, most of all, you wanted to show your mother-in-law life goes on after a loss. Yet you're not willing to take your own advice and move on."

"But I am moving on."

"Yeah. As long as wherever you go, you're working with a safety net. That's not always going to happen, no matter how well you plan." He rubbed his jaw and sighed. "This trip to see the surgeon… You wanted to know what happened. The injury occurred at the same time I lost my partner in an op that got shot to hell. And it was my fault he died."

He had never stated the truth that plainly to anyone but himself. "I can't discuss an open case, and the details aren't important, anyway. What matters is, my partner on the op and I were undercover, working at a warehouse targeted for a raid.

"I'd had a bad feeling about the perps we were dealing with. And though my partner hadn't had his cover blown, he'd run into some trouble with them. He outranked me and had the bigger role in the op. The day the raid was scheduled, he wanted to stay in role and canvass the warehouse ahead of the team."

"If he was in charge, then how could what happened be your fault?"

"Because I didn't follow my instincts."

"He made the decision, you didn't. And you said he had seniority."

"Yeah. He pulled rank, and I gave in."

"I still don't see where you're at fault."

"I knew—I *knew*—he shouldn't go near that warehouse. And because I didn't stop him, because I didn't listen to my gut, he was caught in an ambush."

She closed her eyes, the way she had done at the inn. Her face turned pale.

This time, he was the one to look away. He didn't close his eyes. Experience had taught him he would see the scene too clearly. "By the time I got inside, he was dead and so was one of the perps. The other turned his sights on me. I managed to get off a couple of rounds, but my weapon was nothing against his AK. It blasted my knee—and that was the good news. It was the only thing that saved me. I landed flat on my ass just as our backup stormed in."

He looked at her and saw her eyes shimmering with tears. He had to get some distance before he could tell her the rest. He walked to a corner bookshelf, where he stood looking down at a photo of Jed and Paz and the Garland clan.

"They slaughtered my partner," he said, knowing he had to keep his voice low or he'd lose control altogether. "He was only a few years from a full pension and had a wife and three kids. They carried me out on a stretcher, but they took him away in a body bag. Because I didn't follow my damned gut."

From behind him, he heard her choke back a sob. His throat tightened. He looked down at the photo again and took a deep breath.

Then he turned back to Andi. He could see the horror in her tear-filled eyes.

"If ever a time could have come when I would debate handing in my shield, it would've been then. But even with all that—surgery and rehab and knowing I could have saved my partner if I'd done the right thing—even after all that, I'm still on the force. I told you, it's what I do. But it's more than that." He sighed.

"I know what you're looking for, Andi. And I know how you feel. But if you can't accept the work I do, there's nothing more I can say. Because for me, being a cop isn't just a job. It's who I am."

Chapter Eighteen

In his surgeon's offices in LA, sitting half-undressed and freezing his butt off in an examining room, Mitch flipped through an outdated magazine, studied the anatomy charts on the wall and tried to guess the number of surgical gloves in a monster-size carton near the corner sink.

Anything to keep from thinking about his last conversation with Andi.

The doctor entered the office carrying a file folder. He usually looked like a blue-eyed basset hound who'd had his last bone stolen. Today, he appeared to have gotten a new treat.

"Good news, Doc?" he asked hopefully.

"The X-rays show improvement. Let's see how the rest measures up."

The man put him through his paces, checking range of motion, stability, flexibility and a list of other things. Mitch aced the tests, gave ratings of pain on a scale from one to ten, and earned another smile.

"You seem to be following the exercise program."

"Yeah." He thought of his night in Santa Fe with Andi and knew he probably had her to thank for some of these improvements.

He also realized he'd now have to accomplish any future progress on his own.

The doctor went over the list of modifications to the exercises, scribbled something on a form, then finally slapped the file folder closed. "Questions?"

"Any idea when I'm going back on duty?"

He knew his return would also depend on the shrink's report but felt sure he would ace that evaluation. He was more concerned now about questions he couldn't put into words. Mentally, he was back where he should be, but physically…

The man gave him his basset-hound smile. "As you know, the final decision regarding your status isn't up to me.

"At this rate," the surgeon went on, "I would anticipate seeing you back to full strength by your next appointment with me. But from this point, everything depends on you."

"And I'm nothing if not reliable."

He froze, waited, considered. A few weeks ago, he'd have had second thoughts after making that statement. Now, nothing. Except the knowledge it was true. "Don't worry, Doc. You can count on me."

The surgeon eyed him for a moment, then nodded. "Good. And I'm recommending your immediate return to desk duty."

He hadn't noticed he'd been holding his breath until he exhaled and felt ten tons of pressure leave his chest. He hadn't realized how much he'd had riding on this report.

Even as a kid, he had been athletic, and while he didn't expect or want to be star quarterback again, he wanted to do his job…now more than ever, since it seemed likely the job might be all he ever had.

AT THE STATION, he shook a lot of hands and received a lot of back slaps. He heard stories of ops that had ended in disaster and of cops who had recovered and moved on.

He had begun to believe he was past the worst of the memories…until he took a turn down the hall leading to the interrogation rooms and almost ran over a woman who stopped dead in her tracks in front of him. She looked at him through the familiar bright red–rimmed glasses that went with her bright red hair. She went by the familiar title of department shrink.

"Hello, Mitch."

"Janice." He nodded. "What brings you to my neighborhood?"

"I needed to discuss a few things with the chief. You haven't forgotten our appointment?"

"Wouldn't miss it." With luck this afternoon's meeting would be their last.

She peered down at her watch. "I could fit you in now if you'd rather not wait till later."

"At your office?"

"Why not right here?" She gestured to a couple of open doorways.

He didn't much go for the idea of meeting in an interrogation room, but the space was available, and he did want to get this over with.

After a quick word with the desk sergeant, he escorted Janice into a free room. She set her briefcase on the scarred tabletop and settled back in her chair.

He took the one opposite hers.

"How have you been sleeping?" she asked.

"Better. Much better. Like a baby, in fact." And it was true. As he had told Andi, she had helped him sleep. *I'd rather dream about you than have nightmares any night.* What he hadn't said was what an accomplishment that had been.

"How's the knee doing?" she asked.

"Great. I just got cleared for desk duty by the surgeon this morning."

"Ah. How does that make you feel?"

He'd learned to hate that question.

He set his jaw and stared at the blank white wall behind her for a moment before looking back. "We're closing in on our final session." He smiled to soften his words. "Shouldn't we be moving on? Aren't these meetings supposed to show progress on both sides?"

"Some of my clients seem to think so," she said drily. "What they sometimes don't want to acknowledge is that progress can mean taking a few steps backward. When we do that as a team, I can help them face reality. And that also often involves sharing their feelings."

He laughed. "Come on, Doc, I've told you before. I'm a guy. And a seasoned cop." Again, he thought of what he had told Andi. "I don't do feelings."

"Except at the appropriate times."

He narrowed his eyes. She might have gotten him into a claustrophobic interrogation room, but she wasn't trapping him in this conversation. "Such as?"

"When you're trying to get a suspect to crack, you play on their emotions."

"Well, yeah. Whatever works."

"If you're confronting someone holding victims at gun- or knifepoint, you talk them down."

"Sure. Basic negotiation."

"And when you have a friend upset about a problem, you help him think the situation through."

"Of course." He laughed shortly. "Okay. If you want to talk about dealing with reality, take a look at this scenario. A woman with two kids. Recently lost her husband. She thinks her in-laws are having trouble letting go. They don't want to believe he's dead, are trying to act like nothing happened, and—" Swearing silently, he cut himself off.

"And they don't want to talk about how that feels." She tugged on her glasses to eye him over the frame. "Like someone else I know."

How many times had she tried leading him down that road? *Not sleeping at night, having those nightmares, might be a sign you need to voice your feelings.*

As she stared him down, he sighed. "All right. You don't need to beat me over the head with it."

She laughed. "You know I would never do that. This woman is someone you know personally?"

Intimately. He shrugged and shoved his hands into his pockets. "We…went out when we were teenagers."

"You saw her again on your visit back home."

"Yeah. For the first time in a long time. Since we were teens, as a matter of fact."

"That must have brought back memories—"

"It sure did."

"—which are often based on feelings. And those feelings frequently hover just beneath the surface—or even come out into the open—when those memories are being shared."

He grimaced. "You got me there, Doc."

"I don't want to get you, Mitch. I want to help you. The way you want to help your friend." She smiled. "You could start by asking her—"

"I already know. She told me how she feels."

"Then maybe it's your turn."

"I did tell her. She doesn't want to listen, and I've got nothing more to say."

"Sounds like it's time for negotiation…if you want to see progress on both sides." When he didn't reply, she added, "Now we *are* close to the end of our sessions,

I'll ask you the same question I did in our first meeting. How do you feel you've been affected by the trauma you suffered?"

He shrugged. Drummed his fingers on the edge of the table. Looked away from those all-seeing eyes. "I'll have to get back to you on that one."

Again, he thought of Andi.

How could he expect something of her he couldn't manage to do himself?

IN THE DAYS Mitch was away, any time Andi found herself on her own, she couldn't help thinking of him. So she did her best to make sure she was never alone.

That wasn't as difficult as she had expected.

During preparations for the rehearsal dinner and wedding, she found a never-ending list of jobs to keep her mind on business.

Once the bridal party and wedding guests began arriving, she had even less time to brood. Her family, including Ginnie, had less time to question her about Mitch. They were all so busy entertaining the Hitching Post's guests.

Once in a while, she had to sidestep a comment about him. She managed that. What she couldn't bear was Trey's puzzled expression when he looked around a crowded room, then asked, "Where Mitch?"

It was only in her room at night, when she tossed and turned and watched her children sleep, that she stopped fighting her thoughts.

Mitch hadn't contacted her once. She mulled over everything they had said to each other since their last conversation, ran through every bittersweet moment of their one night together and wondered about the results of his doctor's appointment.

She thought of his accusation about not being willing to move on. She *had* moved on…except when it came to him.

Most of all, she thought about the story he had finally told her. She couldn't begin to imagine the horror he had gone through at losing his partner. She didn't want to think about the pain and guilt he had carried ever since. And she couldn't find the words to tell him how much it hurt to know everything he'd had to face.

All things she had to put behind her, too.

By the time the wedding reception ended on Friday night, she was both physically and mentally worn-out.

She sank onto a seat in the banquet hall and propped her feet up on the chair beside hers.

"Sandra made a beautiful bride," Tina said from two seats away.

"And a happy one," Jane admitted from the opposite side of the table. "I had my reservations, but everything all worked out. She ended up raving about every one of our services."

"I can't wait till we see Abuelo in the morning." Tina smiled. "He'll be so thrilled to know the wedding—"

"—went off without a hitch!" After chorusing his familiar phrase, all three of them burst into laughter.

"Really," Tina added, "you did a great job, Andi."

"We all did," she said. "It was a joint effort. Plus it was fun."

"And look at it this way," Jane said, "after you-know-who, any other event here ought to be a piece of cake."

They all laughed again.

"I'm going to take these platters to the kitchen," Tina said. "See you in the morning." She headed out of the banquet hall ahead of Andi and Jane, who rose more slowly to follow her.

"It must be a relief to feel you're off the hook." Jane smiled. "Since you agreed to stand in as planner only for this first wedding, you are now free."

"Yes." Free to move on. Free to leave Cowboy Creek.

Free to walk away from Mitch. This time, forever.

Chapter Nineteen

Mitch stepped into the Hitching Post's lobby and saw just the woman he wanted to see.

Andi was standing near the reception desk talking to Tina, who stood in her office doorway. Even as he froze, his training kicked in. He saw the new wreath on the front of the desk and the garland draped along the edges. He noted the rows of Christmas cards hung from strings across the wall behind the desk.

In the same swift glance, he took in Tina's welcoming smile and Andi's apprehensive expression. A second later, he felt the tightness in his chest when she looked away.

"Well, you're an early bird," Tina said with a laugh. "I'm not sure Abuela even has the coffee going yet. I'll go check."

Mitch held up a hand. "That's okay. I'm only here for a few minutes."

Tina nodded. "Then I'll get back to work." She went into her office behind the reception desk.

He looked at Andi and tilted his head toward the empty sitting room. "Got a few minutes?"

Andi nodded, and he followed her into the room. There were changes in here, too, a stuffed snowman standing in one corner and a ceramic Santa-driven sleigh and reindeer prancing across the mantel. On the shelf beside the chime clock sat a wooden donkey with a tilted sombrero and a red Christmas bow.

He smiled. "Looks good up there."

"I had to put him out of Trey's reach." She took a seat on one of the couches.

He stood near the fireplace and counted reindeer. "Looks like you've got a full crew."

She nodded. "Speaking of crew, we've got the waitresses who worked the reception last night coming in soon. Did you say you only had a few minutes?"

"Yeah. I'm headed to the sheriff's office to see my dad. I wanted to talk to him about a few things. And I wanted to run them by you, too."

She looked surprised, but said nothing.

"My appointment went well. I'll be going back to duty soon. And I have to admit, this enforced leave from the job has had its benefits. Besides getting to see you again, it's given me some time to think. Getting involved in the op in Arizona has done that, too. And now I hear my dad's planning on retiring. Everything coming together like this has helped me make some decisions."

Still no reaction. He pushed on. "There's going to be an opening for a deputy sheriff here in Cowboy Creek. And I intend to apply for it."

The positive reaction he had expected didn't come. Instead, her expression went completely blank, as if she couldn't summon politeness or even a passing interest. He couldn't take her silence. "No comment?"

"What do you want me to say?" She kept her voice low, but he could hear the repressed emotion. "I love you. You know that." She took a deep breath. "No matter what you think about my situation with Ginnie, that has nothing to do with what's between us, except for the fact that I *am* moving on."

"That's irony for you, isn't it? When I encouraged you to do that, I didn't mean away from me."

"I have to, Mitch, for my kids."

He took a half step toward her.

She shook her head. "Please don't. And if you've somehow tied us in to your decision to stay in Cowboy Creek, please don't do that, either. Don't make us your reason for giving up your job in LA." She stood and wrapped her arms around herself as if she'd felt a chill.

This time, he didn't move.

"I've told you how I feel about getting close to someone in a job like yours. I can't." Her voice broke. "I can't face the thought of Trey and Missy someday finding they've lost another daddy."

He stared silently at her. He had nothing more to say.

Andi stood frozen in place and watched Mitch turn and walk away. It broke her heart to see him go.

She wanted to change her mind. To call him back. To run to him and tell him—

Her thoughts were interrupted by a scream.

"Jed! *Dios mio—ayudame!*"

Andi started. The cries had come from the hallway leading to the kitchen.

The office door opened. "Abuela," Tina said in a hushed voice, her eyes wide. "She needs help."

Mitch was already across the lobby when Paz appeared in the doorway.

"Jed," she gasped. "On the floor. He won't wake up."

Mitch brushed past her and strode down the hall.

Paz followed. Andi rushed across the sitting room and ran behind Paz and Tina.

In the den, they found Jed sitting on the edge of the couch, flapping his hand as if to shoo Mitch away.

"I'm fine," he insisted. "Just had a weak spell. Nothing a drink of water won't cure."

"Sit back, Jed," Mitch said quietly. "You've got all the ladies worried. Let's just take a look to put their minds at ease."

From behind her, she heard running footsteps in the hallway. Robbie and Trey burst into the room.

Wide-eyed, Robbie gasped. "Grandpa's sick?"

"Sick?" Trey echoed.

"Grandpa's resting," Mitch said firmly. He made eye contact with Tina. "Didn't Pete say Daffodil was waiting to see the boys this morning?"

"Yes," she said quickly. "Yes, he did. Come on, you two, Abuelo's busy. We'll come back to see him after we visit Daffodil." With one hand on either boy's shoulder, she steered them from the room.

Mitch glanced over at Paz.

Andi looked in her direction, too. The older woman stood wringing her hands and staring at Jed.

"How about a glass of orange juice for this guy, Paz," Mitch suggested.

She nodded. "Yes, I'll bring it right away."

He had said just the right thing. Giving Paz something to do in her kitchen would calm her.

"Andi, could you call for an ambulance?"

"Ambulance?" Jed roared as Mitch pulled the afghan from the back of the couch and draped it around his shoulders. "Don't you do it, girl. I don't need an ambulance."

She was relieved to hear the strength in his voice, but wasn't about to give in to the demand.

As she crossed to the desk, Mitch said evenly, "Jed. Paz found you out cold on the floor. If the situation were reversed, you would want reassurance. Your family deserves that, too."

Jed glowered at her. She reached for the phone.

"I trust Mitch, Grandpa. If he thinks you need to get checked out at the hospital, I'm calling for the ambulance."

ANDI KEPT A close eye on Jed as he ate from the tray table pulled up to his hospital bed. "You make sure you finish every bite," she told him.

"I'm your granddaddy, not one of your kids," he grumbled.

But at the twinkle in his eye, she sighed in relief. She would never forget that ride in the ambulance Mitch had convinced Jed to take to the hospital.

Thanks heavens, his episode had turned out to be short-lived, stemming from a case of vertigo and a missed meal.

"I just can't believe you skipped dinner last night, Grandpa. Everyone might have been busy serving at the reception, but if you felt hungry, you should have raided the refrigerator."

He shrugged. "With all you women running in and out, it was more than my life was worth to set foot in that kitchen."

Tears sprang to her eyes. "Don't say that!"

Sheepishly, he patted her hand. "And don't you take on, girl. It's just an expression."

"One I don't ever want to hear again."

"You won't." He pushed the empty tray aside. "But I make no guarantees about what you'll hear if a doctor walks in here. I don't know why they feel the need to lock me up in this place overnight."

"It's just for observation. They want to make sure

you're hydrated properly before they send you home in the morning. You know that."

"A beer in Paz's kitchen would do me just fine."

"Oh, Grandpa," she said, laughing weakly and shaking her head.

The scare this morning could have been so much worse. Jed could have been facing a more serious condition. He could have hurt himself when he'd fallen to the floor. He could have passed out while Mitch wasn't around to take charge and counter all Jed's arguments.

As if he had read her thoughts, he said, "That young man of yours certainly knows his mind."

He wasn't her young man. Her fiancé. Her anything. She forced a light tone. "Sounds like some other bullheaded man I know."

He attempted to glare at her, but his lips twitched in a smile.

This morning, once they had arrived at the hospital and she had been reassured Jed was in good health, her thoughts turned to Mitch again and again.

He cared about Jed. About her. He was so good with the kids. As Grandpa had once said, he would make a good daddy someday. She already knew he was a wonderful lover.

But his choice of career—what he did, who he was—meant he could never be the man for her.

As tears sprang to her eyes again, she made a pretense of straightening the hospital sheets.

She had watched Mitch in action, calming everyone down and quietly taking control of the situation. Today, he had been her hero.

"What else is on your mind?" Jed asked quietly.

"Grandpa… Mitch and I aren't really engaged." She sighed. She hadn't planned to tell him this way, but she couldn't keep up the pretense any longer. And she had a feeling Jed had suspected all along.

He sat back and rested his folded his hands on the sheet, as if settling in for a long chat. "I'd guess there's more to the story than that."

Vainly, she tried to decide the best way to handle this conversation.

As if he had seen the struggle in her face, he said, "You know how I like to hear my news, girl. Flat-out straight."

Her laugh ended on a sob. His familiar phrase always made her smile, but she'd never heard him say it so gently.

She gave him a shorter version of what she had told Mitch about her worries over Grant's family, and especially her concerns about Ginnie. She left out the arguments Mitch had used to convince her to accept his idea, but confessed what they had hoped to do by pretending to be engaged.

"Your hearts were in the right place, I'll give you that," he said. "Family's important, more important than the two of you probably know yet. Look at what we've lost in the past few years, Andi. Not having your mama and your husband with us is sad enough. And look at how the rest of us have all grown apart. Time and distance both take their toll. It's important to keep in touch. To stay close."

She blinked hard to hold back a rush of tears. "You're right, Grandpa. And of course, I want to stay in touch with Ginnie. I'm planning to tell her exactly what I told you. I just wanted to help her and the rest of the family forget their grief and move on."

"Then you can, too."

You're not willing to take your own advice and move on.

Mitch's words hurt as much now as they had then.

"You already know this," Jed continued gruffly. "I'll say it, anyway. Life's too short not to keep moving while you've got the chance."

Blinking back tears, she nodded.

ANDI TOOK ONE last glance into the dresser mirror. Her gold-spangled party dress had looked great on the hanger but did nothing to make her feel ready for a party. She smoothed her hair, tried to soften the frown lines in her forehead and plastered a smile on her face.

Quickly turning from the mirror, she left the bedroom and went down the hall to Ginnie's room. She tapped on the door and waited till Ginnie called for her to come in. Her mother-in-law, in a tea-length red dress, stood in front of her own mirror.

"You look great," Andi said.

"And you look beautiful."

"Do you have a few minutes to talk before we go downstairs?"

"Well, of course. Come and sit." Ginnie took a seat on the chair near the window. "Did you get Missy up from her nap?"

"Yes. She's already downstairs." She crossed the room to sit on the edge of the bed.

"Good. Since Jed and I started taking turns holding Missy all day, I'm afraid we've made things harder for you with her nap schedule. Between the two of us, we have her spoiled. But that's what grandparents are for, isn't it?"

"Yes, it is. I'm glad you're getting the chance to do that this week. With me working and now with Missy and Trey and I all staying here at the ranch, I know you don't get to see the kids as much as you'd like."

"That's true. Although even if you were all living with

me, the way you and Grant did for a while, I don't think I could get enough of having you around."

"I know. We're your connection to him."

"You're all much more than that, Andi. Yes, Grant lives on through the children, but they're also the next generation, both of the Price family and my own. And you…" She smiled. "You're the daughter I always wanted."

Andi's throat tightened. At that moment, she couldn't respond. Fortunately, she didn't need to.

"I remember the day Grant brought you home to meet us," Ginnie continued. "I knew right away you were special to him, and that made you special to me. That's why it worries me to see you upset. There's been something bothering you, hasn't there?"

She nodded and gripped the edge of the bed on either side of her. "I…I have a confession to make. Mitch and I aren't really engaged."

Pursing her mouth, her mother-in-law nodded. "I wondered, when you two were 'old friends' at my house one night and then making your announcement two days later. And when, on the night between at Trey's party here, you didn't look like a couple who had just gotten engaged."

"I'm sorry." Sighing, she braced herself for what else she had to say. "I wish I could tell you I didn't plan to deceive you—or anyone—by pretending to be engaged. If it's any consolation, I was trying to keep you from getting hurt."

"It looks to me like you were the one hurt in the process," Ginnie said sadly. "But why would you think I'd be hurt to see you happy again?"

"It wasn't that." Haltingly, she explained, keeping the focus on her need to take care of her kids. "I want to be able to support them myself."

"And knowing you, I wouldn't expect anything less. You're a terrific mother. Of course you would want to take care of Trey and Missy, to put them first in your life, as you should."

"Thank you. But it's more than that," she went on. "I need to be independent for my own sake, too. The kids and I love you, Ginnie. And you've always been there for me. But I feel if you continue to be there for me, I won't learn to stand on my own."

Ginnie smiled wryly. "Are you suggesting I drop you from the family tree?"

"No." She laughed. "But maybe let me go out on a limb once in a while."

"And this is why you felt the need for your so-called engagement?"

Silently, she nodded.

Ginnie came to sit beside her. She shook Andi's arm gently. "I need to knock some sense into you, as Jed would say. You're putting a roof over your family's head and raising your children—my grandchildren—all by yourself. How much more independent can you be?"

"I don't know." She flushed. "Sometimes, I just feel that I need to…"

"Cut the cord to the Price family?"

Again, she couldn't respond. She had never felt so tongue-tied or as sure of ruining a situation as she did this one.

"When I first married," Ginnie continued, "there were times I felt the same way."

"There were?"

She nodded. "Being a Price is a privilege, but it also carries obligations. It wasn't long after I married into the family that I went looking for some independence, too.

"And I got lucky."

Andi blinked. "How?" She was fascinated by this new view of her mother-in-law.

"Eventually, I managed to find my independence and my niche *within* the family." She smiled. "That's my solution, not yours. I knew you would have to find your independence on the outside. And you already have."

Her throat tightened again, but she managed to blurt her thanks. Mitch had been right, after all, as Ginnie's obvious concern for her proved.

"But, Andi," she said gently, "though you're on your own now, you'll never *be* alone. Through Trey and Missy, your link to me is as strong as the bond you share with Jed. We're all *family*. And we all love one another." She wrapped her arm around Andi's shoulders and gave her a quick hug.

"I know life's not always the way we want it to be," she went on. "And I realize life may take you farther from me in miles than you are now. But can we make a deal?"

"Of course."

"Good." Ginnie smiled. "As for my not seeing the kids as much as I like… I'll be honest, twenty-four hours a day wouldn't be enough. But whenever I *am* able to see you and the kids, promise you'll let me spoil them just a bit. And when I can't see you all, I promise to do only a little grumbling."

Andi laughed. "All right, that's a deal."

"Good," Ginnie said again. "Now, since I'm leaving for home in the morning, let's go find a couple of grandkids for me to spoil."

Chapter Twenty

Andi stood beside Jed in the hotel lobby to greet their guests for the open house. She, Tina and Jane had all assured Paz they would take turns staying by his side.

He seemed as healthy and steady as Andi had ever seen him and twice as energetic while he talked about hosting the party. But Paz, who was busy running her kitchen, was worried about him overdoing it.

The front door swung open, pushing a drift of early-evening air into the lobby. When Andi saw who had stepped through the door, she felt grateful for the cool breeze.

As she watched Mitch make his way toward them, she held Jed's arm—not because he seemed unsteady but because she needed to brace herself. The Weston family had arrived earlier, and though her heart had plummeted when she saw Mitch wasn't with them, she had told herself it was for the best.

As he reached them, her heartbeat seemed to flicker like the twinkling lights on the Christmas tree.

He smiled at her, then reached to shake hands with Jed. "They let you out already. I can see why. You're looking good."

"I'm feeling even better. Must be all this clean living

and a clear conscience. Which is more than I can say for you, after that stunt you pulled about your engagement."

"Grandpa." She was grateful for the voices and laughter all around them. "Please don't blame Mitch. It was my decision. He was only trying to help me."

"Some help." Despite his gruff tone, she could see the loving concern in his eyes.

"It was my idea," Mitch said just as stubbornly as he had the morning they had returned from Santa Fe. "I'm as much at fault for this, if not more."

"Either way," Jed said, "seems like neither of you did a good job of sticking to your plan."

She flushed. "No, we didn't."

He stared at them both for a long moment, then patted her arm. "Well, I'll be off. Someone's got to be the life of this party, and I'm sure you two have some talking to do."

"Oh, but, Grandpa—"

"Calm down, girl. Tina's just three yards north of us. I'll go take my turn standing with her now."

Swallowing a laugh, she watched him walk away.

"Do we?" Mitch asked.

She started. "What?"

"Have some talking to do."

She took a deep breath. "Yes, I think we do."

MITCH FOLLOWED ANDI up the stairs, knowing she was leading him to the suite the women had been using for the wedding preparations.

The overhead hall light struck her gold dress, making it sparkle, but he had already been dazzled by her the moment he'd seen her standing in the lobby.

In the suite, a mountain of paperwork still covered the bed. She pushed some of it aside and took a seat. Mitch remained by the closed door.

She linked her fingers and took a deep breath. "I'm glad you're here tonight. I was so busy with Grandpa yesterday, I never even thanked you for everything."

"I don't need any thanks. That's part of what I do."

"Be a hero."

"I'm nobody's hero, Andi. I'm just me. I sure found that out recently." He shook his head, ashamed at how long it had taken him to discover the truth.

"Tell me," she said softly.

Why was it so hard to do just that, to tell her he'd received as much help from her as he had tried to give? He sighed. "Look, I already explained I don't do feelings. I've also always refused to let anything get to me, always thought I was invincible, I guess. What happened brought me to my knees, literally. That's what taught me there aren't any guarantees in life. And it tore me up with guilt. Not just over my partner, though that was most of it."

He crossed to the desk and took a seat close to her. He didn't want to share the admission he was about to make, but if that was the road to progress, he was taking it.

"After the incident, I believed I'd let down my family, too. My dad was always my hero. So was my granddad. You know he was on the force, too, before he retired?"

"Yes. I remember. You once told me that was why you wanted to become a cop. Because of them."

He nodded. "That was partly it. Law enforcement is in my blood. It's the only job I want to do. And I felt I let down my family and myself by not being the cop I should have been."

"You weren't at fault."

"I know. Now. You helped me see I couldn't have outtalked a fellow cop who was following his own gut feeling, especially when he pulled rank. It was a hell of a way for me to confirm I can trust my own instincts, too."

He smiled briefly. "But I *can* trust them, especially the one telling me to take the job with the sheriff's department. What happened with Jed yesterday proved that to me. I didn't become a cop for the thrill or danger of the job, but to serve and protect. Becoming a town sheriff satisfies that need.

"As for my other needs…" He ran his fingertips down her cheek. "Andi, no woman but you will ever satisfy me. And I want to live the rest of my life right here—with you and our kids."

"Mitch—"

"Don't say it, please. I know how you feel about my job, but Cowboy Creek is a much safer place than LA to raise a family." He held her gaze. "I'm not going anywhere, no matter what. And I'll wait, no matter how long it takes you to feel ready to go forward with me. And if you're never ready, I'll still be waiting."

She sighed.

His heart missed a few beats.

Then she gave him a small smile. "While you were gone, I took your advice. I did a lot of thinking. And after you became *our hero*," she said firmly, "I thought some more. And you're right—there are no guarantees. I learned that with Grant. With my mom. On that ride in the ambulance with Grandpa. And when I thought I'd lost you—again."

He smiled. "Sounds to me like we've made some progress on both sides."

"We have. And I'm thankful you're taking the job here in Cowboy Creek, for all the reasons you said." She touched his cheek. "You're a good cop, Mitch, and a wonderful man. And we've postponed our happy-ever-after long enough. I'm ready *now*. For always."

He got down on his knee beside the bed and pulled a small white box from his pocket.

"Oh, no," she cried in mock disappointment. "You're not letting me choose my own ring?"

"Where's the romance in that?" He tucked a strand of her hair behind her ear just for the chance to touch her again. "I love you. I always have."

Her eyes glistened.

He flicked open the jewel box and showed her the ring inside, a diamond offset by two small blue sapphires. "You're the diamond in the middle, Andi, and Missy and Trey are the stones on either side." He slid the ring onto her finger. "I love you all. Will you marry me?"

"Will you serve and protect us?"

"You know I will."

"Will you love, honor and cherish us?"

"I already do."

"I already do, too, Mitch. You know that."

"Yes, I do. But this engagement won't be official until you give me your answer."

She laughed. He reached up to brush a tear from her cheek. "Yes," she said. "We'll marry you."

Epilogue

Christmas morning

His arm around Andi, Mitch stood near the Christmas tree in the Hitching Post's sitting room. They had been engaged—for real, this time—for all of a day, and already he knew he was part of the Garland clan.

Jed grinned at him from his seat near the fireplace. "I gather you'll be here for Paz's Christmas dinner this afternoon."

Mitch held Andi more snugly against him. "I plan to be around for all the holiday dinners from now on."

"And you're really taking a deputy's job in town?" Jane asked.

"If they'll have me."

"Oh, they will," Jed promised. "I've got an in with the sheriff."

Paz set a glass on the small table by Jed's elbow. "You forgot this in the dining room."

"Don't fuss, woman," he snapped. But he smiled up at her before taking a big gulp of water.

He looked around the room at his family. Mitch could see the tears in his eyes. "You girls have made me proud," Jed said gruffly. "The Hitching Post has been put on the map, with the first wedding going off without a hitch… so to speak."

All three of the man's granddaughters laughed. Jed grinned at them. "I've outdone myself with this final matchmaking assignment, if I do say so myself. And thanks to Tina and Cole, I'm going to be a great-granddaddy once again." He nodded in satisfaction. "Darned good work, for an old man with a dream."

Mitch knew not one of them in the room could disagree.

He had a lot to be thankful for, too.

His parents had been solidly behind his decision to apply for a deputy's position. He had talked to his dad at the office, as he had told Andi he would. But first he had spoken to his mom.

Nothing will make your dad happier than knowing you're joining the department, too.

And you?

Sweetheart, you know I just want whatever will make you happy.

Coming home to Andi and the kids…to his families, old and new…to a job in Cowboy Creek… All that fit the bill.

He even felt thankful for Jed's matchmaking scheme.

And when his bride-to-be led him to the sitting room door and the dangling sprig of mistletoe, he knew right down to his bones he was exactly where he belonged.

* * * * *

Keep reading for an excerpt of a new title
from the Western Romance series,
THE COWBOY'S HOMECOMING by Donna Alward

Chapter One

Crooked Valley Ranch had changed since Rylan had last been here.

He drove slowly up the driveway, the Ford 4x4 and hybrid camper he towed behind moving easily over the gravel lane, not a pothole to be seen. Duke must have had it leveled this spring, he mused.

Ry touched the brakes and stared at the house. A fresh coat of white paint was on the front porch and flowers bloomed in a profusion of color in front of crisscross lattice skirting. The barns could use a new coat of paint as well, but there was an air of neatness and organization that had been missing before, too. It looked as if his sister hadn't been kidding. Crooked Valley Ranch was on its way up.

"I'll be damned," he breathed, a smile touching his lips. He never would have thought his dyed-in-the-wool military brother, Duke, would turn out to be a rancher. But if outward appearances meant anything, Duke was doing a damned good job revitalizing their granddad's spread.

Rylan scowled a little, chafing against the demand-presented-as-a-request he'd received from Lacey. Duke was staying on at Crooked Valley. Hell, he was married and had a baby on the way—a family to support. Lacey had taken over the administration aspect of the operation, and she and the ranch manager, Quinn Solomon, were planning a June wedding. Joe Duggan's will required all three of his grandchildren to take their place at the ranch before the year was up or else the place would be sold. Lacey had totally guilted him into coming "home," as she'd put it.

"It's not forever," she'd assured him. "Just use this as your home base. That's all we ask. We've never asked anything else of you, Rylan. Please help us keep it in the family. Once everything's settled, Duke and I will find a way to buy out your third."

Roots. He tried to avoid them whenever he could. Still, it kind of stung that Lacey had just dismissed him as having no interest in the ranch. Not that he wanted his part of it, but that they hadn't expected it of him. No one ever expected anything of him, did they? He should have been used to it by now.

He pulled into a big vacant spot next to the horse barn and cut the engine, which also cut out the comforting sounds of the music he'd had blaring on the radio during the drive from Wyoming.

Truth was, he'd known since February that this day was coming.

His arrival must have made some noise, because a little girl came rushing out of the barn, brown curls bobbing. Amber, Quinn's daughter. Rylan grinned. Little-known secret: he liked kids. Kids were easy, and honest, and thought being a grown-up meant doing what you wanted to do and not what someone told you. At least with kids, he never had his choices judged. To them, he was "cool."

"Hey, short stuff!" He hopped out of the cab and slammed the door.

"Hi," she offered, but stopped short, tilted her head and stared at him. "Are you going to be my Uncle Ry now?"

Yep, blunt honesty. He grinned back at her. "Looks that way. I'm okay with it if you are."

She nodded. "I gots a dog. Her name is Molly."

"Congratulations."

With a happy giggle, Amber turned around to run back to the barn, but stopped when she saw Quinn coming around the corner. Rylan liked Quinn, and he was happy for his sister. They'd make this work out somehow… He knew his brother and sister didn't realize it, but he actually did care about their happiness. That was the only reason he'd come back.

That and the heavy sense of inevitability that told him he probably should face his demons at some point.

And then a blond head appeared, the streaky strands of hair twisted back in a braid. His gut clenched. Maybe it wasn't her. Maybe he could be that lucky. He wasn't ready for the confrontation he knew would be coming.

The woman came around beside Quinn, both of them talking, and he recognized the long legs, curvy figure and slight sway to her walk. Kailey Brandt. He held back a groan. Why did she have to be here right at this particular moment? Why couldn't he have had time to prepare, to work out something to say?

He hadn't spoken to her since Valentine's Day, when she'd hopped into his truck and had gone back to the motel with him after the benefit dance at the Silver Dollar. He'd slipped out the morning after, before she woke. It had been a coward's move and one he wasn't proud of. He figured he deserved whatever she would sling his way. He'd just hoped to avoid it for a little while longer.

"Daddy, Uncle Ry's here!" Amber's sweet voice broke the silence and both Quinn and Kailey looked up. Quinn's face broke out into a smile while Kailey's...

Damn. His gut twisted again. She looked ready to commit murder.

"Rylan," Quinn greeted him, holding out a hand. "Glad you're finally here."

Rylan shook his hand. "Me, too, Quinn. Congratulations on your engagement. Glad my sister isn't marrying some pansy-ass."

Quinn laughed. "To the point. And a compliment, I think."

"It is."

His gaze slid over to Kailey. Her lips were set in a thin, unrelenting line, her eyes as cold as January ice.

"Hello, Kailey."

She looked down at Amber, who was within earshot, then pasted on the falsest smile he'd ever seen. "Why, hello, stranger."

Quinn frowned, looking from Rylan to Kailey and back to Rylan again. "Okay, I'm just a guy and even I can tell there's some friction here. What's going on?"

Kailey patted Quinn's arm. "Nothing. Nothing at all. I'd better get back home now. Chores to do and stuff."

Without so much as a nod goodbye, Kailey marched off in the direction of her truck. Rylan noticed it was a year or two newer than his, a V8 with a crew cab and lots of power to tow a trailer full of stock. He had no doubt she could do it, too. She was the prettiest girl he'd ever seen. And one of the toughest and most capable.

Quinn's voice was low. "That have something to do with Valentine's Day?"

No sense making excuses. Rylan met his gaze evenly. "Probably," he admitted.

Amber bounced away to play with Lacey's pup, Ranger, and Quinn blew out a breath. "You know, Lacey insisted that you guys were adults. That I needed to let things be. But let me tell you this. That girl is one of my best friends."

"Warning received," Rylan acknowledged. "I'll make things right. I don't have any intention of hurting her, Quinn."

"Intentions are funny things," Quinn replied. But he let the matter drop, thankfully. "Have you been inside to see your sister yet?"

"No."

"She's thrilled you're here. Just so you know."

Unease settled over Rylan again. He'd come to Crooked Valley as requested, but he fully intended to do his own thing and on his own schedule. That was the agreement. None of this convincing-him-to-stay crap. He'd be on the road most of the summer anyway, hitting as many rodeos as possible in his run for the National Finals title. He had a real chance this year and he wasn't about to blow it.

"I'll park the trailer and make my way up in a bit."

Quinn nodded. "I'll see you later then."

He gave Ry a clap on the shoulder before moving on toward the rambling farmhouse. Rylan looked after him, vague memories stirring in his brain. He'd been little but he still remembered. He remembered Grampa Joe and Grandma Eileen and learning to ride the horses and the sound of his dad's laughter. Grandma had made the best chocolate cake he'd ever had, and Grampa Joe had bought Ry a pony to ride since he was younger and smaller than Duke. The pony's name had been Daisy and he'd doted on her from the first moment, feeding her treats of apples and carrots, and brushing her every day.

His early childhood had been absolutely perfect.

There were other memories, too. He remembered how it had felt to hear the news that his father was never coming home. It had been incomprehensible to imagine a world where Dad wouldn't come thumping in, dropping his duffel and looking so tall and important in his uniform. Ry had spent hours in the barns, sitting with the horses, smelling their warm, pungent hides and trying to make sense of it all. He'd told Daisy all his feelings, burying his face in her coarse mane when things got to be too much for him to understand.

And then even that had been taken away when their mother had moved them to Helena and that small house on a postage-stamp lot. The city, for God's sake. No fields, no chocolate cake and no Daisy.

He would never invest that much of himself in a place again. No commitments meant no disappointments, and that was just how he liked it.

He got back in the truck and found a nice level spot to park his camper.

KAILEY HAD THOUGHT a lot about what she'd say to Rylan Duggan the next time she saw him. She'd also known that Lacey and Duke had asked him to come to Crooked Valley. His presence here would ensure that the ranch stayed in the family, and with two of the three Duggan siblings invested in it now, his agreement was especially important. She understood that.

But to her knowledge he hadn't agreed, and he certainly hadn't advised anyone of his arrival. He'd just shown up, wearing those faded jeans and a cocky grin that had made her traitorous body stand up straight and pay attention.

She hated him for that. Almost as much as she hated that she was just that weak to fall for a sexy smile and fine ass. Well, falling for it and acting on it were two different things. He wouldn't get the chance to burn her again.

Dust puffed up in clouds behind her tires as she drove along a dirt road parallel to the Brandt ranch. Just beyond the next ridge was the bend in the Crooked Valley Creek, where the water slowed, creating the perfect summer swimming hole. She needed some peace and quiet, some tranquility, before she went home. The last thing she wanted to do was take this mood inside.

Sometimes it really sucked being in her late twenties and still living with her parents. Yet it made no sense to do otherwise, when she spent 90 percent of her time working the ranch. The ranch that was going to be hers someday. That had always been perfectly clear. She was an only child. Without her, the ranch would have to be sold.

She loved Brandt Ranch. She truly did. But having the weight of it on her shoulders had come with a price.

Finally, she slowed and pulled off the dirt road, driving carefully down a path that was no more than two tire tracks through the grass. It opened up into a wide, grassy knoll that led to the water. As she climbed out of the truck, she could hear the comforting warble of the creek and the sound of the birds in the nearby trees and bushes.

She picked her way down the bank to the edge of the water and dipped her fingers in. "Brrr." She shivered and pulled her hand back out. It was only May and the creek was higher than usual, fed by the runoff from the mountains. There'd be no swimming today.

But the sun was warm and there wasn't a soul around for miles. She closed her eyes and rolled her shoulders, trying to ease the tension out of the tight muscles, but she could only see Rylan in her mind, his weight resting on one hip, looking calm and sexy and as if he didn't have a care in the world.

It was her own stupid fault. She'd anticipated a no-strings night of fun when they'd hooked up a few months ago. She'd needed it after putting on an "I'm so over it" show for Colt Black. No one had known how serious their relationship had been, or how hurt she'd been when he'd rebounded so quickly and found another girl. Newly single and at the benefit for Quinn and Amber, Colt had danced with her and asked if they could be friends again.

And to demonstrate how very over him she was, she'd flirted with Rylan, danced with him, fallen under his spell despite herself. By the time she'd awakened in an empty bed the next morning, she'd fallen for him. Hard. And she'd seen Rylan Duggan for who he really was.

A heartless bastard.

Worse than that, she hated herself for her moment of weakness. Maybe Rylan had left her high and dry, but she'd put herself in that position all on her own. She'd rather just forget that whole night had ever happened.

Letting out a huge sigh, Kailey sank into the warm grass and lay back against the ground, letting it cushion her body as she turned her face up to the sun. The water was cold, but the sun's rays were gloriously hot. She unbuttoned her plaid shirt, letting the fabric fall away from her chest and abdomen, exposing her skin to the sun. She let the rays soak in, restoring her calm and her confidence. It made her feel feminine, when so often she felt like one of the guys, smelling like the barn and sweat. She loved every second of it, but once in a while a woman liked to feel like a woman.

She'd definitely felt like a woman in Rylan Duggan's arms. After he'd left her at the motel, she'd come to the conclusion that she not only didn't need Rylan, but she didn't need anyone at all. Maybe someday the right man would come along and sweep her off her feet, treat her the way she should be treated. Like an equal. With respect. Someone who wouldn't mind that she already was tied down—to her ranch.

Kailey sighed heavily, a deep, cleansing breath. And if her Prince Charming never showed up, well, that was all right, too. She was fine just the way she was.

Except she sometimes wondered if that were true. First it had been Carrie, now Lacey. Both deliriously happy. And somehow Kailey felt as if she was missing out on something important.

One thing she knew for sure, she thought, as she stretched out in the sun. Rylan Duggan was *not* the thing she was missing out on. She'd learned her lesson there.

If she had her way, he'd be hitting the road for his next rodeo before any of them had time to catch their breath. In and out of her life as quickly as he had been the last time.

ON RYLAN'S FIRST night home, Lacey pulled out all the stops, just as Ry had known she would. Duke and Carrie came for dinner, and Quinn and Amber practically lived at the ranch, though the official move-in wasn't until after the wedding in June. Lacey had made potato salad and Caesar salad, and Quinn was grilling rib-eyes for the prodigal celebration. It was nice but unnecessary. He didn't want any fuss made.

Good luck with that.

They had asked all sorts of questions about Rylan's latest rodeo conquests and were well into the meal when Duke brought up the subject of Rylan's camper.

"I noticed you set up your RV," Duke said as he cut into his steak. "That's a great little rig. You must like it when you're traveling."

Rylan nodded. "It's smaller than some, but there's only one of me. Doesn't take long to set up and suits me just fine." Truthfully, he'd had something bigger but it had been a pain in the ass, heavier to haul, more space than he'd needed. He'd sold it in February and had bought the smaller set-up. On the heels of his latest win, he'd been flush with cash for a few weeks.

Including over Valentine's Day.

"I made up the spare room with fresh sheets," Lacey broke in, handing a basket of buns to Quinn. "Same one you slept in at Christmas."

Rylan put down his fork. "Not necessary, sis." He smiled. "I'm happy in the camper."

"Rylan Joseph Duggan. You are not sleeping in a camper!"

He raised one eyebrow as all eyes turned to look at her. "Wow," Quinn said. "You've got the mother voice down cold."

"Can I sleep in your camper, Uncle Ry?" Amber speared a piece of steak that her father had cut for her. "I's never been camping."

"We'll see, pumpkin."

Lacey regarded him with disapproval. "Rylan, really. There's no need to sleep in the yard when there's a perfectly good room here with your name on it."

Right. Just what he needed. To horn in on her relationship with Quinn. Maybe the manager hadn't formally moved in yet, but it was clear as the nose on Rylan's face that the three of them had a cozy little vibe going on. Besides, the wedding was in less than a month. The last thing he wanted was to be smack in the middle of their newlywed love nest.

"I like it," he contradicted mildly. "I've got my own space. My own privacy. And I won't be invading your privacy either."

"There's a much better mattress on the bed upstairs." Lacey frowned. "You surely didn't come all this way to sleep in that contraption."

"I prefer it."

"What if you have to go to the bathroom in the night?"

Rylan couldn't help it. He burst out laughing and smiles bloomed on faces around the table. "Really? What am I, five?"

Amber lifted her chin. "You can't be five, Uncle Ry. I'm gonna be five in two weeks." She rolled her eyes.

"See?" He reached over and ruffled Amber's hair. "Five, huh? Guess that means you start school in September."

"Real school," she replied importantly.

Amber's insertion into the conversation had mollified Lacey a little bit. "You're sure?" she asked. "There's lots of room."

"I'm sure. I also know how to do my own laundry. Make food."

Quinn stepped in. "You're going to want to take advantage of the food thing. Your sister's a heck of a cook." Rylan watched as Quinn turned a tender gaze on his fiancée. "Even when you don't want it, she's going to press food on you. You might as well accept it and enjoy."

Lacey turned pleading eyes on him. "Yes, Rylan, please eat your meals here."

"I can probably do that," he conceded. The small concession would get her off his back, and he'd eat a lot better than if he cooked for himself.

Duke joined the conversation. "You're always welcome at the bunkhouse, too, Ry. Carrie and I have room. At least until the baby comes."

Which would be in a few months. Carrie was already glowing with motherhood, her hand resting on her rounded belly. And Rylan smiled through it all, feeling incredibly claustrophobic and smothered.

"I'll stick to the camper for now, but thanks for the invites." His jaw felt tight and he forced himself to relax it. "Heck, I'm going to be rodeoing a fair bit of the time anyway. Easier to just hook up and go, you know?"

This would be his home base. No commitments, no ties. He was still going to run this life the way he had for the past several years. On his terms, coming and going as he pleased.

He knew at times it must have seemed as if he didn't care for his family, but nothing could have been further from the truth. That he was here was proof of that. He wanted this for them, if it was what would make them happy, and he was strangely happy that he could finally do something right rather than merely being an afterthought.

He just hoped they could accept that he needed to run his life his own way, too, and understand when the time came for him to leave again.

Western Romance
Rugged ranchers looking for love...
4 Brand New Stories
Each Month
MILLS & BOON